For anyone who's ever wished they could forget that one awful ex and meet a former pro baseball player who doles out Os like a hometown slugger, knocking them out of the park with a grand slam, wham-bam, thank-you-ma'am finish…

this one is for you.

-KS

STARRYCARD CREEK BACHELORS

THE *Baseball Card* BOYFRIEND

KRISTA SANDOR

USA TODAY BESTSELLING AUTHOR

CANDY CASTLE BOOKS

CHAPTER

One

MAGGIE

"EXCUSE ME, honey, you with the strawberry-blond hair and darling button nose who's been crying and stuffing her face with pie since the bus pulled out of Rocky Mountain City. Could we have a word, please?"

At the sound of a stranger's sassy request, Maggie froze.

Even in her shattered state, she knew she was likely the only bawling, pie-hoovering strawberry-blond on the bus. She swallowed her last bite of the delicately savory and perfectly sweet maple pumpkin pie and struggled to get her bearings.

And who could blame her?

It's not every day a girl surprises her boyfriend with a freshly made pie only to find him moaning, "Just like that, baby," as he passionately screwed another woman against the wall.

Yep, the wall.

She'd been with the guy five years—since she was nineteen—and they'd never done it against a wall. In fact, she couldn't even recall the last time they'd slept together.

She tried to banish the sweaty wall-sex image from her mind and focused on the caramel-colored monstrosity resting on her lap. What was once a carefully crafted culinary masterpiece with hand-cut stars arranged in a starry-sky swirl now resembled the aftermath of a wrecking ball's rampage. Crumbs splattered across her jean skirt and exposed thighs. Broken pastry stars were buried like victims of puree quicksand under a layer of maple-infused pumpkin pie filling. The obliterated celestial pattern left only hints of what once was—a lot like the state of her life.

She was a literal, pie-splattered, crust-covered human train wreck. She had no family, no boyfriend, no job, no money, no plan, and no path forward. All she could claim as her own was the pie plate and the contents of an envelope with a note detailing her grandfather's peculiar final wish. The man wasn't one to keep secrets, which made this all the more mysterious.

"We hate to bother you," came another voice, gentler in tone than the last. "But I've got to give you props. You're inhaling that dessert like a pie-eating all-star. However, your commendable exuberance has resulted in a rather large amount of pie in your hair."

Maggie sniffled, then shook her head, freeing the crusty fragments from her locks. They joined the rest of the crust party on her lap. She sighed a whimper of a sound as the throaty grumble of the bus's engine grew more labored, and the items on her lap shifted. She gripped the armrest and steadied the pie plate as the vehicle traversed a bumpy patch of Colorado highway. The brief jostling allowed her burdened brain a second to recalibrate.

Come on, girl! You're making a scene. Reassure these people that you're a normal person.

Unfortunately, nothing was normal about sobbing while gorging on a decadent fall-inspired dessert with a spork. Yeah, a spork.

"Pie makes everything better. At least, it's supposed to," she said and blinked away the last batch of tears. Raising her gaze from the pie catastrophe, she gasped, wide-eyed, taking in her traveling companions seated in the row across from her. "Oh, wow...you're..."

"Absolutely fabulous from the top of our wig-covered heads to our mile-long fake lashes to the strappy stilettos covering our painted toes?" the sassy-voiced person suggested from the window seat.

Maggie admired the woman's piled, platinum-blond wig decked with diamond-like beads. She wore a white sparkly top that reflected the beams of afternoon sunshine bathing the bus's interior. This woman was glorious. Not a soul could deny that she positively glowed.

Unsure of how to answer the stunning diva, Maggie sat there like a stunned, pie-splattered bump on a log. Luckily, the woman in the aisle seat, wearing a sparkly red ensemble, gifted her with a kind grin and appeared to offer less sass than her diamond-encrusted companion.

"We're drag queens. I'm sure the word's stuck on the tip of your pie-devouring tongue," the softer-spoken queen in red answered. Shimmering in the bold, fiery hue, she was the perfect contrast to her glittering, snowy-white companion.

"Right, drag queens," Maggie repeated. "Drag queens on a bus. It's just a normal day crossing the great state of Colorado with ladies dressed to the nines. Like I'm a normal girl who is totally not on the brink of a pie-filled panic attack. Because I'm okay. A-okay. All the okays." *Oh, heaven help her. What a word salad.*

The drag queens narrowed their gazes and pursed their lips. They studied her as if they were assessing the degree of danger posed by a pie-consuming dumpster fire of a human being.

Say something, pie freak.

"You're *stunning* drag queens. Positively radiant," Maggie added, then glanced at the other occupied seats in the motor coach. "Holy moly, you're all drag queens!" It wasn't that she had anything against drag queens. She admired the drag community's style and individuality. Still, how had she missed being surrounded by the brightly dressed and gloriously bejeweled women?

Wait, she knew the answer. After catching her boyfriend in the act of wall fornication, everything became a blur of tears and pie. She hadn't even planned on getting on a bus—but here she was.

She pressed her hand to her heart. "I'm sorry. I don't mean to look so surprised or alarmed. I didn't notice that—"

"That you're the only one on this bus whose mascara is running like it's trying to escape your face before the next stop?" the snarky queen in white offered, but the warmth in her gaze lessened the impact of the stinging critique.

The woman in red clucked her tongue at her companion. "Pay no attention to Diamond Dentures. She's very particular about eyes."

"And teeth," Diamond Dentures added, flashing her pearly whites. Then, in a move that could only be described as disconcerting at best and downright jaw-dropping at worst, the queen dislodged her chompers and waved the dentures in the air to the delight of the others.

Maggie's jaw dropped. Thankfully, her teeth remained firmly in place.

"Enough, queens, we're overwhelming our new friend," the woman in red called, gesturing for the raucous group to quiet down. "Now, we've got a crisis to address. One of our bus mates needs our help. And you, Miss Cry-In-Her-Pie, need to get one thing straight."

"Okay, what's that?" Maggie eked out.

"It's your lucky day. Once you've entered a drag queen's orbit, you are family. Talk to us. Why the tears? Do you have something against pie?" she asked, gesturing to the mutilated pastry.

"No!" Maggie exclaimed. "I love pie. All pies. Fruit pies, cream pies, custard pies, savory pies, nut pies. I'm a certified pie freak."

"I won't debate you on the freak part, honey," the woman in white murmured.

Maggie looked from the drag queens to the marred dessert and then back to the painted woman in red. "May I ask a question?"

"Ask away."

"Am I awake? I don't mean to be rude. But is this really happening, or did I hit my head and pass out?"

A whisper of a grin pulled at the corners of the woman's scarlet lips. "This is real, All-Star."

"As real as my false teeth," the queen in white assured her—which wasn't super reassuring.

"Let me make our introduction," the woman in red continued. "We're the Geriatric Gemstones—fabulous drag queens in our seventies and eighties. I'm Ruby Wrinkles and my seatmate is Diamond Dentures. We've got Sapphire Sags and Jade Jowls in the seats behind you. Across from them are Amber Angina and Tanzanite Tachycardia. The queens further back are Pearl Palpitations, Crystal Cataracts, Silver Stenosis, and Topaz Trifocals."

Maggie nodded, acknowledging the queens, still unsure whether she was awake. "Those are quite the names."

"Our drag queen names play off our age. We embrace where we are in life," Ruby Wrinkles explained. "We travel in our grandest attire to bring laughter, individuality, acceptance, and encouragement wherever we go."

"We get invited to events across the state, like fairs, drag queen story times, festivals, parades—even weddings," Diamond Dentures added with a wave of her hand.

"That's lovely," Maggie answered softly.

"And you, Little Miss Cry-In-Her-Pie, need to hand over that sad excuse for an eating utensil. Where did you even get a spork?" Diamond pressed.

Maggie eyed the plastic cutlery. "I found it on the bench at the bus station."

"*On a bench at a bus station!*" Diamond bellowed as exaggerated gagging echoed throughout the cabin.

"Slide over, Ruby, and sit beside the poor dove. We waited too long to intervene," Diamond Dentures directed, nudging her seat companion.

Ruby waved off Diamond's antics but complied. She crossed the aisle and settled her red sparkling form into the seat next to Maggie as Diamond shifted into Ruby's seat.

"Before we begin this intervention, give me that *sporking* biohazard!" Diamond ordered.

Maggie eyed the cutlery and pouted. "But how will I eat?"

"Child, you have done enough damage to that poor pie. Hand over the spork. It's surely teeming with bacteria."

Maggie's shoulders slumped forward, her eyes lowering before passing the plastic flatware to Ruby, who held it in Diamond's direction.

"Hold your horses," Diamond warned, then procured a glove and plastic baggie from her sparkling white bag. She slipped on the glove, then plucked the spork from Ruby's fingers and dropped it into the baggie. "Good Lord, Little Miss Cry-In-Her-Pie, never use or touch random plastic bus depot cutlery. Do you want Coxsackievirus?"

"Cocks-a what?" Maggie repeated, then dragged her tongue across her teeth like the act could dislodge whatever the heck cocks-a-sack-a virus was.

"Just ignore Diamond. She was an epidemiologist for fifty-five years before joining the Gemstones." Ruby folded her hands in her lap. "Now, we've taken care of the spork. It's time to talk. What's your story, All-Star? Why are you crying in that pie?"

Maggie's eyes filled with fresh tears as the full impact of her new reality hit.

"Let me guess. A man?" Diamond offered.

Maggie wiped her cheeks with the back of her hand. "My boyfriend. No…I'm pretty sure he's my ex-boyfriend now. I was supposed to move in with him today—well, tonight. I wanted to surprise him with a pie. And then I heard a noise. I went into the bedroom and caught him with another woman."

"In the act?" Diamond pressed, wide-eyed.

"Naked and doing it against the wall."

"What a no-good cheat!" the drag queen in white remarked angrily as the other glittery queens nodded and voiced their disgust.

Maggie's shoulders slumped forward. "He's one of those, but…"

"But what?" Ruby pressed.

Maggie shrugged. "Maybe I shouldn't have been surprised. He hasn't always been a…consistent boyfriend."

"Consistent? Elaborate," Diamond demanded.

"It was hard to know how he felt about me. From time to time, he'd say we needed a break, but he'd always come back. He'd say he missed me and loved me. But it felt calculated. It was like he'd swoop in as soon as I was happy and ready to move on. I could be wrong. Maybe I haven't made enough of an effort. I've been preoccupied the last couple of years taking care of my grandparents. I didn't think anything of spending so much time apart. This pie was for him—for us to share to start again. I used to do pie for breakfast or dinner—or even lunch—with my grandparents. We'd stand around the little island in the kitchen and talk and laugh. We laughed so much." She paused, blinking back tears. "This is the last pie I baked at my grandparents' house—the house I grew up in. The house where they raised me," she added, her voice cracking.

Ruby leaned toward her. "Why was it the last pie you baked there?"

Maggie struggled to keep her tears at bay.

"You can tell us. Think of us like grandma glamazons. Unburden yourself," Diamond Dentures offered gently.

Ruby touched Maggie's tear-stained cheek. "Remember, the Gemstones are your family now."

Maggie exhaled a slow breath, her mind racing as she tried to fend off the familiar pangs of anxiety. "I had to sell my car. When that still wasn't enough, I sold the house to a company that acquires homes and everything in them, from the furniture to all the personal items. It was my last resort to get enough money to settle my grandfather's medical bills."

"You lost everything because of medical debt?" Diamond asked, her powdered cheeks burning crimson.

"Almost everything." Maggie touched the edge of the pastel-pink ceramic pie plate on her lap. With a ribbony scalloped edge, it featured an intricate star pattern around the rim.

And just like that, her worries faded away, and tender memories of baking with her grandmother in their tidy little kitchen surfaced.

The stagnate bus air was replaced with the scent of cinnamon. The old oven's warmth enveloped the space. A vintage circular clock with faded black numbers hung on the wall. It ticked away happily with its rhythm hitching at eleven past the hour, the moment stretching as if it held some secret meaning, while her grandma's soothing voice and the low hum of the old radio drifted through the air. She pictured her grandfather in his spot at the cozy kitchen table. Barely able to contain a smile, he'd radiate sheer adoration as he sipped his coffee and watched his wife.

Maggie exhaled an even breath.

For the first time in a long time, a calming peace settled over her. Surrounded by the echoes of her childhood, her grandparents' quiet affection was the purest form of love she'd ever witnessed.

She tapped one of the pink ceramic stars on the baking dish. "This pie plate is all I kept."

"Oh, honey! How unfortunate!" Diamond Dentures lamented, pulling Maggie from her thoughts.

"The pie plate is unique. I'd love to know the ceramist who'd made it," Jade Jowls remarked as she peered over the seat, her green and gold necklace glinting in the light.

"That pastry dish is very important to you," Ruby observed.

Maggie traced another blushing pink star. "It is. I kept it for sentimental reasons. The estate sellers said I could take a few personal items."

"I believe it's quite old. Was it passed down from previous generations?" Jade Jowls continued, eyeing the pie.

Maggie chuckled, her first laugh in weeks. She held up the

plate so Jade could get a better look. "I don't know. It came from a flea market. It cost my grandfather eleven dollars."

"Are those the letters *E* and *B* on the side?" Jade asked, narrowing her gaze as she continued her study of the ceramic dish.

"Yes, we figured it stood for the person who made it, or perhaps a previous owner scratched in their initials. We weren't sure. This was always my favorite pie plate. When I was little, and even now, I found comfort in closing my eyes and brushing my fingertips across the stars."

"What's its story?" Ruby asked, genuine interest woven into the question.

Maggie returned the plate to her lap. "My grandmother was a self-trained baker. Pies were her specialty. She loved experimenting with different flavors and pie crust designs. She taught me everything I know about baking. I memorized all her pie recipes."

Ruby nodded. "How many did she have?"

"Hundreds—maybe more. She had several different pumpkin pie recipes: classic pumpkin, maple pumpkin, pumpkin cheesecake, streusel-topped, chocolate swirl, pumpkin pecan, coconut pumpkin, and gingerbread pumpkin, to name a few. I've been experimenting with a spiced rum pumpkin pie recipe. It's good, but not the flavor profile I was hoping for."

"My, my, our little miss knows pie," Diamond cooed.

"I think there's more to that plate," Ruby added gently.

Maggie smiled as a wave of nostalgia washed over her. "This pie plate meant a lot to my grandparents. My grandfather loved to watch my grandmother bake. It was this sweet little game they played. She was a soft-spoken woman. She'd catch him looking at her, and then she'd blush. My grandpa would say the blush on her cheeks matched this pie plate."

"Isn't that darling!" Diamond exclaimed.

"Before they married, my grandmother was a waitress at a diner, and sometimes they'd let her bake—that's where my grandparents met. She served him a slice of her pie. He ordered another slice and then a third. He said he wanted to marry whoever baked that pie. She blushed and shared that she'd made it. The next day, he passed by a flea market. The pie plate caught his eye, and he knew he had to get it for her—knew she was the one. When he proposed two weeks later, he handed her this pie plate with an engagement ring in the center. My grandma would tease him and say he married her for the desserts, but I knew better. They were soulmates. It brings me comfort to know that they're together now."

"When did you lose them?" Diamond asked.

"My grandmother passed away two years ago—complications arose a few years after she had surgery."

Diamond's eyes softened with sympathy. "And your grandfather?"

Maggie's vision grew blurry as she pulled at a string hanging from her denim skirt. "He passed a month and a half ago."

Ruby pulled a handkerchief from her pocket and offered it. "You took care of them, didn't you?"

Maggie accepted the folded square and patted her cheeks. "I moved back in after my grandmother's health began to decline. My grandparents tried to dissuade me, but they couldn't. I never knew my parents. They passed when I was a baby. My grandparents were everything to me. Family matters to me. I didn't see caring for them as a burden. I liked it. I like taking care of people. And my grandparents were good people. My grandmother and I used to bake for everyone in the neighborhood. There's nothing quite as satisfying as seeing a person's reaction when you show up with a pie." She sighed as the memories faded. That's all they were. That life was over. "But now I'm alone," she whispered, staring at the sad pie remnants on her lap.

"Did you grow up in Rocky Mountain City?" Ruby asked, shifting the conversation.

Maggie exhaled a slow breath. "Born and raised. My grandfather worked for Rocky Mountain University. He didn't go to college, but he was a big RMU Mountain Lions sports fan. He was part of the grounds crew that maintained the athletic training facilities. He mostly worked on the football and soccer practice fields."

"I also worked at Rocky Mountain University for a time. In the athletics department, too," Ruby replied.

Maggie brightened. "On the fields?"

"Something like that."

She mustered the ghost of a grin. "Small world."

"Indeed, it is, *Maggie*."

Maggie?

She held Ruby's gaze. "How do you know my name? I haven't shared it. Do we know each other?"

"Did Ruby not mention we're geriatric *psychic* drag queens?" Diamond said with a wave of her bejeweled hand.

Maybe this was a dream.

"That's a joke, right? You don't see the future, do you?" Maggie asked meekly.

Ruby touched her shoulder and gave it a reassuring squeeze. "It's embroidered on your little pink apron, All-Star. We saw it when you got on the bus."

Her apron?

Maggie looked down and took in the faded fabric. Her grandmother had made the apron and embroidered her name across the top in forest green. It was a gift for her eleventh birthday. Sure, it barely fit, but wearing it this morning had made her feel a little more grounded.

She touched the letter *M.* "I forgot I was wearing this. I was pressed for time this morning. I had to be out of the house early. I didn't realize I still had it on. And then, after I walked in on the…"

"Wall sex," Diamond supplied.

"Yeah, since the wall sex, I've been in a fog," Maggie said, deflating in her seat.

"Chin up!" Ruby ordered. "That's the past. What are your plans for the future?"

Maggie chewed her lip as the warmth from recalling her grandparents' devotion drained from her body. "Plans? My boyfriend—I mean, my ex-boyfriend—is a doctor. He wants to make a name for himself in his field out of state. I told him I would join him wherever he found an opportunity. But that's no longer in the cards for me."

"Those aren't your plans. They're *his* plans. His path. What do you want?" Ruby pressed.

"Me?" Maggie whispered.

"Yes, you," Diamond chimed.

Maggie froze as an emptiness settled in her chest. "I haven't thought about what I wanted in a long time. I don't regret taking time off to care for my grandparents. But it hasn't left much time for me to think of myself. I was supposed to foster a dog. My ex-boyfriend went to pick him up, but by the time he got there, the dog had just been adopted."

"What were eleven-year-old Maggie's passions? What did she want to do when she grew up?" Ruby asked, employing an even, reassuring tone.

Maggie eyed the drag queen. "What were you before you were a Geriatric Gemstone, Ruby? A therapist?"

"When the job called for it, yes, but we're talking about you."

Maggie touched the pie plate. "Eleven-year-old Maggie loved to bake and wanted to open her own shop, but..."

Ruby raised a dark painted eyebrow. "But what?"

Maggie's chest tightened. Doubt flooded her mind in a looping soundtrack listing all the reasons why she'd fail. This happened when she dared to dream. She shook her head. "I can't run a business. I don't have a fancy degree. Last I checked, I had one hundred and eleven dollars. I'm not on any path. If anything, I've been running in circles for years."

"You're on this bus," Ruby said as if she were choosing her words carefully. "That's a path of sorts and the beginning of a plan. Are you taking it all the way to the end of the line to Dennison, Colorado? It's just south of Durango."

"That's where we're headed," Diamond shared.

Maggie glanced out the window. "No, I'm getting off at the next stop."

"At Starrycard Creek?" Ruby asked, a crease forming on her brow.

"Yes."

"Do you know someone there?"

Maggie flicked her gaze to the pie. How was she supposed to answer? "Yes…no…I mean, everyone knows him. I need to meet with a professional baseball player—well, a former professional baseball player named Christian Starrycard."

"Is that so?" Ruby replied, a thread of surprise in her voice.

"Miss Maggie, you blushed when you said the ballplayer's name," Diamond purred.

"Did I?" Maggie touched her cheek—her heated cheek.

"Poor Christian Starrycard. His last Major League ball game was a real heartbreaker," Jade Jowls said, shaking her head.

"And to think the man will never play again," Diamond added. "And Ruby, you—"

"Are a Rocky Mountain City Rattlers fan as well. Like all of us," the woman in red replied with a curious edge to her voice.

The queens grew quiet—even the sassy chatterbox Diamond Dentures held her tongue. Maggie glanced around the bus and took in their solemn expressions. Still, it wasn't a surprising reaction. Christian Starrycard's downfall was a tragedy. Footage of the man's career-ending injury had looped on TV for weeks, and his subsequent public outbursts had made the news. Social media had recorded his drunken antics, which provided fresh fodder for the tittering online masses. But the gossip and speculation seemed to have died down over the last several weeks.

"Maggie," Ruby continued, "what's got you headed to see Christian Starrycard?"

"This." Maggie pulled a worn envelope from the pocket of her jean skirt and removed the contents.

"Well, look at that," Ruby remarked, a wisp of wonder infused into her words.

"What is it?" Diamond pressed, leaning into the aisle.

"A card and a small rock with a number scratched on it," Maggie answered, eyeing the deep midnight blue stone with subtle veins of soft pink running through it. The blushing streaks added warmth to the smooth pebble's appearance. Two faint lines that appeared manmade were carved down the center. An eleven. She moved her hand into the light and noticed something she hadn't observed earlier. The sunshine revealed tiny, shimmering silver inclusions that resemble stars scattered across a twilight sky.

"Who's on the baseball card?" Diamond asked.

Ruby touched the corner. "It's Christian Starrycard. It's his card from when he played in college. How did you get these things, Maggie?"

"My grandfather had them. He was quite upset after the game where Christian Starrycard was injured." Pressure built in her chest as she recalled the resounding crack. Christian had hit the ball hard. It sailed over the stands. A home run. But he didn't run. He'd dropped the bat, gripped his left shoulder, then fell to his knees like a lightning bolt had struck him. She studied the baseball card, focusing on the man's charismatic and confident boyish half-grin.

"Maggie," Ruby said softly.

"Yeah?"

"Did your grandfather tell you anything about these items—how he came to possess them?"

"No, not really. After the game, he asked me to get a box from the attic. I'm pretty sure these items were inside."

"You don't know?" Diamond asked.

"He took the box into the study where my grandmother had kept this special handmade paper and envelopes and closed the door. He called me in. I could see that the box was empty when he handed me the envelope and made me promise to open it after he was gone. He passed in his sleep a month later."

"What's in the letter?" Jade Jowls asked.

"It was sweet—like my grandfather. He said he wanted me to trust my gut and follow my heart. He wrote that my goodness would lead me to where I belonged. He asked me to return the contents of this envelope to Christian Starrycard and to do it in person—and alone. But I couldn't bring myself to open the envelope until…"

"Until today," Ruby answered.

Maggie touched the corner of the letter. "I'd always kept it with me. I sort of figured one of the objects was a stone, but I wasn't ready to find out what was inside because it would be the last thing I'd do for him." She drew in a shaky breath. "But after seeing my boyfriend with another woman, I started walking and somehow ended up at the bus station. I opened the envelope, read his last words, and…"

"And here you are," Ruby finished.

Maggie glanced down at herself. "Here I am, broke, wearing a child-sized apron with a massacred pie in my lap and crust remnants in my hair."

"You're here on this bus. Isn't that a plan?" Ruby asked.

"Maybe," Maggie whispered, but something happened inside her—something good. Ruby's words had stirred a flicker of hope, hinting that the universe might still have a plan for her—a path for her.

"You poor little dove," Diamond cooed. "You've lost your grandmother and your grandfather and caught the man you thought you'd be spending your life with banging another woman."

Maggie slumped in the seat. "And our dog passed away a few days after my grandfather."

"And you lost your dog?" Diamond wept, tears streaming down her cheek.

"I never really thought about it all at once, but yes, that's been my life."

"Perhaps we should let her eat the entire pie, spork bacteria be damned," Diamond offered, sniffling and sobbing as she dug through her bag.

"Experiencing the loss of loved ones, betrayal, and the death of a pet in such a short period are profoundly traumatic events, Maggie," Sapphire Sags said as Jade Jowls and Ruby nodded. "It's important to acknowledge the immense weight of these losses and the impact on your psyche."

"My psyche?" Maggie repeated.

"Sapphire is a retired neuropsychologist," Ruby explained.

"Have you spoken with anyone—a behavioral health professional or a close friend?" the drag queen continued.

Maggie shrugged. "Not really. My boyfriend was always busy with work, and I lost touch with most of my friends after I moved back in with my grandparents. And my psyche's been preoccupied settling medical debts."

"My God, Maggie, if anyone needs a little luck, it's you," Diamond lamented, holding the baggie with the spork. "You deserve the world—the freshest of fresh starts. Not a bout of Coxsackievirus." She scowled at the utensil, then dropped it back in her bag. "I changed my mind. No matter how dire and depressing your life is, I can't let you use that spork. Explosive diarrhea is no way to begin again."

"And it might be headed her way," Ruby said with a curious lilt to her voice.

"Explosive diarrhea is headed my way?" Maggie asked and rested her hand on her stomach. *Was that her belly churning? Was she experiencing the beginning symptoms of Coxa-a-whatever?*

"No, not explosive diarrhea. I'm talking about luck. It might be headed your way." Ruby gestured to a digital clock above the bus driver. "Look at the time. It's one ten in the afternoon—a minute until one eleven. Didn't you say you have one hundred and eleven dollars?"

"I did, but I'm not sure how it being one ten and me having barely enough cash to pay for one night in a crappy motel is lucky."

"You and your superstitions, Ruby Wrinkles," Diamond remarked, clucking her tongue.

"What's superstitious about one eleven?" Maggie asked, eyeing the red digits that still blinked 1:10.

"It's what some call an angel number. If you encounter a series of ones, it means you're on the right path."

"But I don't know what path I'm on. We've established that," Maggie said, leaving the letter on her lap as she slipped the base-ball card and stone into her pocket.

"I have a feeling your next life choice might have been written in those stars on your mauled pie," Ruby mused.

Maggie frowned. "What's the choice?"

"The choice to be brave and blaze a new path."

"I don't know what that means."

Ruby leaned in. "Forget the old Maggie."

"How?" she pressed, shaking her head. "A person can't simply transform, especially me."

"Why couldn't you change?"

"I've always been plain old Maggie. I think I always will be."

Ruby's expression sharpened. "You're surrounded by men in their seventies and eighties dressed in full drag. Do you think, for a second, we knew this was our path? We took a chance and embraced what was right for us."

"But you are much braver than me." Her chest tightened. "And I get…anxious. My nerves take over. I babble on and on like a lunatic." Simply conveying that information kicked up her pulse. But she couldn't have a panic attack—not here. She inhaled slowly and recalled her grandfather's gentle voice.

"Maggie," Ruby said, looking her over, "have you considered that your grandfather might have wanted you to embark on this journey to create a new path and transform your mindset? Today can always be your first day."

"First day of what?" she asked when movement on the horizon caught her eye.

"Your first day living, learning, and chasing—"

"A dog!" Maggie cried, interrupting Ruby. She peered out the bus's windshield as the digital clock flipped to 1:11.

Ruby frowned. "I was about to say *dreams*. But, sure, you can chase a dog."

"No, not chase a dog. A black dog is on the tracks." She focused on the bus driver. "Sir, driver!" she called, determination edging out her anxiety. "Aren't you going to stop? Can't you see that there's a dog in trouble? It's stuck on the train tracks. See, it's pulling but can't get off."

Toot! Toot! Toot! Toot!

Toot! Toot! Toot! Toot!

"And there's a train coming!" she exclaimed, handing the pie to Ruby as she climbed over the drag queen and into the aisle.

"Oh, poor pup!" Diamond exclaimed.

"Stop the bus!" Maggie cried, holding on to the top of the seats as she charged down the aisle.

The driver caught her eye in the mirror. "We're on a schedule, lady. I can't stop for some dog. And you need to sit down."

"What are you doing, Maggie?" Ruby called.

"I have to help that dog." She eyed the train and the defense-less animal, then hurried down the steps toward the folding door. "Open it!" she demanded, pegging the driver with her piercing gaze.

"We're moving, lady! I can't open it!"

"Stop the bus, or I'll pry open the door and jump out," she threatened, pressing her hands against the glass. It wasn't like her to be rude or cause a fuss, but an animal's life was at stake. The train was barreling down the tracks, kicking up plumes of dust through the mountain valley. Its whistle echoed off the steep cliffs, getting louder by the second.

And she was running out of time.

She wedged her fingertips into the tight space and prepared to force the glass doors open.

"All right, all right," the driver said and hit the brakes. The bus came to a jarring halt. He pushed a button, and the doors hissed open, allowing gusty mountain air to sweep inside.

"Maggie, what about your things? Your letter, your pie plate, and your purse and bag?" Diamond called.

Maggie looked beyond a sprawling ranch and grand house close to the tracks where the dog was stuck before shifting her focus back to Diamond.

There was no time to worry about material things.

"I have to go. I have to help that dog," she answered and bounded off the bus.

"I can't wait," the driver called as the train horn wailed.

"Neither can I," she replied, casting one last look at the wide-eyed, slack-jawed drag queens with their noses pressed to the windows.

The bus doors hissed closed, and the brakes released with a sharp puff of sound. Bits of rock and earth pricked her legs as the vehicle pulled away.

She scanned the terrain, then zeroed in on a faint dirt trail snaking through the brush toward the tracks. "There's my path," she whispered, heart pounding, and without a second thought, she took off running.

CHAPTER

Two

CHRISTIAN

TOOT! *Toot! Toot! Toot!*

Toot! Toot! Toot! Toot!

Christian Starrycard groaned a ragged, restless sound as a distant whining pulled him from paradise. "Don't go," he mumbled sleepily, but it didn't matter. He knew what was coming. He winced as the agony returned, and an image imprinted in his mind faded—her image. The face of the mystery woman who'd appeared each night since he'd lost everything. She'd become his only respite. His one escape. When he slept, there was no pain, no expectations. Just her and a peace he hadn't known since the day his body betrayed him.

But she came at a price—and she was getting harder to find.

As he transitioned from slumber to the land of the living, a persistent pounding echoed in his head. The room was too warm. The air, too dry. The wind howled outside, rattling the windows and sending drafts through every crack, making the indoors feel even more suffocating. His muscles resisted any attempt to move. He worked to part his lips, and Christ, his mouth was devoid of moisture. What he did taste was probably a hell of a lot like the grimy floor of a dive bar.

Where the hell had he passed out last night?

He squinted against the light seeping in. It stung his bloodshot eyes, and he exhaled a tight breath. "Fuck me," he uttered, meeting the day like a drunk in the gutter.

Dammit, he better not be in a gutter...again.

He tapped his hand against what he'd hoped would be a mattress or even the couch. But the surface didn't give because he was on the goddamned floor. Still, it was better than the gutter—but not by much. He made a second attempt at opening his eyes and spied his arm sling a few feet away in a crumpled heap. He recognized the rug—a silly fluffy white number his young niece insisted he purchase. At least he'd made it to his bedroom. He'd woken up on the front porch yesterday. Pretty pathetic—but it wasn't some random alleyway. No, he was home. A fact that used to comfort him. He twisted and winced as shooting pain spiked through his left shoulder. It was his fault. He knew better than to sleep on his left side. The hardwood planks mercilessly pressed against the tender joint, and another jolt of pain ripped through his bare torso.

"Dammit!" he hissed, hoping it wouldn't get any worse until the blast of a train horn reverberated through his skull.

Toot! Toot! Toot! Toot!

Toot! Toot! Toot! Toot!

The airy cry used to mark the day like an old friend arriving. Now, it only added to his torment.

Ping! Ping!

And speaking of skull-rattling torment—his cell phone chime brought him no comfort either.

He groaned as the train continued blowing the whistle, then gripped the top of the bedside table with his right hand. His fingertips brushed his cell. And like some bad comedy routine, the damn thing tipped over the edge and struck him in the center of his forehead before bouncing off his chest and thumping onto the white rug. He ignored his phone and peered at his inked chest —at the message that once motivated him. He barked a mirthless laugh and exhaled a frustrated breath. Gingerly, he peeled his body off the ground and rested against the table leg as the train continued blasting away. "Can a man get a little peace and quiet?"

"Christian? Chris?"

Dammit!

He squinted and read the name blazing on his cell's glowing screen.

Eliza Starrycard-Dunleavy.

He winced. Of all the calls to accidentally answer—on speakerphone, no less—this was probably the worst.

"Christian, can you hear me?" she called a touch too sweetly, like she was auditioning for the role of well-meaning yet extremely nosy sibling. "It's Eliza, your sister. You know, the principal of Starrycard Creek Elementary School, the mother of your darling niece, and the *smartest* Starrycard sibling out of our unruly brood."

Christian grimaced. He could deduce two salient facts from that lively introduction.

One: His headstrong sister was feeling feisty.

And two: He was screwed. That sing-song voice meant something was in the works.

He cleared his throat and prayed the brain cells he hadn't killed off with excessive alcohol consumption could produce a witty response. "Don't let Kieran hear you think you're the smartest Starrycard sibling—or Finn or even Owen or your own daughter. I'm sure they'd all disagree. Come to think of it, Caroline probably thinks she's the smartest one. But I'm still older than you, Liza. So there," he rasped like a man who'd been lost at sea and hadn't spoken in weeks, which wasn't that far from the truth. Except, he'd made a dire mistake in his response. Not only was it *not* a witty reply, but he'd also broken an unspoken rule. Don't get sassy with Eliza Starrycard-Dunleavy—at least before he'd had caffeine or grain alcohol or a fucking lobotomy.

"You, dear brother, are only a year older than me. I might be the fifth born, but I'm the first-born daughter. And you know what that means."

He rubbed the sleep out of his eyes. "No, I have no clue. What does that mean?"

"It means whatever the hell I want it to mean. And today, it means that I'm not letting you drown in a river of self-loathing."

Scratch Eliza feeling feisty. His sister was in full-throttle meddling mode, a well-worn trait among Starrycard women.

He massaged his left shoulder and flinched. "I don't have the energy to fight, Liza. Why are you calling so early?"

"It's not early. It's the afternoon. A little after one."

"One," he barked, a parched, mirthless laugh at the mention of the digit. "One, one—power-hitter number eleven, from Starrycard Creek, Colorado, Christian Starrycard," he slurred, imitating the ballpark announcer.

"Are you drunk?" Eliza asked softly. The sharpness in her tone receded. It should have made him grateful she'd lost her biting edge, but it only amplified his emptiness. When Eliza softened, shit got real.

"I'm not drunk. I just woke up." He retrieved the phone from a clump of rug fluff, then hauled his muscled frame off the floor to sit on the edge of his unmade bed.

"You cannot mix that Stumble Juice bathtub hooch you make with your meds."

He eyed the arm sling. "I'm doing what I have to do. You should go easy on your ailing brother."

"An *ailing brother* who should be doing better. It's been eleven weeks since your surgery. I know a physical therapist at Creek County Hospital. He mentioned they hadn't seen you there in a while. Are you skipping out on your appointments?"

Christian groaned, exhausted to the bone. "I don't need to go to the hospital for PT. I know the exercises. I was a kinesiology major back at RMU. Hell, I could show up at the Starrycard Creek Senior Center and teach the Stretch-and-*Fucking*-Shine class to the geriatric crowd. But it doesn't matter if I go to physical therapy or not. This shoulder is done. I'm fucking done."

And there it was. The cold, hard truth.

"Doctor Driscoll said the surgery went well, Chris. You'll have to be careful with your left arm, but you'll live a normal life."

Normal life. The phrase hit like a punch to the gut.

"My normal life *is* baseball." He swallowed, a dry, tortured movement. "I mean, it *was* baseball. Whatever the hell I'm supposed to do now is anyone's guess," he hissed, utterly lost. The once regimented, methodical man was now trapped in an endless cycle of aimless days, each one punctuated by throbbing pain. Or maybe the shoulder pain had dissipated, and the agony now came from his heart. What did it matter? The life he'd loved beyond measure was over.

"Chris," his sister said gently, "you need your family. You need connection. You need direction. You need a challenge—a goal. It's who you are. You find that one thing, and you're golden."

"It's a challenge to button my damn shirt. It's a challenge to look at myself in the mirror. It's a challenge to wake up every day. Do those count as challenges?" He glanced around his room, taking in the World Series Champion ball caps and the pair of rings he'd accumulated from two back-to-back wins.

"What about volunteering?"

"I'm not a celebrity anymore. Who gives a fuck what I do? I'm just some guy now. I'm not..." He paused. "I'm not *me* anymore." He exhaled a tight breath. "Fuck, I don't know what that means. I'm just groggy. I'm not making any sense," he said, waiting for his sister to make a snarky remark. Seconds passed, and nothing. "Liza?" he rasped.

"Chris, I'm worried about you. It's not good to close yourself off and hole up at the ranch. Lean on us. Let us help you. Get out of the house. Hell, hire someone to help with the house. The last time I dropped Kenzie off, she said it looked worse than the mess she's got going on under her bed—which is a biohazard. I found a moldy PB and J under there. The cats and dogs won't even venture into her room anymore. Anyway, back to you. I've decided to take matters into my own hands and—"

"Eliza, stop," he blurted. He hated cutting off his sister, but he'd said too much. He had to put her mind at ease. The last thing he wanted was a full-on Starrycard family intervention.

He glanced at the assortment of painkillers strewn across his bedside table. And then something else caught his attention—one of his lucky stones. He peered at two lines carved down the center and shook his head. So much for luck. His goddamned luck had run out. With a swift flick of his wrist, he brushed the item off the bedside table. It ricocheted against the wall and dropped behind his bed, where it could live beneath an inch of dust.

His gaze shifted past the clutter to a picture taped to his window. And dammit, the emotional arrows to his heart kept coming. His bone-deep rage morphed into soul-crushing grief. Tears blurred his vision as he stared at a picture. His seven-year-old niece had drawn a sketch of the two of them with bright, ruby-red smiles. She'd adorned him with a cape. It fluttered beside him like a superhero. It was the first thing he'd laid eyes on after surgery. His niece had captured him—the old, joyful him. The always cheerful celebrity athlete. Damn, how he used to love to smile—how he'd embraced life.

Baseball had fed him a constant feast of sensory delights. The crack of the bat making crisp contact with the ball would send a rush of endorphins flooding through his body. He loved the lights, the cheering crowds, and the scent of fresh-cut grass. He'd inhale the earthy aroma of the infield dirt. It sustained him. Now, there was nothing but the tick of the clock counting off empty minutes, hours, days, and weeks. He'd lost his ability to dial into life. Was this his fate? Pills, alcohol, blacking out on the floor, desperately hoping to catch a glimpse of his mystery woman's face?

He cleared his throat. "You caught me at a low moment. That's normal in recovery. Ups and downs. I need time on my own, a little more time to think and figure things out," he said, trying to appease his sister.

"Listen, Christian, don't get mad. I asked Owen to stop by and see how you're doing. Mom and Dad agreed it's a good idea."

Dammit! The Starrycard family's intervention had already started.

"So…everyone's talking about me," he said, shaking his head.

"Yes, we are," she snapped. "Your family loves you. I have a feeling you're falling apart. I know you're eating like crap. And don't even get me started on the alcohol…"

But she'd already gotten started.

His sister continued speaking, but he couldn't focus on her words. A flicker of movement outside caught his eye. He peered out the window past the gurgling creek and fall-kissed dried grasses and spied a woman running toward the train tracks. Dressed in a jean skirt, boots, and some type of pink bib, she looked both entirely out of place and strangely at home.

What the hell kind of thought was that? Perhaps Eliza was right about him needing to cut down on the booze.

Still, this woman shouldn't be there.

The ranch was on the outskirts of Starrycard Creek. It wasn't far from town, a ten-minute bike ride at most, but it was far enough that stragglers didn't often appear. And it was private property. No matter who this woman was, she wasn't allowed to be here.

"Liza," he said, eyes trained on the trespasser, "I need to go. Something's happening outside," he mumbled, abruptly ending the call. He tossed his phone on the bed and went to the window to get a better look.

Toot! Toot! Toot! Toot!

Toot! Toot! Toot! Toot!

His foggy mind cleared. He'd spent enough time living by the tracks to recognize the signal patterns. And holy shit, those continuous, sharp horn blasts meant something—or someone— was in the train's path. The breath caught in his throat. That had to be why the woman was on his land.

There was trouble on the tracks, and that could be deadly.

Barefoot and clad only in jeans, he dashed through the house. He flung the front door open. The unforgiving autumn mountain winds whipped his bare skin. But he didn't feel any pain. His body was on autopilot, as if it were being pulled by an invisible force. His heartbeat thundered in his ears as he zigzagged past a trio of evergreens, and the horrifying scene unfolded in front of him. A dog was stuck on the tracks, and the woman was running straight for it. But they weren't alone. A freight train barreled toward them—closing in on the pair at full speed.

Goddammit!

The last thing he wanted to do today was take on a freight train. He had his own problems—and those didn't include getting obliterated by a steam engine. He huffed, then looked between the woman and the dog, and there it was—that undeniable pull.

He had to go to her.

"Of all the days to play the hero," he muttered, then took off running toward the tracks.

CHAPTER
Three

CHRISTIAN

TOOT! *Toot! Toot! Toot!*

Toot! Toot! Toot! Toot!

"Hey!" he shouted, sprinting toward the pair. "You've got to get back! The train can't stop!"

She didn't acknowledge him. She probably couldn't hear him over the blaring whistle and rumble of the approaching train. He took note of its location and speed. They had ninety seconds—maybe a little more, but not much to get the hell out of its path. He turned his attention to the trespassers. The woman was slight. Her halo of reddish-blond hair blew wildly in the wind. She'd dropped to her knees, bent over what looked like a skinny black lab. And Christ, the poor canine was in a tight spot. Trapped in a precarious downward dog position, with its head and neck pressed to the center of the track and its rear in the air, the animal was pinned to one of the wooden slats.

The train's whistle screamed. There was no more time to think.

He had to act.

He shook the woman's shoulder. She turned toward him, her hair whipping across her face, concealing her features.

He narrowed his gaze. Did he know her?

"Help me!" she called above the rhythmic clatter and the whooshing wind. "We can't leave him on the tracks. He's stuck."

Toot! Toot! Toot! Toot!

Toot! Toot! Toot! Toot!

"Is this your dog?" he hollered.

"Can you help us?" she cried, her hair flying in all directions.

"Yeah, yes, of course." He dropped to his knees beside her and examined the dog. The scrawny creature's eyes were wide with fear and confusion as he struggled in vain.

"He keeps pulling," the woman yelled. "I can't get his collar off. It's too tight, and I need him to let up and give me some slack to unfasten the buckle. But he's scared. I can't get him to calm down. His collar is caught on something. I can feel it. We've got to pull it out. I've been trying but can't get it to budge."

The animal whimpered and wiggled. They didn't have time to earn its trust and get it to settle. Luckily, while the animal was anxious, it didn't appear vicious.

"Easy, now," he said to the pup.

He worked his hand beneath the trapped creature, and his fingers found the culprit: a bent nail. The rusty metal hooked around the collar like a curved finger. As a pro athlete, he'd been in plenty of clutch situations, but this was his first do-or-die scenario. Still, his body took over and followed the familiar steps.

Focus. Plan. Execute. Succeed.

The train's whistle grew louder, but he blocked out the noise. He regulated his breathing, then leaned toward the woman so she could hear him over the roaring rumble and punishing winds. "Hold the dog. He's stuck on a nail. I'll pull it out. Once he's free, I'll get us off the tracks. Say you understand."

She peered at the barreling train. "It's so close!"

They had twenty seconds at best.

He got closer to her, his lips a breath away from her ear. "Forget about the train. Say you understand. Come on, we're a team. We do this together. Every storm passes. Now, say you understand."

"I understand," she replied, her voice steady.

"Hold on to him!"

"Lucky," she said as she encircled the creature.

"What?"

"It says Lucky on the collar. It must be his name."

He got a glimpse of a tarnished gold plate on the leather collar. Sure enough, the unluckiest dog on the planet appeared to be named Lucky. "Okay, hold on to Lucky." He slipped his right hand beneath the dog's neck and pinched the rusty piece of iron. "I've got the nail," he called as the seconds ticked away. He gave it a few tugs, but the damned thing wouldn't budge. He required better leverage. He wrapped his left arm, his damaged arm, around the woman. Anchoring himself to her, he channeled every ounce of force into his right hand. Inhaling, he summoned his strength and heaved the metal upward. The train's roar was now deafening, its vibrations shaking the ground beneath him.

"Every storm passes. Every storm passes," she repeated over the thunderous sound.

While she'd only echoed what he'd said, hearing her say it triggered something inside of him—a reserve of strength, a well of resilience. With a swift, decisive motion, he pulled. And there it was. That little bit of movement, that oomph, that last bit of might —ever so slight, but the motion that tipped the scales. He dug deeper. "Come on," he cried, pleading with the piece of old wood. And holy shit, the damned slat listened. The metal parted ways with the weathered board with a final, furious tug.

"He's free," he cried.

Toot! Toot! Toot! Toot!

Toot! Toot! Toot! Toot!

The woman scooped the pup into her arms. "I've got him!"

Toot! Toot! Toot! Toot!

Toot! Toot! Toot! Toot!

The train's shadow loomed over them.

Christian tightened his hold on her, and she buried her head in the crook of his neck with the dog cradled in her arms.

It was time to fucking move.

The roar grew deafening. The earth quaked beneath their feet, each tremor a deafening, heart-pounding reminder of the train's unstoppable power. The blaring horn reached an earsplitting crescendo. It reverberated through his body, shaking him to the core.

Toooot!

This was it.

With his heart pounding and muscles straining, he summoned every ounce of strength. He bolted to his feet and whisked them off the tracks. Like a lynx, he lunged back as the train thundered past, inches from where they stood. The lightning-sharp *clackity-clack-clack* crackled in his ears. The heat from the chugging engine whirled through the air. Gravel and dust scraped against his bare skin. He stumbled back a few more paces, his heart galloping in his chest, every nerve electrified. He turned his back to the tracks, shielding the woman and dog as his breath came in ragged gasps.

"We're okay. We're safe," he said, relief infused into the words.

He rested his chin on the crown of her head and tightened his hold on the trespassers. This activity wasn't what the doctors had in mind when they told him he could begin to use his left arm for everyday tasks, but he wasn't in pain, and he sure as hell couldn't—*wouldn't*—let go. He continued back a few more paces, then dropped to his knees, allowing his legs to bear the brunt of the load. Taking his first even breath, he looked over his shoulder as the end of the freight train drew closer and spied another engine. It wasn't surprising. To traverse the mountains, lines of boxcars were bookended by engines, the front engines pulling while the back pushed. A train operator craned his head out the window. Christian waved, and the man theatrically wiped his brow—providing the universal *phew* gesture.

Phew was right. Jesus, that was a close call. Had they waited another second—another half second—it would have been over for the three of them.

Christ, he'd almost died with a stranger and a stray dog on a railroad track.

But he didn't. And the storm passed.

"Are we alive? Are we really, really alive? Like one hundred percent alive?" the woman stammered, her voice laced with panic.

He shifted the bulk of his companions' weight to his right arm. "Yes, we're okay. Just breathe. I've got you," he said softly, holding her to his bare chest, feeling her lithe body tremble in his arms.

"I can't open my eyes. They're sealed shut. I can't move. I'm frozen. I'm immobilized. I might be stuck like this permanently," she rattled off, then, contrary to what she'd stated, she shifted slightly, brushing her bare arm against his exposed torso. "Um… sir?" she said meekly.

"Yeah?"

"Were you always shirtless?"

He couldn't help but smile—and an ease he hadn't known in ages radiated through his body. "Yes, on the shirtless part. But I don't usually run around half-naked saving dogs and damsels in distress from runaway trains like some half-dressed romance book cover model. However, I do have some good news for you."

"And what's that?" she asked as the roar of the freight train became a distant thrum.

"You're not completely immobilized. Your mouth appears to work," he said as the howling winds followed the locomotive and the world stilled.

She chuckled. Her breath tickled his skin as she smiled against his neck. The sensation of her cheek muscles moving sent a ripple of heat through him, and his entire being became attuned to the nearness of her presence. She relaxed into his embrace, and time ceased to exist. In that quiet, relief-laden moment, nothing else mattered. It was just the two of them—well, the three of them, united by their profound connection. Thank God they'd survived. He closed his eyes and held her as gratitude washed over him—a gentle wave, soothing and all-encompassing. Damn, it felt good to feel something besides rage and clawing disappointment. He settled into the moment and inhaled notes of maple and cinnamon—her scent.

It was as if he'd rescued the goddess of fall and her skinny canine companion.

"We're alive, and I can talk," she said, continuing her adrenaline-fueled stream of conscious chatter. "That's good. That's probably the best outcome—being alive and not splattered across the tracks. Yikes, that's quite a visual. And sorry about the verbal vomit fest. I did that with the queens, too."

"Queens?" he repeated. He must have misheard her.

"Yep, queens. You see, I'm a nervous talker. I talk when I'm anxious. I guess that means the same thing. You get it, though, right?"

"Yeah," he said, spellbound by the woman.

"And sometimes, I talk to myself," she continued. "Okay, a lot of times I talk to myself. I'm alone quite a bit. So, heaps of solitude. But I'll stop talking. Or maybe we could keep talking but change the subject. Or maybe my brain is about to explode, and I should reserve as much oxygen as possible and shut my trap, but I don't think that's how brains work, so there's that." She paused. "And—I must emphasize this—I can't tell you how much I wish I could jam a giant slice of pie in my mouth to stop this stream of blathering. Oh my gosh, another jarring visual. And if you feel something sticky, I might have pie in my hair. But for the record, pie does make everything better."

Damn, she could talk.

He lowered his head. "I agree with you about pie making everything better. I don't detect anything sticky, but I smell cinnamon and…" He paused. "Maybe maple syrup?"

"Wow, you've got a good nose. I'm sort of covered in maple pumpkin pie. It's one of the best pumpkin pie flavors, in my opinion. Top five, possibly top three. There are so many delicious ways to make a pumpkin pie that it's hard to rank them. But it sounds like I just did. Okay, I'm closing my mouth."

Her off-the-rails pie commentary was adorable, but it wasn't all pie jabbering. He caught the part about her being alone. Her words struck a chord within him, awakening what felt a hell of a lot like a tiny fragment of his past self—the part that cared, the part that never gave up.

"You're okay. You're safe," he said, rubbing lazy circles on her back. "You're coming down from an adrenaline high. It can make you do strange things, feel strange things, see strange things—"

"What about *say* strange things?"

"That, too. It's a normal physiological reaction," he answered, then gasped as something warm and moist tickled his side. "And when I mentioned feeling strange things, it's like whatever's going on against my ribs."

"Oh, that's licking, but it's not me. I'm not a licker. Sorry, I am a licker—especially with whipped cream or ice cream, which are delicious served with pie or on top of pie. Pie à la mode. Oh my God! I don't know what's happening with my mouth. But I promise, I'm not licking you."

He continued making slow circles to help her unwind. "Don't worry. I never pegged you as the licker. You're clearly too busy talking to get in any licking. How is Lucky? I assume he's the culprit."

She relaxed and laughed a light and airy sound. "This guy is quite a little lover. Let's get a better look at you, Mr. Lucky." She straightened slightly, and something—no, a couple of items—fell from her pocket. They tapped his leg, then hit the ground.

He started to look just as the dog's coal-colored nose peeked out from beneath her curtain of tousled hair. "Hey, little guy," he said, directing his attention to the jet-black animal's soulful brown eyes.

She scratched behind his ears. "Are you okay, buddy? I don't think you're hurt. You don't seem to be in pain. That was scary, wasn't it? But you are such a brave, good boy," she cooed.

Again, Christian couldn't wipe the damn grin off his face. She had the kind of voice that tugged at something deep inside him. He could listen to this woman read the phonebook and deem it time well spent. He tried to get a look at his damsel, this enchanting stranger, but that curtain of strawberry-blond hair still hid her face. It seemed almost surreal that he couldn't describe the appearance of the person he'd shared a life-or-death experience with, yet there was something thrilling about the mystery—an intriguing allure.

And speaking of allure…Lucky's allure appeared to be his puppy-dog eyes and enthusiasm for tasting everything within range of his little pink tongue. Christian studied the canine train enthusiast as the dog went to town on his shoulder. Lucky resembled a lab mix. He had to be around thirty or thirty-five pounds. He wasn't a puppy but didn't seem fully grown, either.

Christian patted the dog. "He's scrawny and could use a meal and a bath, but he's—"

"No worse for wear," she said, her words matching and overlapping with his.

And holy hell, what was going on? Were they already finishing each other's sentences?

She trembled in his arms.

Had she felt it, too?

"I can't thank you enough for what you did. You saved me. You saved us," she said softly.

She shifted in his lap. Turning into him, she raised her chin, and his pulse kicked up as her strawberry-blond locks parted. The fall sun lit her face, and his heart leaped into his throat.

No way!

He blinked, thinking the light was playing tricks on him, but it wasn't. He was face-to-face with the woman he believed only lived in his dreams. He studied her features. Her cheeks glowed with a natural warmth, and her button nose gave her a subtle charm—just like in his dreams. Perhaps it was a trick of his subconscious, but in his dreams, he didn't know her eye color. Still, something inside him knew if he had identified them in his slumber, they would have looked like this—a dazzling hazel, flecked with mesmerizing shades of greens and golds.

"It's you. How can it be you?" he whispered, overwhelmed by the realization that his dream girl was right in front of him.

"How can it be *you*?" she shrieked, wide-eyed. She bolted from his lap, moving so abruptly her elbow collided with his left eye.

And Christ, she had some power for such a tiny thing. His face ached, but the possibility of a black eye was the least of his concerns. His mystery woman clung to the dog, holding him close.

She took a step back. "I didn't know it was you. I didn't real-ize..." She peered at his chest. "I didn't know you had a tattoo. Give what you love everything you've got," she said, reading the words he'd had inked above his heart.

Words he'd been trying to forget.

She shook her head as if to order her jumbled thoughts. "What are you doing here?"

What was she up to?

He watched her closely. "I live here."

"You live in Starrycard Creek. Everyone knows that. You're Christian Starrycard."

He frowned. This was getting stranger by the second. "Lady, you're in Starrycard Creek."

"No, I hadn't arrived yet."

Was she okay? Was he?

Perhaps the surge of adrenaline, mixed with the meds and alcohol in his system, had caused him to hallucinate. He caught a glint out of the corner of his eye. He peered at the ground and noticed a stone that wouldn't be found out here by the tracks and a baseball card—his college card from RMU. These had to be the items that had fallen from her pocket, and his need to know who this woman was grew stronger by the minute.

The card was rare—only a limited quantity were printed. But the rock glinting in the sun next to it was the true mystery. He'd brushed a similar stone off his bedside table. Starry quartzite—the unique stone found only around Starrycard Creek. But this wasn't any starry quartzite stone.

This one was marked.

The rock alone would have been curious but not jaw-dropping. It was the two lines carved down the center that left him speechless. Add in that, until thirty seconds ago, he believed a woman who looked exactly like the one standing before him was merely a figment of his imagination, and boom. This had to be the definition of a complete mind fuck.

They stared at each other, disbelief radiating between them. It was as if everything in their lives had led to this moment.

He walked toward her as if an invisible force called him to her. "Who are you? How do you have these things?" He lifted his hand and tucked a lock of hair behind her ear, needing to touch her again to make sure she was real. His hand lingered on her neck. Her pulse beat a rapid rhythm that echoed in his racing heart. And that wasn't all. Her skin was impossibly soft. It was as if he already knew every curve, every contour.

Tangible energy thrummed between them, bringing with it an understanding that settled into his soul—this woman, the person in his dreams, was real and meant to be his.

"I'm Maggie," she said softly, blushing the most beguiling shade of pink, then gifted him with a smile he'd only known in his dreams.

"Maggie," he repeated, saying the word like a prayer. The two syllables curled around him like an embrace. "How is this real? How are you real?" he asked, holding her hazel gaze.

"Chris, Christian!" came a voice—his brother Owen's voice.

The man's panicked cries popped the bubble of wonder and awe. Maggie startled, then took a step back with the dog wriggling in her arms. She wobbled on the loose rock.

"It's okay. It's my brother." He picked up the card and the stone. "What are you doing with these? Why are you here?"

"I'm here because—"

"Jesus, Chris, your arm!" Owen exclaimed, fear and exasperation shining in his eyes. "Are you okay? I saw what happened from the road. Did you jack up your arm? Should we call the doctor?"

Christian pocketed the items. "I'm okay. Calm down, O."

"And you, miss. That was insane. The train just missed you," Owen continued, looking her over. "Are you hurt? Is the dog all right?"

"We're fine," she replied. Her blush had faded, and she'd turned ghostly pale.

"You're shaking. You should sit. Both of you should sit. Chris, are you in pain?" Owen went on, going into older brother mode. "Miss, I can take the dog from you. Here, let me help." He reached for the animal, but Lucky wasn't having it. The pup wriggled, worming into Maggie's embrace. She wobbled back a few more steps to counter the animal's frantic movements.

Christian zeroed in on the rocks behind her. "Don't move! Don't take another step!" he shouted, urgency coating his words.

The dog twisted and struggled in her arms. She inhaled sharply and swayed, her body arching toward the tracks.

She was going down.

Instinct took over. He sprang forward. He nearly had her. He was so damned close, but she slipped through his grasp. Their eyes met for a fleeting second before her head struck the iron edge of the railroad track with a sickening thud. The dog scrambled to his feet, whimpering as he licked her face, but she didn't respond —didn't open her eyes, didn't move a muscle.

Christian dove to the ground. Panic tore through him as he knelt beside her. Her chest rose and fell slowly. She was breathing —at least there was that—but she was unconscious. And there was blood coming from the back of her head. Playing ball, he knew a thing or two about head injuries. They could be bad, life-altering. He gathered her into his arms. "Owen, call for help! And give me your jacket. She's bleeding. I need to stop it."

His brother hesitated, his attention darting between Christian and the unconscious woman. "I didn't mean to scare her," he stammered, anguish etched on his face.

"Owen, call for help. I don't have my phone. We need an ambulance. And give me your jacket now. I have to put pressure on her head to stop the bleeding."

"Yeah, of course." He whipped off his coat, handed it over, then pulled his cell from his pocket. "We have a medical emergency at the Donnelly Ranch. A woman hit her head and is unconscious. Send an ambulance." He stilled, listening to the dispatcher. "Her name? Chris, what's her name?"

Christian cradled Maggie's head in his lap. He looked up to find his brother gazing at her. The man seemed just as struck by her as he was.

"Chris, who is she? What's her name?" Owen repeated, anxiety coating his words.

Christian peered at the woman from his dreams—at the face that had given him peace these last few torturous months. He couldn't lose her. Not like this. Not at all.

"Her name is Maggie."

"The name on her apron?" Owen asked.

Christian spied the green letters. He hadn't even noticed them. "Yeah."

Owen nodded and continued the call.

Christian pressed the jacket against the gash on her head. "Maggie," he rasped, his heart lodged in his throat. "Breathe, Maggie. Keep breathing." He stroked her cheek, the warmth of her skin a fragile lifeline. Her arrival with the stone and his baseball card had to mean something. He felt it. His heart knew it. He leaned in and lowered his voice. "I'm here, Maggie. You're not alone. I just found you, and I can't lose you."

MAGGIE SIGHED AS A STEADY, distant tap wove through the dreamy haze.

No, it wasn't quite a tap. It was a *ting.*

Ting, ting, ting.

Like a metal measuring spoon meeting the edge of a mixing bowl. A pleasing sound, a comforting sound. But something was amiss. A scent? A taste?

What a curious thought.

She inhaled a slow, steady breath.

The sterile scent of antiseptic mingled with the aroma of fresh flowers. She didn't know what she should be smelling, but whatever was in the air was not what she'd expected. Her fingers twitched against cool sheets. She had to be in bed. Okay, that was a start. She moved her thumb, brushing it along the soft fabric, and was rewarded for the effort. A warm hand enveloped hers as a gentle voice pierced the groggy layer of slumber.

"Maggie, can you hear me?"

She focused on the voice—a man's voice laced with tenderness. It coaxed her from the sleepy shadows. She wanted to open her eyes, but her eyelids were heavy, so heavy. Still, his voice anchored her to the present, guiding her out of the misty darkness. She opened her eyes and blinked, not recognizing the man. He watched her intently, like she was the center of his world.

She swallowed, a tight, labored motion. "Who is Maggie?" she whispered.

He leaned in. "You are. You're Maggie." The concern in his eyes gradually gave way to relief, and he gifted her with an endearing half-grin.

"I'm Maggie? That's me?" she asked. Why was confirming her name a difficult task? Why couldn't she access this information? It was an odd sensation, like walking through a library and finding every book filled with blank pages.

"Yes, your name is Maggie," he answered, his smile fading as his worried expression returned.

"Who are you?" she asked.

"I'm Christian."

"Christian," she repeated. She stared into his sage-green eyes, which were striking despite the dark circles underneath them. One eye appeared to be a touch black and blue. *Strange.* There was an unkempt attractiveness to his appearance. His sharp jawline was covered in messy stubble, giving him a rugged, mountain man air. He wore a ball cap over a dark tangle of hair. His wrinkled white T-shirt had writing on it. *Starrycard Creek Paper Company.* The shirt stretched across his broad chest. He was a big man with a muscular build, the kind who must command the attention of a room without even trying. A sling on his left arm hinted at a recent injury. Despite her close examination, she couldn't place him.

"Do I know you?" she asked, her gaze darting to their clasped hands. Logic told her to let go of the stranger's hand, but a peculiar connection held her back.

"You were on my land. We rescued a dog together."

"We rescued a dog?" she repeated, unsure if she was awake or dreaming.

"He was stuck on the railroad tracks, and a train was coming. Do you remember that?" Christian continued.

"No, I don't remember." Her brain felt like a bowl of three-day-old oatmeal. How could she forget about saving a dog from an oncoming train? It sounded memorable—and remarkably terrifying. "Is the dog okay?"

Christian squeezed her hand. "Yes, Lucky's fine. He misses you."

"Is Lucky my dog?" She didn't recall having a pet.

What was happening?

"No…well, yes, maybe? He might be *ours* now."

"Ours?"

"There haven't been any reports of a missing dog. My niece has been taking care of him for us."

Us?

She tried to recall the animal but came up with nothing. And *coming up with nothing* might as well be her mantra. Who was this guy? She peered at her left hand. No ring. That seemed to rule out the man being her husband. "Are you my boyfriend? Are we related?"

He glanced away. "No."

She took in his sling and his eye, then gasped. "Did you get hit by the train?"

"No, I had shoulder surgery a couple of months ago for a condition called avascular necrosis, and the eye…"

She eyed the discolored skin. "What about your eye?"

He cringed. "You did that to me."

What kind of person was she? "I punched you in the eye?" she exclaimed.

"It was an accident. You got me with your elbow."

Her life was getting crazier by the second—and she didn't recall even one iota of it.

She inhaled a shaky breath. "Let me get this straight. My name is Maggie. You and I saved a dog from being hit by a train. A dog that may or may not be mine or ours. Then I elbowed you in the eye?" she asked as if she wasn't quite familiar with the rules of this place that she sure as hell hoped was Earth.

"Yes, that's right."

"My name is Maggie," she repeated, hoping it would jump-start her addled mind.

It didn't.

Christian shifted in his seat. "You told me your name was Maggie. It was also embroidered on your child-sized apron."

Child-sized apron? Forget crazy. They'd hit Bonkersville.

"Why was I wearing an apron made for a child? Where is this apron? Can I see it?"

"It's not here. McKenzie, my niece, the one who's been caring for Lucky, has it. She's seven. It fits her, and she wanted to wash it for you. My family's been coming by to see how you're doing. That's where all the flowers came from," he said, gesturing to the windowsill.

She peered at the line of vases. "Do I know your family?"

"You briefly met my brother after we saved the dog. Do you remember Owen?"

Owen?

"No." The room went topsy-turvy. She blinked, struggling to regain her bearings. She pushed up onto her elbows. She was on some type of incline and needed a better look at her surroundings.

"Careful," he cautioned, releasing her hand and rising to his feet. Gently, he slipped his good arm beneath her and helped her sit up. His touch was familiar, like he'd held her, like he knew her body. But who was he to her? Try as she might, she couldn't connect the dots.

And where the heck was she?

She looked around, taking in the sterile white walls, the rhythmic beeping of medical monitors, and the IV stand next to her bed. She peered at the needle in her left arm. "Am I in the hospital? Am I sick?"

Christian returned to his seat and took her hand. "You hit your head on the railroad tracks after we saved the dog. You lost consciousness."

"Was I in a coma?"

"Yes."

She patted her face, chest, and shoulders. "Am I awake? I don't mean to be rude. But is this really happening?" She paused as a fuzzy half-recollection hit. "I feel like I've asked that question before."

"This is real. You started to wake up yesterday. The nurses told me it was a positive sign, and then your neurologist said that your last scans were good. The swelling in your brain had gone down. But then you were out again. They left an IV in your arm for fluids."

Holy wow!

"Have you been here with me?" she asked, peering past him at a stack of to-go boxes with the words Goldie's on the Creek stamped to the side. A slew of empty water bottles around the trash can joined the mound of take-out containers.

"Yeah, I've been here the entire time."

She watched him, wishing her brain would give her something. "Again, I apologize if this sounds rude, but who are you to me?"

His mouth opened and closed like a confused flounder.

Why was he struggling to answer what should have been a simple question? He traced slow circles on her palm with his thumb, a movement that felt like a distant memory, before offering her the hint of a boyish grin. "I'm someone who didn't want you to be alone when you woke up."

They didn't have a relationship, but they'd saved a dog together, and he didn't seem to know her beyond that.

She frowned. Nothing was adding up. "How long have I been here?"

"A week."

"A week?" she whisper-shouted, anxiety seeping in.

Whoever she was, she'd been missing from a life she didn't recall for seven days. *Seven days!* What if she had a job and a family? There had to be someone out there worried about her, right?

A nurse peeked in through the open door. "Well, well, it's good to see you awake, Maggie. I'll get the doctor. How's our patient doing, Christian?"

"She's a bit confused," he replied, concern flickering in his eyes.

"A week," Maggie whispered, unable to focus on the nurse or put the pieces of her life together because there were no pieces.

Nothing.

Christian continued rubbing slow circles against her palm. "Just breathe, Maggie. It's okay. Let's take it slow. Tell me anything you remember. How about your last name."

She shook her head. "I should be able to tell you my last name." But she couldn't. She wasn't even sure if her name was Maggie or Margaret or Marjorie, Magdalena, Magnolia, or Marguerite. And hello, jolt of panic, take three? Four? Five? The beeping increased to a rapid thrum. The frantic sound amplified like somebody had cranked up the volume.

"Let's stick with Maggie. You're my Maggie. Just keep breathing. Focus on me. We're in this together," he said gently, squeezing her hand.

What was this man talking about?

"I'm *your* Maggie? I thought we just met. What's happening?" she demanded.

For the space of a breath, pain flashed in his eyes. "Yes, sorry, I'm a little sleep deprived. You're just Maggie. I think you were coming to see me when you noticed a dog stuck on the tracks. I saw you and ran to help."

She kept shaking her head. Nothing made sense.

She pegged him with her gaze. "Why do you think I would come to see you?"

"You had these items with you." He reached into his pocket and retrieved a stone and a baseball card.

"No purse? No ID? No phone? Just those things?" she pressed.

"Yes," he answered softly, like he'd wished he could give her more and ease her anxiety.

She studied the peculiar items. "That rock is a lovely little thing." She touched the surface. "I wonder who would scrape two lines on it and…" She looked between the card and the man. "Wait, that's you. You played baseball for Rocky Mountain University?"

"Yes."

She perked up. "I could have gone to school there. We could have met there. The school is in Colorado, right?" Okay, she knew something. Hooray for basic geography. "What state are we in now?" she asked, excitement beginning to edge out fear.

"Colorado. You're in Starrycard Creek, Colorado."

She nodded, working to weave together the fragments. "I'm probably from this state. That has to be how we know each other."

She figured he'd be thrilled by this information. But his pained expression conveyed the opposite.

"I know we didn't meet there."

"How do you know?" she pressed, grasping at anything that could give her a window into her life.

"Even if you did attend RMU, I'm pretty sure I'm older than you—old enough that we wouldn't have attended at the same time."

"How old are you?"

"Twenty-nine."

"And I'm…" She paused as another fact about her life came up blank.

"I'm guessing you're closer in age to my youngest sister. She's in her early twenties. So even if you went to RMU, we wouldn't have met there, and…" He brushed his thumb across her knuckles.

"And?" she repeated, her voice a wisp of a sound as his touch set off butterflies in her belly.

Why was she reacting to a stranger's touch like a starry-eyed schoolgirl?

"And if I had met you, I would have remembered." His boyish half-grin returned.

Yowza! He was a beautiful man. Despite the void where her memories should be, she felt an inexplicable bond with him, as if her soul recognized him in a way her mind couldn't.

But could she trust him?

A knock snapped her out of it. She slipped her hand from his grasp and peered at a woman in a white coat standing in the doorway. "You must be my doctor."

"Yes, hello, Maggie, I'm Doctor Ironside, a neurologist here at Creek County Hospital. It's good to see you awake. How are you feeling?" The woman had a grandmotherly warmth about her.

"I'm confused, doctor," Maggie began. "I can't remember anything. Has anyone come for me who knows me? Has anyone called looking for someone named Maggie?"

The doctor offered a placating grin. "No."

"Are you sure?"

"We've taken the extra steps of sharing your description with the Sheriff's Department since you were admitted as Maggie with no last name."

Maggie froze. Every muscle in her body tensed, her eyes darting wildly as if searching for some rational explanation. "And nobody's looking for me? The police haven't heard anything?"

"No, but Mr. Starrycard's been with you the entire time."

Maggie glanced at Christian. A man who barely knew her had stayed by her side while she was in a coma, and nobody else on the planet seemed to know she was missing.

No, no, no! This could not be happening.

She wrapped her arms around her body. After a week's absence, someone must be worried. Or did she have no one? A knot formed in her belly.

Who was she?

"May I check you over?" the doctor asked, removing her stethoscope from around her neck.

"Yeah...okay," Maggie answered, trying to stay calm, but it was getting harder by the second to remain composed.

"Let me share what we know," the doctor said gently. "We've

been monitoring your vitals, and I've gone over your scans. Mr. Starrycard reported that you hit your head on the railroad track. You suffered a cerebral contusion. That's a bruise on your brain tissue. The condition is often accompanied by swelling. This led to a loss of consciousness."

Maggie searched the woman's face for answers. "I don't remember falling."

"What do you remember?"

Maggie closed her eyes. Feeling Christian's gaze on her, she worked to access something—anything. Again, she failed. She sighed, her heart racing. "I don't remember anything about myself or how I got here. And you're sure no one is looking for me?" She glanced at Christian. His jaw had tightened as deep concern welled in his eyes.

"No, I checked again before coming in," the doctor answered. "No one has contacted the hospital or law enforcement looking for anyone named Maggie or anyone with your description."

Christian reached out, his hand trembling as he took hers. "We'll figure this out. I promise," he said, his voice thick with emotion.

She blinked back tears and turned to the doctor. "What's happening to me? Why can't I remember?"

"You've experienced head trauma, leading to amnesia," the doctor explained, her expression growing solemn.

"Amnesia," Maggie repeated, wide-eyed. "That really happens to people?"

"It's rare, but it does occur. The brain is incredibly complex. It processes mental and physical trauma differently in each person, which is why your memory loss is wholly unique to you. The good news is that with the brain's ability to adapt and recover, there's hope for regaining some or all of your memories over time."

Maggie exhaled a shaky breath. "How do I do this? Where do I do this? I don't know where I live. I'm alone."

"You're not alone, Maggie," Christian countered.

"But we just met," she said, fear taking over.

"That might be true, but I believe you came to town to return the stone and card to me. You're here because of me and…I'm here because of you."

I'm here because of you? What did that even mean?

She drew in another uneven breath. Her body ached to move, to get out of this room, this place. She studied the IV in her arm. "Doctor, can you remove the IV? I don't think I'm comfortable in hospitals. I'm feeling anxious, and this needle in my arm isn't helping."

"I can do that," the doctor replied. "Aversion to hospitals is something you have in common with your companion. My cousin sends his regards, Mr. Starrycard."

Christian's gaze flicked to the ground. "Give him my best."

"I also hear the physical therapy department misses you," the doctor chided, eyeing Christian before peeling back the medical tape and removing the IV.

Christian released her hand and stood back to let the doctor work, but the man was agitated. His tense demeanor spoke volumes. "I'm aware I've missed a few appointments."

"Maggie, I'm not sure if you know this, but Christian Starrycard is our local celebrity," Dr. Ironside continued.

Maggie studied the man. "You're a celebrity?"

He shrugged. "I used to be a professional baseball player. That's what I did after college." He adjusted his sling. "What are Maggie's next steps for her care, doc?" he asked, his demeanor still tense as he changed the subject.

But she didn't need Christian to advocate for her. She knew what she wanted.

"I'd like to leave the hospital…now," she blurted before the doctor could answer. "Getting out into the world might be the key to unlocking my past."

The doctor pursed her lips. "While your labs and scans are normal, I'd like you to stay a bit longer in the hospital for observation. You shouldn't be alone so soon after gaining consciousness."

"But I need to go. I can't be here," she said as forcefully as she could.

Worry creased the doctor's brow. "Let's wait a few days. It's dangerous to be alone after a head injury. And your memory loss gives me more reason to keep you here."

Maggie shuddered. It was as if the walls in the tiny room were closing in on her. "No…please…I can't stay here. Hospitals make me anxious. I don't know if that's something I always felt or if it's new, but I'll do whatever you tell me to do—just not here."

"Maggie will stay with me," Christian said, stepping forward. "She won't be alone, doc. I know a thing or two about head injuries. I've had teammates get clocked. I'm familiar with the protocols. I know what to look for if Maggie needs medical attention."

"You'd do that for me? You'd let me live with you?" she asked, wide-eyed. *Who was he to her? There had to be something he wasn't telling her.*

"I have an enormous ranch. Twelve bedrooms—all suites. There's plenty of room. Think of it like a bed-and-breakfast for—"

"People who can't remember their last name?" she said, cutting him off. *And where did that sassy comment come from?*

But Christian seemed to like it. He offered her the hint of that boyish half-grin. "Sure, it's a niche market. The Amnesia B and B. Our motto: You won't remember if our service sucks."

"You should probably come up with a better name," she replied, staring into his eyes as a calmness washed over her. Ten seconds ago, she was on the cusp of a breakdown, and now she was joking about memory loss. Whoever he was, this man seemed to steady her.

His whisper of a smile widened. "I'll work on the name."

The frenzied emotions swirling inside her eased up a fraction. She had a place to go. Now, she had to convince the doctor she was well enough to leave.

She held the woman's gaze. "I'd like to check myself out of the hospital and stay with Christian…Mr. Starrycard. The guy with a ranch. The man with twelve rooms catering to amnesia, which sounds rather silly. And I know there's nothing funny about memory loss or a ranch for people who can't remember their last name or how old they are. Because it's never nice to make fun of a medical condition. That's cruel, but sometimes you've got to laugh, or you'll cry, right?" *What was happening with her mouth?* "I'm sorry," she said, touching her lips after spewing that word salad extravaganza. "I don't know why I'm blathering on."

"It's something you do when you're anxious," Christian answered.

She stared at the man. "Is it? How do you know that?"

"You did the same thing after we saved the dog."

That had to be a promising sign.

She pegged the doctor with her gaze. "Look, I did something pre-amnesia Maggie would do, so I must be on the road to recovery."

Dr. Ironside tapped the side of the bed, her lips pursed as she appeared to mull over the situation. "We certainly don't want to keep you in a distressing environment." She paused, then nodded to herself. "All right, Maggie, I'll allow you to leave, but I'd like you to start taking a medication that will help with your anxiety."

"I can do that."

"And you must promise me that you won't be alone," the doctor continued.

"I'll be with her. I won't let her out of my sight. You have my word," Christian said, his tone commanding and resolute.

The doctor's demeanor sharpened. "If you experience any dizziness or nausea, I want you back at the hospital. No toughing it out. No ignoring symptoms. And you need to take the meds and let me know if you experience any side effects. Can you agree to that?"

"I can," Maggie said, her voice trembling with relief.

Dr. Ironside removed an iPad from her jacket pocket, entered some information, and gave Christian a once-over. "It appears you're in good hands, Maggie. I'll have your discharge papers and that medication sent immediately. It'll also have resources to help get you back on your feet. I encourage you to get follow-up care."

"Do I have to return to the hospital for that?" Maggie glanced around the sterile room, her chest tightening as if it were preparing for another pang of anxiety.

"Not if you don't want to."

"Oh, good."

"The Starrycard Creek Senior Center offers counseling, therapeutic, and rehabilitation services. That goes for you as well, Christian. I'm sure they'd welcome you with open arms…now," the doctor added, biting back a grin.

"Perhaps," he murmured, not meeting the woman's gaze.

What was that all about?

No, she couldn't worry about that. She had enough on her plate.

She released a heavy breath, her shoulders relaxing. "Thank you, Dr. Ironside, for everything."

The doctor rested her hand on the end of the hospital bed. "Be patient with yourself. I know it's easier said than done, but don't stress too much about trying to remember everything at once. Routine and structure are important. Spend time outside and follow a schedule. Fall is a glorious season in the mountains."

Maggie nodded, excitement building, so close to getting out of this place. "Routine and schedule. Got it."

The doctor took a step toward the door, then stopped. "And if anyone contacts the hospital looking for you, we'll get in touch."

"Thank you."

"One last thing," the woman said, watching Christian from the corner of her eye. "Get a notebook. Start journaling. Track your new memories and experiences. Write whatever comes to mind. That should be something Mr. Starrycard can help you with."

"Do you journal?" Maggie asked, watching her new roommate closely.

With the mention of journaling, the coolness in his demeanor thawed a fraction. "No, not really. I believe the good doctor is referring to my family's artisan papermaking business. We make pretty spectacular notebooks."

She glanced at his shirt. "Is that a papermaking business? The Starrycard Creek Paper Company?"

"That's it," he replied, warmth returning to his tone.

"I have a final piece of advice," the doctor said from the doorway. "Be open to new experiences. I believe your memories will return, Maggie. I have a feeling you'll find your path."

Her path. Why did that feel familiar?

"I hope you're right," she answered as a fleeting flash of red echoed in her mind.

"Are you okay?" Christian asked after the doctor left the room.

She brushed off the feeling and examined the pink hospital gown. A fading glimmer of recognition returned, then receded. She strained to recall why another color called to her—doing exactly what the doctor had told her explicitly to avoid. She wrote off the odd inkling and met Christian's gaze. "I don't know what I enjoy."

He lit up. "You like pie."

"Pie?" she repeated.

Wide-eyed, his jaw dropped. "You don't remember what pie is? The dessert. It's like crusty cake but not really cake."

"No," she said, unable to stop herself from laughing at the crusty-cake line. "I know what pie is. It's just a totally random thing for you to know about me. Did I tell you that?"

"You did. We didn't talk much. We were mostly engaged in freeing the dog and not getting hit by a freight train, but after we were safe and coming down from the adrenaline high, you mentioned pie. That was when you went off on a tangent. And you smelled like pie. You might have had some pie in your hair." He said these things like they were endearing, not mind-blowingly bizarre.

"And for some reason, I had your college baseball card and a scratched-up rock that might belong to you?" she asked, mulling over the facts.

"I'm not sure how you got them or why you have them, but they had to be what led you to me," he replied, then looked away like he had when the doctor put him on the spot.

He was leaving something out. She could feel it. Or was her mind playing tricks on her? Whatever it was, she'd worry about it after they'd left the hospital. She peered at a stack of clothing on a chair with a pair of brown boots beneath it. "Are those mine?" she asked and gestured to the neat pile.

"Yeah, I washed them for you," he said, handing them over.

She held the items to her chest and waited for him to leave, but the man didn't budge. "I'd like to get dressed."

"Okay."

"Can I have a little privacy?"

He stood his ground. "I'm not taking my eyes off you. You heard Dr. Ironside's instructions. You shouldn't be left alone."

"You want to see me naked?"

His eyes nearly popped out of his head. "No, Jesus, no way! I mean…I'm not saying *no way* like I would be turned off by it. You're beautiful, absolutely perfect. You might have the cutest nose I've ever seen. Your eyes. They're just right. Hazel with flecks of gold and green. Christ, they're spellbinding. And your body is… I mean, who wouldn't want to see you naked? *Shit!* I meant that as a statement of fact. But that sounded wrong, really wrong. And sexist and creepy, and I'm not a creepy guy. I realize only creepy guys will probably tell you they're not creepy, but I promise you, I'm not creepy. I'm *un-creepy, anti-creepy.* Those aren't words, and…now I sound like you did after the train."

His anxious rambling was rather charming.

"How about you close the door and look away for a moment?" she suggested, suppressing a grin.

Knowing he was nervous made her more at ease.

He exhaled an audible breath. "That's a solid plan, but first, I'm helping you out of bed."

She waved him off. "No, I can do it."

He frowned, his gaze darkening. *And holy intensity!* This was not the awkward man from thirty seconds ago. No, this man was not messing around. "I'm sorry if I wasn't clear, Maggie," he said, coming to her side. "I wasn't *asking* for your permission to help you. How many times do I have to say this? You're not doing this alone."

Wowza! The man could take charge.

Her gaze didn't waver. "Okay," she answered, her voice carrying a breathy, sultry note.

He slipped his good arm around her. "Is this okay?"

"Yes," she whispered, striving to maintain control, but his touch sent her pulse racing.

"Are you feeling dizzy or lightheaded?"

She turned toward him, a motion that her body seemed to recognize. "No, I'm steady. But what about your shoulder? I don't want to hurt you."

"You could never hurt me," he said against the shell of her ear, his voice a low rasp.

She nodded. It was all she could do.

With a steady hand, he helped her off the hospital bed. Her bare feet hit the cold linoleum, and the sudden icy shock forced a gasp from her lips. She shivered, and he tightened his grip, holding her close.

"It's just the floor. It's a bit cool. You can let go," she said, her tone far more breathless than she'd anticipated.

"No, not yet. Take a second to acclimate yourself. Your only movement this past week has been from the passive range of motion and mobility exercises I performed on you while you were comatose."

What?

She looked up at him. The man was stone-cold—or linoleum cold—serious. "What did you perform on me?" she asked, rethinking his *un-creepy* line.

"Stretches and some mobility exercises."

She stepped away from the man. "The hospital let you do that to me…on me…for me?"

He shrugged, but a smirk played on his lips. "It's amazing what they'll let local celebrities do."

She scoffed. "You said you were *un-creepy*. That sounds super creepy."

"Okay, ease up there. For the record, no, I didn't ask if I could do it, but I studied biology and kinesiology in college. When it comes to the body, I know what I'm doing. Bodies are made to move. They heal more quickly that way. You feel okay standing, don't you?"

She did a little march in place, testing her balance. "I feel great. Oddly solid."

That slightly cocky half-grin appeared. "Good. The chair is right there if you need it to maintain your balance," he said and kept his gaze locked on her.

"Christian?"

"Uh-huh?" he replied, that sexy smile still gracing his lips.

"Turn around."

"Right, sorry," he stammered, losing the sweet swagger as he closed the door and stared at it.

She wriggled out of the pink hospital gown, eyed the unfamiliar clothing on the chair, then started dressing.

"Do your clothes fit?" he asked, his back still to her.

She zipped the jean skirt. "Yes, why?"

"It's good you have amnesia. You probably don't recall that your shirt was white."

She studied the garment. "It's light pink now."

He shifted his stance. "That's because I accidentally washed your clothes with a red T-shirt of mine. I didn't know it was even in the washing machine. The thing is a beast. The last cleaning person must have left it in there."

"When did you do my laundry?"

"My mom convinced me to head home to take a shower yesterday, and I decided I'd wash your clothes while I was home."

"I see."

"And then I washed them on hot. In my defense, I've never run the damn thing before. It has a control panel like something off a space shuttle. I just pounded on the keyboard till it started."

She stifled a chuckle. "You don't know how to run a washing machine? I have amnesia, and I'm pretty sure I could figure it out."

"I've used a washing machine before. I have five siblings. Growing up, we had chores, and laundry was one of them, but the washing machine I had put in at the ranch is next level."

"Oh, I bet," she said through a giggle.

"Are you laughing at me?"

"No," she said, now doubled over with laughter.

"It sounds a hell of a lot like you're laughing," he replied with a sly teasing edge to his words.

"Maybe a little," she replied, regaining control as she put on her socks and boots. She finished dressing, then peered at herself in the mirror. She smoothed her blouse, taking in her appearance. Her strawberry-blond hair was braided. The tail curved past her shoulder and around her collarbone. "Hello, Maggie," she whispered, peering at the stranger.

"Did you say something?" Christian asked.

"No, just mumbling. I'm ready. I'm dressed," she answered, severing the connection to the girl in the mirror.

He turned and froze. His eyes softened, and he swallowed hard. His confident demeanor dissolved into quiet awe as he drank her in.

"Is something wrong?" she asked after a lingering stretch of silence.

He looked at her like he'd seen her face a thousand times and wanted to see it a thousand more. "No, you're exactly what you're supposed to be."

She tried to decipher the man's words but couldn't. She touched the tail of her braid. "Was my hair like this when we met? It feels different."

He took a step toward her. "Your hair was loose when we met."

"Did you braid it?"

He chuckled. "No, ask my niece. I'm a disaster with girls' hair. I tried to put her hair in a ponytail once. It took me damn near an hour. My sister, Eliza, my niece, my sister-in-law, Izzy, and my brother Finn's fiancée, Hailey, were all in on the braid decision and execution."

"Wow, that's quite an operation for braiding." She glanced at the flowers. "And they've all visited me?"

"Yes."

"That was kind of them. They sound lovely," she said as a whisper of longing tugged at her heart.

The ghost of a grin curled the corners of his mouth. "You might feel differently when you meet them. They're good people —the best. But they're also…a lot."

She couldn't help but smile, her heart warmed by the sight of his genuine affection for his family. "I think you like *a lot*."

His expression grew serious. "I've liked this time, the quiet times, here with you."

"While I've been in a coma?"

He touched her cheek. "I'll take you whatever way I can have you."

And there it was again—that boyish ghost of a grin. He looked at her with such wonder and awe. There was something between them—there had to be. *What was it about this man?* Her mind had forgotten him, but a part of her recognized him and this connection they shared.

"Christian, how do you know me?" she whispered, searching his face.

Pain flashed in his eyes just as the door to the room opened.

"Maggie, last name to be determined," a stout man with a nasally voice called as he entered the room, a stack of papers and a pill bottle in his hands, his hospital ID badge swinging around his neck.

Maggie, last name to be determined?

She blinked, regaining her bearings. "Yes, I guess that's me."

"I've got some meds and information for you."

Her pulse kicked up. "Did someone contact the hospital asking about me?"

"No, I'm Bob from patient services. Here's the medication the doctor wants you to take," he said, handing her a bottle of pills. He held up a couple of sheets of paper. "And these are your discharge instructions. The last sheet is your medical billing invoice. There's a number for a payment plan if you're not able to cover the cost."

She pocketed the pills, then scanned the second page, tracing line after line of charges. Her breath hitched as the air left her lungs. "So many numbers. So much money," she whispered.

"Maggie, Maggie?" Christian called, but she couldn't reply.

Her stomach twisted into knots. "Medical billing. Payment plan," she stammered. Trembling, she fought the encroaching blackness as the edges of her vision blurred. No, this could not be happening. She couldn't afford to faint. If she collapsed, they'd surely revoke her discharge order.

She latched on to one frantic thought.

Don't pass out. Don't pass out.

MAGGIE'S HEART POUNDED. It drowned out the other sounds as the world grew blurrier by the second. She gripped Christian's T-shirt, desperate for grounding. And thank God for the man. In the storm raging inside her, he was her anchor.

She stared at the sheet. Scores of numbers jumped out at her like a swarm of angry wasps. She raised her gaze and read the words again.

Medical billing payment plan.

They were words. Only words.

Just as she was about to be swallowed by darkness, Christian snapped the paper from her hand and shoved it into his pocket. He wrapped his arm around her and held her close. "Maggie, look at me."

Trembling, she lifted her chin and locked on to his gaze.

"I'm taking care of your bills. I've already spoken with the hospital administrator."

"Christian—" she said on a pained exhale.

He sharpened his gaze, assessing her. "Breathe. I know what you're feeling. It's a panic attack. Listen to me. The storm always passes. You're safe. I've got you."

The storm always passes.

She clung to the words. The imagery of dark clouds parting and sunlight kissing her face pulled her back from the brink.

Steadying herself, she shook her head. "I can't allow you to pay my bills."

His gaze sharpened. The sheer force of his drive and focus left her speechless. "I'm not asking your permission to do this. It's done. You don't have to worry about medical debt." He shifted his attention to the man with a stack of papers. "Your name is Bob, right?"

The short man swallowed hard. "Yes, yes, sir. I'm Bob. Officially Robert Kramer, but yes, I'm Bob."

"This is a mistake, Bob. Call someone. Check your piles. Do whatever you need to do, but confirm it's a mistake for Maggie's peace of mind." His voice was calm, but there was an unshakable firmness beneath it that made it clear he meant business.

Bob wiped the sweat from his upper lip. "Um..." he began nervously, "my shift just started, and this billing sheet was on the top of my stack." He shuffled through the pages and zeroed in on another sheet. "Yikes, yes, it is a mistake. I'm sorry, ma'am. Sorry, Mr. Starrycard, I didn't see the updated patient invoice record."

Still holding on to Christian's shirt, she nodded to the man.

"Mistakes happen," Christian said, forgetting the billing guy and holding her gaze. "Storms always pass, right?"

"Storms always pass," she repeated, and the pressure in her chest eased.

Christian turned to the man. "Are we good to go, Bob? I'd like to get Maggie home."

"Yes, you're free to leave. But..."

"Yes?" Christian replied, commanding tone still in place.

Bob shifted his stance. "I wanted to say that it's awful what happened to you—your shoulder injury and losing your spot on the Rattlers. I've been a fan of yours since you played college ball for the RMU Mountain Lions."

Christian pulled her in a fraction closer and tensed. It was a slight movement. The billing guy didn't appear to notice, but she felt it. He'd protected her. Now, it was her turn to be the strong one. She rested her hand on his hammering heart. He turned to her and covered her hand with his left hand. Still bound in the sling, it trembled against her.

Her heart hurt for him. He hid it well, but this man was in pain.

"You were on track to be one of the great ones," Bob continued, oblivious to Christian's discomfort. "Number eleven. Power hitter one-one. You would walk up to the plate, and the entire stadium would hold its breath, wondering how far you would hit it this time. You could have been up there with the greatest players ever. It's heartbreaking your career's over. You were truly in your prime."

How often did he have to endure conversations like this?

"I appreciate your kind words," Christian replied, putting on a brave face, but anguish rolled off him in silent waves. "We should be going. Thank you for clearing up the billing issue, Bob. We appreciate it," he said and guided her out of the room and down the hallway.

She wrapped her arm around him as they walked. His pain was still palpable. And more than anything, she wanted to help him like he'd helped her.

"Christian, stop, please."

He stilled, his gaze trained ahead.

"Are you okay?" she asked, making slow circles on his back like he'd done for her. "I didn't realize your injury was life-changing. I have the feeling I might be the only person who doesn't know what happened to you. I'm so sorry you're hurting."

He watched her, again looking at her like they were connected beyond that train encounter. "I try not to think about it. I've been trying not to think at all lately. You've helped me."

"How could I have helped you?"

"Your...your touch...back there. It helped because..." he stammered, then peered at his injured arm.

"You can tell me."

He shook his head. "It's nothing. I'm good. How are you? You were on the cusp of a panic attack."

"I don't understand why that happened. The billing guy was doing his job. He wasn't rude or pushy."

"Sometimes our bodies know things our minds don't or…" He offered her the teasing whisper of a grin. "Maybe Maggie without amnesia really hates guys named Bob."

She chuckled. "I don't recall any Bobs, but who knows. Screw the Bobs," she said with a pinch of gusto.

"That's the spirit," he replied, the color returning to his cheeks. "Bobs can go to hell. Fuck Bob."

"Fuck Bob! Every Bob can take a long walk off a short pier," she added, enjoying slipping back into this playful dance.

His expression softened. "I'm sorry about that guy. I didn't want you to have to concern yourself with any of that." He took her wrist in his hand and applied gentle pressure. "Your pulse is still elevated, but it's slowing. That's a good sign."

"The storm does pass." She glanced down the hallway, her body aching to leave. "But can we keep moving? Every cell in my body is screaming for me to get out of here. Evidently, I really don't like hospitals. It seems like you're not crazy about them either."

"Yeah, I'm no fan. Let's get out of here, but first, we need an exit plan." He released her to pull his cap lower, shielding his eyes.

Exit plan? What was he talking about?

"Can't we walk out the door?" she asked, watching the stress return to his expression.

"It's not that simple." He surveyed the empty hallway. "There might be people recording us or taking pictures as we leave. It doesn't happen as much in town, but people from all over the region come to Creek County Hospital. It's happened a few times since I've been here. I'm always polite, but we'll keep walking, okay?"

What a life. On top of enduring strangers bringing up his most soul-crushing moment, he had to be perpetually ready for the spotlight.

With the thought of every pair of eyes on them, she glanced at her outfit. "Do I look all right?"

His expression warmed. "You're beautiful—straight out of my dreams."

She watched him closely and homed in on one word. *Dreams.* He'd likened her to something out of his dreams at least a couple of times in the short time since she'd awoken.

He cursed under his breath. "There I go, sounding like a class-A creeper. I meant to say that you look like a normal woman wearing mundane women's clothing." He shook his head. "There's nothing mundane about you or your clothes. You're *un-mundane.* Dammit, that's not a word." He exhaled a pained breath. "You're the only one who can get me tongue-tied."

Again, she couldn't shake the feeling that he knew her beyond their train encounter.

"Why are you doing this for me, Christian? I'm nobody to you."

He winced, as if her words cut him to the bone. "I'm doing this because I can," he said and offered her his hand.

Not sure what to do, she took it. And like everything else with him, the action felt both new and practiced.

"What's the plan?"

He gestured with his chin. "The elevator is at the end of the hall. We'll head down and make a straight shot through the lobby. My car is parked right outside. It's a little after seven, and things usually quiet down at the hospital around this time."

"Sounds easy enough."

They entered the elevator without encountering a soul—a positive start. A few seconds later, a pleasant pair of pings announced their arrival to the lobby. The doors opened, and Christian laced his fingers with hers, tightening his grip as they walked. The man's presence was unmistakable, even with his hat shading his face. There were a dozen people in the lobby. Each one they passed couldn't resist a glance, some murmuring to each other. Christian nodded to a man who called his name. A few cell phones came out, and she did her best to look away.

"Almost there," he whispered as the exit came into view.

The automatic doors parted, and they cleared the building's threshold.

She exhaled, not realizing she'd been holding her breath. "That was quite an experience."

"That was pretty tame," he replied, relief coating his words as they slowed to a leisurely stroll.

She squeezed his hand. "Hold on. I need to stop."

"Are you feeling dizzy?" he asked, releasing her hand to cup her cheek.

His hand radiated warmth against her skin as the crisp breeze enveloped her. She inhaled deeply. The air was rich with the earthy scent of pine, fallen leaves, and a faint trace of minerals. She felt an extraordinary stillness, like the tranquil aftermath of a thunderstorm. Her heartbeat slowed, syncing with the serene environment as she listened to the rustling of leaves and the gentle whisper of the wind.

"Maggie?" he said, searching her face.

She exhaled, the tension draining from her body. "I'm the opposite of dizzy. My life is a complete mystery, but I've never felt so grounded."

Beneath the golden glow of the exterior lights, Christian's features softened. His eyes shined with warmth and what looked a whole lot like adoration. The lines of stress and fatigue at the corners of his eyes disappeared, revealing the boyish charm beneath, and her heart fluttered—positively fluttered—captivated by his attention.

She locked onto his gaze. "We made it out. We're free. What should we do first?"

He stroked her cheek with his thumb, and her body came alive beneath his touch.

Was he about to kiss her? Was she about to let him?

"Maggie," he said, his voice a low rasp.

His eyes burned with a mixture of uncertainty and desire. In the space of a breath, this man—this stranger—had become her entire world. His presence overwhelmed her senses. Were they floating? Were they on the ground, or had they joined the stars twinkling in the night sky? He leaned in, and their breath mingled in the space between them like some force was at work, drawing them together.

"Christian," she whispered, the only word she could produce.

Wonder shined in his eyes. "It's wild to hear you say my name," he whispered, and it sounded more like a confession than a statement.

She drew her tongue across her lips, and his gaze darkened with an unmistakable hunger.

Being seconds away from engaging in a lip-lock session with a stranger was hardly appropriate behavior for someone with no recollection of her past, but it seemed like the natural choice. Calm and centered, her thoughts weren't clouded with worries, and her actions were in harmony. She moved seamlessly, pressing up to her tiptoes as he lowered and came toward her.

Her gaze flickered between Christian's eyes and his lips. Every nerve tingled with anticipation. Time slowed as she waited, her body steady, her heart open, anticipation building for that singular moment when his lips met hers.

Ping, ping, ping!

Like a jarring alarm pulling her from slumber, she gasped and stumbled back.

Christian caught her, keeping her upright, but the longing in his gaze had turned to agitation. "That's my cell," he mumbled and removed the chiming device from his pocket.

She smoothed her skirt, feeling her cheeks heat as she tried to understand what almost happened.

She could not kiss this man.

What was happening to her? Did her bump on the head leave her perma-horny?

Perma-horny? What was going on inside her amnesia brain?

She twisted the tail of her braid and watched as he eyed the screen and groaned.

"What is it?"

His jaw tightened, the muscles flickering beneath the skin like they were straining to hold back his frustration. "We're not free yet, and...we've got company."

Six

MAGGIE

THE BEAT of footsteps drew closer as a little girl bounded down the walkway, pigtails swishing from side to side.

"Hi, Uncle Chris, and hey, Maggie, you're awake," she called, waving as she charged toward them with a dog's head bobbing on her shoulder. As the child got closer, the picture sharpened. The girl was wearing an apron and carrying a black pup in a backpack.

Christian waved to the child and pocketed his phone. "That was my grandmother. She's here with my niece. Brace yourself."

The little girl skidded to a shaky stop. "Maggie, your apron fits me. Both our names start with the letter *M*."

Maggie knelt and eyed the powder-pink connection to her old life. "You must be McKenzie," she said, looking between the child and the garment—a garment that didn't spark any memories.

The child's smile lit up her face. "I'm McKenzie Fiona Starrycard-Dunleavy. I'm everyone's favorite Starrycard. And look! Your dog fits in an old doggie backpack we had at our house."

The dog.

"Hello, Mr. Lucky," Maggie said, meeting the pup's soulful brown eyes. She surveyed what she could see of the pup. Lucky had a sleek, black face, curious eyes, and a shiny black nose. An endearing little scar above his left eye added to his charm. She couldn't place the animal, but she knew without a doubt that he belonged with her.

And Lucky appeared to feel the same.

The dog whimpered and wiggled, trying to get to her, licking her face and hands as she scratched behind his ears.

"Easy, boy," Christian said, taking a knee beside her.

She laughed as the dog's head bobbed back and forth, licking her, then licking Christian.

"He's a licker," Maggie said as the dog showered her with kisses.

"He's only like that with you guys," McKenzie said, scrunching her face as a few of Lucky's kisses brushed her cheek.

Maggie and Christian stood to relieve the child of the copious dog kiss-fest.

"Thank you for caring for Lucky," Maggie said, grinning at the girl. "How's he doing?"

McKenzie beamed. "You don't have to worry about Lucky. My dad's a veterinarian, and he says Lucky is a healthy dog. He gave him a bunch of shots and checked all his parts. But you don't want to know where the thermometer goes."

"Kenz," Christian chided, but there was nothing but amusement on his face.

Maggie chuckled. "That was very nice of your dad."

McKenzie twisted from side to side like she had ants in her pants. "Okay, I'll tell you, Maggie. It goes in the butt. The thermometer goes in the dog's butt," she finished, wide-eyed.

Maggie bit back a grin.

"McKenzie!" Christian exclaimed, then pressed his lips together to suppress a grin.

Maggie caught Christian's eye. "I can see why she's everyone's favorite," she said, doing her best not to burst into a fit of giggles.

McKenzie looked over her shoulder. "Oh, hey, Uncle O! Look, Maggie's awake," the child called, then waved her in. "Hey, Maggie, that's my uncle Owen. He can help get Lucky out of the backpack because my uncle Chris isn't supposed to lift heavy stuff yet, and Lucky weighs thirty-four point six pounds. And that's too much for you because part of your shoulder bone didn't get enough blood and broke and died, right, Uncle Chris?"

Christian mustered a weak grin, but his tight posture and the tic in his jaw gave away his discomfort. "Something like that, Kenz." He shifted his stance and lowered his voice. "I thought you came with Goldie and Great Grandpa Rex," he continued with a hint of unease in his voice.

"Nope, it's me, Goldie, and Uncle O. Me and Goldie parked next to Uncle Owen in the parking lot, but then I started running because Goldie said I could do the hundred-yard dash up the sidewalk. I'm a crazy fast runner. "

A man who looked strikingly like Christian but with longer hair and a leaner build approached them.

"I didn't know you were coming," Christian said, his tone tinged with a slight edge.

Maggie looked between the men, attempting to get a read on the situation.

"That's because my mom said we should take turns coming up to the hospital and hang around in case you needed any help, Uncle Chris," McKenzie explained, filling the stretch of silence and spilling the beans. "I told her I wanted to go after school today, and that meant riding up with Goldie. And then Uncle O said he wanted to come again even though he comes here all the time. Can you get Lucky out of the pack, Uncle Owen? He really wants to be with Maggie."

Maggie checked the brothers again. Christian didn't seem to enjoy being managed, and it appeared his family's concern wasn't only for her welfare.

"Kenz, you are a walking and talking encyclopedia," Owen said dryly and removed the dog from the pack.

"Here, Maggie," Owen said sheepishly, handing her the pup. "It's good to see you awake."

She nodded, then glanced at the glowering Christian.

What was going on?

"Here's his leash," Owen continued. He attached it to the dog's collar and handed it to her. He took a step back and raked his hand through his dark tumble of hair. "I'm so sorry about what happened."

What was he talking about?

Maggie studied the man. "I don't understand. What are you apologizing for?"

Concern creased Owen's brow. "I'm the reason you fell and hit your head."

"You are?" she asked and looked at Christian.

Christian took a step toward her, his arm brushing hers. "Everything happened quickly. Owen, it's not your fault. I've told you this."

"What exactly happened?" she pressed, holding Owen's gaze. She wasn't going to get much from Christian. The man had taken on a protective demeanor. But why would he have to protect her from his brother?

Owen raked his hands through his hair again. "I tried to take the dog from you after the train passed. He wiggled, wanting to stay with you, and you lost your balance on some loose rocks around the tracks. That's how you ended up here. Don't you remember?"

Maggie chewed her lip. That would be a no on remembering anything. But how was she supposed to share that? *Hey, I think I'm Maggie, and I've got amnesia* sounded both ludicrous and highly distressing—and she didn't want to make Owen feel any worse.

"About that..." she began, tossing another look Christian's way when an attractive older woman headed toward them.

The woman donned a smile as wide as McKenzie's. "My goodness! It's wonderful to see you up and around, Maggie. When did you wake up? What are you doing out here? Yesterday morning, you were still in a coma."

"This is my grandmother, Goldie Starrycard," Christian said, his voice softening slightly.

Goldie's blue eyes sparkled with a mix of relief and concern. Her silver hair brushed against her shoulders with every movement.

"I asked to leave. I'm not comfortable in hospitals," Maggie replied, forcing a weak grin, still unable to figure out what was going on between Christian and Owen. The brothers had barely acknowledged each other.

"We heard your harrowing dog rescue tale. How's your head, dear?" Goldie asked, then glanced at Christian and Owen and pursed her lips.

Was she picking up on their tension, too?

Maggie maintained her forced, pleasant expression. "The scans showed no permanent damage. The doctor just discharged me."

McKenzie gasped.

"What is it, little star?" Goldie asked.

"It's me, Goldie. I made Maggie wake up. I made a wish this morning, wrote it on a piece of Starrycard Creek paper, and put it in the wishing wall before I got to school."

"The wishing wall?" Maggie repeated.

"It's town folklore," Christian answered.

"It's more than town folklore," Goldie countered. "If you write your heart's desire or true wish on a piece of Starrycard Creek paper and tuck it into one of the old rock wall's nooks and crannies, if whatever you ask is meant for you, it'll come true."

"I did my wishes this morning when Goldie walked me to school. I wished for a dinosaur—again—and didn't get it yet, but I had another piece of wishing wall paper in my pocket, so I also wished that you would wake up, Maggie," the child gushed. "Oh, and then Goldie wrote something on that paper before I put it in, but I didn't see it. Did you write that you wanted Maggie to wake up and be happy?"

"Something like that," the woman replied.

Maggie looked from McKenzie to her grandmother. "Well, thank you to you both. I'm happy to be awake."

"Is there anyone we can call for you, dear? Your family? We've been asking around and alerted the authorities to your arrival, but they haven't come up with anything," Christian's grandmother shared.

Maggie maintained her beauty pageant smile. Again, what the heck was she supposed to say? Her life sounded like a soap opera.

She looked down at Lucky as the dog settled himself between her and Christian. "About that...I—"

"Maggie is having some issues with her memory, but we're addressing it," Christian said, schooling his features.

"What kind of issues?" Owen pressed.

She shifted Lucky's leash from hand to hand. "I don't recall anything about my life. I only know what Christian has told me about our encounter with the dog and the train."

"You don't remember meeting me?" Owen asked, his question tinged with disbelief.

She gave the man a small, hesitant smile. "No, I don't."

"She's experiencing amnesia, but Dr. Ironside is optimistic her memories will return. That's all you need to know," Christian hissed.

Why was he being so cagey with his family?

"Oh, Maggie," Goldie lamented and pressed her hand to her heart. "You seem to be in good spirits despite this news. You don't know us, but our entire family is here to support you however we can."

"That's very kind. And Christian's been..." Their almost kiss flashed before her eyes. "He's been so...helpful." She met his gaze, expecting warmth, but was taken aback by the desperation etched on his face as if he feared losing her.

"You don't remember anything? Do you know your middle name?" McKenzie asked, wonder aglow on her face.

Maggie gathered herself and released a nervous chuckle. "No."

"Do you know your last name?" the child continued.

"No."

"Do you know your house address?"

"I don't."

"Wow," McKenzie breathed, wide-eyed. "Do you know what this is?" she asked, lifting her foot and shaking it around.

"It's a sneaker."

The child cheered and clapped. "Yes! You haven't forgotten everything. How about this?" the child continued and pointed to a towering evergreen.

"It's a tree."

Owen frowned. "Where were you two going? Where are you staying if you don't know who you are or where you're from?" he pressed, cutting off the child's questions.

"She's staying with me. That's the end of it, Owen. And we should be going," Christian answered and rested his hand on the small of her back.

Whatever this was, it didn't seem to be about her.

"Wait, I have another question for Maggie." McKenzie pointed inside the hospital toward the gift shop near the entrance. "What about that? Do you know what those are?"

"It's a poster with flowers and chocolates."

"Goldie, can we get some chocolates?" the girl begged.

Goldie studied her grandsons, then gifted McKenzie with a coy grin. "Yes, little star, this appears to be a very good time for a treat. Excuse us," the woman finished, taking the child by the hand and leading her inside.

Once Goldie and McKenzie entered the hospital, Owen pegged his brother with a piercing gaze. "What are you doing, Chris?"

Christian's hand trembled against her as if he was fighting to stay composed. "I told you. I'm taking Maggie to the ranch. She's staying with me."

"But you're…" Owen shook his head. "I don't think that's a good idea. You can stay with me, Maggie. Christian is still recuperating."

She looked from one brother to the other, her heart beating a mile a minute. The intensity between them crackled, a dam of unspoken words and raw emotions threatening to burst.

"It's been three months since my surgery, O. I'm only wearing the sling out of an abundance of caution. I'm fine, and I have plenty of space."

"I have an extra room," Owen countered.

Christian rubbed slow circles on her back, his touch growing steady and possessive. "I have *eleven* extra rooms."

"Dammit, Christian," Owen hissed, pacing. "Fine, Maggie doesn't have to stay with me. She could stay at Starrycard House with Mom and Dad."

"She's coming home with me," Christian said, his tone laced with an unmistakable warning.

Breathless, a tingle traveled down her spine as she looked between the brothers. Christian's eyes burned with a fierce intensity. His entire presence resonated with a determination to move mountains to keep her by his side.

Owen raised his hands defensively. "I'm not trying to be difficult, Chris. I care about you. I want what's best for everyone. But we can't ignore your issues," he said quietly.

"I don't have any issues," Christian shot back, his voice steady.

"Really?" Owen countered, incredulity dripping from his words. "Because the press would beg to differ. And why do you think I came to check on you last week? The entire family is concerned. You could use some help with...with fucking everything."

"Enough," Christian barked. "I'm not overdoing it anymore. I haven't had a drop of alcohol in seven days. You know this. The family's obviously been keeping an eye on both me and Maggie. I might be your younger brother, but I'm not a child. I don't need to be minded like a toddler. And it only makes sense that Maggie would stay with me. She came to Starrycard Creek for me. She's here for *me*."

Maggie's breath hitched. The raw possessiveness in his tone sent a delicious tingle down her spine.

"You met her while she was saving a dog. She's not *yours*," Owen said through clenched teeth, but his expression softened as he turned to her. "Do you even know why you're here, Maggie?"

She peered up at Christian. He could have easily told his brother—and his whole family—about the baseball card and the stone. The card tied her to the man, albeit loosely. But he didn't say a word. *Why didn't he want them to know?* His gaze intensified. He offered her a minute shake of his head—a barely there movement. And she understood what he was silently conveying. He didn't want her to mention the items. *Why?* There had to be a reason he'd kept this information from his family. Between this and his strange dream references, she needed to figure out what was going on with the man. Not to mention, the last thing she wanted was to have the brothers fighting over her.

She gasped as something warm and wet made contact with her waist and found Lucky resting his front paws on her leg. He nipped at the hem of her blouse, and his action sparked a plan.

Thank you, Mr. Lickster Lucky.

She helped the pup onto all fours, then stood between the brothers. She looked from one towering man to the other. In addition to her plan, these men badly needed a little reality check when it came to her welfare. She might not have her memory, but she remained in control of her choices. "Hi, I'm Maggie. Remember me? And *I* would like to weigh in on where *I* am going to live," she announced.

"What?" Christian and Owen barked, with matching confused expressions.

"First of all, the decision is mine. And second, I need a job," she said, praying her plan would work.

"Why do you need a job?" Christian pressed.

Here goes everything.

"Doctor's orders. You were with me. You heard the doctor say routine and consistency could help me retrieve my memories. A job would provide that. Now, I don't know exactly what I'm qual-ified to do, but I'm pretty sure I could work a…*washing machine.*" She paused.

Would Christian catch on?

"A washing machine, you say?" he repeated, and the knowing glint in his eyes sent her pulse racing like they were speaking a language only the two of them knew.

"Uh-huh," she continued casually. "Do either of you know anyone who might need help with *housekeeping*?"

Christian nodded, pretending to connect the dots. "I have a particularly complex washing machine and could use help around the ranch. My family's been harping on me for weeks to hire someone to assist me while I *recuperate*, right, Owen? I think you and Eliza discussed the topic about a week ago."

Owen's gaze darted between her and Christian like he sensed he was being played but wasn't one hundred percent sure. "Yeah, we did discuss hiring someone to help out at the ranch." His expression softened. "Listen, Chris, we love you and care about you. And Maggie, we want what's best for you. But my brother is—"

"All right then," she said, cutting off the man, acting decisively —and a bit deceptively. *Was she decisive and deceptive? Were those traits of hers?* Oh, forget it. She couldn't worry about whoever the old Maggie was. If she wanted answers, this Maggie had to cement her stay with Christian. She focused on Owen. His deep concern showed how much he loved his brother, and she had to smooth things out between the men. "I appreciate your kindness and your offer to let me stay with you. I can tell you have a big heart and that you want what's best for everyone—me included. But I won't be *staying* with you or Christian."

Owen frowned. "What will you do? Where will you live?"

She lifted her chin. Despite the fog of amnesia and her uncer-tainty about…well, everything, a surprising sense of self-reliance surged through her veins. She scratched behind Lucky's ears, and the pup winked at her like he'd read her mind and approved her plan. Emboldened by the pup's support, she smiled sweetly at Christian. "From what your brother says, it sounds like you've got an opening for a housekeeper at your ranch. I assume it comes with room and board."

He watched her for a beat. The corner of his mouth twitched as if he were suppressing a grin. "It does," he answered smoothly.

"What do you say? Would you be willing to hire me for the position?"

"Maggie, last name to be determined," Christian said, his tone even.

"Yes?" she answered, her heart in her throat.

Christian's eyes sparkled with a mix of amusement and admiration. "The position is yours."

CHAPTER
Seven

CHRISTIAN

LUCKY WHIMPERED and scratched the bedroom suite's solid oak bathroom door. Christian patted the dog's head, wishing he could morph into a pup and do the same damn thing. He was close to pressing his ear against the slab of wood to get a clearer picture of what was happening beyond his view.

No, he couldn't do that.

By any assessment, that would be considered creeper behavior, and thanks to whatever was happening with his mouth, he'd already plunged head-first into that end of the pool.

Still, he was concerned. And a responsible citizen would insist on garnering information, especially when it came to safe-guarding another person's health, right?

Somewhat satisfied with his thinking, he leaned in, his ear an inch from the door, when Lucky wiggled in. The pup pushed him back a few steps and sniffed the space between the door and the doorframe. The animal's curiosity was growing by the second. Christian exhaled a pained breath and studied the animal. It appeared they were suffering from the same condition: Maggie Withdrawal Syndrome.

Now, was she truly gone?

Oh, hell no. He wouldn't have allowed that.

She was here at the ranch, and currently behind said door, soaking in a bubble bath.

He'd figured she'd ask for the tour of the main ranch house when they'd arrived. Most people did. The exterior of the two-story, thirteen thousand-square-foot ranch house sported massive wooden beams, stone accents, and expansive windows that reflected the land's rugged beauty. But she wasn't like most people. Instead, she'd made two requests upon setting foot inside the palatial mountain abode.

She'd asked to be taken directly to her room, then requested for privacy to take a bath.

While he couldn't offer her complete isolation—per doctor's orders—his post outside the bathroom had been their compromise.

And that's where he and Lucky stood guard—or lurked.

Dammit, what was he doing?

He rested his forehead against the door and pictured her hazel eyes. She'd barely said a word on the drive from the hospital to the ranch. Since they'd gotten home, her gaze had grown muted and guarded. She'd drawn inward. And for the life of him, he couldn't pinpoint what was going through her head.

He'd wanted to congratulate her on coming up with the housekeeper job, wanted to revel in how they connected, and how it ensured her decision wouldn't hurt his brother. Sure, she must be wondering why his family thought he couldn't care for himself. His pissing match with Owen had to have given her plenty to contemplate. A sharp pang in his chest rippled through him at the thought of sparring with his brother. He couldn't fault Owen for his reaction. The man had always carried guilt with a heavy heart. He was an artist. He had an artist's acutely introspective soul. It was no surprise O felt obligated to help Maggie. It was also not shocking that Owen was worried about him. If only he could have shared what Maggie meant to him, who she was to him. But sweet Jesus, if he'd told anyone he'd been dreaming about Maggie and that she'd suddenly materialized out of thin air, they'd have him in a padded room at the hospital awaiting a psych eval.

Here's the thing. At the minimum, he expected Maggie to pepper him with questions the second they got into his truck, but she didn't. Instead, she'd asked him to tell her about Starrycard Creek. Maybe she needed a distraction. He couldn't deny that it was a welcomed respite.

He'd taken the long way home and played tour guide. He'd explained how the town was founded by his ancestor, William Starrycard, and his wife, Fiona Donnelly Starrycard, in 1880. Beneath the glow of the streetlights and the starry night sky, he'd driven along the rushing creek that cut a watery path through the heart of the town. She nodded as he explained how his father, Hank, and two brothers Finn and Owen ran the family's artisan papermaking company. He'd shared that his mother, Maeve, was the mayor, his eldest brother, Kieran, was the town manager, and that Kieran's wife was the region's environmental land steward as they passed the town hall. He'd pointed out Starrycard Elementary School and told her about Eliza's post as principal and how Finn's fiancée, Hailey, taught second grade there. He'd capped off the Starrycard Creek mini excursion by sharing that his grandmother owned the town's local restaurant and that his grandfather pretty much did whatever the hell he wanted and was happiest with a good cigar and a glass of whatever alcohol was strong enough to knock a horse off its feet.

The horse line was the one time he managed to coax a faint chuckle from her. But he couldn't fault her reticence. She'd endured a hell of a lot in a short amount of time. For Christ's sake, she'd had amnesia.

Amnesia.

Talk about a damned curveball. He'd been on pins and needles this week, waiting for her to wake up. Questions had been whirling through his head. Who was she? How had she ended up with his college baseball card and the starry quartzite with two lines carved down the center? And why he couldn't shake the feeling that his soul was intertwined with hers.

Still, as much as he craved answers, two things stood out with blinding clarity.

She was here because of him.

She was meant for him.

And damn, he'd wanted to kiss her.

His heartbeat quickened as he recalled her beautiful face—the face in his dreams. Her gaze had pierced through him, igniting a storm of feelings he could barely contain.

And he'd almost done it, almost given in. He was right there, teetering on the edge. Had his damned chiming cell not interrupted them, he would have lost control. He would have held her face in his hands and feasted on the curves of her lips. He'd fantasized about kissing her while he'd watched her sleep. He'd envisioned her taste as a blend of cinnamon and maple syrup, the very scents that had enveloped her when they'd first met. The fantasy had played out a million times over the last seven days.

He was never one to go slow. Speed and power were his trademarks. But not when it came to daydreaming about kissing Maggie.

In his head, he'd taken his time. He'd run the tip of his tongue along the seam of her plump lips. He'd kissed the corners of her mouth, then slipped his hand inside her panties and made deliciously slow circles against her most sensitive place. In his mind, she'd gasped at his touch, her lips parting as she rocked against his hand.

He'd imagined her voice, a heated and feathery rasp saying, *"Kiss me, Christian,"* as she blushed that rousing shade of pale pink that made him ache to have her, possess her, and provide her with the kind of pleasure that would keep her cheeks hot and flushed for hours.

Woof!

Lucky let out a sharp, staccato bark—what seemed like the dog version of *knock it off, human.*

The dog was right.

Christian squeezed the bridge of his nose. "Calm the hell down," he whispered, scolding himself.

And he needed to be reprimanded. He couldn't lose control. He had to think of her mental state. She didn't know him—she didn't know anyone, herself included. She was as vulnerable as a person could get. He had to tread carefully. Still, when she'd come up with the idea of working for him to relieve Owen's guilt, he'd read her play, and he was right. They'd connected. It was like when he was back playing baseball, and the team pulled off a double steal, every player knowing exactly when to act.

He'd never had that connection with anyone he'd dated. He'd never experienced that unspoken synchronicity, that seamless blend of minds and intentions. It was exhilarating and terrifying all at once.

Lucky dropped another low woof and narrowed his chocolate-brown eyes. Again, it was as if the dog could read his mind.

He yanked off his college baseball cap, raked his fingers through his tangled hair, and shoved the hat back on with a frustrated sigh. "Don't worry, boy. I'm not going to drop this on her. I know she's been through a lot. I know she probably has a life out there. A world beyond what she is to me," he whispered as an icy shiver passed through him and a revelation hit.

There was a very good chance that if her memory returned, she'd leave. Sure, she'd mentioned she was lonely, but that didn't mean she didn't have a life waiting for her—or a man. She could be with someone, dating someone.

A muscle ticked in his jaw. His body tensed. But if she was involved with someone, the douchebag hadn't come looking for her and certainly didn't deserve her. The notion of an unworthy man laying claim to Maggie's affections ignited his competitive side. The determined, driven part that rallied the Rattlers to back-to-back World Series wins kicked in. Of course, he wanted her to regain her memories, but that didn't mean he couldn't try to win her heart.

Lucky pawed at his leg and cocked his head to the side—as if he were asking, *do you hear yourself, tall human? You're losing it.*

"You're right, Lucky. You're right. This isn't a game. It's a woman's life." Christian stared at the door. "A woman who is naked and soaking in a steamy bubble bath." He traced a line with his fingertips a few inches down the door, unable to stop himself from wishing he was in the oversized tub with her, touching her, trailing his fingertips between her wet breasts to the hollow of her neck. He pictured her resting between his legs, her back against his chest as warm water swished gently. "Christ," he growled under his breath, his imagination running wild. "All the things I could do to you in that tub."

"Did you say something about a bathtub, Christian?" Maggie called from the other side of the door.

Had she heard him?

He damn near fell over. "Um…no, I wasn't talking. Well, yes, I was talking, but I was speaking with Lucky. Yes, he really wants to make sure you're okay…in the tub. That's why I said the word *tub*. I wasn't thinking about you being in the tub. Even though I know you're in the tub—a bubble bath, a bath with bubbles. And people are usually naked when they bathe. Just a fact."

Fuck!

Splash!

"Maggie?" he called.

"Sorry, I was rinsing the shampoo out of my hair. I didn't catch what you said."

"Thank God," he mumbled, listening as the gentle splash of water, soft patter of droplets hitting the floor, and muffled thump told him she was out of the tub. Seconds later, the gurgling rush of water confirmed the bath was complete. He focused on the sounds—the rustle of the towel and then the swish of her dressing.

"You can go. I'm finishing up in here. I feel fine. You don't have to worry about me," she called.

He leaned against the doorframe. "I can't leave you. Doctor's orders."

"All right, then. I got dressed in here. I'm coming out." She opened the door and offered him a sheepish grin before Lucky zipped past him.

His damned heart nearly stopped as he watched her crouch to pet the dog. Fresh from the bath, her skin looked smooth and radiant, almost ethereal. She had on a white tank top and yoga pants. She must have dressed hastily because a few water droplets shimmered on her shoulders. Lucky licked them off, and he'd never been more jealous of a dog in his life.

"Go lay down. You could use a rest. I could hear you making quite a ruckus out here," she said to the pup.

The dog pranced around her a few more times, then conked out on the white floofy rug in front of the bedroom's stone fireplace.

"So here we are, Christian." She stood and held his gaze. Her eyes sparkled with a mix of curiosity and bewilderment. "Shouldn't you be wearing your sling?"

"I don't need it. I kept it on last week as a precaution. I've got limited mobility and have to watch how I use it." He glanced into the bathroom. "Do you need anything? There should have been toothpaste and a toothbrush in there. I used to pick up hotel samples from when I was on the road and leave them in there for Kenz."

"I found everything I needed." She exhaled a shaky breath and surveyed the room. "This just got very real."

He needed to get out of his head and focus on her. "It must be so strange being here," he said, taking in her tense posture.

"I think it would be strange for me to be anywhere since I can't picture my home." She chewed her lips and checked her outfit. "Um...are you sure your sister won't mind me wearing her clothes?"

He had to put her at ease.

"No, she won't mind. She probably forgot she left them here. I believe they belong to Eliza, but they could easily belong to someone else. Women's clothing is scattered throughout the ranch. You could probably assemble a whole wardrobe with what people have left behind."

"You've had a lot of women here?" she asked, glancing away, color rising to her cheeks.

Damn! That wouldn't put her at ease. The last thing he wanted was for her to think he was a man-whore.

"I don't mean clothing from the women I've slept with. It's clothing from either my sisters, mom, or grandmother. I've never brought a woman to the ranch. Women have been here, like I said, family and my brother Kieran's wife and my brother Finn's fiancée. But I've never had sex. I mean, I've had sex—lots of sex. I was a professional baseball player, for Christ's sake. What I mean is, I have never had sex with a woman here." *Oh, for fuck's sake!* He broke into a cold sweat. *What was happening to his mouth?* He gathered himself and tried again. "You're a woman, so I've brought one woman to the ranch. Numero uno. And we haven't had sex." He shook his head. "*Dammit,*" he murmured, staring at a knot in the wood floor. "Only you do this to me. I'm usually a pretty smooth talker. And my trash talk is next level—not that I would trash talk with you. It's a baseball thing." He clamped his mouth shut. *Fuckity, fuck, fuck, fuck!*

"And that's your bedroom?" she asked, peering past him at the door leading from her room to his.

Had she not heard his bizarro sex babble?

He glanced over his shoulder. "Yep, yeppers, that's me. Right there, mere feet from where you'll be sleeping."

Yeppers? So much for being a smooth talker.

He had McKenzie to thank for the bedroom situation. Upon learning Maggie would be working for him and living at the ranch, the child insisted Maggie stay in the Donnelly bedroom—a bedroom decorated with old photos and sketches of his Donnelly ancestors. It was the room Kenz used when she spent the night. The bedroom that happened to be next to his, with an adjoining doorway. It made sense to be close to McKenzie in case she had a bad dream or got sick in the night. But was it too close for Maggie's comfort?

He gestured to his room. "We can close the door. It locks. But not tonight."

She cocked her head to the side. "Why not tonight?"

"I should watch over you. Dr. Ironside doesn't want you to be alone."

Maggie nodded, looking as if she were lost in a dream, and padded past him. "That's a nice rug."

"Christ, that rug! My niece begged me to get it. She saw it in a store in town. Now her uncles have them in their houses."

Maggie chuckled softly, the tension in her shoulders relaxing a fraction. "Sounds like McKenzie has her uncles wrapped around her little finger."

"She does, and she knows it," he answered, grateful the conversation veered toward his precocious niece.

"McKenzie told me to look at a sketch next to the bed. She said it's one of her favorites of Kathleen and Seamus. Who are Kathleen and Seamus? Your niece was speaking so quickly I didn't catch it if she'd mentioned it."

"Fair warning, Kenz will do that. She's got a speed all her own." He tapped the framed drawing. "That's a pencil sketch of Kathleen and Seamus Donnelly. They're the ones who started ranching on this land. They're my ancestors from Ireland. Before they came to America, Seamus was a farmer, and Kathleen was an artist and schoolteacher. After they arrived here, they had one son, Brian Donnelly. He married a woman named Martha Riley, and they had two children. Michael was their first, and ten years later, they had Fiona."

Maggie perked up. "Fiona, like McKenzie's middle name."

He watched her closely. "How did you know that?"

"It was one of the things your niece said that I do recall. She told me when she introduced herself. McKenzie Fiona Starrycard-Dunleavy."

He nodded. "She's named after Fiona. Fiona married William Starrycard. He's my ancestor who founded the town of Starrycard Creek."

Maggie's brows knit together. "If we're at the Donnelly Ranch, aren't we in the town of Donnelly?"

"No, we're in Starrycard Creek."

"The Donnelly's didn't have their own town? It sounds like they got here first."

"They did. But their situation is unique." He gestured to a painting of a mountain landscape. "Kathleen painted this. It was before there was anything out here. It was a wild time back then. The land this ranch is on has a unique history. Do you recall the Louisiana Purchase?"

"Yes, I couldn't tell you my birthday, but I know Thomas Jefferson purchased a big chunk of land in 1803, and it was called…drum roll… the Louisiana Purchase. Whoever I am, I paid attention during history class."

He pointed to a map above the dresser. "We're on the very far edge of that land or…" he paused, "we're in what used to be Spanish territory. There were quite a few boundary disputes back then in these parts, and how Seamus and Kathleen got the land is quite a story."

"I'd love to hear it."

This was good. Talking was good. He could sense her relaxing more with each passing second.

"To tell it properly, I've got to show you something in the kitchen. It's part of the story, and you've got to see it to believe it. Come with me," he said, offering her his hand. She stared at it like she wasn't sure what she was supposed to do. "I want to hold your hand in case you get lightheaded," he added—not a complete lie.

She twisted the hem of the tank top. "I don't mean to be weird. And I appreciate you letting me live and work here. I sort of railroaded you into it—no pun intended. But I can't seem to figure out what the rules are with us?"

He held her gaze, reveling in her hazel eyes. "I guess we get to make them as we go."

She watched him for a beat, then nodded. "Okay," she said, resting her hand on his. Her expression brightened. "So, how did Seamus and Kathleen get this disputed land that wasn't quite Spanish land and wasn't quite part of the Louisiana Purchase?"

He loved telling this story—and this part was a real crowd-pleaser. He schooled his features. "Seamus wrestled a mountain lion."

"What?" Maggie exclaimed. "He wrestled a mountain lion?"

"Come on, Lucky," he said, calling the pup as he led them to a back staircase. "Quick tour before I continue the story," he said as they started down one of the ranch's two cavernous walkways. "The south wing has a fully equipped gym, therapy room, and an indoor pool."

She craned her neck, taking in the aquatics area. "That pool is huge."

"There's one outside, too."

"You have two pools? That's awesome!"

He smiled. He'd hoped she'd like the place. "And here's the—"

"It's the scene of the great pink shirt debacle," she finished, a glimmer returning to her eyes as they passed the laundry room.

And damn, it did his heart good to see her relaxed.

"This is the main living and dining room. I jokingly call it the lobby."

"I can see why. This space could easily double as the rustic lobby of a lodge."

He gestured with his chin. "The north wing is where you'll find the library, the home theater, and the room where I brew beer and distill spirits. I've got more equipment for distilling in the small barn."

"You make beer and spirits?"

"I usually do it in the off-season. My ancestors were prolific at supplying the region with bathtub hooch during Prohibition. I keep up the tradition."

They continued through the lobby toward the back of the house.

"What type of spirits?"

"Stumble Juice."

"What's Stumble Juice?"

"An old family recipe for moonshine. The taste is unique."

"Can you describe it?"

He paused, reflecting on the flavor—a flavor unlike any other hard alcohol he'd tried. "It's made with water from Starrycard Creek. It's replete with minerals that only exist in a certain concentration here. Like my ancestors, I use Colorado-grown barley and wheat. I'd say that gives it an earthy, malty flavor."

"So, it's a whiskey?" she asked.

"Not really. I guess you could call it malt whiskey moonshine. My ancestors used what they had—not much corn here. That's what's used in traditional moonshine. Also, whiskey is aged in barrels, and the Starrycards before me had to get their product out the door quickly. No time to wait around."

She nodded, clearly intrigued. "What else goes into it?"

"Wildflower honey and juniper berries. They give it a piney, slightly sticky-sweet flavor. Does that make sense?"

Methodically, she twirled a lock of hair around her finger. "Oddly, it does. I'm able to imagine it."

"I almost forgot. There's one last ingredient—molasses from sugar beet trees. It gives it a caramel-like finish."

"Caramel," she repeated with a furrowed brow. Her eyes narrowed as if she were trying to grasp a thread of a memory hovering just out of reach. Her features smoothed, and she smiled up at him. "That's quite a description. Sounds like you're good at what you do."

"I've had more time to devote to it recently. Maybe too much time," he said, glancing away, a heaviness setting in.

"But you're doing better, aren't you?" she asked softly.

He held her gaze, and she shined her warmth his way. And God help him, he wanted to tell her that she was the reason he was standing there—that her presence was like a beacon pulling him from the darkness. But he couldn't. At least not yet. "Yeah," he said softly, "I'm doing better."

"I believe you."

Those three words bound to his heart. He nodded and mustered a grin. Had he tried to speak, he might have broken down with relief and gratitude so deep it would have spilled over in a torrent of tears.

She slipped her fingers from his grip and turned in a slow circle, taking in the vaulted ceiling, wide beams, and expanse of windows framing the starry night sky. "This place really could be the Amnesia B and B—better name to be determined," she added, tossing a teasing glance his way, her cheeks growing the most beguiling shade of pink. And damn, that color was his salvation. The hint of a smirk curled the corners of her lips. "It couldn't have always looked like this back in the eighteen hundreds, though, right?"

"It didn't look like this. Not even close," he replied, so at ease with the woman of his dreams by his side. He brought her to a bookshelf littered with framed photos and old sketches. "Seamus and Kathleen's original ranch house had three rooms. Brian and Martha added to it, making it seven rooms. They also built a small barn. I keep the distilling barrels there. I built this house during my second year playing for the Rattlers after I signed a big deal with an apparel company. But that's not my life anymore." The darkness seeped in like a suffocating fog. He'd been so proud that the fruits of his labor were able to make the ranch a place for his family and the generations to come to enjoy. *Was this to be his only contribution to Starrycard Creek?*

"Hey?" Maggie said tenderly.

He swallowed hard. "Yeah?"

"Don't go there."

"Where?"

Worry welled in her eyes. "Wherever you went in your head when your expression fell, and the light left your eyes."

"I'm trying, but I don't know who I am anymore."

She offered him that sweet whisper of a grin. "Me neither."

He drank her in, and the fog lifted. She had no idea of the power she held over him.

Mischief glinted in her eyes. "Perhaps I have an inkling as to *what* I am."

"What do you think you are?"

"A professional wrestler," she said coolly.

"Why would you think that?" he asked, laughing, so damned happy to have her here.

"I'd really like to see this Seamus Donnelly the Mountain Lion Wrestler memorabilia—so much so, it makes me wonder if Pre-Amnesia Maggie wore outrageous costumes and fake gut-punched people for a living."

"Pre-Amnesia Maggie elbowed me in the eye," he tossed out.

"See, anything is possible. The storm always passes, right?" She smiled like she did in his dreams. And damn, he wanted to kiss her, wanted to keep her close like a good luck charm. He patted his pocket and felt the stone she'd brought with her to Starrycard Creek.

"It does, and you won't believe what I'm going to show you," he replied, snapping out of his Maggie-induced stupor, and again feeling settled and secure like his old self. "It's in the kitchen." Lucky trotted ahead as he guided her into the space. With Maggie beside him, it seemed as if anything were possible until they entered the room, and the joy coursing through his veins turned to ice.

CHAPTER

Eight

CHRISTIAN

CHRISTIAN'S BODY WENT RIGID. Shame burned through him. His skin prickled with a fiery heat, and his stomach twisted in a painful knot. His gaze darted around the space, seeking an escape, but his humiliation held him in place.

Crusty plates were piled high in the sink. A greasy pizza box with a congealed slice sat on the table like a frat house centerpiece. The large island in the middle of the room was a disaster zone. Wrapped gift baskets, hastily tossed on their sides, were scattered among takeout containers, crumpled napkins, and a box of cereal with more than half its contents spilled onto the floor. Empty prescription pill bottles added a disconcerting pop of orange. It wasn't just the unsightly mess; the air was thick with the mingling smells of stale food and something faintly sour.

Lucky whimpered.

Even the dog knew this was an utter clusterfuck.

"I forgot I left it like this. I'm not usually…"

"Living in a pit of despair, completely at a loss for what you're supposed to do now that you've lost your ability to play baseball?" Maggie supplied, nailing it.

He sighed. "That's pretty much it."

"We're two peas in a pod. I'm completely at a loss for everything, also. *Literally everything.*" She squeezed his hand. "It's a messy kitchen, Christian. No biggie. It can be tidied up. We'll do this together. That's what you said to me in the hospital, right?"

He nodded, shame still gnawing at his heart. "I don't usually need help," he confessed. It wasn't a lie. He'd always been the best at whatever he set his mind to accomplish.

"Well," she said, theatrically dusting off her hands, "I'm here, and there's no sense crying in your pie."

Crying in your pie? He'd never heard that expression before.

He cocked his head to the side and watched as she padded into the room.

"Do you have trash bags and a recycling bin?" she asked casually, like she'd just breezed into the local coffee shop and not the place where moldy takeout containers went to die.

He regained his bearings. "They're under the sink. I think they're still there—or around there. I'm not sure. I used to have people come to clean and do the—"

"Laundry. I know," she said, surveying the scene like a general assessing the battlefield.

He stuffed his hands in his pockets and felt the cool stone, but it brought him no comfort. "I forgot it was this bad. I didn't want anyone to see this—especially you."

She removed a green recycling tub and a large black plastic bag from the cabinet and held them in the air. "But I'm not simply anyone. I'm your housekeeper and glorified washing machine technician." She set the bin on a stool and secured the trash bag to the back of a chair. "But this is a two-person job." She glanced at the dog. "No, it's a two-person and one-dog job. Lucky, you'll tackle the cereal on the floor. All-Star, you're going to fill up this bag. Think you can lift that pizza box?" There was no judgment in her eyes, no moment of doubt in her movements. She acted with determination, her presence ushering in a sense of calm like she did in his dreams.

His anguish ebbed. "I can manage, *All-Star,*" he said, tossing back the curious term of endearment—one he knew well.

"I called you that, didn't I?" she replied.

"You did. Do you know baseball?"

She shrugged and turned a gift basket right-side up. "I know what it is. There's a pitcher. He tosses a ball to a guy with a bat. He hits it, and then he runs. Ask me something technical. That's how we'll know."

"Do you know what it means to…sit on a pitch?"

She scrunched up her face like he'd asked her to eat the congealed slice. "Sit on a pitch? Like, sit on the ball once it's thrown? How would you even do that? Do players flip around and let the ball hit their butt? That sounds insane and painful."

He laughed, and fuck, it felt good. "It's safe to say Pre-Amnesia Maggie was most likely not a hardcore baseball fan."

Maggie schooled her features and projected an aura of strength, and damn, the woman looked invincible. "You know what I bet Pre-Amnesia Maggie was really good at?"

"What?"

"Organizing and tidying up," she said, grinning from ear to ear. "I've got a whole system of attack in my head. I know just what needs to be done and how we'll do it." She pressed her hands to her hips. "Enough talk. I need you to clear off the table, then hit the island. I'll take the dishes and wipe down the counters. We'll worry about the floor tomorrow. This space is massive. It's like a chef's dream kitchen. And look, our Lucky is a natural," she added, gesturing to the dog happily hoovering Cheerios like a vacuum. "You make plans for exiting hospitals, Christian Starrycard. I forge the path through domestic challenges."

Domestic diva Maggie was a sight to be seen.

"Yes, ma'am, that appears to be the case," he said, knowing he had to be starry-eyed as he watched her start in on the dishes without an ounce of hesitation.

Again and again, she was the sun slicing through his shroud of darkness.

"Tell me about Seamus, Kathleen, and this mountain lion," she said over her shoulder, her voice rising above the swish of water and clinking plates.

With a spring in his step, he tossed the pizza box into the trash bag. "Seamus Donnelly and Kathleen Conners met in Ireland and fell in love. On their journey to find land to settle across the ocean, they came across a young Spanish girl. She'd been separated from her party, and when they found her, she was cornered by a mountain lion."

"Oh, no!" Maggie chimed. "What happened?"

He broke down a few boxes and added them to the recycling container. "Seamus was a big guy, like all the men in my family. Without a second thought, he stepped in. He diverted the beast's focus from the child, and the mountain lion pounced on him with savage fury."

Maggie caught his eye. "How terrifying!"

Christian settled into the rhythm of tidying up. "Yeah, terrifying…for the mountain lion."

She flipped a dish towel onto her shoulder. "The mountain lion?" she repeated, confusion coating her words.

He grinned from ear to ear. He loved telling this story. "It's said that Seamus rushed the creature, wrapped his burly arms around him, and flung it against a boulder. With one crack of his head, the animal died instantly."

Maggie leaned against the counter, wide-eyed. "That sounds like something straight out of a movie. What happened to the young girl? Was she okay?"

"The kid didn't have a scratch on her. Kathleen spoke a bit of broken Spanish and was able to learn the girl's name was Mariana Salidoro. She and her mother were part of a group en route to meet up with her father, a Spanish nobleman. Sadly, everyone in her party, save for her, grew ill and died. Her mother included."

"How awful! What happened to Mariana? Did she ever find her father? Could Seamus and Kathleen even help her?"

"Seamus and Kathleen were good people. They'd never leave a kid to fend for herself. And they were superstitious folks. They believed it was a sign that their path crossed with Mariana's—that the child would lead them to a place that would be safe for all of them. Mariana had a rough map, and Seamus was able to follow it and safely deliver her to her father. The man was overcome with gratitude and was also the Spanish crown's agent for dispatching land grants. He bequeathed this plot of land to Kathleen."

"To Kathleen?" Maggie repeated, now arranging the litany of gift baskets and organizing their contents.

"Seamus insisted. You see, Kathleen was content to stay in Ireland. It was Seamus who craved land and adventure. When he proposed and shared his plan to seek a new life abroad, he promised she'd always be protected and in control of her destiny. He lived by this motto. *Give what you love everything you've got.* Seamus loved Kathleen, so this land was hers."

"That's very romantic and progressive. When exactly did they arrive here?" Maggie's cheeks warmed to that sweet shade of pale pink that made the breath catch in his throat.

"1813," he answered, unable to take his eyes off her.

"What is it?" she asked, the color intensifying.

Again, he wanted to kiss her, wanted to gather her in his arms, set her ass on the edge of the counter, and lock lips with the woman until he couldn't see straight.

"Christian?"

Calm down, man.

He shifted his stance and gestured toward a wooden hutch. "Check out the little weathered wood framed box over there."

She wiped her hands on a dish towel, then peered at the old keepsake. "Is that the mountain lion's tooth?"

He joined her. "It sure is. Seamus and Kathleen kept one canine and gave the other to Mariana so she could remember how brave she was when she was alone. Kathleen cut them out of the cat's mouth. She used to wear the tooth on a bit of twine around her neck. Thanks to one unlucky mountain lion and one lucky little girl, this land belongs to my family and is now considered unincorporated Starrycard Creek."

"That is an incredible tale," Maggie remarked as she eyed another framed photo near the box. "Who are they?"

"That's Brian—Seamus and Kathleen's son—and Brian's wife, Martha. She's holding their baby, Michael."

"The parents of Fiona, too, right?"

"Yes."

"What's their story?"

"Sadly, Martha died in childbirth when Fiona was born. Michael passed away seven years later."

"How old was Michael when he died?" she asked, returning to the counter.

Christian studied the trio. "Seventeen."

"Was he a sickly child?"

Christian kept his gaze trained on the photo. "No, the opposite. From every account, he was an athletic guy. He set up hunting, fishing, and shooting competitions, and even though baseball was in its infancy in the 1860s, he'd heard about it from people passing through."

"Baseball?" she said with a coy twist to the word.

"Yeah, I guess that's where I got it."

"How did he die? Do you mind me asking?"

"He was mending the roof and fell."

"I can't imagine how hard that had to have been for them," she replied, her voice carrying genuine sorrow.

He nodded, listening as the refrigerator opened and closed, soothed by the gentle taps and thumps of Maggie's movements. Lucky came to his side. He knelt and scratched the dog above the little scar over his left eye. "It's why Brian was so protective of Fiona. His daughter became his entire world. It's said he turned away twenty suitors asking for her hand."

"Why was he okay with William Starrycard marrying her? Was it the Starrycard charm?" she asked with a sparkle in her eyes as she flitted around the kitchen.

He chuckled, gave the pup one last pat, then placed the last of the takeout containers into the garbage bag. "Something like that.

That's how the folklore behind Starrycard Creek paper was born. William Starrycard was a papermaker from England who came to America to make a name for himself. He never planned on marrying, but when he met Fiona, it was love at first sight for both. Knowing Fiona's father was a tough but fair man, he made a special paper using botanicals from the ranch and creek water and wrote to the man. After receiving the letter, Brian agreed to the marriage, but no one knows exactly what he wrote on that paper—only that it was written on handmade Starrycard Creek paper."

"You don't have the letter? How do you even know it exists?"

"We have William's journals, and he recorded the story there. But nobody knows the location of the physical letter. Still, I don't think it was just the letter that won over Brian Donnelly."

"What do you think it was?" she asked, back to opening and closing cabinets.

He gathered the empty water bottles and filled the recycling bin. "A combination of what William wrote and the craftsmanship of his paper."

"He showed the man what he was capable of with his actions," Maggie supplied.

"That's my guess," he agreed.

Maggie drummed her fingers on the counter, seeming to mull over his theory. "Give what you love everything you've got. The Donnelly motto. William Starrycard gave Brian Donnelly the fruits of his labor to prove his love for his daughter."

"Yeah, that's what I believe," Christian answered, so entranced with the woman of his dreams who'd become his reality.

She walked the perimeter, surveying the scene. "We've made a pretty good dent getting this place in order. Sit, please."

"Me or Lucky?" he asked, sliding the recycling bin back in place.

She gestured to a stool at the island. "You. Lucky's got a few more Cheerios to take care of. Get to it, boy."

He—and Lucky—complied.

"What are you doing?" he asked as she plucked items from the island he didn't even know he had.

"I'm making a quick bite to eat." She glanced at the clock on the microwave. "We deserve an eleven o'clock-ish snack."

He shifted in his seat. "I'm not sure I have much to snack on. I've relied heavily on takeout—if you couldn't tell."

"You've got more than you think," she replied, presenting a tray covered with a clean dish towel. "Ta-da!" she sang. With a flourish, she whisked off the cloth to reveal a platter adorned with bite-sized delicacies and petite pies. The spread looked straight out of a high-end specialty market.

His jaw dropped. "When the hell did you put together a charcuterie board?"

"While we were tidying up, and you were talking. It's mostly stuff from the gift baskets. I don't know how good the pre-packaged mini pies will be, but they don't look terrible. You had a few things in your fridge. The orange marmalade pairs beautifully with the nutty Gruyere cheese. It'll taste delicious with the multigrain crackers."

He smiled, taking in her masterpiece. "My grandmother makes the marmalade."

Maggie bit into one of the cheese and marmalade crackers, closed her eyes, and sighed. "Utter perfection in one bite."

She passed him one, and he devoured it. "Damn, that's good. You know your flavor combinations."

"I sure seem to, huh?" she replied, eyeing the tray, then looked up and gave him the once-over.

"What is it?"

"I do have a few questions about your pickle consumption." She plucked a spear from the medley of deliciousness and pointed at him. "I'm a little concerned about how many giant jars of pickles you've got stashed in this place."

He took the pickle from her and knocked it back in two bites. "The pickles belong to my brother, Finn. He needed somewhere to keep the extras. He bought every jar in town back in early June."

"Why?" she asked, laughing.

He shrugged. "Love. Hailey likes them."

"And there's four frozen cakes in your freezer. Are you a cake fanatic?" she continued.

"I'm not one to turn down cake. I keep them around for when Kenz stays with me. They came from my brother Kieran and are here because of love…again. His wife, Izzy, is crazy about cake. He brought in a ton for his proposal, which turned into their wedding day. They're definitely meant for each other. I helped him win her back. Actually, it was a team effort with the whole family pitching in."

She smiled, but the emotion didn't reach her eyes.

Was it his mention of love?

"Here, eat some more," she said, making him another loaded cracker.

He ate the bite-sized treat and watched as she ignored the platter. She peered out the window that framed Starrycard Mountain beneath a sea of stars.

"You're not eating. I figured you'd go straight for the pie," he said, trying to uncover what had caused her darkened demeanor.

"I'll pass on the pie. I might be a fresh-pie-only kind of gal," she answered, gaze trained on the inky sky.

"Maggie, look at me," he said gently.

She turned, and the tears in her eyes damn near broke his heart.

He reached across the island and took her hand in his. "What is it?"

"Your family…they're good people, aren't they?" Her voice trembled like a leaf in the wind.

"They are," he said, treading carefully. "They can meddle and drive me insane, but they love me, and their intensions are always in the right place. I wouldn't trade them for the world. But tell me what's going on in your head. Did I say something? Did you remember something?"

"No, it's not you, and I didn't remember anything, but…" Her bottom lip trembled.

"Maggie, talk to me."

A tear trailed down her cheek. "What if I'm a terrible person?" she whispered, her distress palpable.

He came around the island to be closer to her. "Why would you think that? I met you saving a dog. You were risking your life."

She touched the edge of the platter, tracing a wobbly line along the curve of the dish. "You said the items I had with me were rare, valuable even—things not many people could get. Do you have them with you?"

He removed the card and stone from his pocket and slid them toward her.

She focused on the stone. "What's important about this rock? I noticed the way you look at it, the way you tap your pocket to make sure it's there. It means something to you."

"I carry it for luck. It's starry quartzite. They're only found in the creek in this part of Colorado. But the lines are what make them valuable to me."

"Why?"

"Because of my family's paper company. We use special drums and beaters to prepare the pulp to become paper. Every so often, a rock slips past the sorting process. The beaters have divots. When they hit the stone just right, they carve a line. It was uncommon to strike once, but it was extraordinarily rare to happen twice. And when that happened, it made the number eleven. That's always been my number. Before my first game, back when I was a kid, I was so nervous. I loved baseball and wanted to grow up to be a Major League player. Starrycard Creek is a superstitious place. We write our hopes and dreams on paper. But I needed something more, something that was completely mine. I saw the eleven on the stone, took it as a sign, and put it in my back pocket. I hit my first home run that day. I've never played a game without one— well, almost never."

"You must have known one was missing?"

"Not really. I've lost a few over the years—especially in college when life was pretty chaotic between school, practice, and games. When I hit the majors, I had a little pocket sewn into my uniform. I've got three here at the ranch: one that I chucked behind my bed last week and two in my top drawer. When my shoulder started hurting, I thought they'd protect me from whatever was happening with my body."

"What did happen? Do you mind telling me?"

"No, I don't," he said and meant it. Unlike when others asked, he wanted her to know—to understand. He gestured to his affected side. "The blood flow to my shoulder joint got messed up, and the bone started breaking down. I had to get surgery to fix it, but the damage was already done. I'd felt the pain for years, but I didn't want to acknowledge it. Still, a part of me knew it was more serious, but it's..."

"Scary to acknowledge that you have no control over what happens," she supplied, reading his mind.

He nodded.

She held the rock, turning it in her hand to allow the inclusions to glitter in the light. "Does anyone know about your lucky rocks?"

"No, I've never told anyone—not even my family. I'm superstitious like that. I don't want to jinx it by talking about it." He gazed into her hazel eyes. "Only you know what they mean to me."

She placed the stone on the island's white marble surface. Pain flashed in her eyes as if a heaviness clung to her heart. "What if I stole it from you? What if I got it by some shady means and wanted to get you to pay me for it? I can't figure out why I'm here with it. I worry that my intentions weren't good. What if that's who I am? What if I crave being bad? I have amnesia. How would I know if I'm that type of person? A person the people in your family surely wouldn't like or trust."

While he'd bet the ranch that she wasn't a bad person, he

couldn't deny he was curious about how she'd gained possession of the stone. He glanced at the platter, zeroed in on the three sad little pies, and recalled how he handled issues on the field.

Focus. Plan. Execute. Succeed.

That's how he'd make it better for her.

"There's only one way to find out if you like being bad," he said, lowering his voice as a plan formed.

"And what is that?"

"Maggie…last name to be determined, also known as Maggie TBD," he continued, borrowing Bob's ridiculous moniker, hoping it would lift her spirits.

"Yes?" she replied, the tears in her eyes giving way to a twinkle and a smile—that smile he saw in his dreams, the smile he knew by heart.

He glanced at the clock.

11:11 p.m.

The universe just weighed in on his plan with a big thumbs-up—a sure sign of success.

Emboldened, he gently tipped up her chin and inched toward her. "Let's be bad. *Let's be very, very bad.*"

MAGGIE PEERED down the shadowy alley.

The coast was clear.

Her conscience?

Not so much.

She inhaled the crisp night air, her emotions swirling between eager anticipation and a creeping sense of dread. "Christian, are you sure we won't get in trouble?"

"For a bad girl, you worry a lot about getting caught," he teased, his back to her as he slid a thin, flat tool between the sash and the frame of a first-story window that looked out into the alley.

Lucky whined. He'd pressed his front paws against the building's brick wall, his eyes locked on Christian's every move, his ears twitching with each creak and click.

And speaking of creeks—the watery kind—she yearned to lose herself in the soothing murmur of Starrycard Creek. It flowed, babbling and bobbing a block away. She would have also loved to spend more time gazing at the night sky. The stars were truly *the stars* of the night, casting a gentle glow over the silhouette of the mountains as a layer of dark clouds built in the distance. The raw beauty of the place was almost enough to quell the storm of anxiety brewing within her.

Almost.

"It's okay if you can't open the window. Going out for a drive in the middle of the night was exciting enough. We're really breaking the rules," she said, aiming to add excitement to her statement, but it landed as flat as a deflated balloon.

"What rules?" he asked, turning his baseball cap backward to allow him to get his face closer to the window.

Good question.

She paced. "The rules about needing eight hours of rest. It's got to be close to midnight. Our sleep will be impacted."

Tap, tap, tap. Creak!

"What do we need to wake up early for?" he asked, gaze trained on the latch.

Gah! Another good question.

"Um…work. Because I work for you, and you need to recuperate, even though you are clearly agile enough to break into a building. But sleep allows people to follow a daily schedule and such and so on and so forth as prescribed by my neurologist, Dr. Joan Ironside, MD." Maggie clamped her mouth shut. *Stupid, nervous rambling!*

"I've just about got it," Christian said under his breath, maneuvering his large frame as he worked, unmoved by her word salad.

A faint click signaled the latch giving way, and her heart raced. He lifted the window, then held her gaze in the inky darkness. "What did I tell you?" he said, his voice brimming with satisfaction.

She shrugged. "You didn't tell me anything. You said we were going to be bad."

"And we are the *baddest* of bad, aren't we, boy?" Christian cooed to the dog. He swayed from side to side as Lucky pranced around him—the dog equivalent of a high five.

Despite her nerves, she chuckled and shook her head. The pair could have been lifted straight from a quirky heist flick—Christian with his exaggerated swagger and Lucky with his tail whirling like a helicopter blade. She glanced past them into the sea of darkness behind the window. She had no idea what type of business was inside. The wind whipped through the alley as the clouds blew in with a smattering of raindrops. She shivered as a chill came over her.

"Here," Christian said, taking off his coat and draping it over her shoulders. He glanced at the sky. "A storm's blowing in. That's common this time of year." He looked her over. "First thing tomorrow, we're getting you an insulated coat, a raincoat, and a fleece jacket." He rubbed her arms, and she stared up at him, captivated. His hat, still backward, gave him a roguish allure. As her eyes adapted to the dark, the man seemed to grow more handsome by the second. Everything about him radiated a boyish charm.

Stop! She could not let her mind go there. Even if her head injury had rendered her perma-horny, she had to control it. Christian Starrycard was her boss—sort of.

She held his gaze. "I'm not sure I'm a bad girl. In fact, judging by my pounding heart, I may be a very, *very* good girl."

A wicked grin stretched across his lips. "A good girl, huh?"

This man.

"You're terrible! You know what I mean."

"This is the bad girl experience. Go big or go home."

She chewed her lip. "Go home sounds good."

"That's not what you want. You're intrigued. Admit it."

She exhaled a heavy breath. "I'm intrigued, but we're breaking and entering."

He waved her off. "We're barely breaking and entering, and we won't break anything. We certainly won't be robbing the place. Wait, I've got to take that back. We'll partake in the amenities and offerings, but nobody will be none the wiser."

Excuse me?

"Hold up. Amenities? Offerings? We're not at a bank or a jewelry store, are we?"

He inhaled a hiss of a breath. "A liquor store."

"A liquor store!" she whisper-shouted. "Why are we robbing a liquor store? You have a whole liquor-making room and a mini barn stocked with even more alcohol."

He laughed, and the warmth of the sound resonated through her. As much as she loved seeing him in good spirits, she couldn't take part in robbing a liquor store.

"Why are you so excited?" she demanded.

"We're not at a liquor store. I was messing with you."

"Where are we?"

"The Starrycard Creek Senior Center."

That was no better.

Her jaw dropped. "We're robbing senior citizens?"

"No, we're not fleecing old people. Trust me. Growing up, I used to do this all the time with my little sister, Caroline."

She narrowed her gaze and pursed her lips. "Just Caroline? None of your other siblings? Why just her?"

The man cringed.

"Christian, enlighten me," she pressed, absolutely sure she was on to something.

"Caroline's the youngest, and she was the easiest to convince," he answered, rubbing the back of his neck with a nervous chuckle.

"You are not making a compelling case for sneaking in," she shot back.

But her attempt to cut their night of breaking and entering backfired when that maddening half-grin bloomed on his lips.

He tucked a lock of hair behind her ear. "Come on, Maggie TBD, it'll be great. It's harmless fun. And Lucky will love it, too. I mean, look at him. He's on his best-boy behavior."

She surveyed the pup. The man wasn't wrong. The dog had ceased his wild ways and sat like a disciplined soldier beneath the open window.

"What if someone sees your truck?" She did another check of

the darkened alley, her defenses waning but not completely depleted.

"Nobody will see it. And even if they do, they'll figure someone from the senior center left their car here overnight."

"What about the Starrycard Creek Police?"

"It doesn't exist. We're under the Creek County Sheriff's jurisdiction."

"What if they come by?"

"They won't. There's basically no crime in Starrycard Creek."

"But we're *crime-ing*," she whisper-shouted.

He watched her, his lips twitching as he stifled a grin.

So nice to know he'd found this exchange amusing.

She peered down the darkened alley again. "Maybe I should stay out here and keep watch. There are bad girls in movies who act as lookouts. That could be my level of bad girl."

He placed his hands on her shoulders, and just when she thought he couldn't leave her more breathless, the jacket slid down a few inches, allowing his warm skin to brush against hers. A delicious shiver danced through her, leaving her yearning for more as his expression grew earnest. "I'd never do anything to hurt you, Maggie. All I want is to make you…"

"Go on," she murmured, her body tingling.

He parted his lips as if to finish his thought, but he hesitated.

Was he reconsidering her go-home plan?

"On the badness scale of one to ten," he continued, "what we're about to do is barely a one. Probably more like point five. We can go home, if you're not up for it, but I know you'll like what's inside. Will you trust me?"

Little did he know, she was powerless to say no.

"Okay. Let's do it."

"You're sure?" he pressed, his nervous grin slowly transforming into that boyish expression that made her weak in the knees.

"Yes, but we're not calling it *breaking in*."

"We're not?"

"We're not burglars," she reasoned. "We're acting in the capacity of...security guards. Yes, we're monitoring and ensuring safety," she continued, feeling much better about what they were about to do. She glanced at the dog, and her smile widened. "We're the Volunteer Creek County K-9 Unit."

"That's the spirit. I used to tell Caroline we could sneak in because we were invisible."

"And she believed you?"

"Until around Christmas. She thought she could be invisible whenever she wanted. One afternoon, she left my family's paper shop and went to the candy store—a very packed—candy store. She jumped the counter and started gorging on chocolate peppermint fudge. She didn't think anyone could see her."

"Did she get in trouble?"

"We both did. She ratted on me."

"I bet she was furious with you."

Vibrating with silent laughter, he removed his hat, ran his fingers through his hair, and then replaced the cap firmly on his head. "She punched me in the eye. The kid was half my size, and she knocked me out cold."

Maggie chuckled. "I don't know the woman, but I like her already."

"Well, you both have socking me in the face in common."

She touched the skin below his bruised eye. "I wish I remembered doing this to you."

His body went rigid, and he pulled back.

What a strange reaction. He must want her to regain her memories, right?

Heavy raindrops peppered the ground. "Come on. Pretty soon, there'll be a downpour." He gestured to the open window. "I'll climb through. Pass Lucky to me, and then I'll help you in."

"What about your arm, your shoulder?" she asked, her eyes narrowing against the intensifying rain.

"I'll be careful. It's much better since I started doing my

mobility exercises. I can use it. But it'll never be the arm of a power hitter."

She nodded, noting that the usual torment lacing his words when he spoke of his injury had softened.

"I want to share this with you, Maggie. This place means something to me."

There was no way she could say no now.

She nodded as Christian slipped through the window like a lynx. Barely a second passed before he reached for Lucky.

"Here we go, boy." She lifted the pup and handed the dog to Christian, who cradled him briefly before setting him inside. Then, extending his good hand, he helped her, his grip firm as he guided her through the window into the darkened interior.

He shut the window, removed his coat from her shoulders, and rested it on an old chair. She glanced around, her eyes adjusting to the darkness. Bookshelves lined the walls, and tables were strategically placed throughout the space, giving the impression of a makeshift library.

He came up behind her. "Close your eyes."

"Why? It's dark," she replied, the heat of his presence stirring an intoxicating sense of anticipation inside her.

"Just do it, Maggie TBD."

"Are you going to keep calling me *TBD*?" she asked with a pout, but when he said it, the ache of not knowing her last name didn't sting quite as much.

"Yes, I like it. Baseball players love nicknames. We'll stick with it."

"What's your nickname?" she continued.

"I didn't have one."

"Then why do I need one?"

"Because I want to give you one. Now, be a good girl, *TBD*, and close your eyes," he said in that cocksure, commanding tone that threatened to turn her knees to jelly for what had to be the hundredth time since they'd left the hospital.

She exhaled a slow breath. "Fine, my eyes are closed."

He clasped her hand, and a wave of warmth washed over her —a sensation she was beginning to crave.

"Oh, shit," he whispered under his breath, leading her deeper into the building.

"You should never say 'oh, shit' while trotting someone around with their eyes closed."

"I forgot something."

"Should we turn back?"

"No, we'll make do. Okay, we're here." He stopped. "Stay like that. Don't move. I need to open the door."

Lucky brushed against her legs as she heard a click, then listened to the door emit a slow, drawn-out whine. She inhaled and identified their destination. "Are we at an indoor pool?"

"Open your eyes, TBD, and see for yourself."

Bingo! She was right.

The air was thick with the unmistakable scent of chlorine. It blended with a faint mustiness that hinted at the pool's age. The only light came from the underwater bulbs. They cast a bluish glow that danced across the water's surface, creating shimmering reflections on the tiled walls and ceiling. A diving board jutted out over the deep end. Despite its simple rectangular design, the place had an undeniable charm, especially when imagining Christian and his little sister sneaking inside for a midnight swim.

She peered up at the man. "It's hauntingly beautiful. You're right. I'm glad we're here, but you have an indoor pool at the ranch."

A wide grin stretched across his face. "Not with a diving board and what comes next. Come on, Lucky." He jogged toward the deep end, kicking off his shoes.

And that's when it hit.

They were here to swim, and she wasn't wearing a swimsuit.

She stood like a gobsmacked statue, looking on as he stripped down to his boxer briefs. His broad shoulders tapered down to a chiseled chest and defined abs. Despite no longer being a professional athlete, his body exuded raw athleticism, and it left her breathless.

"Take it down a notch, Miss Perma-Horny Brain," she whispered.

"Did you say something?" he called.

"Um…no," she uttered, grateful she could even produce two syllables.

Christian set his hat and clothing on a bench. "I forgot we needed swimsuits. I'd always make sure Care had hers on under her pajamas, but underwear works. Are you good with that?"

She blinked. *Speak, woman.*

"TBD, all good?" he repeated, one foot on the ladder that led to the diving board.

His hella hot bod must have triggered her brain to reboot.

She cleared her throat. "Yeah, yes, sure. Underwear for the win…for the goal…for the…"

Splash!

She gasped as Christian hit the water.

Splash!

Lucky sprang into the pool on the man's heels.

Christian emerged from the shimmering blue depths and shook the water out of his hair. "Hey, water dog," he crooned as Lucky paddled around him. "TBD?" he called.

"Yeah?"

"Check out Lucky. You like the water, huh, good boy," he cooed to the pup as the pair swam and frolicked. "Water's perfect. It's warm. That's how the old people like it."

She pointed to the far end and started walking that way. "I'll wade in at the shallow part—just to be safe, in case I can't swim."

"Good call. I'll be right there," he said, his gaze locked on her as he glided through the water toward the steps. "Want me to look away as you undress?" he asked as he approached the shallow end.

She tugged at the hem of her shirt. "Yeah, just give me a second." Her breath quickened as she untied her sneakers and slipped off her yoga pants and tank top, feeling the humid air against her bare skin. She silently thanked Pre-Amnesia Maggie for choosing a matching pale pink bra and panty set trimmed in lace. Nothing over the top, but at least it wasn't granny panties or a teeny-weeny G-string stuck in her butt crack. Still, her heart raced.

Calm down! This is just a midnight swim in her underwear with a gorgeous former pro ballplayer who was built like a brick house.

She ran her hands down her torso, feeling the delicate fabric cling to her curves. *Just a swim, just a swim.* She dipped her toe into the water as Lucky bounded up the steps leading to the pool deck. The pup shook vigorously, sending a spray of water droplets all over her. And God bless that dog. It was the tension breaker she needed. She laughed. "Hey, no need for the preview. I'm getting in," she said, giggling. She took another step into the pool, expecting Christian to comment on the dog's antics, but the man didn't make a sound.

He stood in the shallow end, gaze locked on her. Wide-eyed and jaw flapping, it was as if he wasn't quite sure if she was real or something from a dream.

She dragged her fingertips across the water's surface. "The old people really know how to choose a pool temperature," she remarked, like an idiot, unsure of what to say to the person currently staring at her like she was the most fascinating thing he'd ever seen.

"Christ, TBD," he got out. "I could look at you forever and it still wouldn't be enough."

"What?"

He cleared his throat. "Um," he murmured, like his brain needed a reboot, too. "I don't know what that was. Would you like me to help you? I won't let you sink. Even if you could swim, I wouldn't let you drown. That would be pretty shitty of me. Fuck...I'm gonna shut up, but you should know that you look..." He stilled, his lips parting like a confused goldfish.

"Yes?" she said softly.

"You look like a woman wearing underwear. Underwear is not exactly swimwear, but it's similar in function and in what it covers and doesn't cover. And I fully support everything it doesn't cover and, of course, the parts it does cover." He grimaced. "Goddammit, I don't know what just poured out of my mouth."

And, like earlier, his nervous rambling put her at ease.

Feeling empowered by his word salad jabbering, she waded into the pool, the water rising until it reached just below her breasts. She schooled her features and held Christian's gaze. "Would you say I look like a good girl or a bad girl in my swimming attire?"

That shifted his attention. His mortified expression vanished, and his half-grin returned. "That depends. How do you feel?"

"I feel like a little of both," she replied, moving toward him, the water now kissing her shoulder blades.

But what if she was wrong? What if her naughty overpowered her nice?

"What is it, Maggie?" he asked, coming to her side.

"I'm worried I might be..." she said, continuing further into the pool as she recalled what had gone down outside the hospital, and that sense of clawing worry took over.

"What?" he asked, losing the playful tone.

"I was thinking about how I behaved with your brother, with Owen, when I made up the housekeeper position. It was deceptive and—"

"It was genius, Maggie, and I understood what you were doing."

"But I tricked your brother."

"No, you were being kind to him—and to me. You were trying to smooth things over and lighten the load on the guy. He's prickly on the outside, but he takes everything to heart. I picked up on what you were doing immediately."

"Okay, that's what I hoped was happening. It was like you could read my mind, like we were..."

"Like we were what?" he asked, the blue light highlighting the sharp cut of his cheekbones.

How was she supposed to answer? He'd already made the case for them not knowing each other before she'd materialized out of thin air to save Lucky from the train. And yet, she couldn't shake the feeling that he did know her, and that knowledge was intimate.

Intimate.

Her chest tightened as a damning realization dawned.

Christian was a well-known baseball player. A celebrity. He wasn't married. He didn't have a girlfriend. He could probably have his pick of women. She was nobody—literally and figuratively. What if she'd had a one-night stand with him? What if she'd stolen the baseball card and the stone? What if that was what he wasn't telling her? Maybe that's why he didn't want her to mention the card and the stone to his family.

The watery world grew topsy-turvy. She could barely draw a breath. She took one unsteady step, then another before a dizzying sensation took hold. The room blurred. Her vision darkened, and before she could draw another breath, her body slipped beneath the water's surface.

CHAPTER

Ten

MAGGIE

MAGGIE'S BODY WENT LIMP, her limbs rising as if she were weightless. The transition from the air to water stopped her spiraling thoughts as an otherworldly quiet took over. She descended into the depths, her hair floating around her head like a halo, moving in a slow-motion dance. She closed her eyes and relaxed, lightening, fading, gently fading. But just as she was about to succumb to the watery embrace, strong arms encircled her. She opened her eyes and saw Christian's face, his features drawn tight, his hair flowing in dark, swaying waves. The anguish on his face stirred something inside her. And then she heard a noise.

Crack!

As she peered at him, the sharp sound echoed in her mind like a memory attempting to rise to her consciousness. But the recollection vanished as he shuttled her through the water. He broke the surface, and the air hit her cheeks with an icy blast as Lucky's panicked bark reverberated through the space. She coughed and struggled for breath.

"Take it slow," Christian urged, his grip firm and protective. He pressed her against his chest, his heartbeat hammering in her ear. He maneuvered them to the steps where Lucky sat, whining and yelping anxiously.

"I'm all right, boy," she rasped, her hand trembling as she stroked the pup's neck.

Christian helped her out of the pool and onto a bench. He grabbed a towel off a nearby stack and wrapped it around her shoulders. "What happened, Maggie? Is it your head? Are you in pain, or was it another panic attack?"

She shivered, her breathing finally evening out. "I think it was a panic attack. I couldn't make it stop. This thought kept rattling around. It took hold and wouldn't let go."

"What thought?" he asked, taking her hands as he knelt before her with Lucky at his side.

She couldn't tell him.

"It's not important. I didn't really eat earlier. I'm pretty hungry. That could have made me lightheaded and exacerbated things."

He tightened his hold on her. "What thought sent you spiraling?"

She shook her head.

"Tell me so I can help you," he pleaded, his words ripe with agony.

"You really want to know?" she asked, finding her voice.

"Yes, of course, I do. I hate seeing you upset."

Here goes everything.

She centered herself and locked onto his gaze. "I know that you know me, Christian. That's the thought that's been eating at me. I can't understand why you won't tell me how we know each other unless the reason would hurt me. And that got me thinking about our current situation. You're a famous athlete." She looked away, breaking their connection. "You've probably been with a lot of women."

She could feel the intensity of his gaze as the air between them thickened with tension.

She focused on one of the pool deck's cracked tiles and forced herself to go on. "Did we sleep together? Did we have a one-night stand? Could I have taken the stone and the card then? And what kind of person just shows up? Am I a stalker? A jilted lover? Was I trying to get money out of you? Am I some crazy girl who couldn't get over you?"

"Stop! Stop, and look at me, Maggie, please," he begged.

She complied. The torment written across his face was raw and unguarded as a sea of emotions roiled in his eyes.

"Do you think I would keep something like that from you?"

"I don't know what to think. I don't know much, but I know there's something between us. I feel it. I've felt it since I woke up and saw your face. I feel it every time you touch me. Say it, Christian. I can handle it, and I need to know. It's tearing me apart inside. How are we connected?"

His hands trembled. He tightened his hold and spoke. He'd said one word. One syllable. But she must have misunderstood.

"Say that again. How are we connected?"

He swallowed hard, the muscles in his neck tightening. His gaze flickered to the floor before meeting hers again. "I said… pie."

———

The light from the refrigerator cast the senior center's kitchen in a pale, ghostly glow as they stood before the appliance stocked with a bounty of pies, each covered in clear plastic wrap.

"Pick one. You'll want something in your stomach for what I'm about to tell you," Christian said, his voice barely a whisper.

She couldn't figure out what was going on with him. He was only making it worse by dragging out the explanation. "Christian, this is insane. Just tell me."

Still dripping wet, she adjusted the towel around her shoulders. Clad in only her bra and panties, he'd led her to a space resembling a Home Ec classroom. He stood beside her, his bare chest exposed, a towel cinched at his waist, and another looped around his neck. He stared into the refrigerator like the aluminum pie tins held the answers to life's greatest mysteries.

"Humor me, Maggie. Choose a pie."

"Why?" she snapped.

"Pie is delicious, and it makes everything better," he replied, the despair in his eyes unmistakable.

"Who says pie makes everything better?"

His expression softened. "You do."

"Me?"

"You made that claim after we saved Lucky during one of your damned adorable word salad soliloquies. Now, pick a pie, TBD. The seniors won't miss it. I've been eating their pies since I was a kid."

"You mean stealing," she countered.

He shrugged and offered a roguish grin. "Fine, stealing. But I did donate a shit-ton of money to put in new appliances here a few years ago. As far as karma goes, we're good."

Her frustration prickled through her. "You'll only tell me how we know each other if I pick a pie?"

"Yes."

This man.

She scanned the room to check on Lucky. The pup had nestled into a recliner in the corner and slept in a ball, exhausted from the late-night antics. She was exhausted, too. Exhausted by Christian's stalling. She returned her attention to the infuriating man. He turned on one of the banks of lights, setting the room in a dim glow. The strain in his expression told her he was nervous, but she was pretty freaking anxious also. The difference was that he held the cards. He had the answers. She huffed—so he'd know she wasn't pleased—then studied the tins. Each pie was labeled. She narrowed her gaze, reading the scribbled writing, then glanced at Christian. "They're all some variation of pumpkin pie."

"It's close to the town's fall festival. We call it Donnelly Days. There's a pumpkin pie-making contest. Martha Donnelly, Fiona's mom, started it. Caroline and I would sneak in a lot more during this time of year. Many of the seniors baked them here. They've got a culinary club. They start testing recipes early and the fridge was always stocked."

She scanned the labels. "Bourbon Pumpkin Pie," she said, her interest piqued.

"That's a good one—smoky with a little kick. But it won't get you hammered. Care and I each hoovered two in one night to see if we would get wasted. The results weren't pretty. The next day, we couldn't stop puking. It took a good five years before I was able to even think about pumpkin pie without gagging."

"Bourbon Pumpkin Pie it is then," she said, wanting to be angry at the man but unable to hide her amusement at the imagery of the pair gorging on pie, thinking they'd get a buzz.

"That's more like it," he said softly.

"What's more like it?"

"You're smiling. This is how I always see you—smiling with that sweet blush."

What did that mean?

He pulled open a drawer and grabbed two plastic sporks while she retrieved the pie and placed it on the stove next to the fridge. Carefully, she peeled back the plastic wrap as if she were opening a gift. An oddly familiar sensation washed over her like this pie, and the work that had gone into making it, was someone's present to them.

He handed her a spork, and she stared at it intently.

"Are you okay?"

"Yeah," she said, probably the first person to be rendered gobsmacked by plasticware.

"I could look around for real silverware," he offered.

"No, no, this is fine," she answered, pushing aside her puzzling spork fascination.

He gestured with his chin toward the tables. "Do you want to sit?"

"No, pie for dinner should be eaten standing."

He cocked his head to the side. "Is that some unspoken pie rule I've never heard?"

Again, that peculiar familiarity returned. "I don't know why I said that."

"Standing it is. Ladies first. Dig in."

She took a bite, eyes widening as the rich, smoky flavor hit her tongue. The smooth texture and bourbon's subtle kick stirred an uncanny sense of recognition.

"What do you think?" he asked, then loaded up his spork.

She closed her eyes and concentrated on the flavors. "It's delicious. I taste a little ginger, too. A nice addition." She turned her attention back to the pie, took another bite, then rested her spork on the counter. "But we're not here to talk about pie—even a pie as good as this one. Please, tell me how we know each other. There's no doubt we're connected. You called me 'my Maggie' in the hospital. You told me that you're here because of me. You said you'd take me however you could have me. And the way you look at me, it makes me feel like…" Her heart fluttered.

"Like what?"

She gazed into his sage green eyes. "Like you adore me. Like I'm the girl of your dreams. Am I losing my mind?"

That beautiful, boyish grin graced his lips. "No, you're not. You hit the nail on the head."

"I don't understand."

"I didn't want to do this so soon. I didn't want to put too much pressure on you. You've got amnesia. Everything is new."

"Christian, tell me now," she said, voice trembling with emotion.

"Here it is. The truth. Maggie, you *are* the woman of my dreams."

She waited for him to smirk or to offer a teasing shrug, but he stood there, his eyes steady and his posture unwavering.

"Christian, answer me truthfully," she demanded, raising her voice. "I ate some pie. I'm done playing games. I'm about to lose my mind. Where did we meet?"

"I'm telling you the truth. We've never met, but you are the girl of my dreams."

She shook her head, pure fury surging through her. *Forget this guy!* Sure, he had shown her kindness, and their bond was undeniable, but she was done with this endless back-and-forth. "I don't have any memories, but I'm not an idiot," she seethed. "I'm done being treated like one. I'm leaving. I'll walk around in the rain and sleep on a bench or something. Make sure Lucky gets back to the ranch."

Fuming, she turned to walk away but didn't make it an inch. In a fluid motion, he slammed the refrigerator door shut. His hands seized her hips with a fierce urgency. He pushed her back against the hard surface, caging her in, trapping her with the intensity of his hulking presence, their breaths mingling in the charged air between them.

"Don't go. Let me explain. What I'm about to tell you will sound crazy. It's why I didn't want my family to know what you had with you when you showed up."

"I'd prefer hearing something crazy over nothing. Tell me, or I am leaving. I'll go to the police. I'll see what services they provide to help people like me."

Agony flashed in his eyes. "I'm not lying to you, Maggie. I've never met you. But I know you because I've been dreaming about you for months—since my injury."

"I'm literally in your dreams?" she repeated, sure not expecting that.

"Yeah, I see your face. You're outdoors, and there's a subtle breeze. Wisps of your hair catch the light as they move. You're concerned at first, but then you smile at me. I see your face, that smile, the gentle blush on your cheeks, and I'm me. I'm whole. I'm at peace."

Her anger dissolved, and her heart filled with a raw, aching tenderness for the man. She softened her expression. "Could you be dreaming of someone who looks like me?"

He shook his head, pain welling in his eyes. "It's you, Maggie.

You're the woman in my dreams. I didn't know your name. I only learned it when you told me after we saved Lucky. I know what it feels like to be with you. It's how I feel now. It's how I've felt from the moment I saw your face, touched your hair, and held you. You're a ray of pure sunshine, this goodness and light in my life. You're the only thing that's mattered to me since I lost my ability to play ball. You're what keeps me going. And it's been rough. I didn't want to put this on you, to burden you. You just woke up from a fucking coma with amnesia," he said, voice cracking.

"I want to know, Christian. I want to know everything, or it's over. Whatever this is will end."

The man was hurting, but she had to hold her ground. The air was thick with tension, and each word between them was a spark threatening to ignite the charged atmosphere.

Christian's eyes darkened, a storm brewing behind them. "You want it all? The good, the bad, and the ugly?"

"Yes, I told you. I want *everything*." Her voice was barely above a whisper, but it carried the weight of her resolve.

He stepped closer, heat radiating from his body. "Then, Maggie TBD, that's what you'll get."

Eleven

MAGGIE

MAGGIE WAITED, watching Christian stare at the ceiling, his eyes shining with unshed tears.

He looked at her with a raw, deep ache etched on his expression. "There were days when I couldn't see a path forward, when I couldn't see the value of going on another day. There was pain, and the only thing that got me through was hoping that if I got drunk enough to black out, I'd get to be with you and gaze at your face and feel like a person again," he finished and stroked her cheek.

"Christian," she whispered, leaning into his touch.

"It's hard to put it into words, but when I saw your face after we saved Lucky, I knew it was you. My heart knew you were the woman in my dreams."

"As sweet and romantic as that sounds, it doesn't make sense. There must be a reason—something besides a dream that connects us."

His body tensed like it was fighting to accept this notion. "I know you're right, but I also know what I feel for you is real, and nothing will convince me otherwise."

Donning a mock-serious expression, she looked him over.

"Are you sure you don't have memory issues?" she asked, trying to lift the weight of sorrow that pressed down on him.

He chuckled, the tension draining. "Christ, who knows? Can I confess something else to you?"

"Of course."

"I got myself into a bad place. I was at the point where I'd do anything to get to you. I'm a big guy. It takes a hell of a lot of alcohol to even get me tipsy. I started drinking nearly nonstop. When I was still at my place in Rocky Mountain City, I'd go out and get hammered. I got arrested a few times. Thank God they didn't file charges. I went down a dark path. I fired my management team. I lost sponsors and deals. I became the epitome of a washed-up ballplayer. I moved back to the ranch to get out of the limelight and to keep drinking. My family was right to be worried. I had a lot of pills on hand and plenty of alcohol. If you hadn't shown up when you did…"

She pressed her fingertips to his lips. "Don't talk like that. Just because you can't play baseball doesn't mean that part of your life is over. People turn their lives around. I'm sure there's a place for you in it. Coaching? Commentary?"

"No, that chapter is closed. It's not who I am anymore. I can't be on the sidelines. I'm either in the game or out. It's who I am, but I have a new path."

She watched him closely. "What path are you on?"

That ghost of a grin curled the corner of his mouth. "A fresh path. I'm a superstitious guy. Most ballplayers are. We look for signs. We hold on to trinkets. You've been in my dreams for months. You showed up at one eleven."

"One eleven?"

"It's my number, and when you encounter multiple ones, it means you're headed in the right direction. I learned that in college. You had one of my good luck charms with you and my card—my card printed on Starrycard Creek paper. Paper that brings what's meant for you your way. But I think there's more to it. You're not only here *because* of me. I believe you're here *for* me."

"For you?"

"When I saw your face and learned that you were real, it was like rediscovering a part of myself I thought I'd lost forever. This feeling of solidness was how I used to feel about baseball—this unshakable certainty. Being near you, watching you sleep while you recovered, you'd become my compass, guiding me back to a life that made sense. I stopped drinking. I know it's just a week, but it's a start. My focus was on you. All I wanted was for you to be okay. And Christ, the freedom I'd felt when we stepped out of the hospital was like breaking free from chains that had been holding me down. It was dark out, but you were my light, my bright and constant star. I believe you're my future, Maggie. My path led me to you, and yours to me."

"My path," she repeated as a shadowy inkling came over her, a feeling like there was something on the tip of her tongue, a notion just out of reach.

"The second we left the hospital, I wanted to kiss you. I've never wanted anything more." He looked away and grimaced. "I'm sorry. I shouldn't have said that—all that. It's a lot to put on you, especially when you don't remember anything. And I'm not only about the physical stuff. I don't want you to think—"

"I wanted you to kiss me, too," she said, cutting him off, needing him to know she understood.

He met her gaze. "You did?"

"I blamed my brain for feeling that way. I thought my injury might have rendered me perma-horny."

"Perma-horny?" he said, amusement dancing in his eyes.

"I don't think it's a medical term."

"It should be," he replied, drinking her in. "So, you feel a connection to me, TBD?"

She smiled up at him, kind of loving that he'd given her that nickname. "Yeah, I feel it."

He glanced away, nodding bashfully with that dreamy half-grin.

His sweet reaction emboldened her. "Hey, Number Eleven?"

If he could come up with a name for her, she could come up with one for him. Was Number Eleven creative? Not really, but it felt right.

"Yeah?" he said, smile still in place.

"When your phone chimed, it ended the moment, but before that, you hesitated. What held you back?"

His brow furrowed as he pondered her question. "I guess I was sitting on the pitch."

There was that baseball term again.

She cocked her head to the side. "You were waiting for me to throw a ball at your butt?"

Christian's bare, muscled chest heaved with laughter. "Sitting on the pitch is when a batter passes up pitches—even ones they could get a hit off—while they wait for the one they want. It's a strategy players use depending on several factors, one of them being the batter's strengths. You're waiting for a pitcher to throw a certain pitch, like waiting for the right moment. There's risk involved. You could let something good pass you by. But if you've read the game right, it could mean the difference between a win and a loss."

"I'm glad you don't want me to chuck a ball at your butt," she murmured.

He shrugged. "I mean, if you're into that."

"Stop," she said, swatting his chest. She studied him. "I wish you would have told me how you felt after I woke up in the hospital."

The mischievous glint in his eyes disappeared. "I probably should have. But I didn't want to scare you, and I knew I needed to keep you close. All I could focus on was being the best version of myself and finding a way to prove that I'm the kind of man who deserves you."

His words almost knocked the breath clean out of her. "You feel that strongly for me?"

"I do."

"But what if I have someone in my pre-amnesia life? I don't

think I'm married. I didn't wake up wearing a ring. But what if I'm dating someone? What if I'm in love with someone who I can't remember?"

Color rose to his cheeks. "If you are, he's not worthy of you," he growled, his possessive, resolute tone sending a titillating tingle down her spine.

"How do you know that?"

His expression tightened. "He's not looking for you."

She flinched.

He tipped up her chin. "I didn't say that to hurt you. I said it because, if you were mine, I wouldn't let seven days go by without knowing you were safe. Hell, I wouldn't let seven minutes go by. I would move heaven and earth to protect you, to make you smile, to see you blush that sweet shade of pink that I cannot get out of my head. And now you're here with me, and I have a chance to win your heart. I promise you—I won't waste a second of it worrying about someone who doesn't measure up."

Her pulse quickened under the heat of his gaze, everything else fading away. "How does this even work? How do *we* work? We don't know who I am?"

A gentle calm washed over him. "That's the best part, TBD. It's like I said before, we make the rules."

She looked down, her voice barely a whisper. "But I still want to know who I am. It might not be pretty. It might get complicated."

He lifted her chin, gently forcing her to hold his gaze. "We'll figure it out."

"It could be really bad, Christian." Her voice cracked, fear seeping through.

He broke out the boyish half-grin. "Why couldn't it be really good? Why couldn't we trust that every sign got us here and believe you were supposed to be with me? And even if it does get complicated, scary, or confusing, every storm passes."

Every storm passes.

The words resonated deep within her.

"But what if we learn something big stands in the way? What if the storm can't pass?" Her heart raced, and those gnawing thoughts threatened to take over again. "I understand believing in signs and trusting your gut. But how can you be so sure? What about—"

He pressed his finger to her lips. "I'm going to stop you right there and kiss you."

"What?" she stammered.

"I'll kiss you and we'll see how it feels."

This was getting very real.

"I don't have any memory of ever being kissed. I might not even know how to kiss. What if I'm a runaway nun?" She bit her lip, a nervous laugh escaping.

"I doubt runaway nuns wear lacy bras and panties—and that little jean skirt and those hot as hell boots. If you're a nun, nuns have gotten way sexier since I last encountered one."

He was trying to lighten the mood, but she couldn't let go, not yet.

"You seem so invested. I don't want to disappoint you."

"You could never disappoint me. And by the way, TBD, you've just upped the bar for this kiss. If it has the potential to be your first kiss, it's my duty to make it memorable."

"Do you think you can do that?" she whispered, her heart pounding.

"Is that a challenge?" he purred.

And heaven help her. That voice. Her body hummed, alive with an undeniable need to have this man's lips pressed to hers.

Casting aside her doubts and fears, she clutched the towel wrapped around his shoulders and let her gaze wander over him, savoring every detail. This man—this beautiful man—wanted her. And he wasn't playing games—at least, it didn't feel like it. And that notion, that intense clarity, while certainly surprising, felt new, like perhaps even Pre-Amnesia Maggie hadn't experienced such a display of affection. A quiet certainty set in alongside a bubbly breathlessness, like standing on the edge of a cliff, staring at a sparkling lake below, and wondering if you'll leap or back away.

She lifted her chin. She wouldn't let her fears take over.

And she knew exactly what to say.

She tugged on the towel around Christian's neck and brought him closer, asserting her power. "What are you waiting for, Number Eleven? Are you going to sit on the pitch or swing?"

The glint in his eyes darkened as his gaze grew positively carnal. "Don't you worry, TBD. I'm a master at knowing when to swing, and I've been thinking about kissing those perfect lips of yours for months. I've got a plan, and I'm prepared to execute it."

She offered him a sly grin. "You always seem prepared."

"And I will succeed," he continued, laser focused.

The air crackled, drawing them together. And heaven help her. The man's intensity nearly set her aflame.

"Close your eyes," he said, his voice a low, commanding rasp.

Like the good girl she might be, she did as she was told.

He held her face in his hands, and tenderly, so, so tenderly, he drew the tip of his tongue across the seam of her lips.

Sweet Lord above, she loved when he took control.

She exhaled a shaky breath, her mind barely able to process the sensation of being adored. With maddeningly gentle pressure, he pressed the whisper of a kiss to the corner of her mouth. Her breath hitched as he removed the towel from around her shoulders. It fell to the ground, pooling at her feet. Her wet locks dripped on her arms as he forged a trail of kisses down her neck and across her collarbone. He stilled, then gently bit her shoulder.

"That's...wow," she breathed as he licked the droplets of water from her skin. A move that was both erotic and gentle.

"I'm still wet from the pool," she murmured, her hand clumsily bumping the stove dials as she searched for something to steady herself. He hadn't even officially kissed her, and her knees were already threatening to give out.

"You're about to get even wetter. Can I touch you here?" he asked, tracing the band of her panties.

"Yes," she whispered, her core pulsing as the air electrified.

He nipped at her neck. "And fair warning…"

"Uh-huh," she said on the cusp of losing the ability to string words together.

"I used to be the king of hard and fast on the diamond. I was a power hitter, and I could steal a base like a thief in the night. But that's not how our first kiss is going down."

"It's not?" she replied, gasping as he grazed his teeth against her neck.

"I'm going to savor every second." He slipped his hand into her panties and cupped her most sensitive place. "We're going to slow it down." He massaged her in precise circles with the same deliberate, perfect pressure he'd used when he made the motion on her hand and her back. Rhythmic and firm, like he could read her mind and anticipate her every desire.

She trembled. The buildup to this first kiss alone might be the death of her. "Christian?" she managed.

"Yes."

"I need you to kiss me," she pleaded, mustering the last of her brain power to form a complete sentence.

He smiled against the corner of her mouth as he continued working her with his hand. "That's exactly what you say when I fantasize about devouring your perfect mouth. And sweet Christ, Maggie, I want to give you everything."

What could a girl say to that?

Nothing—literally nothing. Between his touch and his voice, she was near delirious. She parted her lips and moaned a low, sensual sound.

"There's the pitch," he whispered.

Heat pulsing between them, he claimed her mouth. But this first kiss wasn't demanding or overwhelming. He savored her, moving slowly, building, tasting, indulging with each unhurried roll of his tongue. He *worshipped* her mouth and worked her sweet bud, easing into a groove. She'd only known him for a handful of hours, but it was as if her soul had already intertwined with his. And this bond felt both profoundly timeless and thrillingly new.

Her core pulsed, tightening, pleasure mounting. She traced her fingertips down his hard, wet torso, exploring every sculpted ridge. No longer able to form a coherent thought, she tugged at the towel wrapped around his waist and let it slip free.

"Maggie," he said against her lips, then deepened the kiss and quickened the tempo. He curled one finger and slipped it inside her hot, wet center, massaging her, teasing her.

The man was delivering a first kiss with a side of orgasm—like a slice of pie with a trailer truckload of whipped cream.

Maybe she had died when she'd hit her head, and this was heaven.

She rocked her hips, riding his hand with reckless abandon, done debating whether she was of this world or not. A fire burned inside her, accelerating, growing, consuming. "Don't stop. It's so good," she moaned, a sultry mix of yearning and lust lacing her breathy words.

"I'll never stop. You're glorious, Maggie—the most beautiful thing I've ever seen. Take it. Take every drop of pleasure and make it yours. It's all yours. I'm yours," he growled against her lips.

His words and the dizzying tempo tipped her over the edge. Her release washed over her in decadent waves. Ripple after ripple, pleasure coursed through her. With her lips parted, she opened her eyes and locked onto his gaze, and a sharp clarity flooded her mind.

She belonged *with* him, and she belonged *to* him.

What they had transcended time and space like he was imprinted on her heart, and she was embedded in his soul.

He kept her in a state of carnal rapture, using his hand to keep her roiling in the waves of ecstasy. She swayed and writhed, taking, feeling, grinding against him. And just when she was sure her spirit was on the brink of departing her body, he slowed, easing her back. Her limbs lightened like a feather drifting to the ground. She loosened her grip on the stove and collapsed into his arms.

He kissed the crown of her head. "You are spectacular, TBD."

She pulled back a bit. "Yeah?"

"Hell, yes."

She leaned against the refrigerator door and peered up at him. "I felt it—that bond. It was there like an invisible thread connecting us."

He gathered her into his arms and held her close. "Now you know how I've felt from the moment I saw you, and why I was fucking terrified you wouldn't wake up from the coma. I couldn't bear to lose you."

She couldn't help but smile up at him, tears welling in her eyes. Even without her memories, she felt an overwhelming sense of having missed this sort of affection—the certainty of being protected. In his embrace, she was safe. She exhaled a shaky breath as a tear trailed down her cheek.

"What is it?" he asked, brushing the tear away with his thumb.

"I'm really happy," she whispered.

"Your happiness means everything to me, and…" He watched her, and the corners of his mouth curled upward. "It also appears I've found my new calling in life."

"And what's that?"

"Making you come on my hand as much and as often as possible."

Oh, this naughty man.

She rested her forehead on his chest. "Sounds like a plan. Lucky for you, you don't seem to have much else on your plate," she teased.

"That's true," he said through a chuckle, his hard body vibrating with amusement.

And talk about hard. His rock-hard cock pressed against her, sparking an idea that was sure to settle the bad girl good girl question.

She lowered to her knees. "Perhaps I need a new calling, too," she said, holding his gaze as she peeled his damp boxer briefs down his long, muscled legs. "Maybe Pre-Amnesia Maggie wasn't a professional wrestler. She could have been a..." She winced, feeling her cheeks heat.

"You didn't think that one through, did you, TBD?" he said, biting back a grin as he gazed down at her with so much adoration in his eyes it left her feeling irresistibly alluring.

With a coy grin, she slid down his boxer briefs and tossed them into the air. "I guess we'll find out." And holy moly, she'd put some power into the throw. The underwear went up with such force it hit the ceiling, then landed perfectly on the stovetop.

"Easy there, Miss Rocket Arm," Christian teased, his voice growing husky.

"Maybe I'm a power hitter or...a power *sucker*."

Lust and a flicker of surprise glinted in his eyes. "TBD, you are the perfect blend of good girl and bad girl. No, I take that back. You're fucking perfect the way you are. Period."

His words ignited a newfound courage within her like she could conquer the world.

She took him in her hands and swirled her tongue around the tip of his hard shaft.

He hissed a sharp inhale and tangled his hand in her hair. "Maggie," he rasped.

She wrapped her lips around his cock—his thick, beautiful cock—and took him deep, then deeper.

"Fuck, that's amazing," he said, gritting out the words.

The bad girl in her seemed to outweigh the good because sweet heaven above, she loved turning this man into a growly, rasping heap of hotness.

Finding a rhythm, their rhythm, she sucked hard, grazing her teeth along his shaft, making sure he felt every curl and caress of her tongue. She worked him with her hand, admiring his velvet cock, glistening with his arousal, then looked up and saw Christian and...fire.

Fire?

She gasped and fell onto her ass.

"Maggie?" Christian said, confusion marring his features.

"Fire!" she exclaimed. "Your boxers—they're burning! I must've turned the burner on during that earth-shattering orgasm."

"Earth-shattering?" he repeated.

How was he not freaking out?

"Christian, I was giving you a you-know-what, and now there's a fire, and you're standing there naked and sexy and with an enormous hard-on."

"Enormous," he repeated, that cocky half-grin blooming.

She gestured to his manhood. "Are you not able to think with that thing fully erect? Christian, listen to me. There is a fire!"

He glanced at the smoldering underwear and waved her off. "It's nothing. There should be a fire extinguisher close by. Turn off the burner. I'll find it."

She fiddled with the dial, but the dang thing wouldn't budge. "I can't turn off the gas."

"What?" he said, losing the naked swagger.

She searched desperately for a safe spot to grip so she could remove the boxers from the flames, but she nearly burned her fingers trying to rescue them from the growing inferno.

Beep, beep, beep, beep!

The fire alarm sliced through the silence, jolting Lucky awake. The dog sniffed the air and bolted toward the commotion.

"No, Lucky, stay back," Christian commanded, frantically rummaging through cabinets for a fire extinguisher.

Billowing smoke thickened, swirling around them as Christian's boxers smoldered, sending sparks flying. In a desperate panic, she grabbed a nearby towel to smother the flames, but fire hungrily devoured it.

Lucky bounded across the room with frantic energy, leaping up to rest his front paws on a dish rag beneath a precarious stack of loose-leaf paper piled high on the counter next to the stove.

It was like watching a car crash—or fire disaster—in slow motion.

"No!" she cried as the tall tier of papers, aka tinder, fluttered onto the towel and flaming underwear, feeding the fire.

The smoke grew denser.

Beep, beep, beep, beep!

Click!

"Found the fire extinguisher!" Christian yelled, holding it up as another click sounded.

Barely two seconds later, the indoor sprinklers burst to life, unleashing a torrent of ice-cold water.

She shrieked as water doused the room. Lucky jumped, trying to catch the water droplets in his mouth, as Christian, still naked, aimed the extinguisher at the flames. A plume of white foam peppered with streams of water enveloped the stovetop.

The water cut off, and she knelt beside the barking dog as the last drops fell to the ground. "It's okay, boy. We're okay."

Christian opened a window, allowing the smoke and extinguisher fumes to escape. Shivering and dripping, she looked up at him. "This is my fault. I touched the knobs. I must have jammed it. This is bad. I am a bad girl. A very, very, very bad girl."

"Hey, TBD?" Christian said, lowering to the ground to wrap his arms around her and Lucky.

"Yes?"

"I feel like we handled that well."

She stared at the cooktop carnage. "What about the damage?"

"I'll take care of it. My mom's the mayor. My brother is the town manager. We'll work it out internally."

"But the cost."

"Maggie, I have plenty of money. I own a ranch and a helicopter," Christian said calmly.

"You own a helicopter?"

"I bought it right after I got injured."

"Where do you keep it?"

"Behind the big barn," he replied, a small smile tugging at his lips.

"What's inside the big barn?"

"My cars. A few snowmobiles. A plow for the roads."

"You're rich, rich," she eked out, wide-eyed.

"Rich enough to take care of this. We're okay."

"But your underwear, that towel, and those papers caught on fire because of me," she said, her voice cracking with guilt.

His eyes twinkled with amusement. "You're really living the dream, TBD. We better get you that notebook. Dr. Ironside said to try new things, and just look at you."

"Arson?" she shot back, incredulity coating the word.

He gave her the sweetest half-shrug. "You've got to begin somewhere."

She couldn't help but laugh. "How have I only known you for five hours?"

"No, it's not five hours. You've been showing up in my dreams for three months."

She surveyed the room and sighed. "And are you sure you're not worried about what will happen when people learn we were in here and set the place on fire?"

"Full disclosure. My family will initially freak out, but that's their default. It's a big family. Deciding what game to play on game night entails fifteen minutes of debating. But they know what matters. They'll know I'm okay. I'm not drunk. I'm not disorderly. Fire and water damage can be repaired. And we've got an ace up our sleeve."

"And what's that?"

"My grandma will get it. She'll calm everyone down."

"Why?"

"She's a strong believer in the town folklore and trusts that fate and destiny will intervene—sometimes in the most surprising ways. She'll calm everyone down because I know she saw something when she looked at me today. My guess is it confirmed whatever she wrote on McKenzie's piece of Starrycard Creek wishing wall paper."

"What could she see?"

"How much you mean to me."

"She won't question why we have feelings for each other? What about the rest of your family? We'll need a better story than me hijacking your dreams and making you fall for me while you were unconscious. We need another plan."

"That's easy. When they see us together, they'll know we complete each other. My family is already half in love with you, and most of them haven't even seen you conscious. I'll be my usual charming self. Honestly, you won't be able to resist me. I'm loaded, devastatingly handsome, and I've got an enormous cock. What else could you want?"

"A little humility?" she teased.

"How about this," he said, helping her to her feet, his gaze softening. "I want to be the reason you never stop smiling. I want to learn everything about you. Let's get that notebook and fill it up with everything we want to do together. We'll tell my family that I'm helping you unlock your memories while you're working for me and keeping me accountable with my PT and mobility exercises. Nobody will be surprised when we decide it's the right time to tell them how we feel about each other. Here's the thing," he paused, his eyes locking onto hers, "William Starrycard fell ass over elbow in love with Fiona Donnelly the moment he saw her."

"Love at first sight," she said, her voice soft with wonder.

He brushed his fingers gently against her cheek. "Yes, that's it. I just happened to meet you in my dreams when I fell in love with you."

"Love?" she whispered.

"What else could it be, Maggie? Love at first sight runs in my family," he said, his voice filled with certainty and warmth.

A wave of emotion washed over her. Tears welled in her eyes. "Maybe it runs in mine, too." She gazed down and squeezed the skin on her forearm.

He furrowed his brow, leaning in closer. "What are you doing?"

"Pinching myself because I feel like I'm the one who's dreaming now."

"You're not dreaming. This is as real as it gets, and so is my love for you."

All she could do was smile. She looked him up and down and couldn't help but stare at his very erect cock. "You know you're still naked, and you're…"

"Oh, this?" he said casually, glancing at his manhood. "It's hard not to be turned on when I'm staring at my dream girl, and you did call my cock enormous. So, he's kind of reveling in the vibe."

This man.

She shook her head and felt her cheeks heat.

"That's it," he said, his voice a low rasp.

"That's what?"

"You're blushing."

"Of course, I'm blushing. You called me out—for the second time—for calling your penis…"

"Enormous," he supplied, stupidly sexy, half-smile in place. He glanced around the room. "You spend your life in a locker room, you get used to letting it all hang out. Hold on." He strode across the room, pulled a rainbow-colored crocheted blanket from a cupboard, and wrapped it around his waist. "Better?"

She was speechless, captivated by the intensity in his eyes— eyes that held unwavering certainty about her, about their connection, about his love for her.

Love.

He cupped her face in his hands and kissed the corner of her mouth. "These pink cheeks are going to ruin me."

"Speaking of ruin. Ruin seems to be my thing. I appear to love setting underwear on fire and getting off while standing. I know you think I'm a little bit good and a little bit bad, but I'd venture to say that I'm part of Team Bad Girl after tonight."

Mischief danced in his eyes. "Why don't we head home and find out just how bad of a bad girl you really are."

Home? Could this place be her home? A gal could certainly do worse than shacking up with a rich and handsome former athlete who dished out orgasms and looked at her like she was the answer to his prayers. And he loved her. Sure, he believed he'd fallen in love with her in his dreams, but the doctor did encourage her to explore new interests. Activities that involved her body writhing with pleasure seemed like an excellent place to start.

She parted her lips, ready to tell him that's exactly what she wanted, when the distant wail of sirens pierced the air, growing louder and more urgent by the second. Lucky barked and whimpered as the sound grew near deafening.

"Is that what I think it is?" she whispered, her voice tinged with alarm.

"It'll be okay," he said, wrapping his arm around her as a thunderous crash reverberated through the building, followed by a sharp crack and clatter of glass shattering.

"This is the Creek County Sheriff's Department! Come out with your hands up!"

CHAPTER

Twelve

CHRISTIAN

CHRISTIAN TUCKED a lock of Maggie's hair behind her ear and stroked her head, gazing at the woman as she slept. She'd fallen asleep curled against him with her head resting on his lap. Her hair spread across his legs and caught the scant rays of morning light. With her lips slightly parted and her eyelashes fluttering gently against her cheeks, she was the picture of serene beauty. He sighed, listening as her breath matched the rhythm of her chest rising and falling.

Everything about her was perfect.

The environment where she'd fallen asleep?

Not so much.

Now, had he wanted to spend the night with her?

Absolutely.

He'd dreamed of the moment he'd sweep her into his arms, carrying her to his bed as if they were living a fairy tale—because having her here felt like a magical miracle. Knowing she felt the same connection only deepened his conviction that their destinies were entwined.

What he hadn't expected was for this night to take place in a Creek County Sheriff's Department holding cell.

Yeah, they'd bunked in jail.

"Here's Lucky, Mr. Starrycard. I took him on a nice walk and got him some kibble and treats from the guys in animal management," the smiling young officer said, stepping into the holding area. He handed over the leash as if he were presenting a prized possession, his grin wide and genuine.

Christian mustered a tired smile. "I appreciate you allowing us to keep him here."

Lucky trotted into the cell, his tail wagging as he approached Maggie. He sniffed her with a familiar affection, as if reassuring himself that his favorite person was okay. Once satisfied, the dog turned his gaze on Christian. No, not just a gaze—a glare filled with silent reproach.

Christian let out a resigned sigh, patting the pup's head. "I know, boy. I know. I screwed up."

That was the understatement of the century.

The officer, who had kindly taken Lucky to the closest patch of grass, closed the cell door behind him. The lock clicked with a sharp clang, but instead of heading over to the area lined with desks a few paces away, the young man lingered. He smoothed his uniform shirt, then drummed his fingertips nervously against his thigh, clearly hesitant to leave.

Christian watched him and knew what was coming. The man either had a baseball question or wanted an autograph. His celebrity status had served them well so far, even if the circumstances were less than ideal. Once the cops realized they were arresting a baseball legend, they were pretty accommodating after holstering their weapons. Still, that didn't take away from the situation being an absolute clusterfuck.

The officer shifted his stance. "Sorry we've had to keep you locked up overnight. Do you need anything? Any more snacks? Drinks? Another blanket?"

"We're good, and I understand you're doing your job."

The officer glanced over his shoulder at the empty desks, then leaned in slightly as if sharing a secret. "We heard about you getting picked up in Rocky Mountain City and thrown in the drunk tank a few times."

Here it comes.

Christian maintained a forced grin. "Yeah, that was a tough time, but I'm doing much better."

"When we got word that you'd come back to Starrycard Creek, the fellas and I were wondering if we'd get to arrest you, too," the officer added with a hint of excitement, as if this were some long-awaited event.

Christian let out a dry chuckle. "It appears dreams do come true."

"They do," the man replied, bright-eyed. "Picking up *the* Christian Starrycard—wearing nothing but a blanket wrapped around his waist after accidentally setting fire to a senior center— is a story I'm sure I'll be telling my grandkids someday."

"I'm pleased to be of service," he replied flatly, sensing that his strained smile was on its last legs.

The officer's expression darkened. "I've got to say, I hate what happened to you—your arm and all."

Christian nodded. "I appreciate your kind words," he said, recycling the same phrase he'd used countless times.

The officer perked up again, as if eager to make a connection. "I went to high school with your little sister Caroline. She's two years older than me. A real ballbuster."

"Yes, she still is," Christian answered, itching to leave this cell and return to the ranch with Maggie. "Any information on when we can leave? I'm happy to pay a fine or take care of posting bail."

Color rose to the officer's cheeks, and he nervously scratched the back of his head. "Sorry, I wish I could do that for you, but the judge insisted we keep you overnight."

"The judge?" Christian repeated, a knot twisting in his belly. *Shit!* This newbie cop must have filed charges.

"Yes, Judge Ironside."

"Ironside?" Christian stammered, the name sending an icy chill down his spine.

No, this couldn't be! Not him!

"Yeah, you've got to appear before him."

"There's nobody else?"

"No, sir, not that I'm aware. He's the acting magistrate."

Dammit! Judge Ironside was as crusty as they get, and he had a history with the man.

"Does the clothing work?" the officer continued, back to making mind-numbing small talk. "I figured you'd prefer those over orange jumpsuits. I've got to say. It was an honor arresting you."

Fuck.

Christian peered at Maggie, sleeping in an oversized heather gray Creek County Sheriff's Department sweatshirt and sweatpants. He had on a matching pair.

"We appreciate it."

"And your…" the officer said, gesturing to the woman still asleep.

"My Maggie," Christian answered, his gaze softening as he looked at her.

"Your Maggie really doesn't know her last name?" the officer asked, his brow furrowing in disbelief.

"No, she doesn't."

"Wild to think she's got amnesia," the officer mused, shaking his head. "What a night! You're my first celebrity arrest, and she's my first arrest without a last name."

Christian hadn't slept a wink and felt his patience wearing thin. "Is there anything I can sign for you to celebrate this exciting milestone in your career?" he asked, hoping to bring an end to the conversation.

The officer's face lit up. "Ah, man, I'd love that. I was trying to figure out how to bring it up in conversation and do it before the other guys came in for their shift." He hurried over to a desk drawer and pulled out a sports magazine. "It's an edition of *Baseball Times*. The one that came out after you hit the winning run for the Rattlers in your first World Series. Can you make it out to me,

Johnny Gandy?" He passed the magazine through the bars, along with a pen, just as the phone rang on the desk.

Christian took the magazine and pen and signed the cover. As he did, he couldn't help but overhear the officer's curious conversation.

"Hey, yeah, I know who this is. You beat me in the Creek County High School arm wrestling contest," the officer said, then frowned, confusion marring his expression as he listened to whomever was on the other end of the call. "I don't know. We're really not supposed to—" he continued, then snapped his mouth shut, his eyes nearly bulging out of his head. "Okay, okay, whatever you say." The cop walked the phone over, stretching the cord to the holding cell. "You've got a call. It's Caroline Starrycard."

Christian eyed the phone. "My sister is calling the station?"

"Take the phone, dude!" Caroline's voice boomed through the receiver.

"Thanks, Officer," he said, exchanging the pen and magazine for the phone. He pressed it to his ear. "How'd you know I was in here, Care?"

"Your buddy Officer Gandy posted in the Starrycard High School alumni group that he'd made his first arrest at the Starrycard Creek Senior Center. He noted a party of three and the lack of clothing. I'm pretty sure we're the only two people ridiculous enough to break in. So, I figured it was you, and it looks like you convinced a lady friend to do it with you, and you brought a dog. Have you completely lost your mind? Do you have turd burgers for brains thanks to all that bathtub hooch? Seriously, Chris, what's going on?"

He pinched the bridge of his nose. His sister's words were like a hammer to his already throbbing head. "It's complicated."

"Did you think you were invisible, or were you trying to outdo me as the most screwed-up Starrycard sibling? Sure, your latest antics had you in the running, but I had a solid grip on that title until you decided to burn down a building naked as the day you were born, no less."

"I wasn't naked, and I didn't burn down an entire building. The only part affected was the culinary classroom. I'll pay for the repairs. It'll be fine."

"Did you get any pie action before the pyro action?"

"Yes, we had pie," he answered warily, knowing where this was going.

"Did you get any *action-action*?"

"Caroline," he growled, his eyes darting to Maggie, who shifted in her sleep, oblivious to the conversation.

"That's a yes," Caroline said triumphantly, not missing a beat. "How is Maggie? I assume that's who you're with. Kenz has been keeping me apprised of her condition while I remain happily abroad."

"Abroad where? Bali, Italy, Antarctica? Have you found yourself?" he asked, trying to divert her attention.

"Very funny. Just so you know, I'm about ninety percent of the way to getting my life together."

"Ninety?" he repeated warily.

"Oh, fuck off! I'm a solid seventy-five—no, like sixty-eight point five."

Jesus, this family!

"Do you need cash? Did you tap out Dad?"

"No, jackass, I don't need money," she blasted. "I'm a damned good graphic designer and make decent money doing my thing online. If Starrycard Creek Paper ever wanted to dip its toe into the digital age, I'd know just what to do."

"Good luck getting Finn and Owen on board."

"Forget them," she replied, barreling on like a steamroller. "I'm calling to help you. I need to talk to you before Mom and Kieran get there."

Shit!

"Mom and Kieran know I'm in jail?"

He glanced at the clock on the wall. Dammit, it wasn't even eight in the morning, and the entire family had probably mobilized.

"Yep, the sheriff called Mom about an hour ago. Kenz spent the night with Mom and Dad at Starrycard House and heard the call. She texted me the deets immediately. She's good like that. I've got her trained. I'm up to date on your progress—or lack of—and all the Maggie amnesia particulars. The woman doesn't recall a thing. That's crazy."

"Are you having a seven-year-old spy for you?"

"She's a pro, and she said she did it for Finn when he was keeping tabs on Hailey. I'm simply expanding our niece's skill set."

Christian hung his head. "We're gonna ruin that kid."

"She's fine," Caroline quipped. "Now, I'm just going to say this. Listen up, slugger."

"I'm in jail, Care. It's not like I'm going anywhere."

"Christian William Starrycard…"

"Yes?" he said, sensing the seriousness in her tone.

"I know you're in love with Maggie."

WTF.

His mind went blank for a second, unable to process how in the hell his sister would have any idea about what he felt for Maggie. "Caroline, what are you talking about?" he blurted, the best response he could muster.

"You brought her to the pool…and you got her arrested, which is not the most romantic of choices, but you brought her to the senior center, and that's so telling."

How had she connected love to breaking into the center?

"I didn't intend on getting arrested, and I thought the pool might help her retrieve her memories." His pulse quickened. He hadn't lied but hadn't told the complete truth either. "Why would you connect the pool to being in love?"

"Do you remember Wade Willigan?"

Who the hell was Wade Willigan?

"No, and what a fucking awful name."

"I was sure you'd remember," Caroline lamented. "Anyway, I had a big crush on Wade Willigan in third grade. I wanted to bring him along with us to the pool one night, and you said only people you love, like family, can sneak into the pool because we're the only ones who can become invisible."

Damn, she was right.

He sighed. "I forgot I said that. In my defense, I told you a lot of bullshit back then."

"Yeah, you did, and I'm permanently banned from the candy shop because of it," Caroline replied, a touch of humor laced with the seriousness of her words. He could picture her smirking, but the weight of what she was about to say kept his heart in a vise. "But somewhere in your head, or maybe your heart, you decided to bring Maggie there."

"What are you saying?" he asked, his throat tightening.

"I'm saying it's okay to care about her, but she's got to be fragile, and you are, too."

"I could bench press you, even with my jacked-up shoulder," he said, trying to lighten the conversation, but the quiver in his voice betrayed him. He flinched. There was no way Caroline wouldn't catch it.

"I'm not talking about physical strength, Chris," she said gently. And like with Eliza, when Caroline stopped razzing him and softened her voice, shit was about to get real. "You never do anything halfway," she continued. "You throw your whole heart into everything. Just be careful. She might have a life out there—a life that doesn't include you."

"You don't think I know that?" he replied, emotion seeping through despite his best efforts to remain composed.

For a beat, Caroline didn't say a word, and her silence spoke volumes.

Of course, he wanted to tell his sister that she was right. That he loved Maggie—that he'd dreamed of her, that she'd brought him comfort when she was a figment of his imagination and now brought him pure joy, but he couldn't.

"Listen, I've got to go. Just be careful. I love you, little star," she said, using the Starrycard family's term of endearment.

The words brought back a flood of memories. He pictured her as that fearless eight-year-old with a gap-toothed grin and eyes full of excitement, always ready for their next escapade. He sighed as a sentimental grin pulled at the corners of his mouth. "Right back at you, Care."

"Hey," Maggie mumbled sleepily as Caroline ended the call, and the line went dead.

"TBD," he said, shifting his attention to her. "Did you sleep okay?"

"Yeah. Who were you talking to?" she asked, easing off his lap.

"My sister Caroline called," he replied, watching her intently.

"She called the station?" Maggie's brows knitted in mild confusion.

"Yes, my family knows we're here," he admitted, the reality of their situation pressing down on him.

"I'm making quite an impression," she said with a wry smile, though he could see the concern lurking beneath her light tone.

He reached out, gently brushing a stray strand of hair from her face, his fingers lingering as if to reassure her. "They'll know this is my fault."

"But it wasn't just you. It was us." Maggie's voice was firm.

Sensing the tension, Lucky nuzzled between them.

"The three of us," she said, her voice lighter as she kissed the top of Lucky's head. "We're a real menace to society." She turned back to Christian, her expression shifting to one of concern. "Did you get any rest?"

"Not really."

"Did I keep you up? I didn't mean to fall asleep on your lap," she said, guilt flickering in her eyes.

"Watching you fall asleep in my lap was the best part of not sleeping. I probably wouldn't have slept even if we weren't here. I couldn't stop looking at you, knowing you're real."

Maggie blushed that shade of pink that had imprinted itself on his soul, and then she looked away and smoothed her hair. "I must be a mess."

"No, not even close. Don't you get it?" He lifted her chin, guiding her to meet his gaze.

"Get what?" she asked, her voice barely a whisper.

"You're stunning."

She smiled, but doubt lingered in her eyes. "Even now, after spending a night in jail?"

"Especially now. Maggie, you will always be the most beautiful thing I've ever seen, whether you're in that cute-as-hell jean skirt or rocking Creek County's hottest inmate hoodie. You're perfect because of who you are to me."

"But we don't know who I am?"

He took her hand in his. "You're the girl of my dreams and always will be. We'll figure out the rest. You know I'm right. You feel it, too, don't you?"

"Yes, I feel it." She smiled the smile from his dreams—warm and soothing, like a soft light breaking through the darkness. Her lips curved gently, and her hazel eyes sparkled with a kindness that seemed to wrap around him like a warm blanket.

He traced his knuckles down her jawline, and she hummed the sexiest little sound.

Instantly, nature took over.

He leaned in and lowered his voice. "Do you know how badly I want to make you come again? Do you know how much I'd give to watch you part your perfect lips and beg to be kissed?"

She glanced down, then met his gaze, a sly smirk on her perfect lips. "I have a pretty good idea, thanks to those snug gray sweatpants."

"There's the bad girl," he replied, his tone low and teasing, but he was cut off by the sound of a voice clearing.

"Um…Mr. Starrycard, Miss…Maggie, no last name of record," Officer Gandy said, interrupting the moment and reminding Christian exactly where they were—in a freaking jail cell—and he was rocking a very inappropriate boner.

"Yes," Christian replied, desperately trying to think of every chaste thought he could muster.

Another officer had joined Officer Gandy.

"Judge Ironside is ready for you," Gandy began. "I'll keep an eye on your dog. Officer Miles will escort you to the hearing room. We need to get moving. The Honorable Morris T. Ironside doesn't like to be kept waiting."

Maggie's eyes widened slightly, a flicker of recognition crossing her face. "Ironside?" she repeated, her expression brightening. "That's my doctor's last name. Do you know if they're related?"

"Your doctor is his cousin," Christian explained.

"That's fantastic news," she replied, her voice tinged with hope. "We should be okay, right? Dr. Ironside is kind and helpful. I'm sure her cousin is, too."

"Nope," Officer Gandy interjected. "He's the scariest guy I ever met. And word is, the second he looked at the docket, he got extra grouchy. And you two are the only thing on it. We don't get a whole lot of crime around here."

"Oh," Maggie uttered, her optimistic expression dimming.

The knot of dread in Christian's stomach tightened, twisting painfully as he watched the shift in her demeanor.

"Why would he be extra grouchy?" Maggie asked, her voice wavering slightly as she searched his face. "I thought everyone adored you around here."

His heart ached to comfort her and tell her it would all be fine, but there was no sense in sugarcoating it. "Everyone pretty much does. Everyone except for Morris T. Ironside."

Thirteen

CHRISTIAN

CHRISTIAN SAT in a stiff wooden chair beside Maggie, facing a narrow table in the cramped hearing room. Every tick of the clock seemed louder, each second stretching out the suspense. Harsh fluorescent lights flickered overhead, casting an unflattering glow over the room. He turned to Maggie. She sat with her hands in her lap, her fingers intertwining and releasing in a restless dance.

He placed his hand gently over hers, stilling their movement. "The storm—"

"Always passes," she finished, offering him a weak grin. "I know. I keep saying that to myself. But could we end up back in jail? Surely, the judge must know that it was an accident, and we meant no harm."

That was the million-dollar question.

"Let's hope the judge is feeling reasonable."

"Aren't we supposed to have a lawyer?" Maggie asked, scanning the room.

"Things run informally around here. Ironside is a magistrate. If he decides criminal charges are worth pursuing, it'll escalate. For now, we present our case, answer the judge's questions, and hope for the best."

The doors in the back of the room swung open, and the rapid clap of sneakers hitting the tile floor echoed through the space.

"Uncle Chris," McKenzie chimed, then skidded to a stop behind him. Decked in Maggie's apron, the kid beamed at them.

He reluctantly removed his hand from Maggie's, noticing the way his perceptive niece's eyes flicked to the movement, taking it in with silent curiosity.

"Hey, Kenz," he said with a nod. "You're wearing Maggie's apron."

"I hope you don't mind, Maggie. I like the way it feels, and I like that your name and my name start with the letter *M*."

"I don't mind at all. It looks great on you," Maggie answered, her smile gentle and genuine.

Kenzie beamed and twirled. "It's a teeny-tiny bit big, but I bet it'll fit perfect when I'm ten or eleven."

"Yeah, maybe when you're eleven," Maggie repeated with a far-off bend to her words.

His brow furrowed. He turned his attention to her, searching her face for any sign of what was troubling her. "Are you all right?"

"Sure, yes," she murmured, but something was on her mind—a whisper of a memory? He couldn't tell.

"Were you guys holding hands, or do they make people who get arrested hold hands like the kindergarteners at school who have to make a big, long chain when they walk down the hall so nobody gets lost or runs away? I don't have to do that anymore because I'm in second grade. I bet you're wondering why I'm here," McKenzie said, in full-on McKenzie speed-talking mode.

"I am wondering that," he answered.

"I came with Grandma Maeve. I had a sleepover at Starrycard House last night and I begged and begged her to let me come. And I told Aunt Caroline I'd get her the *deets*. It rhymes with beets but means details, and that's the stuff I hear adults saying and see adults doing when they don't think I'm paying attention, like you guys, holding hands. Hi, Maggie!" Kenz continued, not missing a beat. "I like your jail sweatshirt. It looks big and comfy."

"It is."

"Do you get to keep it? Is that what you get when you get arrested? Like a party favor?" McKenzie inhaled a deep breath, which was never a good sign. "And thanks for getting arrested on a Saturday. If you got arrested on a Monday or Tuesday or Wednesday or Thursday or Friday, I'd be at school. Since it's Saturday, I can be here. Unless it's a school break or a teacher-only workday, and then I have those days off. Maggie, did you know my uncle Finn and almost aunt Hailey, who is also my teacher, are getting married on Christmas Eve? I get to be in the wedding. I get a big puffy dress and fancy shoes. Uncle Finn is helping me practice being quiet because you can't talk a lot during weddings. So, when I visit him and Uncle O and Grandpa Hank at the paper shop, we play the quiet game. Guess how long I can be quiet, Maggie."

"Five minutes?" Maggie speculated, suppressing a grin.

"Eleven seconds," McKenzie replied, then looked him over. "Your pants are too small, Uncle Chris. "You remind me of this one time my school took a field trip to see ballet dancers. I liked the tutus, but the boy ballerinas don't get them. So, I stood up and yelled, 'Hey, ballerina, you should share the tutus with the boys.' I had to wait on the bus and missed a bunch of the dancing, but that was okay because the bus driver had a bunch of crackers in her purse, and she shared them with me. Do you like crackers, Maggie?"

"Wow," Maggie whispered.

Wow, was right.

"Hey, Kenz, where is everyone?" he asked, overwhelmed by McKenzie's torrent of wild tangents.

"Every Starrycard or every Starrycard and Dunleavy or everyone in town? Because I know the answer to every one of those questions, but first, I need to check Maggie's memory. Maggie, do you know what that is?" McKenzie asked, plowing through her signature stream-of-consciousness banter and pointing upward.

"A light."

McKenzie clapped. "That's right! I think your memory is getting better."

"Maybe," Maggie answered and pressed her lips into a hard line, clearly working overtime not to laugh.

He sat back and drank in his chatterbox of a niece. "Kenz, you are something else," he said warmly, sharing a heartfelt look with Maggie. Thanks to McKenzie's unique charm, a rosy hue had returned to Maggie's cheeks. The lines of worry on her face had softened.

"That's what my dad says. Remember, Maggie, I told you about my dad. He puts thermometers in dogs' butts."

"Yes, I do recall you sharing that with me," she said through a chuckle as a click and a creak echoed from the back of the room.

Kieran and his mom entered, followed by his grandparents. Goldie waved, and his grandfather nodded to him. Armed with snacks and a water bottle that definitely wasn't filled with water, the senior citizens settled in, munching on turnovers while likely enjoying mimosas—or perhaps they skipped the light drinks altogether and went straight for the hard stuff, sipping on Stumble Juice.

Kieran approached and rested his hand on McKenzie's shoulder. "Kenz, please take a seat with Goldie and your great-grandpa Rex. Your grandma Maeve and I would like to have a word with your uncle and Maggie."

"Okay, Uncle Kier. Bye, Maggie. Bye, Uncle Chris. Ask the officers if you can get bigger pants if they want to keep you here. Or there could be a jail ballerina club. You could join that."

"Thanks, Kenz, lots to think about," Christian said, and damn, they better not end up back in the holding cell.

Once McKenzie had skipped to Goldie and Rex, Kieran suppressed a grin. "Christian, did it slip your mind that invisibility isn't one of your many talents?"

At least Kier was getting some amusement from the situation.

Christian shook his head as his brother offered Maggie his hand. "I'm Kieran Starrycard. I visited you when you were in a coma. My wife, Isabelle, helped braid your hair, and now my brother's gotten you arrested. Welcome to Starrycard Creek."

"Thank you?" Maggie replied, appearing stunned, like someone who'd gone through a car wash with the windows down, which was a sensation akin to spending time with his family.

"Hello, little star," Maeve Starrycard cooed, joining them. She pressed a kiss to his cheek and offered her hand to Maggie. "Hello, dear, we haven't officially met. I'm Maeve O'Leary-Starrycard, Christian's mother and the mayor of Starrycard Creek. I helped braid your hair and wiped a little drool off your chin when you were in a coma. It's so nice to see you conscious. I'm so sorry to hear about the amnesia, and I must apologize for my son's encouragement of committing criminal acts. I thought you learned your lesson, young man," she chided like he was a gangly thirteen-year-old.

Jesus, his family was coming in hot on the crazy train.

Maeve turned to Kieran. "Did Chris think he was invisible again?"

It was as if he'd been transported back to his childhood, where his mother would turn to her eldest child, seeking a detailed account of the younger siblings' mischievous antics.

"Mom, I know I'm not invisible," Christian said, waving his hands.

"That's a relief," she replied, then turned her attention to Maggie. "Did my son share the story of his swimming pool and pie-eating adventures with his little sister?"

"He did."

Kieran crossed his arms, lips pursed. "If Chris and Maggie testified that they believed they were invisible, we could easily make an insanity argument."

Christian pinched the bridge of his nose. "Kier, we're not

pleading insanity. What happened last night was an unfortunate accident."

His mother clucked her tongue. "Maggie, dear, I'll tell you about an *unfortunate accident*—and that's what happened in the kids' bathroom after Christian and Caroline wolfed down two pies each. The place looked like a pumpkin patch massacre, with orange goop clinging to every surface. Before that day, I never knew children could have such violent and explosive diarrhea."

Holy fucking too much information! If Ironside didn't kill him, the embarrassment—courtesy of his family—might just do the job.

"Explosive diarrhea," Maggie repeated, her brows knit together with that pensive look she'd had earlier.

Dammit! Now, he had the woman of his dreams marinating on the image of him violently losing his innards.

He looked between his mom and brother. "No more talk of past bathroom events. Listen, just in case you need to hear it, for the second time, I am aware I can't become invisible, and neither of us is insane."

"Nor do you appear to be experiencing explosive diarrhea. That's a good sign, especially with those snug pants," Kieran deadpanned.

This had to be hell. Cause of death: extreme embarrassment.

"Coxsackievirus can cause explosive diarrhea," Maggie uttered, then frowned.

Christian watched her closely. "What's Coxsa-blah-blah-virus?"

Her eyes widened, and her mouth fell slightly open. "I have no idea. I don't know why I said that."

"Putting invisibility, insanity, and explosive diarrhea aside, I'd like to extend a word of advice. When Judge Ironside arrives, don't agitate the man. Don't poke the bear," Kieran said calmly, displaying the composed demeanor of an unshakeable lawyer.

"Yes, don't poke the bear. He's already in a mood," his mother echoed. "Goldie tells me they were out of maple pumpkin turnovers when he stopped in at Goldie's on the Creek to pick up breakfast. He had to go with an apple turnover. It's my under-standing he snipped at the gal running the register. He said he needed to keep his palate focused on pumpkin or something strange like that."

"Why did Ironside have breakfast in Starrycard Creek? I thought he lived across the county in the middle of nowhere."

"He recently moved to a bungalow in town," Kieran answered.

"Do you know why he moved here?" Christian pressed.

"It's my understanding that he wanted to be closer to the senior center," Maeve replied as the doors at the front of the room opened with a long, gnawing whine. The perfect sound to intro-duce the ill-tempered judge.

Ironside skulked to the bench, and Jesus, the guy hadn't changed. With cropped salt-and-pepper hair, lips a thin slash, and wire-rimmed glasses poised precariously on the tip of his nose, the gruff old judge wore a mask of severity. He grumbled some-thing about apple turnovers, then slammed a paper bag and a few files onto the wooden surface. A court reporter settled in at a desk close to the judge, her fingers poised above the keyboard. The tension in the room grew palpable as everyone awaited Ironside's next move.

"He appears quite agitated," Maggie whispered, worry returning to her expression.

Christian leaned toward her and lowered his voice. "That's his default. The judge hasn't been in a good mood since—"

"The goddamned dawn of time," Ironside bellowed, pegging him with his sharpened gaze. "I might be old, but my ears work just fine, Mr. Starrycard."

Well, shit. So much for not poking the bear.

"Before we begin, I have a letter dated from seventeen years ago, nearly to the day," the judge announced.

Christian's already tight muscles hardened into a tangle of knots. "Oh, no."

Ironside held up a piece of Starrycard Creek Paper. "It's an apology letter for sneaking into the senior center to swim and consume pie. It includes a promise never to do it again. Does that ring a bell, Mr. Starrycard?"

Christian shifted in his seat. "Yes, Judge."

"Ah, and there's an addendum," he said, picking up another piece of Starrycard Creek paper. "Your sister Caroline wrote, using a purple crayon, 'I'm sorry. Christian tricked me. I socked him real good, Mr. Judge. He cried like a baby.'"

Christian felt Maggie glance his way. His cheeks had to be the color of ripe tomatoes. "I didn't cry," he mumbled.

"Excuse me, Mr. Starrycard. Did you say something?" the judge quipped wryly.

"Nothing worth repeating, sir."

The judge rested the letters on the table. "I believe we agreed you'd learned your lesson when you were a youngster."

"Yes, sir, we did."

"It appears you did not."

Fuck.

"Your Honor, I'd be more than happy to pay for the repairs. I'd also like to donate a substantial sum. In addition, regarding Maggie—"

"Let me stop you right there, Mr. Starrycard," Ironside said, butting in. "Of course, I'm ordering you to pay the full cost of damages, but you will not be buying your way out of this situation. Considering what I read in the papers regarding your recent conduct in Rocky Mountain City, I do not believe that a fine is the best way to procure justice." The man leaned forward and pursed his thin lips. "That CCSD sweatshirt looks a bit snug on you. I'm certain we have an orange jumpsuit that will fit you and your accomplice until I can devise a fitting consequence."

The blood in his veins turned to ice. This could not be happening. Forget about his welfare. He could not allow Maggie to spend another second in that cell.

"Your Honor, I'm truly sorry, but Maggie—"

"Was the mastermind behind sneaking in. It was my fault,"

she said, cutting him off. She bolted to her feet. "I'm the reason we visited the senior center after hours."

What was she doing? He was trying to keep her safe.

"Maggie, no," he whispered.

The judge removed another piece of paper from his bag. "You are Maggie, last name to be determined."

"Correct, sir."

"I've never had a defendant without knowledge of their last name," he said, eyeing the woman through his spectacles.

"It's a unique situation that's led me to know someone in your family—Dr. Joan Ironside," she answered sweetly.

"That's my cousin."

"Yes, and she's an excellent doctor. I was in a coma and woke up with amnesia. You can ask her. She's been treating me. I'm happy to share my medical information with the court. You see, I don't remember anything about my life, and Christian was trying to help me spark memories of who I might be. So, if anyone is to blame, it's me."

He couldn't let her do this. Panic surged through him. "Judge, no!" he called out, his voice filled with urgency.

"Hold your tongue, Starrycard," the man snapped, then pinned Maggie with his hawkish gaze and sized her up. "And are you a criminal, miss?"

She released a nervous laugh and strolled around the table to perch on the corner. "Oh my gosh, no, sir, I don't believe I am," she replied, her tone almost playful as she attempted to ease the tension. "Causing mayhem in this beautiful town did not bring back my memory, nor did it feel familiar. However, I did learn one thing last night."

The judge's expression remained stern, though a flicker of curiosity crossed his features. "Don't keep us in suspense," he said dryly.

"The bakers at the senior center make one heck of a bourbon pumpkin pie. I sampled some before…"

"You set the place on fire," the judge finished.

"Correct, sir. And it truly was an accident," Maggie assured him, her voice earnest as she met his gaze head-on.

The judge's eyes softened slightly, as though considering her words. "What did you think of the pie?" he asked, a note of genuine interest creeping into his otherwise stern demeanor.

"It was delicious."

The judge nodded. "I made that bourbon pumpkin pie. It was my recipe. I'd just tweaked the ingredients and tried a new crust."

Christian's eyes widened in surprise, and he quickly glanced over his shoulder at Kieran, mouthing, "Ironside bakes?" Kieran responded with a shrug.

"Was it really your creation, sir?" Maggie asked, a wisp of awe in her voice as she leaned forward.

"It was indeed. And now it's gone. We store our precious recipes next to the stove. We're not keen on putting everything into a computer. Your foolishness erased a year's worth of our efforts," Ironside replied, a hint of sadness creeping into his tone. "Pie is important in this town, especially during Donnelly Days. We're going up against the Dennison Senior Center. They're our biggest competition."

"I see," she said quietly, a note of regret in her voice.

"They're sneaky bastards," the judge continued, then paused and glanced at the court reporter. "Carla?"

"Yes, Your Honor?"

"Strike the bastard part."

"Of course, Your Honor."

"Oh, but they are sneaky bastards," the judge grumbled. "Christian Starrycard!" he blasted.

Christian straightened his posture. "Yes, Your Honor."

"You know how there's a rivalry between Creek County High School and Dennison High?"

"Yes, sir, we played them in baseball when I was in high school."

"You led the team to win state against them back then."

"That's true, sir," Christian answered, praying that win would earn them some brownie points.

"The Starrycard Creek seniors loathe the Dennison seniors with the intensity of a thousand suns," Ironside snarled.

Christian swallowed hard. "That's a lot of hate, sir."

"They won the pumpkin pie-making contest last year," the old man grumbled.

"And the three years before that," Carla added, typing away.

"Dagnabbit, that's right!" the judge exclaimed. "My new bourbon pumpkin pie recipe was a surefire winner—and it's gone —burned to smithereens. And we've lost our facility to practice making new recipes. It's not the same if we work alone at home. The magic happens when the culinary club is together. I bought a bungalow in Starrycard Creek to be closer to the center," the old man roared, his cheeks growing ruddier by the second.

Ironside was on the brink of blowing his top.

"Your honor, I believe I have a solution that will serve everyone and keep Christian and me out of jail," Maggie chimed, as sweet as pie.

Ironside's face scrunched into a suspicious, prune-like scowl. "And what is this solution, young lady?"

"The culinary club can meet at the Donnelly Ranch—Christian's home. It's got double ovens and plenty of room. The kitchen is like something out of a baker's dream. I'm employed there as his housekeeper. And I can help you with your pie situation."

"How? You told the court you've got amnesia and recall nothing of your past. Not even your last name. What could you know about pie? My Bess, God rest her soul, and I started making pies before you could even buy a color TV." At the mention of his late wife, a flicker of sorrow softened the old man's hardened expression. The room grew still, the weight of his tragic loss lingering in the silence.

Maggie nodded, her eyes shining as she radiated empathy. "Your Honor, I might not have as much experience as you and your Bess, but I think I know a lot about pie. And I'd like to prove it to you. Does anyone have a piece of paper and a pen?" she asked, scanning the room.

What was she up to?

Christian waved her over, his gaze bouncing between her and Ironside. "Why do you need paper?"

She gifted him with that grin that owned his heart. "Your mom said that the judge mentioned his *palate* this morning. He used that word, *palate*."

"So, he said palate. What does that tell you?"

Her grin widened. "It tells me that I've found the right pitch to swing at."

"The right pitch?" he repeated, not following.

"I've got a blank Starrycard Creek Paper Company notebook and a pen," Goldie called, pulling the items from her bag.

Maggie beamed at his grandmother. "Wonderful! Thank you!"

"Miss, I will not have my courtroom turned into a circus," Ironside barked, losing his softened demeanor.

"I understand, and that's not my intention, sir. Please, humor me for a moment. For the sake of pie and beating the…Christian, help me out," she asked, glancing his way.

"The Dennison seniors," Christian supplied.

Maggie nodded. "Yes, beating the Dennison seniors."

"Those sneaky bastards," Ironside muttered, momentarily preoccupied with his visceral disgust for the group.

"Here you go, Maggie," McKenzie said, holding out the bound journal.

"Judge, may I?" Maggie asked calmly.

The judge exhaled an audible breath. "Christ, I'm too old for this. Fine, I'll allow it."

Maggie accepted the journal and then opened it to the first page. "Bourbon Pumpkin Pie," she murmured and started writing.

Ironside drummed his fingers restlessly. "Miss, the recipe is lost. What do you think you're doing?"

"It's not lost, sir. I can see it."

He balked. "You can see it?"

Maggie glanced at McKenzie's apron before locking eyes with the judge. "Well, I can taste it."

Ironside observed her with the wary gaze one reserves for someone on the brink of madness. "Miss, I'm—"

"The crust was good, earthy even," she said, cutting off the judge. She scribbled furiously, then slipped the pen behind her ear like a waitress in a diner. "One and a half cups of flour, a half teaspoon salt, a half cup of unsalted butter cubes, and five tablespoons of water—no, six. And…nuts." She chewed her lip, then gasped. "You used piñon nuts. They're native to Colorado, aren't they?"

"That's right. That was the change I'd made, but I don't recall the measurements," Ironside answered, wide-eyed, trading his irritated expression for one of complete befuddlement.

Maggie eyed her notes and paced in front of the judge's table. "You added a quarter cup of finely ground piñon nuts. Could that be the right amount, sir?"

"I'm not completely sure. A member of the culinary club brought some back from southwest Colorado. But yes, it could have been a quarter cup." He stilled, thinking, then slapped the table, a grin gracing his lips. "Yes, actually, I believe it was."

"It was a good choice. There was a light buttery taste I enjoyed," she replied, retrieving the pen and jotting in the journal as she continued to pace in front of the judge. She paused, then closed her eyes. "The pumpkin puree was homemade. It didn't taste like it came from a can."

"No, ma'am. We make our own puree."

"You did a lovely job."

The crusty judge sat a little taller, his wrinkled cheeks blushing. "Thank you."

Maggie tapped the tip of the pen against her chin. "I believe your pie contained three-fourths cup of light brown sugar, a little under half a cup of granulated sugar, one teaspoon of cinnamon, a quarter teaspoon of ground nutmeg, and a quarter teaspoon of cloves. All fresh."

"That could very well be it," the judge said, excitement dancing in his eyes.

Christian peered over his shoulder at his family. Everyone was mesmerized by Maggie TBD, certified pie whisperer.

"Let's keep going," she said, glancing at her notes. "The pie contained a teaspoon of vanilla extract, three eggs—large—not extra-large, and three-fourths teaspoon of salt. No." Maggie scribbled in the journal. "Just a half teaspoon of salt. I could tell you cut back. And you added a touch of fresh ginger. Another good choice. And then the bourbon. A quarter cup. No, a half cup of bourbon. Yes, that's it. Does what I rattled off sound like it could be your recipe, Judge?"

"My God, it certainly could be." Ironside turned to Carla. "Did you get that—the recipe?"

"Yes, Judge."

"How much pie did you eat before the culinary room caught on fire?" Ironside asked, his voice tinged with curiosity.

"A few bites. Don't get me wrong. It's good pie but not extraordinary. Unfortunately, I don't think you'd win a contest with it."

The breath caught in Christian's throat. *Holy hell! What was she thinking?* She had Ironside eating out of the palm of her hand. Why was she trashing his pie?

"Not good enough to win? We've been working on that recipe for a good six months," Ironside shot back, his words brimming with irritation.

Christian sat on the edge of his seat, hinged forward, the damned tiny gray sweatpants nearly cutting off circulation to his freaking balls. But he couldn't focus on the tight pants. His knee bounced beneath the table. She glanced at him, and he held her gaze. Their connection only lasted half a second, perhaps less, before she returned her attention to Ironside, but in that brief slip of time, what he'd glimpsed triggered an intense wave of relief.

His knee stopped bouncing, and he relaxed. It was as if she'd reached deep into his soul, kindling an oddly familiar warmth. An overwhelming sense of certainty told him that he would be okay and that she was the reason. She was his angel, his anchor. He relaxed into his chair and let the woman work her magic.

"I can help you craft a winning recipe," she said, like a pie boss.

The judge reverted to his severe demeanor. "How?"

"My mind is teeming with pumpkin pie recipes, and if you've lost over the last several years, you need new ideas. You need to take a new path. You need me to show you which way to go."

The old man watched her like a seasoned poker player, eyeing the new kid at the high rollers' table. "And you guarantee you can craft a winning recipe?"

Maggie glanced at McKenzie, then returned to her seat. "Correct," she answered, voice steady, chin held high. No nervous babbling, no anxious chatter. Just pure pie swagger—and damn, it was sexy as hell.

Stone-faced, the judge drummed his fingers on the table. "We do our mobility movement exercises before we begin baking. It's always mobility and then baking."

"That's not a problem," Maggie answered sweetly. "Christian's home contains a state-of-the-art gym, and he can lead the exercises. He performed mobility movements on me while I was in a coma. And look at me now." She stood and did a little twirl. "Sir, I was still in a coma less than two days ago. And after undergoing his exercises, I was mobile enough to break into a senior center and set it on fire."

Ironside watched her for a beat, then another, before the whisper of a grin curved the corners of his mouth.

My God! Maggie charmed the crankiest man in Creek County.

"And in case you're still doubting my skills..." Maggie sauntered toward the judge, her hips swaying with confidence, then sniffed the man. "You had an apple pastry for breakfast. I can smell the apples. Braeburn apples, I believe."

Christian's jaw nearly hit the floor. *Now she was an apple whisperer?*

Ironside glanced past Maggie into the seating area, his eyebrows knitting together. "Goldie, are they Braeburn apples?"

"They are indeed. Our Braeburn apples come from a Colorado orchard seventy miles due east."

Christian met his grandmother's gaze, and the woman winked. *What the hell was that about?*

Maggie returned to the table, her eyes alight with a triumphant sparkle as she sat next to him.

And Christ, he wanted to scoop her into his arms and kiss her until he passed out from exhaustion. He glanced back at his family again. Kieran and his mother were a good fifteen to twenty feet away and couldn't hear them if they kept their voices low. "What was that?" he whispered.

"I tapped into something when I saw McKenzie wearing my apron. My brain exploded with pie knowledge."

"That's incredible," he replied, soaking in her radiance and her fucking brilliance. He recognized the gleam in her eyes—the same one he had before a game, a quiet confidence that left no space for doubt.

Ironside cleared his throat, silencing their conversation. "The contest is only a week away. We'd need to start on Monday—two days from now. That ranch better be ready and stocked," he ordered.

"It will be, sir. I'll make sure of it. You'll have everything you need and at my expense," Christian answered.

The old man rolled his head from side to side and grimaced. "And my old bones better get one hell of a stretch. Do you know how to get that done, kid? I can't bake when I'm cramped up."

"Yes, sir. I'll make sure you're loose and limber."

"Here's the deal," Ironside barked, his stern facade cracking slightly as excitement glinted in his dark eyes. "If we win the pie-making contest, I'll drop the charges. But if we lose, you both get seven days in the county jail plus three months of community service cleaning the public restrooms across the county."

What?

Christian's mind raced. "How about jail time for me only, Your Honor? Not Maggie," he pleaded, his voice cracking with desperation.

"I have a counteroffer, Your Honor," Maggie interjected, her tone unwavering.

"That's not how it works," the judge replied.

"Just consider it, sir," Maggie said gently. "If we lose, four days in county jail. One month of community service cleaning toilets. But it won't come to that. We're going to rock this pie contest. People will be talking about it for years to come. Think of the bragging rights when you win. Think of the look on the Dennison seniors' faces when you hold up the blue ribbon. And if you lose, you still get to lock us up for a few days and make us clean toilets."

Ironside studied Maggie. "I need a moment." He turned to the court reporter, giving Christian time to confer with Maggie.

"I won't let you spend another second in jail. We know this was my fault," he said, taking her hand in his.

"We're not headed for jail. This is my pitch, Christian. I'm swinging. I can do this. I don't know how I know it, but I do. This is my path."

"Your path is pie?" he asked, gazing into her hazel eyes.

"My path seems to have led me to pie and…to you," she said, meekly looking at him through her lashes as she offered him the sweet smile from his dreams.

And damn, his heart was ready to explode. Every moment with her felt destined, like the universe had finally aligned the stars to bring his dreams to life. He swallowed past the lump in his throat. "I've never loved anyone like I love you," he whispered, unable to hold back.

"Then let's hope I'm not taken," she teased, but the love shining in her eyes was undeniable.

Still, he wasn't laughing as his protective and slightly possessive side took over. He leaned in closer and lowered his voice. "You are taken. By me."

"Miss Maggie, Mr. Starrycard?" the judge barked, his voice slicing through their tender moment and bringing them back to their precarious reality.

"Yes, Your Honor," they answered in unison, their voices strong and resolute.

Ironside's gaze turned icy, his eyes narrowing as they darted between them. "You drive a hard bargain, Miss Maggie," he said, the words slicing through the air. "I'm not known for making compromises with defendants."

The light flickered, casting ominous shadows on the paneled walls. The room's musty scent mixed with the tension that hung thick as the courtroom seemed to hold its breath.

Oh, no! Was he about to reject Maggie's proposition and throw the book at them?

"But in this rare case and under these rare circumstances..." Ironside continued, his voice dropping to a menacing rumble.

Christian's heart pounded so hard it echoed in his ears. He tightened his hold on Maggie's hand. Whatever happened, they were in this together.

The judge leaned forward and peered down his nose at them. "You've got a deal. And you better deliver."

Fourteen

CHRISTIAN

"THAT'S IT, Maggie. That's everything from the truck," Christian called, then popped a bite-sized piece of beef jerky into his mouth. He closed the pantry door and wiped the sweat from his brow with the back of his hand. He gazed out the kitchen windows. Only a sliver of the sun remained, casting its last rays over the jagged outline of the mountains.

He turned his gaze toward the large kitchen table, now softly illuminated by the fading light of the setting sun. Maggie stood there, notebook in hand, with Lucky sleeping peacefully at her feet, as she carefully assessed a slew of ceramic pie plates and an array of baking tools. She was the embodiment of focused intent and serene dedication. Her hair cascaded around her shoulders and accentuated her delicate features. He took a moment to offer a silent prayer of gratitude. With Maggie by his side, everything made sense. She belonged here. She belonged with him. And he belonged to her. It was surreal to imagine that at around this time yesterday, they'd walked out of the hospital.

He was no stranger to a hectic schedule as a former pro baseball player, but the intensity of his athletic career paled in comparison to the whirlwind frenzy of keeping pace with his pie princess.

The moment they were released from CCSD custody, Maggie was already plotting their next move, eager to gather every supply necessary to host the culinary club.

His dad had picked up his truck. It was waiting for them as they exited the courthouse—along with the clothing they'd left on the pool deck—which was a godsend. He could not have traipsed around the county in those ill-fitting sweatpants. The thought alone made him cringe. And Jesus, the internet would have had a field day if he'd remained in that get-up. While they were out shopping, several people had approached him, eager to take a picture. Even more had snapped covert photos on their phones. He'd never been so grateful for a sturdy pair of jeans. The last thing he needed was the outline of his anatomy plastered online.

Normally, he'd shy away from cameras, but being pictured with Maggie and Lucky made him realize how blessed he truly was. She'd tried to slip her hand from his when she'd noticed the cameras, but he'd held on. He didn't care what anyone thought. He loved her. His family might think they were moving too fast, but he knew they'd eventually understand Maggie was the one for him.

Hand in hand, they'd wandered through the bustling farmer's market. It was like autumn was showing off. The crisp fall air was alive with the scents of fresh produce, spices, and herbs. He'd been surprised when she asked him to pull over in front of an antique shop. She'd sifted through the timeworn kitchenware—items that looked like they could have been housed in the original Donnelly ranch house. He'd suggested buying new pie plates and bakeware, but she'd turned him down. She wanted items that had been used and cherished. He'd watched, captivated, as she meticulously sorted through a bin of rolling pins, her fingers brushing each one as if she could feel their stories. She also selected several ceramic pie plates in delicate shades of cream, pink, blue, and green. Dotted with chips and scratches, she'd gazed at them as though they were old friends.

He quietly stepped behind her, wrapping his arms around her

waist, his touch gentle yet possessive. "Can you commune with old pie plates?" he whispered, watching her reflection in the window as the last wisps of light disappeared behind the mountains.

She melted into his embrace, her head tilting back to rest on his right shoulder, his good shoulder. "Maybe," she replied softly, a hint of a smile on her lips. "I was asking them if they could suggest a winning pumpkin pie recipe."

"Did they answer?"

"Unfortunately, no," she sighed, her fingers absently tracing the rim of an old, chipped pie plate.

Christian tightened his hold, pulling her closer. "Have I mentioned that you were amazing with Ironside? You were on fire in that courtroom."

"You might have mentioned it fifty times, possibly sixty."

"Is that all?" he teased. "But seriously, I've never seen the guy so intrigued. And I didn't sense a trace of anxiety coming from you."

She turned slightly, her eyes searching his. "You'll laugh if I tell you why. I might sound a little crazy."

He held her gaze. "Maggie, I fell in love with you in my dreams. There's not much you could say to top that on the crazy scale."

She gifted him with that gentle smile. "You know how I told you I got a surge of confidence when I saw your niece wearing my apron?"

"I remember."

"It was like something was there with me, guiding me, whispering for me to trust myself, telling me to acknowledge the worry but not let it hold me back," she replied, then tensed, her breath hitching as if she were on the brink of a panic attack.

Christian felt a protective surge and kissed the crown of her head. "What is it? Tell me."

"Now I have to deliver a win," she whispered, her voice trembling as she turned away from him.

"Maggie," he said softly. She looked up, and he met her gaze in the window's reflection. "*We* will deliver. You're not alone. And Jesus, look at your notebook. When we weren't buying out farm stands and antique shops, you were jotting down recipes. How many are you up to?"

"I've got eleven different variations of pumpkin pie."

"That's my lucky number. And if anyone has what it takes to come up with a winning pie, it's you. And I'll make sure you have everything you need. Hell, I'll buy every old pie plate in the damned state if that's what it takes to get your pie mojo going."

She turned in his arms and pressed her hands to his chest. "You'd do that?"

"I'd do anything to make you smile. I want to make you happy. I want this to be your home. Our home," he said, then kissed her bare shoulder. "And that seems to start with chipped ceramic pie plates, weathered rolling pins, and dented measuring cups."

She glanced at the antique baking implements. "They have such charm. I feel so at ease with them." She relaxed into his embrace and rested her head against him. "I might be a baker or a pastry chef, but I only seem to remember pie recipes. Maybe I'm just a pie freak."

He stroked her back, making slow circles. "My brothers could put that on a business card for you. Maggie TBD, certified pie freak."

She sighed. "This pie freak doesn't need a business card quite yet but could use a drink."

He released his hold, sauntered over to the fridge, and opened the door. "We are stocked. I can offer lemonade, strawberry lemonade, cherry lemonade, or cherry-lime lemonade. We also have thirty varieties of loose-leaf tea. I believe we bought out those booths at the farmer's market."

She frowned, her brow furrowing. "The lemonade and tea aren't for us."

"They're not? What about those little dried sausage thingies?"

Her expression turned to one of mild amusement. "Those are for Lucky. They're dog treats."

He swished his tongue around his mouth and grimaced. "Yeah, I might be needing a drink, too. I thought it was jerky."

She burst into laughter, shaking her head in delighted disbelief. "How'd it taste?"

"Pretty damned good." He eyed the dog. "We'll have to share those, boy."

Lucky jumped up and licked his hand, his tail eagerly wagging.

He ruffled the dog's fur between his ears. "Lucky seems okay with sharing them with me. But why can't we have any lemonade? We're swimming in it. We've got gallons and gallons."

"It's for the culinary club. And I don't think plain old lemonade will do it for me. I was thinking of something a little stronger. Like strong enough to knock a horse off its feet," she said, peering at him through her lashes.

He shut the fridge door and leaned against the counter. "You were actually listening when I said that last night? I thought you were lost in your own world."

She smiled softly. "I was, and I wasn't. I was absorbing everything. I think when I'm trying to understand something, I can go two ways—either I spill out every thought in a blustery word salad or go silent and observant. That could be how I process things," she said and drew her fingertips over the edge of one of the ceramic pie plates.

He returned to her and tipped up her chin. "Then it's another thing we know about you."

Her bottom lip trembled. "That drive from the hospital to the ranch feels like a lifetime ago."

"It does."

"What if everything about my past is lost?" she asked, her breath hitching as she spoke.

He stroked her cheek. He had to reassure her. "We'll keep doing new things, visiting new places. We'll make our own memories. I want a lifetime of them with you. And I have a feeling that baking with the culinary club will be good for you. Look what happened in the hearing room. That experience unlocked your knowledge about pies. Look at your notebook."

She nodded slowly, her expression a mix of hope and uncertainty as she cast her gaze downward. She'd gone quiet again, her thoughts seemingly a million miles away.

"Come with me," he said, taking her hand.

"Where are we going?"

"To get you that drink and get the dog-treat taste out of my mouth. Are you coming, Lucky?" He looked over his shoulder. The pup had conked out, curled into a ball with his eyes closed.

"He seems done for the day," Maggie observed, lacing her fingers with his.

"It's been one hell of a day," he replied, leading Maggie out of the kitchen and down a hallway. He stopped at the second door, his hand lingering on the knob. "This is where I make moonshine. We call it Stumble Juice." He opened the door and inhaled the rich, earthy scent of barley, wheat, and molasses mixed with the floral notes of wildflower honey and the piney fragrance of dried juniper berries. He flipped a light switch and a lamp in the corner cast the space in a golden glow. The room had been designed precisely to his specifications. The moonshine ingredients were housed in a large hutch while glass Mason jars of different Stumble Juice batches lined the wooden shelves on the far wall. They sparkled in the light that reflected off the hulking copper still in the center of the room.

Maggie took in the gleaming distillation machine. "This doesn't look like it came from the days of Prohibition."

"No, it didn't. I had this beauty handmade. It's a one-hundred-fifty-liter copper pot still. It's got all the modern bells and whistles. It even self-cleans, but it follows the same basic principles of making moonshine like my great-great grandparents did using dented metal vats."

She ran her hand along the side of the copper pot. "How does it work?"

He leaned against the wall and admired the still's craftsmanship. "There's a whole art to it, but in a nutshell, I start by heating the mash in the big copper pot—that's the fermented ingredients: the creek water, barley, wheat, wild yeast, juniper berries, molasses, and wildflower honey. That heating process turns the alcohol into vapor. That vapor travels to the condenser, where it cools and turns back into liquid, creating Stumble Juice."

Maggie nodded, taking in the information as she surveyed the shelves of past batches.

"I tinker around with the flavor, sometimes adding different ingredients to the mash, but the ingredients I rattled off were what my ancestors used," he added, watching her.

"You're meticulous in noting the fermentation time, batch, and proof," she said, eyeing the tags on each jar.

"It's kind of my thing. I guess this is how I keep a part of my family's history alive."

"It's cozy in here," she said, continuing to study the space.

"It's my workshop and sanctuary," he replied, feeling a sense of pride as he watched her take it all in. "And…"

"Yes?" she said, still eyeing the bottles.

"You're the only person I've brought to this room."

She paused her inspection and held his gaze. "You've never brought anyone from your family in here?"

"They could have looked in, but I make Stumble Juice alone. It's like meditation or something. During the off-season, it kept my mind engaged. I've always needed a focus, and the moonshine culture fascinates me." He grabbed a pair of glasses from the hutch and set them on the table. "Pick a jar. We should try some."

Maggie perused the rows, then stopped. "This one is dated November eleventh of last year. Batch eleven. Mash fermentation time: eleven days, and…" She picked up the jar and walked across the room to the wall covered with framed photos and memorabilia. She tapped the glass case with his college jersey inside. "I'm with number eleven, so we're going with lucky batch eleven," she added, handing him the glass jar. And damn, he liked hearing those words fall from her lips.

"Hell yes, you are," he answered, accepting the moonshine and pouring a little less than two fingers into each glass.

She scrutinized the amount. "That's it? That's like an inch of liquid."

He settled in on the sofa. "This is one hundred and ten proof. Enough of it literally will knock a horse over. You're the size of a baby goat. This is all you get."

"A baby goat?" she exclaimed, joining him on the couch.

He laughed. "Fine. A medium-sized goat? I don't know much about goats. You're a small person. You get what you get, TBD."

She held the glass, moving the liquid from side to side. "I bet I could drink you under the table, Number Eleven."

Jesus Christ, he could not allow her to get blackout drunk after a coma. He bit back a grin. "No, we're not doing that. Drink what's in your glass and tell me what you think. I want your honest opinion. This batch is a little heavier on the honey and molasses."

She watched him, eyes twinkling, then turned her attention to the contents of her cup. She took a sip, then closed her eyes. "It's smooth and malty sweet."

He watched her like a hawk. "That would be from the wheat and barley. The water, too."

She opened her eyes. "But there's more." She finished what was left in her glass. "It's flowery and nutty, and there's a warmth to it, like a caramel finish."

This woman was utterly incredible. He took a sip, assessing the flavors. "I couldn't have said it better myself."

"Not bad for a baby-goat-sized woman, huh?" she teased, the alcohol glistening on her lips.

He placed their glasses on a side table.

Mischief danced in her eyes. "Are you afraid of a little competition from a baby goat?"

"I'll show you what I can do with a baby-goat-sized woman," he said as he gripped her hips and lifted her onto his lap.

Her smile faded. "Christian, what about your shoulder?"

"It's okay. I know how to allow my right side to compensate. I didn't hurt myself. I'm not in any pain. I've been taking care of myself since..." He trailed off, suddenly aware that he had Maggie on his lap, straddling him. His breathing grew ragged. The closeness of their bodies sent his pulse skyrocketing, his cock growing rock-hard as it pressed between her thighs.

"You've been taking care of yourself since I showed up out of thin air," she whispered, losing her teasing tone as she locked onto his gaze.

"Yeah."

She caressed his left arm. "I don't want to hurt you, Christian."

"You couldn't. You're an angel, my angel," he said, losing himself in her hazel hues of green, gold, and brown. This woman was complex. Fiercely knowledgeable when it came to baking and genuinely empathic when it came to caring for people and animals. But she was also fragile. Worry and doubt could send her spinning. He wanted to know every part of her. A sharp pang rippled through him, and that damned thought that plagued him returned.

What if she had someone else out there?

Sure, whoever it was didn't deserve her, but they'd have history with her.

Maggie touched his face. "What is it? Where did you go?"

He pushed the thought aside. "Nowhere...I was just thinking. Can I ask you something?" he said, recovering and recalling a question he did have for her that had to do with her recent past.

"Of course. Anything."

"How did you know the type of apple in Ironside's pastry?"

A blush crept up her cheeks, turning them that shade of pink that made him want her more with each passing second. She looked down for a moment before meeting his eyes. "I guessed."

Holy fuck!

"Maggie, you're—"

"A very good girl with a little bad girl mixed in," she interrupted, a glint in her eyes.

And goddamn, he forgot about any sad sack of shit out there who could lay claim to Maggie's heart.

"I was going to say you're an absolute rock star, but what you said is a hell of a lot hotter. Christ, I love you."

She glanced away. "Have you been in love before? You're famous and handsome. I'm sure you've gotten plenty of attention."

"I've dated a lot of women. I partied and hooked up—more when I was younger—but I've never told another woman that I loved her. That she was the one." He cupped her face in his hands, his touch tender, his thumbs gently brushing her cheeks. "I love you. I don't care how long we've known each other. My heart knows your heart. You are the one, Maggie."

She blinked back tears.

"What is it?" he asked gently.

"I get this feeling that I've never been with anyone who's felt so strongly for me."

"No man could love you the way I do. We're meant to be together. That stone and my baseball card brought you to me. I don't give a damn how or why. You're here, and that's all that matters. I love you," he whispered and pressed his lips to hers.

The scents of the distillation room enveloped them, creating an intimate cocoon. Her lips were soft, so damned soft. Her honeyed molasses sweetness drew him in deeper. She hummed the sexiest little sound and parted her lips, inviting him in. And there's no way in hell he'd turn down the invitation. He kissed her like he made Stumble Juice—slowly, patiently, and methodically. Paying close attention to the rhythm of her breathing, he maintained his unwavering focus. She rocked her hips, moving against him like waves kissing the shoreline.

His hands slid into her hair, pulling her closer as their kiss grew more passionate. "Christ, I want you," he said against her lips. "I want you so badly I can barely breathe."

She tensed and pulled back, breaking the connection.

Dammit! He'd pushed her too far and let his cock override his brain.

"I can wait for you, Maggie. I could kiss you for a thousand years and never want anything more." He watched as her breath hitched and her eyes flickered with something that made his heart clench.

"I don't want to wait," she whispered.

"You don't?" he asked, searching her face for any trace of doubt. He needed to be sure that she was ready.

She gripped his shirt as if she was holding on for dear life. "But I don't even know if I've done this," she confessed, her voice trembling with uncertainty. "And what if I'm not that great at it?"

Tenderness washed over him. "You've done it."

"What? Did we do it before I hit my head?" she asked, her voice laced with panic.

"No, no, hell no," he blurted out. He took a breath, his gaze dropping for a moment as he considered his next words. "And I guess I don't know for sure that you've had sex, but you've got an IUD."

"I do? How do you know that?"

"The doctors wanted to make sure nothing had happened to you since I knew so little about you and where you came from. They ran tests and checked for any signs of trauma or illness. The nurse said it was routine."

"You were there while they checked my entire body?"

"No, not in the room. They wouldn't allow that. I waited right outside, and…"

"Yes?"

"I was sort of listening—but only to make sure that you were okay. Not to be creepy or nosy, which now sounds like I was being really creepy and horribly nosy. I'm sorry."

"Is there anything you know about me that I don't know?"

"Well…" he eked out.

"Christian, tell me."

"You don't have any sexually transmitted diseases, and you have a scar where you must have had your appendix removed."

She blinked, processing this information. "Do you know my blood type?"

He couldn't help the slight smile that tugged at the corners of his mouth. "O positive."

She watched him, wide-eyed. "They probably need thicker walls in that hospital."

"Probably."

She wrapped her arms around his neck, then glanced down to where he was sporting one hell of a hard-on. "So, we can…"

"Yep."

She twisted the hair at the nape of his neck between her fingers. "Anytime we want?"

"Yeah," he bit out, his voice a low rasp.

"Without worrying about me getting…"

"That's right."

She rocked against him. "And you—"

"Haven't been with anyone in months, and I've had so much blood work done, I know I'm good," he replied, damn near out of his mind.

She nodded, then arched her back. The movement was subtle, almost imperceptible, but with Maggie, he noticed everything. She lifted her gaze, eyes twinkling with mischief. "Have you thought about sleeping with me?"

"From the first night I saw you in my dreams," he blathered again. And Jesus, he needed to calm down.

She continued gently twisting the locks at the back of his neck, driving him wild. She paused. "What did you picture? What's your fantasy?"

He couldn't even pretend to play it cool. "You, in my college jersey, and nothing else."

"That jersey?" she asked, pointing toward the framed display on the wall. Encased in glass, the white jersey with bold forest green trim hung next to a framed photograph of the team.

His gaze lingered on the jersey, a wave of nostalgia washing over him. "Yes, that's the exact one."

"There's a latch on the display case," Maggie observed, her voice laced with a sultry undertone.

"Yep," he said, reduced to caveman-like utterances.

"So…it opens?"

"Yes."

She leaned forward, her lips a breath away from his. "Close your eyes, Number Eleven."

He didn't comply right away. Instead, he held her gaze for a beat, drinking in those eyes that left him spellbound—that hazel sparkle that lit a fire in his soul.

She cocked her head to the side and pursed her lips.

"Fine, I'll do it," he grumbled, closing his eyes, hating to look away for even a second.

She maneuvered off his lap, and his senses heightened. He listened to her footsteps.

Tap, tap, tap.

Click.

Creak.

"You've got it, don't you?" he asked.

"I do," she purred.

He inhaled a tight breath. "How long are you going to make me wait?"

"Not long. Is this something all baseball players fantasize about?" she asked.

"Yeah, but we were a superstitious bunch at RMU. As a team, we agreed no one could wear our jersey unless we knew they were the one." He paused. "It wasn't hard for me to stick to that rule."

"Why?"

"I never saw myself with anyone."

A few seconds went by before she spoke. "You never wanted to commit to a person?"

"I thought my life would be baseball, and then it all ended, and my life began again the second I saw you and learned you were real. No woman has ever worn that jersey. You'll be the first and only woman to wear it. Now, will you please let me open my eyes? I've been fantasizing about this for months."

"Okay, you can look."

He opened his eyes, and his breath caught in his throat. She'd twisted her hair into a messy bun, and wisps framed her face. The light wrapped her in golden warmth. He drank in every inch of her body. Only one button was fastened on the jersey, allowing a tantalizing glimpse of her creamy skin and the curves of her full breasts. Desire surged through him, a primal need to possess her.

There was only one thing for him to say.

He narrowed his gaze. "Get that pretty little ass over here."

"You look a little worked up," she cooed, sauntering around the still.

"That might just win the award for understatement of the year."

"You should stretch," she said, gazing at him through her lashes.

"I'm good. Remember when I took Lucky for a walk while you were picking out pie plates and rolling pins in the antique store?"

She nodded, parading around the room like a fucking siren.

"I got in my mobility exercises in the parking lot," he finished.

She stopped next to the wall with the empty display case and traced a line from her collarbone to her cleavage, opening the jersey another inch. "Maybe I should stretch," she mused, her eyes glittering as she held his gaze. And holy fuck, that confident air he'd seen when she'd taken control of the courtroom returned. "Hey, Number Eleven?" she continued, her voice sultry and light.

"Yeah?"

She ran her tongue across her top lip and undid the button. The jersey parted, revealing her mouthwatering curves. She took a step toward him. "I know you like to be in charge. Tell me what to do."

A rush of carnal desire flooded his system. "Tilt your head from side to side. Do it slowly," he said and unfastened his jeans.

"Like this?" she asked, closing her eyes and sensually rolling her head from side to side, a move so erotic, he inhaled another tight breath as he unzipped his jeans and freed his cock.

"What next?" she asked, taking another step toward him, her hungry gaze locked on his hard length.

He pumped his cock. He ached to be inside her, to feel her, to fill her. He worked his shaft and devoured her with his gaze. "Press your hands to the wall. Lean forward and lift your ass into the air. You'll want your hips to be loose for what I'm about to do to you."

She nodded, then turned and walked with a sexy sway. Her hands met the wall above her head, and she leaned in. The jersey lifted, revealing her buttocks. He licked his lips. Goddamn, he wanted to sink his teeth into her soft, supple skin.

"Mmm," she hummed, extending the stretch. She glanced over her shoulder at him. "I think I could go deeper with a little help."

Hell, yes, she could.

He lost his pants, peeled off his T-shirt, and left his clothing in a heap on the floor. He came up behind her, taking in every gorgeous inch of this woman wearing his name and his number.

His.

She was his.

He was hers.

He pressed his lips to the shell of her ear. "Widen your stance and brace yourself. I'm going as deep as you can take."

She took a sharp, uneven breath as he lined up his cock with the entrance to her sweet, wet heat. Using his good arm, he steadied himself, his hand overlapping with hers. He gripped her hip with his left hand, holding her in place.

"Touch yourself, but don't you dare come," he growled.

Her hand slid from the wall, and she slipped it between her legs, her breathing growing ragged as her hips gently rocked.

"Keep going," he said, moving with her, slowly pushing his cock past her delicate folds. He sucked in a sharp breath because, holy hell, he was barely in an inch, and she was wet and so damned tight. He trailed his fingertips from her hip and covered her hand as she worked her sweet bud, observing the cadence of her breath as he threaded his hand with hers, feeling her soft warmth as he took charge of her pleasure.

He pushed in farther. Every fiber of his being wanted to slam inside her, to fill her to the hilt, but he wasn't about to hurt her. "Take a slow, deep breath, then blow it all the way out," he instructed.

It took a few shaky breaths before her body relaxed. On her exhale, he rocked his hips and glided inside. The delicious stretch of her body accommodating his cock sent a lightning bolt of pure lust through him.

"Christian," she whispered, and the raw ache in her voice fueled his need to make her come hard.

"This is for you. Don't ignore any sensation. Let yourself feel everything," he said, working her in steady, rhythmic strokes as he dialed up the pace with his hand. Each touch was a silent promise to learn every inch of her, to make her his own in every way.

"Oh, I'm there. I'm…" she moaned, her body trembling as the rush of orgasmic endorphins flooded her system.

"Take it all. Take everything," he rasped, increasing his pressure between her thighs. She tightened around him, squeezing him, embracing him. He was close to losing it, but this wasn't how he wanted to take her.

She rested her head against the wall, gasping for breath. "I don't think I can walk or even move," she said between heavy breaths.

"You don't have to do anything," he said and scooped her into his arms.

"Christian, your shoulder," she said against his neck.

"I'm good, TBD. My right arm is doing the bulk of the work."

"Where are we going?" she asked as he headed out of the still room.

"I'm taking you to bed. You asked what I fantasized about. It's this. Carrying you to my room," he replied, taking the steps two at a time. "I want to watch you come. I want to look into your eyes, and I want to see your soul while I make love to you."

He kicked open the door to the darkened room and gently positioned her in the middle of his bed. She rose onto her elbows, his jersey drifting off her shoulders as the light from the hallway cast a warm halo on her hair. A sultry smile curved her lips. *God help him!* She was a goddess, a beauty beyond anything he'd ever seen, and his reality surpassed his dreams.

He stood at the foot of the bed, basking in the knowledge that this woman was his entire world. She sighed deeply, her eyes hungrily taking in every hard inch of him. And he could no longer resist simply admiring her.

"Lie back and spread your legs," he said, his voice a low, heated rasp.

She watched him for a beat, then opened to him like a flower welcoming the sun. He prowled the length of her body and settled his cock between her thighs. He cupped her face in his hand, and she smiled up at him. He kissed the corner of her mouth, brushing his lips across hers. "You are my everything. I never believed I'd feel joy again, never imagined I could love so profoundly. I was drowning in darkness. You rescued me with your light." He trembled, shaking from the weight of his emotions.

She gently traced her fingers along his jawline. "Show me what you're feeling."

He fought to keep control, but his feelings were too powerful. He tensed. "It's a lot…it's…I don't want to hurt you."

"You won't. I'm stronger than I look. Show me, Christian. Make love to me," she whispered, and the warmth of her breath steadied him. He could no longer use words to demonstrate what he felt for her. He kissed her, devouring her mouth as he thrust inside, desperate to be one with her. She bucked her hips, moving beneath him, grinding her pelvis against his—an invitation to give her everything. He pistoned his hips, kissing her lips, her cheeks, her neck. Like a starving man presented with a feast, he made love to her, giving her every ounce of himself. Their bodies, slick from wild exertion, slapped with each thrust. He pulled back slightly, observing her parted lips and sweet moans as he rocked into her. Her chest heaved, her breasts pressed against him, her hands gripping his ass.

"Harder," she said on a sultry exhale.

He sure as hell wouldn't deny her.

He roared, thrusting like a beast. The bed creaked. The headboard slammed against the wall. He took every drop of his pain, every moment of pure hell, each clawing thought that had plagued him over the past three months, and let it go, let it evaporate, let it dissolve. With every muscle in his body moving in a rapturous harmony, he gazed at Maggie's face as her core gripped his cock. She was on the edge, and he was right there with her.

"Maggie," he rasped, lost to a whirlwind of sweat and lust and a love so all-encompassing that it threatened to swallow him whole.

She cried out as her orgasm took hold. He kissed her, consuming her cries and losing himself in wave after wave of his release, his soul entwining with hers as they clung to each other. The force of his release ebbed, and soon, the only sound was the one of his breath mingling with hers. He eased off her and gathered her into his arms, marveling at how perfectly she fit against him, as though she were crafted just for him.

"Thank you," she whispered.

"For what?"

"For showing me how you feel, for...loving me." Her voice

trembled, each word fragile, like she was entering unknown territory. There was a vulnerability in the way she spoke the word *love*, and he had a feeling that, while she might have dated or had boyfriends in the past, none of them had loved her completely and fully. In fact, most probably took advantage of her kindness.

He wouldn't be one of them.

"You're mine, Maggie," he said with a fierce tenderness, his hands gently cradling her face. "And I'm yours. I never want to lose you."

"Whatever little we know about me, I know one thing for sure," she said, her fingers tracing his chest over the words tattooed above his heart.

"What do you know?"

She looked up, and her eyes glistened with unshed tears. "Somewhere between waking up in that hospital and getting arrested, my heart started beating for you."

"And I will always protect it. Always." His voice was steady and strong. He needed her to understand that he meant it. She was his path, his future. She was what mattered now. "I have an idea," he said, offering her a wicked grin.

"Do you?" she replied, her eyes now gleaming with desire instead of tears.

He traced the faint line on her abdomen. "We can play find the scars in the tub, and then I'll make you come against the bathroom wall."

"You can go again after what we just did?" she asked breathlessly, her eyes wide with surprise.

He kissed a hot trail to her earlobe and lowered his voice to a husky rasp. "Maggie TBD, I'm not even close to being done with you."

Fifteen

MAGGIE

I don't know if I've ever been this happy.

MAGGIE GAZED at the words she'd penned in the margin of one of her recipes as a wave of pure contentment washed over her. She might not remember who she was, but an extraordinary man loved her with his every breath and being. And this love was uncharted and electrifying.

Of course, it was nothing like anything she'd ever known. She'd lost her memories—she didn't know anything.

But with each touch, kiss, and heartfelt proclamation, his actions filled the void left by the disappearance of her memories. With every passing minute, she worried less about who she was and dreamed more about who she could be—who she could be when she was so utterly and so completely adored. She closed her notebook with a contented sigh and admired the scratched stone and Christian's baseball card on the bedside table. Placing her pen and notebook beside them, she gently touched the corner of the card and traced her fingers over the two lines carved into the surface of the shimmering starry quartzite. "Thank you for bringing me here."

"Thank you for being here," came the gravelly voice of the sexiest ex-baseball player on the planet.

Her entire body buzzed with a sudden, irresistible thrill. She turned her attention from the nightstand to the man lying beside her. The fading light filtering in through the curtains accentuated his sharp cheekbones and chiseled jawline. She brushed a few stray strands of his dark hair away from his eyes and read the words tattooed above his heart.

Give what you love everything you've got.

She nestled into the cozy disarray of the unmade bed. "Did I wake you, Number Eleven?"

He stroked her cheek. "No, TBD, I've been watching you write for a while now. Did you remember another recipe?"

"I did. Rosemary pumpkin pie, and I also wrote about..." She could feel her cheeks heat.

He ran his knuckles down her jawline. "Here it comes. The shade of pink that is my undoing."

And talk about undoing. His voice. His deep, sage-green eyes. And that sleep-sweet half-grin. Her core clenched, and her breath grew uneven at the sight of him. After a buffet of orgasms over the last couple of days, getting hot and bothered by Christian's presence had become an involuntary reflex.

"I'm a new fan of the two o'clock nap. Now, come here, TBD, you're too far away," he said and patted his bare chest.

"I'm right next to you."

"I want you closer," he replied in a gravelly rumble as he welcomed her into his arms.

Between bouts of sweaty, vigorous sex and prepping for the culinary club, they hadn't gotten much rest. But time waits for nobody—not even the perma-horny experiencing mind-blowing orgasmic bliss.

Today was day one of the pie-making grind, and the culinary club was slated to arrive at four.

The countdown had begun.

She had until Friday—at the very latest—to come up with a winning recipe for the Saturday contest.

Now, should she be lounging in bed with Christian? Yes and no. It wasn't like they'd spent the entire day like this. They'd gotten up early to make the final preparations. The house was spotless—even all the bedrooms.

Well, not all the bedrooms.

Christian's room had become their go-to space for a little mattress dancing. And sweet heaven above, they'd been going to town between the sheets.

So, when she'd finished making the last batch of pumpkin puree and her sexy number eleven sauntered into the kitchen and suggested they take a catnap before the group's arrival, she'd agreed, knowing there would be little rest involved. And sweet Orgasm City, she was right—but it wasn't exactly his fault. She'd stripped in front of him, then donned his college jersey. And nothing got him harder than her wearing his number. And she loved this power. She'd embraced this boldness, this confidence, this feeling that she'd found her path. She'd barely taken a step toward him before he'd had her on her back, his cock lined up and ready to rock her world.

Christian kissed her temple. "You're still wearing my jersey, and you know what that blush does to me."

"Every inch of my body knows what my little pink cheeks do to you." She rested against him, careful she was on his right side, his good side.

"Every inch? That's a bold claim," he purred. "As a person who prides himself on going the extra mile and breaking as many records as possible, I better make sure I truly have attended to *every single inch* of your body. I need to make sure I've still got it," he added with a devilish twist of his lips.

She bit her bottom lip as his words sent a delicious tingle down her spine. "I don't know if my body can take it after our naptime romp and after what we did this morning when…"

He shifted to his elbow and gazed down at her. "When you

rode my cock like a professional cowgirl, and I finished you off, fucking you hard and fast against the wall."

Now, that was a way to greet the day.

"Oh, TBD," he said, trailing his fingertips down her belly, "you can handle what I have planned for you."

The heat from her cheeks could probably power the town of Starrycard Creek for the next month. She exhaled a ragged breath and glanced at the clock. "We only have forty-five minutes until they arrive."

"I only need five." He tugged the edge of the open jersey, his gaze hungrily tracing the contours of her breasts. "Maybe less."

Her perma-horny brain kicked in. "What *exactly* do you want to do for less than five minutes?"

Carnal mischief shimmered in his darkened gaze. "Grab a little snack."

"And what do you want to snack on?" she asked, arching her back and putting on a show because little ole Maggie TBD knew exactly what this man was craving.

"You," he growled. He maneuvered his body and had her legs parted faster than a lightning strike. The man settled between her thighs. "How fast do you think I can get you there?" he asked, squeezing her ass as he grazed his teeth across the sensitive skin of her inner thigh.

She purred like a satisfied cat and donned a wicked grin. "I don't know. I've never timed it."

"Look at that. A new record for me to set. You'll want to brace yourself, TBD. I'm going to make this fast, dirty, and so damned good, you'll see stars."

She couldn't take her eyes off the breathtaking man. One thing was certain with him. Failure was not an option. "Someone's feeling awfully cocky," she said, absolutely loving his confidence.

"Can't help it. It's how I feel when you're the first thing I see every morning. Sets the tone." He grabbed a pillow from the mess of bedding and pinned her with his hooded gaze. "Now, lift your pretty little ass and let me get to work."

What gal could say no to that?

"What about you? We don't have much time. Don't you want to…oh, God," she whispered on a tight breath as Christian licked her like she was a triple scoop.

"This is for me as much as it's for you, TBD. Do you know how turned on I get when I find you wet and aching for me?"

"I have a feeling you're about to show me."

His glittering gaze darkened. "This much," he said, holding her hips in place as he lowered his head and feasted between her thighs.

She bucked her hips, greedily receiving everything he was offering. He extended his tongue, the tip grazing her most sensitive place, then teased her as he traced a path around it. Each lick was deliberate. Every glide of his tongue savored her as she melted into a pool of titillating goo. Christian intensified his efforts, building momentum, and this man and his magic mouth had her reeling.

"Forget baseball. This is what you were meant to do," she said on the cusp of losing the ability to speak as she watched him work.

His lips curved into a satisfied smile, and he kicked up his pace, going from teasing her to tormenting her and holding her on the brink of ecstasy in the space of one heated, writhing breath. The tension built, winding her tighter and tighter until it couldn't be contained. Unable to hold back, she threaded her fingers in his hair.

Her breath had grown heavy and ragged, the air escaping her lips in warm, trembling moans. "Christian…Christian…" she cried, the words barely escaping before the coil burst. "I'm there. My God, it's so good."

Her release engulfed her like a surging wave. And as quickly as she went under, the earth shifted on its axis, and she was floating, rising, riding the ripples of sensation, joining the energy sweeping her into a state of pure exhilaration. Her questions vanished, and her worries dissolved. It was only her, Christian, and a universe teeming with infinite possibilities. She sighed, a dreamy, feathery sound, and relaxed into the buttery-soft tangle of sheets and blankets.

"One minute, eleven seconds. My number. I still got it, baby," Christian boasted, grinning up at her, his lips slick with her arousal. "Who's the King of Oral?" he hooted. He zeroed in on her. "You don't have to say a thing, TBD. Your sexy-as-hell blush is telling me everything I need to know."

Knock, knock, knock!

The sharp sound pierced the room like a whip crack, snapping them out of their orgasmic revelry.

"I don't know who the King of Oral is, Christian," a man announced from the other side of the door, "but you've got guests."

She gasped and stared wide-eyed toward the source of the sound.

"Grandpa Rex, what are you doing out there?" Christian called.

She locked onto the King of Oral's gaze. Now, they both sported pink cheeks.

"We've been knocking on the front door for a good five minutes. I decided to use my key," Rex said, raising his rough voice—and the man sounded slightly irritated.

Yikes.

"We?" Christian repeated.

"Yeah, me and the culinary club."

Oh, no! Maggie's heart was in her throat.

"You're not in the culinary club, are you?" Christian asked.

The old man laughed. "Hell no. Do you think your grandmother would allow me to bake? I caught a ride up with them for the booze."

"I should have figured."

Maggie checked the clock and waved Christian closer. "They're early, but we can make this work. First, you've got to tell your grandpa that you didn't say King of *Oral*."

"What do you want me to tell him?" he asked, keeping his voice low.

She nibbled her lip. "Let me think, but don't let him leave."

"Um...Grandpa?" Christian called.

"Yeah, kid?"

"I think you misheard me. I was cheering because I'm the King of..." He looked at her.

"Floral," she whispered. "You're the King of Floral."

"I'm the King of Floral, with an *F*, like flowers. And I'm the King of Floral because..." Christian paused, giving her the international expression for *help me*.

She pressed her lips to the shell of his ear. "Floral, because the wildflower honey in Stumble Juice is such a prevalent flavor."

"I was thinking about Stumble Juice and how I'm getting pretty good at making it."

She nodded and gestured for him to keep going.

"And...how there's wildflower honey in it, and the bees that make the honey must go crazy over the wildflowers in Starrycard Creek. And another word for flowers is floral, so yeah, I'm the King of *Floral*," he said, then cringed as she pressed her lips into a hard line, doing everything in her power not to burst into laughter.

"Yeah, all right, kid, whatever you say." The thud of steps signaled Rex's departure, but then he stopped. "Hey, where's Maggie? I didn't see her downstairs."

Double, oh, no!

Rex's question knocked the giggles clean out of her. She scrambled off the bed and tiptoe-ran into her room—and holy moly, she silently gave thanks to McKenzie for insisting she stay in the Donnelly bedroom connected to Christian's. She slipped off the jersey, put on a robe, and tossed her hair into a towel. She exhaled a slow breath, attempting to compose herself, and mustered a grin, hoping it wasn't the expression of a woman who'd just experienced a mind-blowing orgasm. She opened the door. "Oh, hello, Mr. Starrycard. I thought I heard something out here while I was getting ready in my room. Alone. Not another soul in there with me. I washed my hair. See the towel."

There's her crazy-talk mouth.

Rex looked from Christian's bedroom door and then back to her. "You can call me Rex, and are you two kids doing okay? I heard Christian yelling about flowers."

She plastered a grin to her lips, praying she didn't look like a serial killer or someone who'd had an orgasm in seventy-one seconds. "I can't speak for Christian because I am in my room—*alone*—but I couldn't be better. I'm raring to figure out a winning pumpkin pie recipe."

"And get in some rejuvenating mobility exercises," Christian added, skidding out of his room and into the hallway in gray track pants and a white T-shirt that accentuated his ripped abdomen.

Yummy!

No, no, no. Not yummy. Her amnesia-induced perma-horny brain needed to calm down.

Rex eyed his grandson. "What's on your face, Chris? Is that petroleum jelly? Something wrong with your lips? Are you drying out in the fall air?"

"There is absolutely nothing wrong with your grandson's lips," she purred—and darn her brain, but the words flew out of her mouth. "It must be lip balm," she blathered, trying to make up for sounding like a sexual deviant. "You must have gone downtown—I mean *to town* with that new lip balm we found at the farmer's market." *Maggie, stop!* "Here, use this to clean up," she offered, whipping the snow-white towel from her head and wishing she had a piece of duct tape for her mouth.

"Your hair is dry?" Rex observed. "Didn't you say you just got out of the shower?"

Her plastic smile was about to snap. "Um…"

"There's a reason my towels cost a fortune, Grandpa. They dry anything in seconds. Really fantastic linen or cotton or whatever the hell they're made of," Christian chimed, accepting the magical towel to wipe the remains of her release off his face. He passed the miracle-drying towel back to her with the barest ghost of a cocky grin on his lips. "Must be the lip balm. It is my favorite."

This man.

All she could do was nod and try not to combust into a million sexually charged pieces.

"I'll welcome our guests and lead them through some mobility exercises while you finish up getting ready," Christian said, clearly back in control.

The men headed down the hallway, and she closed the door and leaned against it. "That went about as badly as it could go," she murmured, but she couldn't wipe the stupid grin off her face. Still, she couldn't stand there and moon over the man who made her as giddy as a schoolgirl. There was a contest to win and work to do.

She dressed quickly, throwing on jeans, boots, and a sweater from the haul of clothing Christian had purchased for her while they were out shopping. She tiptoed back into his room to retrieve her notebook and took a second to take in the bed. She picked up his pillow and inhaled his clean, earthy scent. "How could a girl not love you, Christian Starrycard?" she whispered.

While he'd made his love and adoration clear, and she'd confirmed she felt the same way, she hadn't said those three words to him.

Why was that?

Was it because she'd spoken those words to someone else—was in love with someone else?

She'd been missing for ten days. Surely, if someone out there loved her, like Christian said, they would have tried to find her or gone to the authorities.

She looked in the mirror above the dresser, taking in her strawberry-blond hair and the freckles sprinkled across the bridge of her nose. "This is your life, at least until you remember who you are."

She twisted her hair into a bun and headed downstairs. As she reached the first floor, Christian's voice drifted down the hallway. He must have taken the group to the gym. She paused at the bottom of the stairs and smiled, listening as he instructed the participants in a knowledgeable, reassuring tone.

"There you are," Rex said, his voice low and stern.

She gasped and peered into the cavernous gathering room—the lobby, as Christian called it. His grandfather sat on one of the over-stuffed chairs, an unlit cigar in his hand.

"I'm sorry. I didn't see you there," she said and headed his way. "I was about to make sure everything is set up in the kitchen. I also made a few pies for the group. Are you hungry?"

"Hungry and thirsty. Do you know if Christian's got any Stumble Juice on hand?" the man asked as he tucked the cigar into his breast pocket.

"There's some in the kitchen."

"That'll do," Rex said, grimacing as he tried to get up.

Maggie tucked her notebook under her arm and hurried to his side. "Easy. I've got you," she said softly, placing a steadying hand on his arm as he rose.

"My damn hip has good days and bad days. I'm not as spry as I used to be," the man offered with a pained chuckle.

"You should join Christian and the culinary group for the mobility exercises. I'm sure it would help," she suggested, her grip still firm on his arm.

"Maybe I will next time. But I need a word with you." His voice grew firmer, and his eyes narrowed as he fixed her with a penetrating gaze. "And what I have to say is for you and *you* alone."

Sixteen

MAGGIE

WHAT COULD *Christian's grandfather want to discuss with her—alone?*

Maggie peered up at the senior Starrycard, taking a beat to study the man. Rex was tall and burly. A faint scent of tobacco and orange marmalade lingered around him, a peculiar combination that was oddly comforting. His gruff demeanor matched his rugged appearance, but Maggie couldn't help but sense a hidden warmth beneath his tough exterior.

"You want to talk to me...without Christian?" she asked, attempting to get a read on the man.

"Yes," he answered, his expression neutral. "I wanted to see how you're doing with your memory loss, and I also have some Stumble Juice questions."

She breathed a sigh of relief—thank goodness he didn't ask about the oral-floral business.

"I'm happy to answer your questions, but there's not a lot to say. I don't recall any salient facts about my life, mostly recipes, and I think your grandson would know more about moonshine than me."

Rex's gaze softened, the lines on his weathered face deepening with sympathy. "I'm sorry to hear about your memories. I'm sure you're eager to recall your past."

She forced a small smile, trying to push aside the twinge of discomfort. "My neurologist said it could take some time. I'm taking it day by day," she replied, attempting to keep her tone light. "What did you want to ask me about Stumble Juice?"

"Christian's very private about his distilling. Do you know what he's been working on in that little room down the hall?"

Oh yeah, she knew. He'd been working her—hard.

"He showed me around the still room, like a tour," she said, feeling her cheeks heat as she escorted Rex into the kitchen.

No, cheeks, this is not the time!

The man studied her for a beat. "I see."

She turned on the lights and led him to the table. "Let's get you settled. There's a Mason jar with a Stumble Juice batch we tried last night on the hutch. I'll work on that drink and get you some pie."

Rex eased into the chair with a sigh. "You've got a gentle touch, Maggie. You're good with people."

"I like being helpful, but I don't know how good I am at it," she answered, donning a vintage apron, another purchase from the antique store.

"I do, and you are good with people," the man countered, his gruff voice rising with conviction. "I sense that about you. And I can also tell that you're as sharp as they come. I learned that from your performance in the hearing room. It's not often Ironside is left gobsmacked. You believe in yourself, kid. That's not always an easy thing to do."

She stared at an empty glass. "Maybe it's easy because I don't know who I am," she replied, her voice tinged with uncertainty. It was like she was on a seesaw, teetering between two worlds. One moment, she was convinced that this life—her new life with Christian—was where she truly belonged. The next, she was haunted by the possibility that she had another life waiting for her.

"I think you know who you are, Maggie," Rex said, and the sincerity in his tone wrapped around her like a grandfather's embrace.

Her breath hitched as tears came to her eyes. She glanced away and took a moment to steady herself. "I truly don't, sir. I don't even know my last name."

"Enough with the sirs and misters," he said, pegging her with his steely sage-green gaze. "It's Rex, and I don't think a person has to know their last name to know their heart."

She nodded, not sure how to answer. Instead, she focused on cutting the pie and plating a slice.

"My wife was quite impressed with your baking knowledge," Rex said, filling the stretch of silence.

Grateful for the change in subject, Maggie covered the pie with plastic wrap and poured the moonshine into a tumbler. "She's got her own restaurant, right? I saw the boxes in Christian's fridge. Goldie's on the Creek?"

"She sure does."

"Does she bake?" Maggie asked as she returned the top to the Mason jar.

He nodded. "Goldie's specialties are turnovers and muffins. But I know she'd love to have pie on hand."

"Would she?" Maggie replied, setting the slice and Stumble Juice in front of the man.

"I believe she would. You should talk to her."

Wouldn't that be something! This had to be her path.

The man surveyed the liquid in the glass. "What batch is this from?"

She retrieved the Mason jar, a cloth napkin, and a fork and set the items on the table. "Batch eleven, from last year. November eleventh. There are four more jars in this batch."

"Ah, Chris's number. Did you try it?"

She sat in the chair beside him. "Yes, it's smooth and complex. The wildflower honey and molasses stood out to me. Subtle sweetness with a bite."

Rex took a sip and closed his eyes. "Stumble Juice always brings me back in time. My grandmother Delilah, and grandfather Nathan Starrycard, started making Stumble Juice during Prohibition. Delilah was a naturalist and knew her plants," Rex continued. "She came up with the original recipe. My parents, Tristan and Lavinia, tinkered around with the old still, but my dad was busy with the shop, and my mother was the mayor. Once booze wasn't illegal, the need to produce Stumble Juice ended, and we put away the old equipment. Did Chris mention our family's history to you? I could talk for hours."

"He did. After we left the hospital, he gave me a quick tour and even drove by the Starrycard Creek Paper Company."

Rex's eyes lit up as he took another sip, gesturing toward a nearby artifact with his glass. "Did he tell you about the mountain lion's tooth?"

"Yes, it's quite a harrowing story," she replied, a small smile tugging at her lips.

Rex's expression grew more animated, a rough chuckle escaping him. "Kathleen Conners and Seamus Donnelly were two tough motherfuckers, pardon my French," he said, finishing his moonshine and pouring another splash into his glass.

"It certainly sounds like it."

Rex lifted the glass to his lips again, this time drinking slowly, savoring the flavor as if it were a connection to his past. "My family wouldn't be here if it weren't for the Donnellys. Christian looks like a Starrycard man with dark hair and green eyes. A handsome devil like me," he added with a wink, his eyes twinkling.

She couldn't help but chuckle at that, appreciating the resemblance between the generations.

Rex poured another inch of moonshine into his glass, his voice turning more reflective. "But Chris has a lot of Donnelly in him. He can be fiercely bull-headed and won't stop until he achieves what he set out to do. But then there's a softer side to him, the artistry when it comes to distilling. Fiona Donnelly was an artist."

"And baseball, from Michael Donnelly, Fiona's older brother," Maggie added before she could stop herself.

Rex watched her closely. "He told you about Michael?"

"He did."

The man sipped the moonshine and nodded. "I need to ask you another question, and I'd like the honest truth, even if it isn't pretty."

"If I can help you, Rex, I will."

"How is Christian? It takes a lot for a crusty old fart like me to worry, and you may be the only person who knows what's going on inside his head."

She relaxed. That was an easy question to answer. "Your grandson is a remarkable, kind, and generous man, and I..." She traced little circles on the table, the kind that Christian made on her back and hand. "I think Christian and I were supposed to meet—to be there for each other, to take care of each other."

"And how's he doing with this?" Rex asked and tapped the Mason jar.

"He mentioned he'd been overdoing it. He told me about the last three months, but I believe he's turned a corner," she replied, hoping her words would provide the man with comfort.

Rex stared out the window at the mountains bathed in a dusky purple light. "Goldie believes the same thing. I might look tough on the outside, but nothing can turn me into a puddle of blubbering mess like the love for my family. I was an only child. Every Starrycard was until my son and Maeve blessed us with six grandchildren, and now we have a great-granddaughter. I don't mean to get sentimental. Blame it on an old man indulging in a touch too much of the hooch. I just want the kids to be okay," he said, his voice a rasp of a sound as his gaze grew glassy.

She needed to lighten the mood.

"Do you know how I'm absolutely positive Christian's doing better?" she asked, injecting a bit of cheerfulness into her tone, hoping to steer the conversation in a brighter direction.

Rex's gaze sharpened with a curious glint. "How?" he replied, his voice steadier now, the heaviness lifting just a bit.

"I taught him how to use his fancy washing machine yesterday. He single-handedly washed the bedding from every bedroom and these napkins. What else could you ask for in a man? Stick a fork in Christian Starrycard. He's done. He's good," she added, biting back a grin as she held his gaze.

Rex looked her over, then chuckled, a sly smirk curling the corners of his mouth. "You are good with people, Maggie. You seem to know what they need," he replied, then peered out the window at the darkened sky and exhaled a slow breath.

For a minute, perhaps two, they didn't utter a word. But the silence between them wasn't strained or uneasy. It was a serene quiet, a moment filled with an unspoken understanding.

"Do you care about Christian?" Rex asked, his tone serious.

Maggie felt her heart skip a beat. The directness of his question caught her off guard, but she knew the answer without hesitation. "I do," she replied, her voice firm but soft, the truth of it resonating deeply within her.

Rex relaxed at her words, his shoulders easing as he settled into the chair. Another comfortable silence lingered for a moment. "Guess how long it took for me to fall in love with Goldie?" he asked.

Maggie blinked, surprised by the sudden shift in their conversation. She hesitated, trying to gauge the right response. "I don't know. Maybe a month?"

Rex gave a small, knowing smile as he drummed his fingers on the table twice, the sound punctuating the pause. "That long," he said, his voice tinged with amusement.

"Two seconds?" she asked, her tone incredulous, but despite barely knowing the man, she knew it was the truth.

"Probably more like point two seconds. She came into the shop with her father. They were in Starrycard Creek for the summer. And just like that, I knew she was the one."

Maggie rested her chin in her hand. "How did you know? Was it a feeling?"

"Grab yourself a glass, and I'll tell you. I don't like drinking alone."

She rose and returned with a tumbler. With a practiced motion, Rex poured her a measure of Stumble Juice.

She lifted the glass to her lips and took a sip. "All right, let's hear it. I have the strangest feeling that I might be a sucker for love stories."

"This is a good one. I was in the front of the shop, and Goldie walked in like something out of a dream."

"A dream?" Maggie repeated.

"Yes, ma'am. She caught me staring, which wasn't like me. I wasn't interested in dating or marriage. It's funny because the locals here say that love is always in the cards in Starrycard Creek, but I was focused on the company and helping my family keep the paper business and town profitable. Then that fierce woman strolled in and caught me gawking at her."

"And was it love at first sight?" Maggie asked, a warmth enveloping her that had nothing to do with the moonshine in her glass.

A rosy glow lit the man's weathered face. Deep laugh lines formed at the corners of his eyes as he smiled. "I was all googly-eyed. Goldie...not so much. She twisted that beautiful face of hers into one hell of a scowl, pinned me with those blue eyes, and said, 'Take a picture, creep. It'll last longer.' Good God, I was done for after that. I followed her out of the shop and told her I was going to marry her."

"Love at first sight—for you," Maggie said with a giggle.

"Indeed."

She watched the man who appeared momentarily adrift in the past. His story resonated deeply with her, stirring something within. A memory? Did she know of a love like this? Had she experienced something similar?

"That's how it is for Starrycard men," Rex continued, pulling her from her swirling thoughts. "When love hits, it rocks us to our core. Now, that doesn't always mean we don't muck it up before we get the girl. I had to climb a mountain in Peru and sleep in a barn with alpacas to get Goldie back."

She smiled, imagining Rex trying to sleep in a barn was both amusing and endearing. She took another sip of her drink, savoring the warmth of it. "I get the feeling you'd climb ten mountains for your wife," she replied, her voice laced with admiration.

He shifted in his seat. "Not with these old hips. But when I was a younger man, back when I fell ass over elbow in love with the woman, yes." He leaned in, green eyes twinkling. "But thank Christ, it was only one."

She laughed, enjoying his company. But it was more than that —an odd inkling and a strange familiarity she couldn't quite place. Could it be a locked-away memory? She wasn't sure. Whatever it was, though, it brought her peace.

"Like I said, Christian is a unique mix of Starrycard and Donnelly," the man continued. "When he decides what he wants, there's no stopping him. No matter how great the dream. He wanted to become a major league ballplayer—lots of children do. But even when he was a knobby-kneed kid, I knew he'd make it happen. He's got a tattoo. It says, *give what you love everything you've got.*"

She gestured toward the mountain lion's tooth. "From Seamus."

"That's right. But I was worried he'd be lost to his regrets, to his demons. But after talking with you, Maggie, I agree with you. I believe fate brought you here, and maybe even a wish written on Starrycard Creek paper."

"McKenzie and Goldie's wish? McKenzie mentioned the wishing wall paper."

"Perhaps, but I was talking about my wish for Christian. He'd dreamed of becoming a major league ballplayer, and he made it come true. My wish for him was that his life of dreaming big didn't have to end. My wish was for him to have another dream come true."

Wow.

Rex couldn't have known about Christian's actual dreams—dreams of her. Still, it felt like a sign.

"I want that for him, too. I want it very much," she said softly, her heart swelling with emotion. She wanted to tell Rex about how his grandson made her feel like the center of his world. She wanted to thank him for helping to shape the man who loved her wholeheartedly, without games or doubt. She wanted to declare Christian the love of her life, but she wasn't ready to speak those words—not before she said them to him. She exhaled a slow breath, and instead of revealing her feelings, she slid the plate toward him. "Try the pie. Pie always makes everything better."

Rex looked at her, almost as if he could read her mind. He smiled a whisper of a grin, then picked up the fork and took a bite. The man's pensive expression vanished. His bushy eyebrows shot toward his hairline. "I've never tasted anything like it," he remarked, inhaling another heaping forkful.

"It's ricotta pumpkin pie," she said, pleased at his reaction.

"Maggie, this is spectacular," Rex gushed, heartily tucking into the slice.

"You're letting this old loafer eat pie while we exercise?" Judge Ironside balked as he headed toward them with Christian and two others in tow.

Rex finished his last bite and gestured to the lot. "Maggie, you know cranky old Ironside. May I introduce cranky old Judge Wolcott and old Judge Haynes—still cranky, but the least cranky of this bunch of senile codgers."

"Takes one cranky old bastard to know a cranky old bastard," Ironside tossed back with a twitch of a grin. "Wolcott, Haynes," the man continued, "this is the pie lady and possible felon, Maggie, last name to be determined."

She had to hold back her laughter.

The men were a riot.

With his tall, slender frame and neatly combed silver hair, Judge Wolcott wore glasses that gave him an air of authority. Judge Haynes appeared to be his counter. The man was round and bald, his tanned face lined with wrinkles. His gray mustache twitched as he smiled, and his kind brown eyes radiated warmth.

"You're judges, and you bake?" Maggie asked, standing to shake the men's hands.

"Does one preclude the other?" Wolcott pressed, narrowing his gaze.

Yikes!

Her mouth flapped like a flounder. "No, sir, I'm delighted to meet you and welcome you as a baker."

"And this must be Maggie—the mystery woman of Starrycard Creek," said a young man with a rich Italian accent, flashing a wide grin as he jogged into the kitchen, his olive skin smooth and glowing.

She couldn't help but do a double take. Despite the cool fall day, when everyone else was wearing track pants, this man wore the tiniest neon orange shorts she had ever seen. His thighs bulged from the spandex like overstuffed sausages about to burst. Before she could blink, he took her hand and kissed her knuckles.

"Um...hello," she said, not sure of how to react to the exuberant man. She caught Christian's gaze, and he scowled, clearly not amused.

"I am Nico Romano," the man wearing tiny shorts cooed.

"Are you part of the culinary club?" she asked. The guy had to be closer to Christian's age—a good fifty years younger than the other three members.

"Nico's not in the culinary club. Nico drove us here. He's been teaching the mobility class at the senior center until they find a permanent instructor," Ironside explained.

"Unfortunately, I cannot stay. I must leave Starrycard Creek immediately. My flight to Italy departs in a few hours," Nico added.

"I hope everything is all right," she said, trying to focus on the guy, but those shorts were something else.

"It is a joyous occasion. My sister had a baby, and I am a *zio*, an uncle. But I always have a moment to savor the beauty and alluring magnetism that you, Mystery Maggie, exude."

She chewed her lip. *Was this a joke?* "Well, congratulations on becoming an uncle."

"Yeah, you'll love it, man. Let me get the door for you," Christian said, his gaze laser-focused on her hand clasped inside Nico's.

"Not yet, Christian Starrycard," Nico replied, tightening his hold. "I smell something. Is that ricotta cheese?"

"It is. I baked a ricotta pumpkin pie."

The man dropped to his knees as if he were about to propose. "You look like an angel, and you bake pies with cheese from my homeland!"

"Yeah…what a coincidence," she said, still not sure if this guy was for real.

"If I did not have to leave, I would invite you to dinner to tell you about how I learned to make ricotta cheese with my grandfather in a Tuscan village from the milk of the goats that roam the countryside."

Christian cleared his throat, a blush rising from his neck. "Gotta save that gem of a story for another day, Nico. We don't want you to miss your flight, and you can let go of Maggie's hand, like right fucking now."

Nico grinned, undeterred and quite oblivious to Christian's discomfort. "But it is a beautiful hand, Christian Starrycard. A strong, slim hand that must be celebrated. If we were in my village, it would be very good for gripping a goat's—"

Grrrrr.

Maggie gasped. Was Christian growling?

No, it was Lucky, or maybe both Christian and the dog were growling.

Lucky bounded into the room, baring his teeth. The dog locked onto Nico and sprinted straight toward him.

Grrrr. Woof, woof, woof!

"Atta boy," Christian mumbled under his breath.

She tossed a chiding look his way. Nico was harmless. Christian had to know that.

"Lucky, we don't growl at our guests," she said sternly, eyeing the pup and hoping Christian would get the message, too.

Nico released her hand and took a step back. "*Aspetta un attimo!* Hold on a second. I remember you, Lucky the Dog."

What?

"You know this dog?" she asked as she stroked the pup's head.

"I do. I was on one of my forty-mile kayaking and twenty-mile run workouts. I like to head south this time of year. You see, *bella,* I supervise the watersports program here in Starrycard Creek, and that requires I remain in peak physical condition, as you can observe from my well-defined calves and thighs."

"We get it, man. We can see your definition. How do you know Lucky?" Christian pressed.

"Did you see the dog when you were out exercising?" she asked.

Nico's expression grew somber. "Yes, a terrible story. I was far from Starrycard Creek when a car pulled over. It kept rolling, and then the person inside pushed the dog out. The poor animal hit its head on a large rock and started bleeding. Then the car sped off. It was an older car. I got a picture, but the quality is poor. The plate said *boned her.*"

"*Boned her?*" Christian repeated.

Maggie caught his gaze, a silent question passing between them. Clearly, something had been lost in translation.

"Yes, here is the picture. Unfortunately, it is blurred because I was running while I took it," the man said, holding out his phone. The image revealed a blur of red with a *B* and an *O* on the plate— the only readable letters.

"Oh, Lucky, you're safe now," she said, kissing the pup's head above his little scar.

"Hey, boy, we've got you," Christian added, coming to the dog's side and scratching between his ears as she continued to pat his back.

Nico tried to pet Lucky, but the dog rebuffed him with a sharp woof. Nico raised his hands defensively. "I'm no threat to you, Lucky. I see you have your people now, and they care deeply for you."

"We do," she said.

"Yeah, we do. Absolutely," Christian agreed.

"I tried to catch the frightened pup," Nico explained, his voice tinged with concern. "That's when I saw his name on the collar. But he ran, and I lost him in the woods."

Her heart ached at the thought of the poor, scared dog. She looked down at Lucky and gently stroked his head. "He was unwanted," she said softly, her voice barely above a whisper.

Nico nodded. "Yes, sadly, that appears to be the case."

Her breath caught in her throat, overwhelmed by the idea of anyone not wanting such a sweet creature. "Well, you are so very wanted here," she said to the pup.

"Starrycard Creek is your home," Christian added, lifting his gaze from Lucky to lock onto hers. "It will always be your home."

Tears pricked Maggie's eyes as a wave of gratitude and love washed over her, the emotions almost too much to contain.

Before she could respond, Ironside's voice cut through the emotion, his tone stern. "And Starrycard Creek also needs to become the home of the winners of Donnelly Days pie-making contest."

"Of course," she replied, giving Lucky one last pat on the head, and then stood.

"You need to get to your baking, and I must be off," Nico announced. "Goodbye, my mobility friends," he said to the judges, then pegged her with his gaze. "Until we meet again, Mystery Maggie." He reached for her hand, but Lucky's low, menacing growl returned. "Lucky doesn't appear to want to share you," Nico said, taking a few steps back.

"Damn right, he doesn't," Christian said under his breath.

"What was that, Christian Starrycard? Did you say something?" Nico asked warmly.

"Door's right this way," Christian said, leading the man toward the front of the house.

"Let's get to work," Judge Ironside barked. "I know you said my bourbon pumpkin pie wasn't a winner, but I thought if we tweaked a few ingredients, it could be our ticket to beating the Dennison seniors and taking first place."

Maggie shook her head. "No, we need to start fresh," she said firmly. "But first, we're having pie for dinner. Pie makes everything better, and you should never bake on an empty stomach. Also, we're eating at the island, and we're standing."

Ironside balked. "You want us to stand and eat pie?"

She smoothed her apron and rested her fists on her hips. "You're in charge in the courtroom, Judge. But in the kitchen, I'm the boss. And if you want to indulge in Stumble Juice and come up with a winning recipe, you'll join me here," she said, taking the Mason jar from the kitchen table and placing it squarely on the island. "This is the heart of the kitchen. This is where the baking magic will happen."

Ironside glanced between Haynes and Wolcott, then leaned in slightly, lowering his voice as if sharing a secret. "I told you. She's a real ballbuster when it comes to pie."

She caught the mischievous glint in his eye and couldn't help but smile at the comment. Judge Wolcott, however, seemed to take it in stride, resting his hands on the island. "Are you sure you're not a judge, Maggie? You have the temperament," he remarked, his tone light but with a hint of seriousness.

She shook her head and chuckled. "I don't think so, sir. The only things that have come back to me are pie recipes."

Judge Haynes tilted his head, curiosity in his eyes. "You really do have amnesia?" he asked, his voice softening as if he hadn't fully grasped the extent of her situation.

"Yes, but it doesn't seem to have affected my ability to bake and recall pie recipes. I've filled nearly an entire notebook with them."

Haynes frowned, his bushy mustache twitching with discontent. "And we really have to stand?" he pressed, his pout becoming more pronounced.

She set the rest of the pies on the island, carefully arranging them before turning back to the judges. "Just to eat. Then you're welcome to sit on one of the stools."

Wolcott raised an eyebrow, clearly intrigued. "Why?" he asked, his tone a mix of curiosity and skepticism.

She paused. "I have a hunch that standing and eating will help us," she said, unsure of why it felt important, but trusting her instinct that it was a necessary part of the process.

Christian returned to the kitchen and patted Haynes on his back. "A little standing will do you good, Judge. And you need to walk at least twenty minutes a day to build up strength in your ankles."

"Pie for dinner. That's marvelous," Rex boomed. "But if Goldie asks, I had a kale salad with extra kale and a side of kale. And let's hit the hooch."

"The pies do look delicious," Haynes said, his gaze dancing over the freshly baked pies.

Christian came up behind her and pressed his hand to her back. "You handle the pie, TBD, and I'll take care of the Stumble Juice. Does that work?"

"Deal," she said as his hand lingered. She looked into his eyes, wondering how she'd lived her life without this man.

At ease in the kitchen, she cut the pie and served everyone a slice. "We'll start with the ricotta pumpkin pie. Take note of the crust. I used your recipe with the ground piñon nuts."

She watched with bated breath as they took their first bites.

"Damn, this is good pie," Wolcott exclaimed, breaking his stern character.

"I agree, and I'm ready for seconds," Haynes chimed, seeming to forget about his issue with standing.

"Let's get everyone started with a little Starrycard Creek moonshine," Christian said, serving up generous portions.

"I wonder if this ricotta pumpkin pie could win us the blue ribbon," Ironside mused, taking a break from pie consumption to drink his Stumble Juice.

Maggie eyed the last slice of pie on the antique ivory pie plate. "It's a solid recipe, and the flavors are spot-on, but I don't feel that it could win."

"Pie gives you a feeling?" Haynes asked, curiosity dancing in his dark eyes.

She cut a slice of the espresso pumpkin pie and set it onto Judge Haynes's empty plate. "Oddly, it does. Unfortunately, none of the recipes I've remembered feel right for this competition. We're missing something." She peered at the array of pies and drummed her fingers on the table.

"What are you thinking, Maggie?" Christian asked as he added another splash of Stumble Juice to the men's glasses.

She retrieved her notebook, turned it to a fresh page, and studied the judges. "Do you mind me asking how you gentlemen started baking pies?"

Wolcott looked between the men, then held up his tumbler. "Stumble Juice."

"Stumble Juice? I wasn't expecting that," she replied, jotting the name of the moonshine on the blank page.

"This story goes back generations. You'll need to refresh our glasses, Christian," Judge Ironside said, his cheeks growing rosy from the alcohol.

"Coming up," Christian replied, attending to the men's tumblers.

Judge Ironside held up the glass and concentrated on the moonshine. "Our grandparents and our late wives' grandparents had an interesting relationship with Nathan and Delilah Starrycard during Prohibition."

"Define interesting?" Christian said, settling in beside her.

A sly twitch of a grin graced Ironside's lips. "The *illegal* kind of interesting," Ironside replied, catching Rex's eye.

"What?" Christian balked.

Maggie leaned forward. "This just got very interesting."

"Nathan and Delilah produced and shared the Stumble Juice with others during Prohibition. I know that. Was there a coordinated operation to distribute it?" Christian asked, looking to his grandfather.

"We keep this quiet. But yes, there was, my boy," Rex answered, helping himself to another splash of moonshine.

"How did it work?" Christian asked, wide-eyed.

A devilish glint twinkled in Wolcott's eyes. "Our grandfathers and our wives' grandfathers were bootleggers and..." He looked to Haynes.

"Judges in the surrounding counties," the rotund man supplied, rosy-cheeked like the rest of the group.

"They were judges breaking the law?" Maggie asked.

Ironside nodded. "It was the twenties and early thirties, and this was a much wilder West back then, young lady—or at least, that's how my grandparents would tell the story."

"Mine, too," Rex chimed.

"Mind you," Haynes added, "these old-timers—that you're forcing to stand and eat pie—were born in the forties, so some of the folklore may have been embellished when it was shared with us."

"Let's hear it," Maggie said, her voice tinged with excitement.

Ironside's stern expression softened. "I wasn't kidding about it being the Wild West. Many unsavory characters were trying to control the flow of moonshine into Colorado—men willing to murder and bribe to keep their operations running."

Wolcott nodded. "Our grandfathers believed that if they

oversaw the import of moonshine into their counties, that would keep out criminals looking to expand their enterprise."

Maggie served each man another slice of pie. "How did you move it?"

"Paper," Rex supplied.

Ironside nodded. "Counties need paper to function, and even back in the twenties and thirties, everyone knew Starrycard Creek was the place for that. It was the perfect cover."

"No one suspected anything?" Christian asked.

"There was nothing to suspect," Wolcott answered. "They completed the transactions during family vacations. Our grandfathers were commended for picking up the paper and envelopes the county offices needed while they were on holiday with their children and spouses."

"What looked like an innocent gathering of friends and families coming together a few times a year to pick up paper supplies was an operation to quietly get the Stumble Juice out of Starrycard Creek without attracting attention," Ironside added.

"And they took it another step further," Haynes continued. "They'd come during Starrycard Creek festivals and take part in the activities. Our grandmothers and mothers would always enter the pie-making contest during Donnelly Days."

"So, your grandmothers and mothers were bakers," Maggie repeated, fascinated with the people and their history.

"Indeed, they were," Ironside agreed through a bite of pie.

"And…felons," Maggie teased, earning her a cheeky grin from the man.

"When Prohibition was repealed," Ironside said, wiping the corners of his mouth, "the bootlegging part of our grandparents' lives ended. But our families continued to meet up in Starrycard Creek, and it's how we met and fell in love with our wives."

"What a story," Maggie said, a warmth enveloping her.

"Look at that, Ironside. You've made her starry-eyed," Rex observed.

Judge Ironside removed an old photo from his wallet and

passed it to her. "That's me with my wife, Bess. Old Wolly with Meaghan, and Haynes standing beside Cynthia. Our wives continued the tradition of entering the pumpkin pie-making contest. They were excellent bakers."

"Our wives worked as a team and had several titles under their belt," Wolcott explained. "But we weren't much help with the baking back then."

"Better at eating," the rotund Judge Haynes said, patting his belly.

Maggie took in the image of the younger versions of the judges and their lovely, smiling wives.

"A little over a decade ago, we became widowers within a few months of each other," Ironside said, his expression hardening.

Maggie passed the photo back to the man. "That must have been difficult."

"It was. We lost touch. Our wives were the ones who made sure we weren't hermits. But five years ago, we turned up in Starrycard Creek for Donnelly Days," Judge Haynes explained.

"We took it as a sign," Wolcott added.

"People do that a lot around here," Rex said, signaling for Christian to freshen the glasses.

"We ran into Rex, and he hooked us up with some Stumble Juice. He told us that you'd started making it, Christian. After getting well and truly drunk, we decided we'd honor our gals and start entering the contest. Haynes and I moved to the area, and old Ironside just got himself a place in town," Wolcott continued.

Haynes took a bite and hummed his satisfaction. "Baking makes us feel closer to them."

"And that's why we have to win. This year, the contest falls on what would have been my sixtieth wedding anniversary with Bess. But those Dennison seniors are sneaky bastards," Ironside grumbled.

"Crustgate," Wolcott added, jaw tight.

"Crustgate? I don't understand," Maggie said, sharing a look with an equally perplexed Christian.

"We're pretty damned sure the Dennison seniors used store-bought pie crust while claiming they were homemade," Ironside answered.

"And let's not forget the infamous sugar switch-a-roo incident, where they replaced our high-quality cane sugar with some cheap artificial sweetener. They've got a knack for these underhanded tricks," Judge Wolcott hissed.

Haynes finished off his tumbler of moonshine. "Or you bought the wrong sugar, Wolly."

Wolcott's glasses slipped to the tip of his nose. "Never, Haynsey! It had to be them."

"They're always up to some shenanigans, whether it's adding extra decorations to their pies after the judging starts or having a professional baker 'consult' on their entry. This year, we've got to win for Bess," Ironside added, conviction coating his slightly slurred words.

It was time to ease up on the hooch.

"Then we'll win," she said, holding the man's gaze.

"How?" Judge Haynes asked, his expression a perfect match to the other judges' gloomy faces.

Oh, no! This would not do.

"Gentlemen," she said forcefully, channeling something peculiar, but it felt right. "It does us no good for you to be a bunch of Mister...Mister Cry-In-Your-Pies. Our pie entry needs to be unique. It must evoke this place and your history. And we need something no one else, not even the sneaky bastards in Dennison, can replicate." She eyed her judges. They required more—a rallying battle cry. She might as well take advantage of their boozy state. "Come on, fellas! Can I get a hell, yes, we're gonna do this for Bess?"

For a long, nerve-wracking beat, the judges stared at her.

"Hell, yes!" the tipsy judges finally cheered, clinking their glasses. "Let's crush those sneaky bastards for Bess!" they whooped with Rex getting in on the toast as the men continued their rallying cries.

With a heart full of relief, she smiled amid the excitement and as if something on the wind was calling. She looked out the window. Dusk had given way to a clear, dark sky dotted with a sea of stars. She sighed deeply, observing the beauty, then let her gaze settle on Judge Ironside's photo, still resting on the counter. And that's when it hit. "That's it," she whispered, the relief in her heart turning to euphoria.

"TBD," Christian said softly, keeping his voice low beneath the seniors' chatter, "what's brewing in that pretty little head of yours?"

"I've got it, Christian," she replied, her voice brimming with conviction. "I figured out the recipe. I know exactly how we're going to win."

Seventeen

MAGGIE

"THE WAIT IS ALMOST OVER! We have twenty-two minutes until the pies will be cooled and ready to gobble up. Twenty-two minutes until pie time, everybody!" McKenzie exclaimed, wearing the pink Maggie apron and holding a ticking kitchen timer above her head as she marched through the tangle of Starrycards talking and laughing in the ranch house's cavernous lobby-living room.

And what brought a gaggle of Starrycards to the Donnelly Ranch?

The promise of pie and moonshine.

Christian's grandfather had called Goldie to let her know he'd be returning late just as the pies went in the oven. He'd also mentioned eating pie for dinner and indulging in a sip or two—quite an understatement—of Stumble Juice. Christian said that this was the event that triggered the Starrycard group chat to mobilize. Not ten minutes later, the first round of Starrycards arrived—and eagerly indulged in the moonshine. But the pies she'd made earlier in the day weren't enough for the large group, so she'd sprang into action, organizing a spread of snacks and finger foods to munch on. A charcuterie board felt like the ideal solution, and Christian's family couldn't stop raving about the food and knocking back tumblers of moonshine, and little McKenzie was doing her part draining their supply of lemonade.

And it was nearly time to sample their pie—the pie she and the judges had crafted.

"Twenty-two minutes, my little lovelies," she said gently as she inspected the pies cooling on the island. She couldn't help but smile. Her pie-loving heart was hopeful.

The crust was golden brown with a slight sheen.

Perfect.

The edges were crimped and held their shape.

Spot-on.

The deep orange filling was smooth and a touch glossy. The fall color peeked out from behind the golden-brown pie crust cutouts she'd placed on top—a last-minute idea, but, in her opinion, the finishing touch.

She closed her eyes and inhaled. The cinnamon and nutmeg mingled with the earthy richness of pumpkin, but there was a subtle fragrance just beneath. They'd captured a malty sweetness, and there was no denying the caramel-honeyed notes. The full bouquet of scents was enticing and comforting, complex yet harmonious, and soon, she'd know if the experimental recipe tasted like a winner. "Pie makes everything better, and I have a feeling that you are exactly the pies we need to win for Bess," she whispered, then checked her notebook, going over the measurements.

"Are you talking to the pies, TBD?" Christian asked, coming up behind her.

She glanced back at him. "Yes, is that strange?"

"Nah, I used to talk to my bat."

"What would you say?"

He struck a batter's stance. "I'd say, 'Let's smash the fuck out of that ball.'"

She chuckled and looked from one pie to the other. "I don't think that works in this case."

"Probably not. I sure as hell don't want to smash these beauties. They're works of art. You're amazing, Maggie. You're truly talented," he said and pressed a kiss to the top of her head.

She inhaled a sharp breath and glanced around the kitchen, making sure they were alone. "Christian, you shouldn't do that."

"Everyone is too busy and too tipsy to notice."

Suddenly, loud whoops and laughter erupted from the living room, the sound crashing through the moment like a wave. She jumped, her heart pounding.

"Don't worry. That's not for us. No one can see us. My family started a round of hot potato with the couch cushions. And my dad's playing DJ, which is always a dicey prospect. His taste in music is questionable," Christian said as the beat dropped, and a low thumping bass drifted in from the other room. "But as much as I'd love to tell them and let the world know I've fallen in love with the kindest—*and sexiest*—little pie maker on the planet, this may not be the time."

Her heart fluttered as uncertainty mingled with a thrilling sense of joy. "You're serious? You considered telling them now?"

"Yes. It's all I can think about. I don't want to hide my feelings for you, and I sure as hell don't want people thinking of you as just the housekeeper. Maggie, with every minute that passes, I fall more in love with you."

This man.

"Will you tell them about your dreams?"

He brushed his fingertips down her jawline. "I'd worried they'd think I was crazy, but if you can't tell, everyone in my family is crazy, and they're crazy about you."

"They've been so kind and welcoming," she said, feeling an overwhelming sense of belonging.

As the stream of Starrycards had entered the house a couple of hours ago, they'd greeted her warmly—like she was family. But she'd lost track of their names between keeping an eye on the baking pies and preparing snacks and drinks.

He took her hand and led her to the fridge. "It's simply impossible not to love you. I want you right here with me. Always."

"You want me to stand next to your refrigerator? Has your Stumble Juice consumption scrambled your brain?" she teased.

"I haven't had a drop. Somebody has to make sure these lunatics stay in line." He glanced into the living room, then opened the fridge door, blocking anyone's view of them. "I've been wanting to do this all night," he said, gripping her ass in his strong hands as he pressed his lips to hers.

She sighed, melting into his embrace, and wrapped her arms around his neck. Kissing this man with the scent of cooling pumpkin pie in the air and the hum of joyful conversation and music in the background sent a heady rush of bliss through her body.

"You belong with me. I've never loved anyone or anything like I love you," he whispered between kisses, his voice a soft caress. His lips moved with a gentle reverence. He loved her with such ease and such certainty. It filled the empty parts of her heart, the parts left vacant by her memory loss.

She pulled back, her hands gently resting on his chest as she held Christian's gaze. In his deep green eyes, she saw not just her present but every hope she had for the future. Her breath caught as the realization settled in her heart. "I love this life, and I love you," she whispered, her voice fragile yet filled with the weight of every unsaid word. The words spilled out, finally free.

His lips curled into that familiar half-smile that always made her weak in the knees. But this time, there was something more—something deeper. "You love me, TBD? You haven't said the words," he said softly, his gaze unwavering, as if her response held the key to everything.

"With all my heart," she breathed, her eyes brimming with emotion she could no longer hold back.

His grin deepened, eyes darkening. He leaned in closer, his voice dropping to that low, commanding rasp that never failed to make her breath hitch and her core tighten. "You've made me the happiest man on the planet. And…"

"And?" she purred.

"I'd like you to do something for me."

A shiver of anticipation raced down her spine as she gazed up at him. "What would you like me to do, Number Eleven?"

"Once we're alone, I want you in my college jersey, whispering how much you love me while I drive you to the edge over and over until we're both soaked in sweat and too spent to move." He tipped up her chin and leaned in. "That is exactly what I want."

Her blush may become a perma-blush to match her perma-horny brain.

"I believe I can accommodate that request for the man I love," she said, breathless, her body trembling beneath his touch. She sighed. "A girl could get used to a life with a man promising endless orgasms. You're kind of a dream come true."

"*You* are my dream come true, TBD," he replied, his voice heavy with emotion, the sincerity of his conviction evident in every word.

"TB…what?" McKenzie asked.

Maggie gasped as Christian released her ass mere seconds before McKenzie peered around the refrigerator door.

"TBD. It means to be determined," Christian explained.

Maggie pulled two root beers from the fridge, using them as a cover for why she and Christian were standing there. "They called me Maggie TBD at the hospital since they don't know my last name."

"What are you doing in the kitchen, Kenz?" Christian asked, eyeing his niece as he closed the refrigerator door.

McKenzie held the timer in one hand while she hid her other hand behind her back. "Hot potato ended, and I wanted to let Maggie know we've got sixteen minutes left." The child eyed the timer. "Do we have to wait the whole two hours for the pies to cool before we eat them?"

"We do. But it's worth the wait. It allows the filling to set and makes the pie even more delicious. And you are an excellent assistant. You're doing a spectacular job keeping tabs on the pie-cooling countdown. And my old apron suits you. You should keep it."

McKenzie beamed. "Thanks, Maggie! I wore it to school today, and I told everybody that I didn't change my name to Maggie. I said, 'Maggie is my uncle's housekeeper, and her brain doesn't remember anything because she hit her head on a railroad track.' And then I missed a bunch of math problems because I was talking to Logan Laughlin, and I told Ms. Higgins, my teacher and my almost aunt, that I bumped my head on the monkey bars and maybe my brain forgot how to do math. And then, after school, I told my mom that my brain forgot how to unload the dishwasher, but she said my brain better remember fast, or I wouldn't earn my allowance for the week. Oh, and everybody in the living room needs more Stumble Juice."

Maggie looked to Christian to dissect the child's word salad.

"I got this," he said, then turned to McKenzie. "Pay attention in class, Kenz. And no talking to boys. Ignore them until you're thirty. Be careful on the monkey bars. Do your chores. And tell everyone I'll be out with drinks in a second."

"Okay, Uncle Chris," she chimed and skipped away with the timer and what looked like a cell phone behind her back.

Maggie shot the man a wary look. "No talking to boys until she's thirty?"

"Too young? Should I have gone forty?" he teased, his voice brimming with mock seriousness.

She shook her head, then glanced into the living room where their guests were enthusiastically building a pillow tower. "We might want to monitor how much they're drinking."

Christian chuckled. "We might be past that point."

"Chris, we could use some refills," Rex called.

"Sure thing, Grandpa. Let me get another jar."

"You're not getting them more, are you?" she asked, watching the adults stand around the wobbly tower as one of Chris's brothers called out building instructions.

"Oh, hell no," he said, filling an empty Mason jar with iced tea as his mother, Maeve, sailed into the kitchen with a tumbler and an empty plate.

"I have a feeling you're cutting off your grandfather, which is well advised, but your mother, *the mayor*, could use a bit more," the woman said sweetly, holding up her glass.

Christian grimaced. "Mom, are you sure?"

"I birthed you, little star. I was in labor for twenty-nine hours. And as the elected head of this town, it's the law to serve the mayor as much Stumble Juice as she requires," Maeve answered, her movements loose and carefree.

"Mother Mayor, I'm pretty sure that law doesn't exist."

Maeve lifted an eyebrow, and just like that, it was clear she commanded the room.

That's where Christian must get it.

"Let's get you topped off, Mom," he said, choosing a Mason jar containing the moonshine.

Maeve took a sip, smiled, and then eyed the spread on the island. "Maggie, you have outdone yourself," she gushed, adding a few items from the charcuterie board to her plate.

"It's nothing. I threw together some things we picked up at the farmer's market."

"Honey, five different kinds of cheeses, four different types of crackers, roasted butternut squash, charred Brussels sprouts, honey-glazed ginger carrot sticks, and seasoned beet slices is *not* nothing," Goldie said, joining them as she entered the kitchen, sipping on Stumble Juice.

"Don't forget the sliced prosciutto, salami, and chorizo. And Maggie put this together in a flash while keeping an eye on the pies," Christian added, pride written on his face.

"I enjoy doing it." She gazed into his eyes, a gentle heat rising to her cheeks. This man had become a master at making her blush, but she had others watching.

Maeve and Goldie exchanged a glance, sly smirks blooming on their lips.

Maggie cleared her throat and looked away. She could not get swept up in ogling Christian in front of his family.

"Izzy and Hailey tell me you made the hummus from scratch. It's phenomenal," Maeve continued, adding another dollop and a few crackers to her plate.

"Goldie, Grandma Maeve, come watch," McKenzie called. "Great Grandpa Rex said he can do a headstand."

"No, no, no! Not with his bad back and wonky hips, he isn't," Goldie exclaimed, shaking her head and laughing as she and Maeve hurried to the living room.

Maggie's grin grew as she took in the family's lively chaos.

Christian rested his hand on her back and made slow circles. "I'm sorry about my family. I had no idea that my grandpa calling my grandmother would lead to this."

She drank in the laughter from the living room. "Help me out with everyone's names. They told me, but it's all a blur."

"*It's all a blur* should be the Starrycard family's tagline," Christian joked. "You ready? We'll go from left to right."

She leaned into him. It was safe to do so. No one was watching them. All eyes were on Rex as everyone attempted to convince him to remain standing on his feet, not balancing on his head. She sighed and rested against Christian's chest, loving the sturdy solidness of his body. "I'm ready."

"We've got my brother, Finn, and Hailey. She's the redhead."

Maggie nodded. "They're the engaged couple?"

"Yes."

"Okay. Keep going."

"My oldest brother Kieran and his wife Izzy are next to them."

"She's the one who likes cake, right?"

"You got it."

"Moving on, there's my sister, Eliza, her husband, Jack, and you know Kenz. Keeping it going, my mom, Maeve the mayor—and she won't let you forget it—is standing beside my dad, Hank," he said, pointing to the man dropping some serious dance moves.

"He's a papermaker and a dancer?" she asked.

"Sweet Jesus, never tell my dad you think he's a dancer. It'll only encourage him."

"All right," she giggled.

"You know the judges. And you know my grandmother and grandfather."

"I've got it. But this isn't the whole group. We're missing Owen."

"Yeah, he gets a little obsessive about work and art. He's got a project going in his studio, but he sure as hell won't let any of us see it."

"Like you and your distilling room."

He chuckled. "Yes, sometimes I forget how alike we all are."

"And Caroline. She's not in Starrycard Creek."

"No, no! I'm here," came a light, bubbly voice.

Maggie turned abruptly and spotted McKenzie with the timer in one hand and a cell phone in the other.

"I've got Caroline on a video call. She and I are being super spies," McKenzie said, grinning ear to ear. "We've been watching you cuddle in the kitchen."

"We're not cuddling. Maggie was…"

"Chilled. I was chilled," Maggie blurted out.

"Is that what the kids are calling it?" Caroline crooned.

"Care, give it a rest, and Kenz, I just saw you in the lobby," Christian said, frowning.

"I'm fast like that. And super-sneaky. Isn't that right, Auntie Care?" the little girl said, eyes dancing with mischief.

"Super-duper sneaky, Kenz. You are the queen of sneak. Turn the phone so I can see your uncle and Maggie," Caroline requested. McKenzie complied, and the smiling woman on the screen waved. "Hi, Maggie! Hi, Turd Burger!" Caroline chimed. "Oh, and Kenz?"

"Uh-huh."

"Don't say turd burger. You're not old enough yet. When you're twelve, you can call people turd burgers all you want."

"Caroline," Christian chided.

"Got it, Aunt Care. Turd Burger is a twelve-year-old word," McKenzie replied with a resolute nod.

"How are the pies coming, Maggie?" Caroline continued.

"We'll see. We don't have much longer to wait."

Caroline nodded. Christian's little sister, who looked much like their mother and older sister, was lovely with her green, cat-like eyes, curious expression, and brown hair draping past her shoulders. "And it looks like you're getting the full Starrycard experience tonight."

"It sure seems like it."

"Well, I can't wait to meet you when I come back for Christmas. McKenzie's been singing your praises. Do you think you'll still be *working* for Chris in December?" Caroline's question had an underlying spark, as if she knew more than she let on.

How much had she and McKenzie seen?

Maggie glanced at her *employer*, trying to keep it professional, but she couldn't help but grin as her gaze locked with his. "I think I'll still be around."

"In some capacity," Christian added with a teasing smirk.

"Okay," Caroline answered. "Thanks for keeping my turd burger brother in line. And do not believe him if he tells you that you have the power of invisibility."

"Noted," Maggie said, enjoying Caroline's snarky attitude—a Starrycard trait.

McKenzie turned the phone so she could be in the frame. "Auntie Care, do you want to see the pies? We've got eight minutes before they're ready to eat."

"I could look at pie all day, little star. Video pie me!"

McKenzie climbed onto a barstool and held out her phone. "My favorite part is the little stars covering the top," the child said, chattering away with her aunt.

Christian ran his hands through his hair and exhaled an audible breath. "Every storm passes—except for this one. I'm stuck with these people. Sorry, TBD."

"Why are you sorry?"

"I didn't expect you to have to endure a Starrycard baptism by fire so soon—and a Caroline video call."

She glanced at McKenzie and then into the lobby, her heart swelling with joy. "I love this."

"Yeah?" he asked with such warmth in his eyes that it made her tear up.

She blinked away the happy tears. "Yeah," she replied as the bass boomed, and the hip-hop song "Jump Around" echoed through the cavernous room.

"Gotta go, Aunt Care!" McKenzie exclaimed. "Grandpa Hank is playing our favorite song. It's dance party time."

"Dance party time?" Maggie repeated, but before Christian could answer, McKenzie took her hand and dragged her to the living room.

"It's the jump, jump song," McKenzie hollered. "Grandpa Hank and I listen to it and jump around the house." She looked over her shoulder. "Uncle Chris, can I jump on the couch?"

"Jump your heart out, Kenz," he answered.

"Make sure Maggie jumps around, too," the little girl instructed, then pounced onto a sectional.

"TBD," he said, pinning her with his penetrating gaze.

"Yes?" she answered as the lights went out, and a strobe light cast the room in pulsating flashes of electric color. Everyone cheered and hooted. The vibrant, flickering lights created a surreal, almost dreamlike setting.

Christian gestured to his mother. "You let Dad bring his strobe light?"

"There's no stopping your father when he's in party mode," Maeve answered, busting some serious moves.

Maggie turned in a slow circle, peering at the shadows on the walls as the energy in the room soared to new heights. "This is..."

"Ridiculous?" Christian supplied.

"No, it's amazing!" she exclaimed, jumping up and down, losing herself to the beat and her laughter.

Christian joined in, taking her hands as the group clumped together, hopping, jumping, bumping, swaying, and singing. She locked on to Christian's gaze, and her heart fluttered. This was more than a silly dance party. It was a glimpse of a life with the man she loved. And when she thought she might be swept away by sheer bliss, the pleasing trill of the antique kitchen timer pierced the air. Christian's father tapped his phone, and the music stopped, leaving only the metallic clatter of pulsing *ding-ding-ding-dings.*

"Pie time," the group shouted.

McKenzie led the pie-fueled stampede. Maggie brought the pies to the table. Red faced and smiling, the group gathered around, some standing, others sitting, everyone gazing at the culinary delights.

She motioned for the judges to take their seats in the chairs near her, while Christian collected plates, silverware, and napkins.

Goldie handed her a knife and winked.

Maggie nodded to the woman, then looked to the judges. "Would any of you like to make the first cut?"

"No, dear, you do the honors," a rosy-cheeked Judge Ironside answered.

"I'm glad I made two pies," she murmured, delicately slicing each pie into eight slices.

One by one, she plated each slice as Christian handed them out. Lucky wiggled in and sat under the table by her feet, and the room grew still.

She exhaled a slow breath and surveyed the expectant faces. "What you're about to sample is Stumble Juice Pumpkin Pie with a piñon nut crust. We added a swirl of pie crust stars, hand cut in an array of sizes to add to the charm and flavor. The Stumble Juice incorporated in the recipe is from November eleventh of last year. It's the eleventh batch." She held Christian's gaze for a beat, then peered at the group. "Tonight, I was honored to create these pies with some exceptional bakers and storytellers from the culinary club. I've learned so much about the history of Starrycard Creek, the people who love this town, and those who found love here. We baked these pies thinking of Judge Ironside's late wife, Bess. The day of the coming pie competition would have been their sixtieth wedding anniversary." She glanced over her shoulder at the clear night sky. "And I have a feeling that somewhere out there, beyond the stars, she's looking down on this gathering, her love for her husband and baking surrounding us all," she finished, feeling another presence, a warmth, an echo she couldn't quite make out but knew it was there to support her.

As she turned back to the table, she saw the group frozen in place. Their eyes brimmed with tears, but their faces were alight with tender smiles. She pressed her hand to her heart. "I'm sorry. Was that too much?"

Judge Ironside patted her hand. "No, Maggie, it was perfect," he said, a tear running down his weathered old cheek. He wiped it away, then donned his signature scowl. "What are you all looking at? Dig in. It's pie time," the man barked.

In a flurry of fork action, everyone took a bite of pie, and the room was swallowed in a bout of silence. The only sound, the gentle clinking of utensils.

"Is it terrible?" she asked, her voice trembling as she caught Wolcott's eye, searching for reassurance.

"Try it," the man said, his face giving nothing away.

She turned to Christian, her gaze locking with his. The love in his eyes was nearly overwhelming. Taking a deep breath, she picked up her fork, cut a sliver of pie, and let the flavors meld in her mouth. The richness of the filling, the slight honeyed bite, the mellow pumpkin harmonizing with the earthy crust—it was perfect. Tears peppered her cheeks.

"At least I'm not the only one crying," Ironside said, his voice thick with emotion.

She wiped her cheeks, relief flooding her system. "We did it. This is it. This is the recipe."

"Damn right it is, kid," Rex said, nodding approvingly.

The table erupted in enthusiastic agreement.

This is amazing!

Delicious!

I've never tasted anything like it!

Ironside held up his glass. "A toast to Maggie, our favorite felon, one hell of a pie maker, and—"

"The woman I love," Christian declared from across the table, his voice strong and steady.

Once again, a stretch of silence engulfed the room, the weight of his words hanging in the air. She held Christian's gaze, her heart pounding. *What was he doing?*

Christian's grin broke the tension, and he laughed, a light, bubbly sound that filled the room. "I told Maggie I wouldn't do this, but I can't hold back," he said, making his way to her side.

She watched him wide-eyed, her breath catching in her throat.

Christian took her hand, his touch gentle yet firm. "I love this woman," he said, his voice resonating with emotion. "I've loved her since I saw her face in my dreams, dreams that started the night I was injured. The night my baseball career ended."

Maeve's brows knitted together in confusion. "You two knew each other before Maggie showed up in Starrycard Creek?" she asked, her voice tinged with disbelief.

Christian shook his head, his gaze never leaving Maggie's. "No, I didn't know her. I didn't think she was real until I found her on the tracks trying to free Lucky."

Kieran tilted his head, his expression pensive. "You must know her from somewhere," he insisted. "There's got to be an explanation."

"Fate brought us together," Christian began, his voice ripe with conviction. "I never met Maggie before that day. I'm sure of it. I would have remembered her. But she's what kept me going when things got tough. When the pain became too much, I started having trouble sleeping. That's why I was drinking so much. I needed it to knock myself out, to fall asleep to get back to her. And then she showed up on the ranch with a train barreling toward her. When I saw her face, at first, I thought I was hallucinating. But it was her—the woman in my dreams, and I loved her. It hit like…"

"A freight train?" Hank suggested, raising an eyebrow.

"Yeah, thankfully, a metaphorical train," Christian replied, a wry smile tugging at the corners of his mouth.

Everyone chuckled softly, the light laughter weaving through the room. But it quickly died down, as if they could all sense that Christian had more to say, the gravity of the moment settling over them.

"The more time I spend with Maggie, the more our love grows. I've never known anything like this. I love her kindness and her gentle heart, and I couldn't keep that to myself any longer. Everyone at this table is important to me, and I don't want to hide my feelings for the person who's become the center of my world, my north star. I know it sounds farfetched, but this is our story. This is how I know Maggie and I are meant for each other," he said, gazing at her with such love in his eyes, she couldn't speak. All she could do was bask in his unyielding adoration.

"Farfetched?" Goldie repeated with a wry chuckle. "Little star, we're Starrycards. Farfetched love is our calling card. We believe in divine intervention, in the universe listening to the wishes people write on our paper. Love is what stopped William Starrycard in his tracks the moment he saw Fiona Donnelly. Farfetched love is the reason we're sitting at this table. We're the last people who would find anything regarding the pursuit of true love to be impossible or farfetched."

"Maggie, you're into my weird brother? Because we should warn you, he is all sorts of superstitious—like well beyond Starrycard Creek wishing wall paper superstitious," Eliza added, instantly lightening the mood and igniting the Starrycard siblings' fun-loving rambunctious side.

"Yeah, he's a real freak. Remember when he wouldn't change his socks for all of sixth grade because he thought it would be bad luck for the team?" Finn tossed out.

"Remember?" Kieran said, mock disgust lighting his neutral

demeanor. "Chris and I shared a room growing up. I still can't stomach the smell of stinky feet."

Christian blushed, but the smile on his face let her know he didn't mind the gentle ribbing.

"Or when he was a freshman in high school and only ate foods that started with the letter *B*, like *baseball*, because he thought that would ensure he'd keep hitting homers. That boy existed on birthday cake, blueberries, bananas, and bagels," Maeve added.

"I get it. Chris," Kieran's wife, Izzy, chimed. "There's nothing wrong with demanding birthday cake for every meal," she said and kissed her husband's cheek.

"And what about the year he wore his underwear backward?" Hank tossed out.

Rex slapped his hand on the table. "Or when he was little and wouldn't go anywhere without his bat?"

"I had to tuck it into bed with him," Maeve said, laughing as the family shared more anecdotes.

Maggie giggled, eating up the stories.

Christian wrapped his arm around her shoulders. "Are you guys trying to scare off the woman of my literal dreams? I know everyone's pretty tipsy, but can someone at this table say something nice about me?" Christian pleaded as he laughed.

"Do you guys remember when he peed his pants in the car when we took that family trip to Rocky Mountain City?" Finn offered up, clearly not heeding Christian's request.

"Do I remember? I was sitting next to him," Kieran replied.

"I was four years old," Christian balked. "I don't even remember doing it."

"The car smelled like urine for weeks," Hank lamented.

"Uncle Chris peed his pants?" Kenzie chirped.

"No, Kenz," Christian said, then cringed. "Okay, yes, it happened, but I was very young, and I had just downed an entire two-liter bottle of root beer because your uncle Kieran, your uncle Owen, and your uncle Finn dared me to, and my dad couldn't get me to a restroom fast enough."

"It's good you have a helicopter to get you to a potty super-fast, Uncle Chris." The child frowned, the wheels turning in her head. "Or do you pee your pants in the helicopter, too?"

McKenzie's question had the room howling with laughter.

"I sure hope you didn't pee in the pool at the senior center," Judge Wolcott mused.

"We better add a thorough pool cleaning to his tab," Ironside replied, gaining another round of roaring laughter.

"Maggie, are you sure you want Chris? He's a handful," Eliza said, laughing so hard she had tears in her eyes.

Maggie rested her hand on Christian's chest, above his heart. "I'm sure, but…"

"But?" Christian replied with mock indignation.

"I'll be careful to monitor his liquid consumption," she finished.

"Good call," Finn tossed out.

"Thanks to my loving family, you've heard it all. The good, the bad, and the ugly," Christian said, mischief twinkling in his eyes as he leaned in, his lips just a few inches from hers.

Maggie's heart fluttered, and she couldn't help but smile up at him, her gaze softening. "I'll take it all."

Before they could move any closer, Christian's mom's voice broke through the moment. "I think we've got a kiss coming, folks," she chimed.

"Kiss, kiss, kiss!" the group demanded, clapping and slapping the table in unison.

"What do you think we should do?" Christian asked.

She glanced at her hand resting on his chest, feeling the steady beat of his heart beneath her palm. "Give what you love everything you've got," she said, quoting his tattoo.

"Good answer, TBD."

The world melted away. His lips met hers with a tender sweetness that sent shivers down her spine. Her heart swelled with a love so profound it felt as if it might burst. Surrounded by the people who loved Christian the most, she felt an overwhelming sense of belonging.

He ended the kiss, drawing back as the room erupted into a rowdy round of applause.

"We need to celebrate!" Hank exclaimed.

"We've got a winning pie, and Christian and Maggie are in love," Judge Haynes added.

Finn shot to his feet. "Let's go up in the helicopter."

"Yeah, we can buzz by Dennison and let those geezers know their winning streak is over!" Judge Wolcott boomed, shaking his fist.

Judge Haynes rubbed his hands together like a mad scientist. "Yes, let's invade Dennison. We can drop pies on their senior center."

"And store-bought pie crust!" Wolcott exclaimed.

Christian crossed his arms. "Absolutely not."

"You do this for us, and I'll drop the charges. No jail time or bathroom clean-up required. Just pure pie revenge!" Ironside crooned.

"I'm pretty sure the Dennison authorities would slap me with fresh charges for reckless endangerment, and the FAA would most likely revoke my pilot's license."

"What about flour? We could sprinkle it all over town," Haynes added.

Christian maintained his serious facade, but she could sense the man was on the cusp of laughter. "No, Judge. There will be no helicopter rides tonight."

"Boo," the group lamented in unison.

"None of you are in any shape to ride in an aircraft or drive, for that matter," he said again, wrapping his arm around her.

"Everyone should spend the night. We certainly have the room," Maggie said, then tensed.

Was she taking too many liberties with Christian's home?

Christian gazed at her with such profound love in his eyes that it erased the tension. "Maggie's right. *We,*" he began, the adoration in his eyes intensifying, "would love to host you here at the ranch."

"A school night sleepover," McKenzie said through a yawn. "I only get those with Grandpa Hank and Grandma Maeve when Mommy is really stressed out and needs a night to do all the yoga with Daddy. Right, Mom?"

"Kenz…" Eliza and Jack said.

"Before I went over to Grandma and Grandpa's house last time," the child continued, "I heard you talking to Aunt Izzy, and you said, 'I will be doing ALL the yoga tonight, every which way, and in every room in the house. Jack will be *yoga-ing* my brains out until I am a pile of goo.' And then in the morning, when Grandpa Hank brings me home early, Daddy is happy and whistling, but I think that's because he's excited about putting thermometers in dog and cat butts. Remember, Maggie, I told you that's what my dad does at work?" she finished, resting her head on the table.

Wow! Even half-asleep, the child could talk.

Maggie suppressed a grin. "You did mention that."

"On that descriptive note," Jack said, scooping his daughter into his arms. "It's time for us to hit the sack. Chris, Maggie, thanks for the hospitality." He brushed a few pie crumbs from his daughter's cheek. "Say thank you, and good night, little star."

With her eyes closed, McKenzie's head lulled to the side. "Thank you, and good night, little star."

"Pick any room. They're all ready," Christian said as his family wished them goodnight and headed upstairs.

But the judges stayed put, their expressions shifting from light and lively to heavy and longing.

Judge Ironside was the first to rise to his feet. "We're not family. We should go. Christian, could you drive us back to town?"

Christian caught Maggie's eye, and she shook her head.

"No, Judge, he can't take you anywhere. You're staying with us," she said, morphing into pie ballbuster mode.

Judge Haynes stood. "We don't want to impose."

Wolcott nodded and offered a weak grin.

She recognized their expressions. In her soul, she felt their loss and loneliness. She had to make them understand that they belonged—and just as the thought sparked, words came to her. "Once you spend time with me in the kitchen, you're my family," she began, feeling a deep familiarity with the sentiment. "And with me having amnesia and not remembering anything, that makes the three of you my honorary uncles. And I have a feeling that I make a mean pancake breakfast. You surely don't want to miss that, do you?"

"With bacon?" Haynes asked, perking up.

"Yes."

Wolcott's grin reached his eyes. "And sausage?"

"We've got that, too. And eggs," Christian added, catching on to what she was doing.

"And fruit and fresh herbs and vegetables," she continued, then tapped her chin theatrically. "Maybe I'll whip up a quiche, too. A recipe just came to mind."

"And pie?" Ironside asked.

She held the man's gaze. "Always pie. Pie makes everything better."

The judge nodded, then reached out and squeezed her hand. "You've got a good heart, Maggie last name to be determined." He turned to Christian, hardening his expression. "Don't screw it up with her. She's as good as they come."

"I hear you loud and clear, sir. I know how lucky I am," Christian said softly.

Rex ambled into the kitchen, his presence a comforting interruption. "Come on, you old codgers," he called. "I'll get you settled upstairs."

She watched them leave, a soft smile on her lips as she wrapped her arms around Christian's waist and rested against his chest. "Thank you. They needed this," she whispered, her voice full of gratitude.

Christian gazed down at her, his eyes reflecting the depth of his emotions. "You are more than I even dreamed possible. I look at you and think, there's no way I could love this woman any more, and then you go and top it. And all I can do is look at you in awe."

Her cheeks warmed with a blush. "I feel like the luckiest girl in the world. Now, all we need is for our pie to win, and then we'll be home free. Charges dropped and no public toilets in our future."

"TBD?"

"Yes?" she replied, a faint smile lingering.

"Do you want to know what I feel?" Christian's tone was tender, his hand gently caressing her back, making those lazy circles she loved.

"I do," she replied, casting aside her worries about her past and lost memories. Her entire world narrowed down to the promise of a life in Starrycard Creek.

He tucked a lock of hair behind her ear. "No matter what happens on Saturday, standing here, looking into those hazel eyes that own every ounce of my being, I know one thing to be true."

Her pulse quickened. "And what's that, Number Eleven?"

He pressed a whisper-soft kiss to the corner of her mouth, his breath warm against her skin. "With you in my life, I've already won."

Eighteen

CHRISTIAN

CHRISTIAN WHISTLED as he strolled from his family's paper company to the town square, Lucky's leash in one hand and a crate of wishing wall paper scraps tucked under his arm. "Here we go, folks. More wishing wall paper," he announced, placing it on the table.

"Thanks, Mr. Starrycard! I'm wishing to be a baseball player like you," a little boy exclaimed, then frowned. "I'm sad you got hurt."

"I was sad, too, but it's good to be back in Starrycard Creek." He handed the child a scrap of paper. "Here you go. With hard work and lots of practice, I bet you'll achieve exactly what's meant for you. Dream big, kid. And could you do me a favor?"

"Anything for you!" the boy replied with a toothy grin.

Christian pulled a folded slip from his pocket. "Would you tuck this into one of the cracks in the wall? It's my wish."

"I sure will!" the boy answered excitedly, taking off toward the rock wall that followed Starrycard Creek's gentle curves.

Exchanges like that used to slice through him, but not anymore. He slipped his hand into his pocket, his fingers brushing against the lucky stone and the baseball card Maggie had with her when she arrived in Starrycard Creek, along with something else he hoped would make him even luckier.

He watched the child skip to a spot near a cluster of golden aspens and press the scraps into a gap in the rocks.

"I did it, Mr. Starrycard."

Christian gave the boy a thumbs-up, then turned his attention to the town square. Donnelly Days had started a few hours ago with the melodic rush of Starrycard Creek in the background and towering oaks and willowy aspen trees showing off their autumn colors in a sea of vibrant reds, burnt oranges, and golden yellows. The town thrummed with activity as the fragrant aroma of fresh pumpkin pie hung heady and sweet in the fall air.

It was fair to say they couldn't have gotten a better day to celebrate autumn in the mountains. The sky was a stunning shade of blue. Fluffy clouds lazily drifted across the expanse, casting soft shadows on the mountains while dry leaves crunched beneath the feet of the attendees.

Christ, it was good to be alive.

He peered across the square, and a deep sense of contentment washed over him. "There's my blushing baker," he murmured, spotting Maggie wearing her vintage apron and his green Rocky Mountain University ball cap, her strawberry-blond locks cascading over her shoulders.

Damn, she looked good in his hat. His thoughts went to last night when she wore nothing but that exact cap and his college jersey. She'd climbed on top of him, placed his cap on her head, then pressed her hands to his bare chest. The tips of his fingers tingled as he recalled palming her ass. He'd thrusted and bucked, giving her one hell of a ride until she writhed and moaned, taking every ounce of pleasure he could give her. She'd fallen asleep with his cap pressed to her heart. He'd watched her sleep, and when he'd brushed a lock of hair from her forehead, she smiled and sighed. He'd hit homers in front of crowds of thousands of people, but nothing held a candle to what it felt like to fall asleep with his dream girl in his arms.

The possessive caveman inside him wanted to beat his chest and stake his claim for all festivalgoers to see. But it was more than that. Of course, it was. He loved her. An overwhelming need to protect her and always put her first surged through his veins. He drank in the scene, watching her laugh with Hailey and Izzy as they restocked her table with fresh pies.

This was their life.

He adored her. His family loved her, and a fierce sense of pride swelled within him, watching her make sale after sale.

She deserved it.

She'd worked damned hard this week.

In addition to baking a few dozen Stumble Juice Pumpkin Pies with the judges, one of which was entered into the pie contest, she and her culinary companions had been baking machines. From peanut butter pumpkin pie to pumpkin marshmallow pie to a triple-layer beauty made with spiced pumpkin puree, cheesecake, and whipped cream, Maggie's recipes dazzled everyone who'd tasted them.

He'd probably gained ten pounds in the last seven days, but holy hell, it was worth it.

"We're living the good life, aren't we, boy?" he said to Lucky, sitting patiently by his side, watching Maggie like a hawk. "We'll make sure she's always happy, won't we?" he added, scratching the pup between his ears.

"Christian! Christian Starrycard! Can we get a few shots of you for the Rocky Mountain City Dispatch?" a man called, hurrying over with a photographer in tow.

"The Dispatch sent a reporter to cover Starrycard Creek's Donnelly Days? You don't usually cover our seasonal events," he said, pretty sure he knew why they were there. His antics in Rocky Mountain City had sold plenty of papers and earned millions of clicks online.

The reporter, a slim guy with glasses, shifted his weight. "There's interest in your life after baseball. Especially since you've had some troubles." The man pulled a small notepad and pen from his pocket. "People want to know what's become of you."

"What's become of me?" Christian mused, his gaze locking onto Maggie. She must have sensed his eyes on her. She looked up from arranging her pies, blushed that delicate shade of pink, and smiled the smile from his dreams—the smile that had become his perfect reality.

"I might have lost my way after my injury, but I'm where I'm supposed to be," he replied, returning his attention to the reporter and going into professional athlete mode. "While baseball will always be my first love, I've found a new path here at home, and it's more than I ever dreamed possible. Please let your readers know that Rocky Mountain City will always have a place in my heart. I have immense gratitude for the fans and support they've given me over the years when I was a college player under Coach Redmond and in the Major Leagues with the Rattlers."

The reporter jotted a few notes on the pad. "And you have a dog?"

"I do. This is Lucky."

"Any other additions? Anyone special in your life? A model? An actress?" the reporter pressed.

Christian couldn't suppress a grin. "Yes, there's someone, but that's off the record. I hope you understand."

"Fair enough. We appreciate your time. And on a personal note," the man continued, pocketing the notebook. "For a while there, I was worried about you. I'm glad to see you're doing well. You're still well-loved in Rocky Mountain City."

Christian nodded. And just like with the child a few minutes earlier, he wasn't burdened by the comment, wasn't dragged down by the mention of his old life. "It wasn't easy dealing with my injury, and I regret my past behavior, but I'm healing, and like I said, I'm on the right path now," he added as the photographer snapped a few shots of him and Lucky.

"Thanks for the quote, Mr. Starrycard."

"Thanks for coming out. And a word to the wise," Christian

replied, shaking the men's hands. "You don't want to leave town without picking up a pumpkin pie from the table across the square."

"The one with the pink boxes?" the reporter asked, craning his neck.

"That's the one, and then pop over and get a dozen turnovers from my grandmother's booth right next door."

"We'll check them out. Thanks for the tip."

Christian watched Maggie pass a box to a customer, then greet the men and offer them samples. Within seconds of tasting the baked goods, the photographer started snapping pictures of her and her pies as the reporter slipped his notepad and wallet from his pocket.

This was it. This was where she belonged.

"Hey, All-Star, or should we call you the King of *Floral*," Finn called, a sly smirk on his lips. Kieran and Owen flanked him, matching his swagger as the trio advanced with confident strides, clearly up to something.

Dammit, Grandpa Rex!

"How about you go fuck yourself," Christian offered, throwing a sass ball right back at his brother.

"How are your dreams? Did you dream about lottery numbers or the next big tech advance?" Owen pressed, getting in more Starrycard ribbing.

Christian surveyed his older brothers. "O, you're too busy, but Kier and Finn, you are the last two people in this town to give me shit for falling in love."

"He does have a point," Kieran replied.

Owen stared at the pie stand and shook his head.

"What is it?" Christian asked.

"It's nothing."

"Owen, do you have something against pie?" Christian pressed.

"Fuck no. I love pie. And Maggie's great. I want you to be happy."

"But?" Christian prompted, watching the artist closely. His brother had the same odd expression he'd worn when he first encountered Maggie on the tracks.

"I can't shake the feeling that she looks familiar," Owen mused. "It must be a weird artist thing. Or maybe I need more sleep."

"That's a start," Finn said, eyeing the man. "You're probably losing your mind because you never stop. If you're not in the shop, you're in your studio. You need to get out."

"I'm out right now," Owen answered, exasperation coating his words when his phone chimed. He peered at his cell. "I have to go. It's something I'm working on in my studio."

"Case in point," Kieran said as Owen pocketed his phone, issued a backward wave, and headed down the path toward his bungalow.

Finn gestured to Maggie's table. "How many pies has she sold?"

"Over forty. She's killing it. Everyone who meets her loves her and wants to buy one of her pies."

Finn chuckled. "The entire town has fallen under her magical pie spell."

"I've noticed one guy—must be a tourist—eyeing her table," Kieran said.

Christian tensed. "What guy?"

His eldest brother scanned the space. "I don't see him now. He could have been waiting for the line to ease up."

"I don't know, man," Finn said, mischief in his eyes. "Maggie's amazing. You better consider putting a ring on it and soon."

"Oh, I get it," Christian replied, watching an older gentleman gaze warmly at Maggie as she boxed up his pie. "Nico's already tried his moves on her."

Finn and Kieran exchanged a curious glance.

"Nico always tries," Kieran replied, deadpanning the comment in his robotic tone.

"Well, gentlemen, I'm one step ahead of you on the put-a-ring-on-it front, but you've got to promise to keep this between us. Mom and Dad don't know, and neither do Goldie and Grandpa Rex. I want it to be a surprise."

"We promise. What do you have up your sleeve?" Finn asked.

"It's what I've got in my pocket," Christian replied, turning away from the square. He waved in his brothers, then slipped a five-carat pear-shaped pink diamond engagement ring from his pocket.

"Christ, Christian, that's one hell of a ring. I was kidding about putting a ring on it right this second," Finn remarked, wide-eyed.

Christian admired the ring. "I'm not kidding around—not when it comes to Maggie. This girl is the one."

"The girl of your dreams," Kieran said, but there was no sarcasm in the statement. His oldest brother was on the autism spectrum, and while his reactions could often be muted, it was clear he was nothing but supportive.

Finn leaned in for a better look. "How did you get a ring like that so quickly? Pink diamonds are quite rare."

"I reached out to the jeweler who made the Rattlers' World Series championship rings, and she was able to help me out with exactly what I wanted. Being a former pro ballplayer still has some perks."

"That's wonderful news. Truly, Chris," Kieran said with the hint of a grin—an expression that spoke volumes.

"Love is something else," Christian murmured. "One minute, you think you know the exact trajectory of your life, and it's a total shitshow, and the next—"

"Some angry redhead is calling you an axe murderer, and before you blink, thanks to a business card, you've fallen in love," Finn finished.

"Or a birthday card," Kieran added, the whisper of a grin still on his lips. "Speaking of the future, what are your plans, Chris?"

Christian's pulse kicked up. *Plans?* Three months ago, the idea of the future only made him want to guzzle Stumble Juice. Now, he was brimming with ideas.

"Goldie's already asked Maggie to start baking pies for her restaurant. We'll get her set up with her own baking business, maybe rent some space if she outgrows the ranch."

Kieran nodded. "As the town manager, I can tell you that a bakery will be in high demand. The town is growing now that we're developing Starrycard Mountain. Also, our recreation programs are expanding to encompass year-round programming. We'll need someone full-time to serve as the Director of Recreation and Sports Engagement. Someone whose name—*and fame*—might come in handy attracting sponsors, programs, and qualified employees."

Christian kept his features neutral, matching his stoic brother's appearance. "Are you offering me a job, Kier?"

"I am, but it's more than a job. I'm offering you the chance to shape the town's legacy. You'd have complete control. We want Starrycard Creek to be a place where people visit year-round. We're at the helm of ensuring the prosperity of this town for our children and our children's children."

He pictured Maggie baking and building her business while he worked at town hall. He saw nights cuddled in front of the fire, evenings spent with family and friends, Maggie in his hat and jersey smiling at him like the sun bringing light and life to the world.

And children. Their children.

"There is another stipulation," Kieran added.

"Let's hear it."

"The seniors would like you to continue teaching the mobility classes. We received a note in the town's suggestion box that read, and I quote, 'you pricks better allow the felon to keep making our old bones ache.'"

Christian laughed. "Ironside strikes again. I'm happy to continue teaching the class," he replied, blinking back tears, his heart nearly bursting with gratitude.

"Good. I..." His brother trailed off.

"What is it, Kier?"

"I was worried about you," the man finished, a slight hitch to his voice.

"I'm good," Christian replied, hit with another wave of gratitude for this place and a family who loved him fiercely.

"There are my grandsons," his grandfather called, heading over.

"You look flushed, Grandpa," Finn observed, eyeing the man.

Rex removed a handkerchief from his pocket and patted his brow. "Your mother's got me helping out. *Somebody* told her that a bit more movement would help my mobility. Do you know what would really help my mobility?" the old man said with a sly grin.

"I mentioned it to Mom and Goldie. But I come with gifts that might improve your spirits while you move," Christian said, handing the man a slim flask. "That'll put a spring in your step."

"He's a real all-star, like Coach R always said. Oh, and I hear he might be coming today with his crew," his grandfather added, then sipped the moonshine.

"That would be terrific," Christian replied. His day was getting better by the second.

"But we have no time to chat. Your mom's got me on logistics duty, which is a creative way of saying she's making me drag my tired ass across the town square," Rex continued, but the curve to his lips revealed he wasn't bothered by Maeve's request. "Finn," the man continued, "they need your help in the kids' play area. Something is wonky with the jumpy castle. They require a handyman."

"Got it, Grandpa."

"Kieran, did you order cakes from Rocky Mountain City? A van pulled up, and the driver looked confused."

"I'll take care of it."

"I see Maggie is doing quite well," his grandfather said, gesturing to the pie table as Kieran and Finn melted into the crowd. "Her pies are selling like hotcakes. She should look into taking over the retail space that used to be that little café just off Main Street and Creekside Drive. The couple who owned it retired a few months ago, and no one in their family wanted to take it over."

"I was just talking to Finn and Kier about finding a retail baking space for Maggie. That's a great idea, Grandpa. I'll run it by her, and we can check it out."

"Rex, my dear father-in-law," his mother crooned, swooping in and handing his grandfather the crate of wishing wall paper, "there's no time for chit-chat. Your mayor needs you over by the wishing wall with these, please."

"I'm retired, Maeve," the man lamented.

"From making paper, not from handing it out," she replied sweetly and pressed a kiss to the old man's cheek.

The man grumbled, but that didn't hide the sparkle in his eyes. "Duty calls," he said and headed toward the creek.

Maeve surveyed the square. "The judging for the pie contest starts in less than an hour. Did Maggie and the judges get their pie entered?"

"They did. They were the first ones at the tent."

"Excellent."

"And Grandpa mentioned Coach R is coming."

"Yes, the Gemstones are supposed to join us, but I haven't seen them yet. Don't forget, it's *Ruby* when Coach is in his fabulous ensemble."

"Got it," he replied, grinning ear to ear. This was it. Everything was falling into place. Not only was today the day he would propose. He'd get to do it with his beloved RMU baseball coach by his side, rocking full drag.

"What's going on with you?" his mother asked, lips pursed as she looked him over.

He shrugged. "I'm just happy, Mom."

"Do I need to put you to work?"

"No, Madame Mayor, I'm on pie duty. I stepped away because I noticed the paper table had run out of wishing wall slips."

"Always so considerate," she said and patted his cheek. "I'm proud of you and thrilled you're happy. It's good to see you smile like that again."

"Like what?"

"Like you've got everything you want. You'd smile like that in your sleep when you were a boy cuddling your bat. You and Maggie are good for each other. I do wish she'd recall her memories. I'm sure that troubles her. Could you imagine if you couldn't remember this, all our happy years here in this beautiful place?"

"I want that for her, too."

"I know you do, and I'm sure your love and support will help her remember."

He nodded, a subtle weight tugging at his heart.

"Mayor Starrycard, there's a family interested in learning more about the town," a woman called, waving his mother over.

"And now it's back to work," she said, dusting off her hands, then frowned. "I wonder why Judge Ironside, Wolcott, and Haynes are sitting behind Maggie's table? That is quite odd. It reminds me of when I used to put you and your brothers in time-out."

"I'll go see what's up." He crossed the square and weaved through the crowd waiting to purchase Maggie's pies. "Everything okay, TBD?" he asked, keeping his voice low as he positioned himself and Lucky to the side of the stand, then glanced at the judges.

"You missed the excitement," she replied, biting back a grin as she handed a customer their change.

"I've put the judges in time-out," Hailey announced, her auburn ponytail swishing as she went into schoolteacher mode.

He peered at the three men sitting in a row. His mother was right. They were in trouble. "What did they do?"

"They started throwing bits of pie crust at the Dennison seniors," Hailey replied and clucked her tongue.

Judge Wolcott huffed. "But the Dennison seniors started it. They—"

Hailey flashed one hell of a scary teacher look their way,

cutting off Wolcott's whining. Finn's fiancée turned to Maggie. "Please tell the judges—*again*—what the pie plan is."

Christian made a mental note to never piss off Hailey.

"We'll beat them with our baking, and we're doing it for Bess," Maggie said gently as Hailey's phone beeped.

Hailey eyed the judges. "All right, gentlemen, you've had time to think about what you've done. Now you can get back to work and help us sell these pies."

"Yes, Miss Higgins," the men said in unison like a trio of naughty schoolboys.

"Don't worry, Judges," McKenzie said, zooming behind the table. "Miss Higgins will give you a second chance to do your best work. She's nice like that."

"Kenz, are you here to help?" Izzy asked.

"Yup, I wore Maggie's apron, too," the child replied.

"Your job is to bring more pies to the table when it gets low."

"Got it, Aunt Izzy," the child answered, snapping into action.

This pie booth was hopping.

Maggie brushed the back of her hand across her forehead, exhaled a heavy sigh, and blinked a few times.

He watched her carefully and could read the signs. She needed a break.

"Judges, ladies, could I steal Maggie away for a few minutes and leave Lucky at the booth?" Christian asked.

"I shouldn't leave the table," Maggie said, picking up a pie.

"I'll be on Lucky duty," McKenzie chimed.

"Take a break, girl," Izzy instructed, removing the pie from Maggie's hands and handling the sale. "We got here an hour ago. You've been going since before dawn. Just be careful. Those Starrycard boys might try to show you the inside of the paper shop when it's empty. And let me tell you, they are always up to no good," the woman said, biting back a wry grin.

"Where are you taking Maggie?" Hailey asked in a deceptively sweet tone.

These women were truly a force to be reckoned with.

"Just for a walk to give her a breather," he eked out like a kid getting caught stealing cookies from the cookie jar. "But I promise. It won't be long." He held Maggie's gaze. "It's just a little break."

"It's under control, Maggie," Judge Haynes said, offering a kind, bushy grin.

Maggie surveyed the people helping her, and a sweet, grateful grin graced her lips. She met his gaze. "Okay, but we can't be long."

Christian took her hand in his. "We won't be. Come on, All-Star," he said, using Coach R's favorite term.

She threaded her fingers with his. "Are we walking along the creek path?"

He met her gaze and attempted to keep a straight face. But he couldn't, and she read right through him.

"You're taking me to the paper shop," she said, laughing.

"Yes."

"Is this some Starrycard bachelor rite of passage?"

He chuckled. "I didn't think so, but it seems my brothers have brought Hailey and Izzy to the shop when it was empty."

"And what do you think they did there?" Maggie asked, playing the innocent.

He took her down the path that led to the shop's back entrance. "Probably what I've been thinking about doing with you."

"So...talking," she replied, doing a better job than he could at keeping her features neutral.

"So much talking. All the talking," he agreed.

"Will you be providing a papermaking tutorial?" she continued.

"Absolutely...*not*. Listen, I know we're a paper town, and I love my family's business and history. But there's a reason I became a professional athlete."

"You had a dream."

He squeezed her hand. "Yeah, and now you're here."

"I'm talking about your dream to play professional baseball," she said, that lovely blush making her glow from within.

"I know, but I want you to know that you mean more to me than baseball ever could."

She stopped walking, then pushed onto her tiptoes and kissed him.

"What was that for?" he asked, smiling against her lips.

"I love you. I love that you know just what I need, even before I know it. Your love means everything to me. *Everything*," she repeated, beaming at him.

She didn't even know the half of it.

"I have exciting news—baking news," he said, leading her to the shop.

"Really?"

"There's a café that closed in town. My grandpa thinks it might be a great location to be converted into a bakery."

"For me?" she asked, surprise coating the question.

"Yeah, you. The one and only blushing baker."

She paused, framed by the golden yellow leaves of a willow tree. "Do you think I could run a business?"

He took both her hands in his. "I don't think there's much you couldn't do, TBD. And it wouldn't be just you. It's us—together. We're not alone. Goldie knows all about opening a small business. My brother's an attorney and can help with the paperwork. You'll have support, and I'd be working down the street at town hall."

"What would you be doing?" she asked, tilting her head with a curious smile.

"Director of Recreation and Sports Engagement."

"Christian, that's amazing. When did that happen?" she asked, her eyes widening in surprise.

"Like ten minutes ago," he said with a light chuckle, still savoring the moment. "My brother ran it past me. I said yes."

She peered at their joined hands, then smiled as she looked down the trail. "This is our path," she said softly, lifting her gaze to meet his.

"Maggie, Christian? Is that you?" came a familiar voice.

"Yes, hello, Dr. Ironside. It's nice to see you," Maggie chimed as the neurologist headed toward them with a large canvas bag.

"Are you coming to take in Donnelly Days?" he asked.

"I am. My cousin said I had to visit your pie booth. That's why I've got the tote. I'm stocking up for the hospital's break room. And I must say, you've made quite an impression on him."

"He's a wonderful man and a talented baker," Maggie gushed. "Did he tell you the pie we entered in the contest is dedicated to the memory of his late wife?"

"He did, and I must thank you both," the doctor said, a warm smile lighting up her face. "My cousin is a scowly old thing, but he's a good man underneath the bluster. He loved Bess very much, and I'm glad he shared that part of his past with you. And speaking of the past, dear. Have you had any of your memories return? How are you doing on the meds?"

"I'm doing well. I think the anxiety medicine is helping. I feel steady and solid. I still can't recall anything about my identity, but I'm remembering recipes."

"You should see her, doc," he said. "She's filled three notebooks."

"That's excellent progress, Maggie. Don't lose hope. Sometimes, it takes just one thing, a smell, a taste, or even a sound, to unlock memories. Keep living. Stay curious and give yourself time."

Maggie nodded. "I'll keep that in mind. Thank you."

"Anytime," the doctor answered, then held his gaze. "And Christian, I just bumped into Dr. Driscoll."

Maggie peered up at him. "Dr. Driscoll?" she repeated with a crinkled brow.

"He's the surgeon from Rocky Mountain City who operated on my shoulder."

"We ran into each other at a medical symposium a few days ago, and I invited him here," the doctor explained.

"I'll keep an eye out for him. I'd love to see him and let him know how well I'm doing."

"You do seem to be doing quite well," the doctor observed.

He wrapped his arm around Maggie's shoulders. "It's thanks to her."

"That's what my cousin tells me. Take care," Dr. Ironside replied with a sly grin before continuing down the path toward the square.

He turned his attention to Maggie. She was chewing her lip. Something was bothering her. He rubbed her arm. "Are you okay?"

She hesitated before offering a weak smile. "Yeah, I'm…fine."

But he wasn't convinced. "What happened?"

She shook her head, confusion clouding her gaze. "I can't quite explain it, but a pang of anxiety left me feeling off-kilter there for a second. I'm okay now."

"Come on. I think this will help," he said as he brought her to the back entrance of the paper shop. He unlocked the door but didn't open it. "Now, I love the smell of baseball—the grass, the fresh dirt under my cleats, and the roasted peanuts from the stands, but nothing hits like walking into the shop. With your heightened ability to taste and smell, I have a feeling you'll love this."

She watched him with tears in her eyes. "That's why you brought me here?"

"That, and I want to kiss you until you can't see straight."

She laughed, the tension melting from her body.

He stroked her cheek. "That's better. Now, close your eyes, TBD."

She complied, and he opened the door and guided her inside.

"Take a deep breath," he said softly.

She lifted her chin slightly and inhaled. "Oh, Christian, I can smell juniper berries, just like the ones in Stumble Juice, but there's more. There's so much more. The earthy, woody notes have to be the pulp."

"Yes," he said, holding her hand as he led her deeper into the shop where the papermaking happened in large vats.

"There are so many botanicals," she said, smiling as she spoke. "Lavender, rosemary, cherry, cinnamon. Citrus scents and flowery aromas. It's like…like heaven."

He stopped, gazed down at her, and turned the ball cap around so he could see her face more easily. "It is heaven."

She opened her eyes, removed her apron, and took in the vast, cavernous space. "It's so big. There are so many nooks and crannies," she said, resting the apron on a chair. "How did you find your special stones in here?"

He studied the familiar space. Fresh sheets of handmade paper dried over long rods, their edges catching the golden rays of sunlight filtering through high windows. "The first one I found flew through the air before a game," he said, pointing toward a vat.

"What?" she asked with a chuckle.

"One of the beaters in the vat hit it just right to mark it with two lines and then send it flying. I was helping my dad and grandpa, and I caught it. Snapped it clean out of the air. I found the others by chance, hidden around the vats like Easter eggs. When you grow up in a big family, you share everything. Bedrooms, clothes, toys, equipment. But these stones with my number on them were all mine."

"Like that?" she asked, peering past him.

He frowned. "What do you mean?"

She walked a few paces and reached between the drying racks. "The light caught it perfectly, and it shimmered," she said, holding out her hand.

The breath caught in his throat. She held a smooth, midnight blue starry quartzite stone with two lines carved down the center, cutting through the soft pink veins and tiny shimmering specs. "In the hundreds, no, probably thousands of hours I spent in here looking for these marked rocks, I'd found less than a half dozen. You walk in for the first time and spot one in under a minute."

"I guess I'm just lucky," she said with a twinkle in her eyes.

"I'm the lucky one." He reached into his pocket and felt his baseball card, the stone, and the ring. He exhaled a slow breath. This was the moment. There was no time to sit on the pitch. He had to swing.

"Christian, what is it?" she asked, observing him intently.

"It's TBD," he said, his words brimming with conviction.

She tilted her head. "What about it? To be determined. It's what you call me."

"We should change it."

"What would you suggest? I don't recall my last name."

A calm conviction swept through him. Every athlete knew when they were in the zone—that electrifying moment where the world melted away, and all that was left was a perfect harmony between mind and body.

This was the moment.

"How about we change it to—"

"Uncle Chris! Maggie! Where are you?" McKenzie called out, her voice echoing through the space.

He and Maggie exchanged startled glances, their bodies tensing at the unexpected sound.

"Kenz, we're here. What is it?" he asked as they hurried toward the back door.

"Aunt Izzy sent me to get you. The old judges are yelling at a bunch of other old guys. And then Grandma Maeve said that the Gemstones texted her and said they weren't going to make it because somebody named Jade hurt her tooth and had to get an emergency root canal. And then Grandma said Donnelly Days was turning into a big disaster because the Gemstones make everybody happy, but now all we've got are a bunch of old men throwing pie crust at each other."

"What?" Maggie said, blinking like a deer caught in the head-lights from McKenzie's word-a-palooza.

"My college baseball coach and his friends dress in drag and attend events all over Colorado. They were supposed to be here today," he explained.

Maggie stared at him.

"I know it sounds a bit eccentric, but—"

"No, drag queens are terrific. I adore them," she replied, her brow creased like she was trying to piece a puzzle together.

"You've gotta make them stop throwing pie crust at each other," McKenzie said, then gasped.

"What is it, Kenz? Is there more?" he asked.

"My shoelaces are untied!" the child exclaimed.

Christ on a cracker.

"You take care of the shoes. I'll take care of the judges," Maggie said and hurried out the back door.

"What were you doing in here all by yourself with Maggie?" McKenzie asked as he tended to her laces.

"Just showing her around. Let's go, Kenz," he said, but something was off—the day's energy had shifted, and a chill spider-crawled down his spine.

"I'm gonna run, Uncle Chris," the little girl shouted, her voice full of excitement as she took off like a shot.

He sighed and ran his hands through his hair. *So much for seizing the moment.* With his heart pounding, he picked up his pace, determined to get to Maggie. As he rounded the corner, he collided with someone, stumbling slightly. "Excuse me. I'm so sorry," he quickly apologized, his thoughts still racing ahead.

"Well, hello, Christian."

Christian blinked and did a double take. "Dr. Driscoll," he uttered, a bit taken aback.

"It's good to see you. How's the shoulder?"

"I'm healing. Range of motion is improving," Christian replied, trying to keep the conversation brief. He didn't want to be rude, but his mind was elsewhere—he needed to be there for Maggie. Who knows what kind of trouble the judges might have gotten into?

"That's what I like to hear," Dr. Driscoll said with a nod, then gestured toward the creek. "It's beautiful out here. We used to come this way more often when my kids were younger. My sister has a place about forty miles due south," he added, just as his phone pinged. He glanced down at the screen. "It's a colleague. I need to take this, but let's catch up later."

"I'd like that," Christian replied, grateful for the brief chat but even more relieved to cut it short. That nagging feeling of unease still lingered. He scanned the square and breathed a sigh of relief when he spotted Maggie with the judges. He broke into a jog. "Everything under control?" he asked, his voice laced with concern as he reached her side.

"The Dennison seniors saw our pie submission. They snuck into the judging tent and tried adding store-bought sugar stars to their pie to copy us. Wolcott saw the whole thing," Haynes explained.

"And I did what any rational baker would do," the slim judge said, a smug look on his face.

"He threw a pie at them," Izzy said, shaking her head in a mix of exasperation and amusement.

"We've got them shaking in their boots, those sneaky bastards," Judge Ironside declared triumphantly, raising his fists.

Christian couldn't help but chuckle at the absurdity of it all, but his concern quickly shifted. "Where are the Dennison seniors now?" he asked, his brow furrowing as he glanced around the square.

"Your mother is acting as peacemaker. She invited them to the wishing wall and led them down the path to put some space between the competitors," Hailey replied.

Christian let out a breath he didn't realize he was holding. Leave it to his mom to defuse the situation with grace.

Maggie waved in the judges. "Bakers, let's focus. They didn't get away with it, and liars and cheaters never win in the end. We put our hearts and souls into our pie submission. I believe in us. I feel good. I feel very good. My gut is telling me we've got this. Let's hold on to that. Think of your wives. Think of the love you shared, and forget about the Dennison seniors. You know what's important."

"You're right. The heat of the moment took over," Wolcott admitted, his voice tinged with regret.

Maggie offered a reassuring smile. "I understand. Let's take a breath and steady ourselves."

Christian couldn't help but marvel at her strength and composure as he watched her gracefully manage the situation.

"You all look like you could use some cocoa," McKenzie said, looking over the judges. "Chocolate always cheers me up. Let me take you to the booth with the best cocoa around." Without waiting for a response, she grabbed Judge Ironside and Judge Wolcott by the hands, and with Judge Haynes trailing a step behind, she led the trio toward the far end of the square.

"These judges are a handful," Maggie said with a weary sigh. She glanced at her table. "Can you keep an eye on the pies while I go speak to the pie contest committee? I want to confirm that we're still in good standing."

"You got it," he replied, his tone light but reassuring.

She smiled the smile that warmed his heart. "And then you can tell me what you want to call me instead of Maggie TBD."

"I can't wait," he replied, his gaze lingering on her as she weaved through the crowd toward the judging tent. But then something—or rather, someone—caught his eye.

A man. A man making a beeline for Maggie.

Unease settled in the pit of his stomach.

This mystery man looked a hell of a lot like the younger version of Dr. Driscoll. This lookalike gripped Maggie's wrist, and she startled, pulling back instinctively.

Who the fuck was this handsy joker?

The man said something to Maggie, then hugged her. Immediately, her perplexed expression darkened. She pulled away from his embrace and touched her head. She spoke, and he could make out one word.

Amnesia.

The man grinned. What an odd reaction.

Adrenaline coursed through Christian's veins. He had to get to her. He turned to Izzy and Hailey as Lucky whined. Even the dog knew something was wrong. "Can you watch the pies and my dog a little longer? I need to find out who that jerk is and why he thinks he can put his hands all over Maggie."

"We're good. Go," Izzy replied, concern etched on her face.

The crowd had grown. It swelled around him, thick and unyielding. Each step forward was like wading through molasses. Time stretched as he struggled to get to Maggie. Her face had turned an unsettling shade of white that sent a rush of urgency through his veins. Every muscle in his body tensed with protective fury as he reached her side, ready to punch this guy into next week for laying hands on his girl. "Who the hell are you, and why are you touching Maggie?" he growled, the words coming out like daggers.

The man smiled a slippery grin and extended his hand. "I'm Bobby Driscoll, Junior, MD—Maggie's boyfriend."

Nineteen

CHRISTIAN

CHRISTIAN ZEROED in on the man with sandy brown hair and broad shoulders standing inches away from him—the fucker who thought he was Maggie's boyfriend. There was no fucking way. From his plastic smile to how he looked at Maggie like she was some sort of prize, this man could not be her boyfriend.

"Who are you?" Christian demanded. He must have misheard the guy.

"I'm Doctor Robert Driscoll, Junior. I'm Maggie's boyfriend. It's a pleasure to meet you, Christian. I consulted with my father on your surgery, though we never met."

"You're Maggie's boyfriend?" he asked, the words tasting bitter and acrid.

"Yes. For the last five years."

Woof, woof, woof! Grrr!

"Lucky, stop!" McKenzie called.

Lucky sprinted through the crowd, then stopped in front of Bobby Junior, separating him from Maggie. The dog wasn't vicious, but he sure as hell didn't like this so-called boyfriend.

"Easy, boy," Christian said, taking hold of the pup's leash.

"Lucky got all crazy and ran away from the table. I saw him take off and came running to get him."

"It's okay, Kenz."

"Who are you?" McKenzie asked Junior.

"I'm Dr. Driscoll. I'm Maggie's boyfriend."

McKenzie glared at the man. "You can't be. My uncle Chris is—"

"Kenz," he said, cutting her off. "Please take Lucky back to the table. Let Izzy, Hailey, and the judges know we need a moment."

McKenzie glared at the doctor. "Dogs don't like you."

The man didn't reply. His features remained neutral, but surprise flickered briefly in his eyes.

"Kenz, take care of Lucky," Christian said gently, mustering every ounce of strength to remain calm.

His niece watched him for a beat, then nodded.

Thank Christ, the kid didn't ask a million questions. As if she sensed the weight of the situation, she and Lucky headed back to the table. He exhaled an even breath, centering himself, then checked on Maggie. She'd grown another shade paler.

"Let's get you out of this crowd, and we can all talk somewhere more private." He pressed his hand to her back. She walked like a zombie as he led her and Bobby Junior away from the square toward the creek. He spied a picnic table tucked behind a few aspens near the water and helped Maggie take a seat. He took the spot beside her, leaving Junior to sit across from them.

He fixed his gaze on the man. "Maggie's got amnesia. She arrived at my ranch, then took a bad fall, hit her head, and lost consciousness. I rushed her to the hospital, where she spent days in a coma. She doesn't remember a thing about her past."

"That's what she told me," Bobby said, nodding. "I'm so sorry, Maggie. I can't imagine what you've been going through. I didn't expect to see you here. I figured you'd started your trip in Starrycard Creek and kept going."

"What does that mean?" Maggie asked, her voice barely a whisper.

"You had a letter from your grandfather. You don't have it

now?" The man swallowed hard, his nervousness unmistakable. Christian could read people like he read pitches. Junior's unease was undeniable.

"No," Maggie said, her voice tinged with uncertainty. "All I had with me when I woke up was an old pink apron, a stone, and Christian's baseball card. Did you read the letter? Did I share it with you? Maybe that could help me remember."

Bobby's features softened. "It didn't say much...really. He just asked that you return some items to Christian Starrycard."

"So, I came here to drop off the items, and then I was planning to travel around the state on my own? But I didn't arrive here in a car. At least there wasn't one in the area that belonged to me," Maggie mused, her brow furrowing as she tried to piece together the story.

"You had to sell your car to pay your grandfather's medical bills. My only guess is that you took the bus," Bobby offered, his words coated in feigned sincerity.

Christian couldn't hold back any longer. "You're guessing?" he barked, a sharp edge to his voice. "You don't know how your girlfriend planned to get around for a solo vacation?"

"It didn't come up. We'd had a little argument. Do you remember, Mags?" Bobby asked, his voice laced with a saccharine sweetness that felt anything but genuine.

"No, I don't," Maggie replied.

Christian locked onto the man's gaze. "What happened?"

Bobby glanced away. "Just normal couple's stuff. Stress about work and relocating for my job."

"Relocating?" Maggie repeated, confusion and disbelief coming off her in waves. "And I wanted that? I wanted to move out of Colorado?"

"You do," Bobby cooed, his voice softening in what felt like an attempt to reassure her. "You always support me."

Christian bristled. This relocation business was bullshit, and he couldn't get past this guy not knowing a damned thing about

Maggie's welfare for the last fifteen days. "Do you have a car, Bobby?"

The man brightened. "A sixty-seven Corvette Sting Ray. Candy apple red. A real beauty."

"Why didn't you offer your car to her?" Christian pressed.

"It's got a manual transmission. She can't drive a stick shift," he answered smoothly.

That answer didn't cut it.

"Weren't you worried when you hadn't heard from her? She's been with me for the last fifteen days. We've checked with the Sheriff's Department. No one has been looking for her. Not one inquiry has been made," he shot back.

Bobby folded his hands on the table. "Fifteen days is hardly a lifetime." The man turned to Maggie. "We went to Fiji for three weeks. You probably don't remember that when we were watching the sunset, I told you I'd fallen in love with you. It was just after your twenty-first birthday."

Christian gnashed his teeth, holding back his fury.

"I'm sorry, Bobby," she whispered. "I don't remember."

"Come on, man," Christian continued. "Weren't you worried even a little? Jesus, she hasn't called or texted you in over two weeks. She lost her cell. Have you even tried to get ahold of her?"

Bobby kept his gaze trained on Maggie. "You asked for space to process the loss of your grandpa and having to sell your grandparents' house and everything in it to pay his medical expenses. After the house sold, you wanted to get away and clear your head."

Christian scrutinized the man. That wasn't the truth—or at least not all of it. Years of reading players told him this guy was holding back.

"What happened with my grandfather? What about my parents or other family? I don't remember anything," she said, pain infused in her words.

"They've all passed. Your parents died when you were just a baby. You never knew them. Your grandparents raised you in

Rocky Mountain City. We met when you were nineteen. I was a resident at Rocky Mountain Hospital and assisted in your late grandmother's hip surgery."

Maggie exhaled a shaky breath. "So, I have nobody, and I've lost everything?"

Christian's heart twisted as anguish panged in his chest. Bobby looked at him, studying his expression, then offered Maggie that slippery smile. "You have me."

Christian shook his head. This wasn't adding up. "You're a doctor. Your father is a doctor. You couldn't help her with the expenses?"

"She...wouldn't let me." He reached into his jacket pocket. "Here, maybe this will help you understand our connection, Mags."

Mags.

Christian glared at the man.

Bobby took out his phone and opened the photo app. "Here's a shot of us after I passed my boards. Here we are at an event at the hospital. I earned an award."

"Oh," she said, staring at the pictures.

Christian's heart sank.

There was no doubt Maggie and this man had history.

"Here's one of you and your grandparents when you were in culinary school, but you dropped out to care for your grandmother. She had trouble after her surgery, and you insisted on being with her," he said, handing her his phone.

"Those are my grandparents? What were their names?" she asked, peering at the picture.

"Fred and Constance Michaels."

"I'm Maggie Michaels?" she asked, wonder edging out her anxiety.

"Yes. Margaret Kathleen Michaels."

Holy shit!

"Christian," she said, a faint smile on her lips, "my name has

Michael and Kathleen in it like…" She trailed off and glanced at Bobby.

Like his ancestors.

His pulse kicked up. He wanted to bang the table and proclaim her name to be the proof needed to secure her as his. But it wasn't proof. It was all she had to cling to in a life obscured by amnesia.

"May I see?" he asked gently and gestured to the phone.

She passed it to him, and he zeroed in on her. Her hair was shorter in this picture, but her kind smile remained the same. His gaze shifted from her to an elderly woman whose hazel eyes radiated warmth. He studied the older gentleman in the photo and gasped. "Oh my God."

"What is it?" she asked, worry creasing her brow.

He set the phone on the table and stared at the man. Instantly, the scent of the mountain air was replaced with the smell of the leather of his glove, the faint tinge of sweaty socks, and the freshly cut grass of Rocky Mountain University's practice fields. "I know him. I know your grandfather. I met him briefly when I was eighteen and still in high school. It was the day I showed up for RMU's prospect camp."

She shook her head, confusion clouding her gaze. "I don't know what that is."

"A day where the baseball staff evaluates high school athletes to decide who they want to recruit. I remember that day like it was yesterday. I was nervous. I had my lucky stone with me, and I'd misplaced it somewhere in the locker room before they called me out. Your grandfather was passing through. He had a badge clipped to his pocket. He worked there. He saw me searching the floor."

Maggie looked at Bobby. "Did my grandfather work at RMU?"

"Yes, Fred was part of the crew that maintained the football and soccer facilities. Perhaps he moved around to the other fields. I'm not sure. I never asked him much about his work," Bobby supplied, his gaze flickering with a hint of impatience, as if the topic was unworthy of his time.

"Well," Christian continued, holding Maggie's gaze and ignoring Junior, "your grandpa was on the baseball side that day. I was frazzled and nervous, the way you get when everything seems to ride on one moment. He must have seen it on my face because he asked if I was okay. I told him I'd lost something important—something that was meant only for me, and that I was due on the field, and this item could make or break the rest of my life. He patted my shoulder and said, 'Just breathe, kid. Every storm passes. Go out there and give them everything you've got.'"

"Every storm passes, and give them everything you've got?" Maggie repeated.

He nodded, the faint whisper of a grin on his lips. "Yes, it made me think of Seamus, and then I kept repeating 'Every storm passes' to myself. It got me through camp. It got me on the team."

"He must have found your stone," Maggie said softly, nervously tracing circles on the table.

"Yes, that's what I'm thinking."

"What about the card? How did he get it?"

"I made sure all the maintenance and support staff received one."

"I see," she replied, then stilled.

"What is it, TBD?"

She searched his face. "Why didn't he just give you back your stone?"

"That was the only time I'd interacted with your grandfather. Perhaps he meant to. He might have put it in his pocket or a drawer and forgot about it. I don't know."

"That wasn't the only time," Bobby chimed.

Christian's jaw tightened. *Fuck!* That guy was still here. He pegged him with his gaze. "What are you talking about, Bobby?" he demanded, his voice a low rumble.

"Let me show you. There's a video. Maggie's in it, too."

Christian watched as the man tapped his cell's screen, an edge of impatience and dread creeping in. "What video?"

"At the ball game—the one where your shoulder went out. Look," the man said, holding up the phone like it was the key to some long-lost treasure.

Christian leaned in as a chill ran through him. The video showed him on his knees, his face twisted in agony, desperately searching the crowd.

The camera zoomed out and panned to the stands as if to follow his line of sight, and there she was. His angel. His dream girl. While everyone else held up their phones, recording the horrific moment, she stood beside her grandfather, who looked like a shadow of his former self, his face hollow with age. Maggie's hand rested over her heart. "Just breathe. Every storm passes," she mouthed, her gaze locked with his, as if her very soul was reaching out to him, urging him to trust in her words and find solace in her unspoken promise.

"Maggie's neighbor had season tickets and couldn't attend the game. He gave the tickets to Fred. It was Maggie's first Rattlers game. She was never into sports, though, and went because her grandfather wanted to go," Bobby supplied.

"That's how you know me," she whispered with tears in her eyes.

Christian shook his head. "No, there's no way. I would've remembered," he replied, his heart sinking as if the ground beneath him was giving way.

Bobby pocketed his cell. "Listen, Christian," he began, mock sincerity dripping from his words, "I understand that you feel protective of Maggie and care about her. She was injured, and you helped her. I'm a doctor. I understand trauma and trauma responses. Given Maggie's memory loss and the life-altering injury that cost you your career, it's understandable that the two of you would form a bond. Stress can amplify and accelerate that connection. But Maggie and I have been together for five years. That's five years of memories and love. You've been with her for fifteen days, not even a month. I'm here now. I can take care of her and give her what she needs."

A muscle ticked in Christian's jaw. Sure, the doctor's fancy words sounded logical, but his gut disagreed. His heart disagreed.

"What do you need, Maggie?" he asked, searching her pained expression when McKenzie's voice cut through the heavy tension.

"Maggie, Maggie!" his niece called, running toward them. "You won. Your pie won. The pie people put the ribbons on the winning pies. The Stumble Juice Pumpkin Pie got first place, and those mean old guys who tried to cheat didn't even get a ribbon."

Maggie blinked as if being pulled from a dream. "That's... that's great news."

"You won a pie contest?" Bobby asked, raising an eyebrow.

"My team did."

"It's such a great little hobby. She can bake one hell of a pie," the man said, then brushed a few fallen leaves from the table's surface.

This guy didn't give a damn about Maggie.

Sweet Christ, Christian had the urge to punch him in his smug face.

"McKenzie, will you do me a favor?" Maggie asked.

"Sure! What do you want me to do?"

"Please tell everyone I'm so proud of them. I just need another minute here," she said evenly.

He could tell she was drawing on every last bit of strength to stay in control. It damn near killed him to see her in pain.

"Okay!" McKenzie chimed before skipping to the table with the winning pies.

Bobby's phone pinged, drawing his attention as he casually glanced at the screen. "It's my dad. We need to get back to Rocky Mountain City. He has to consult on a case and always appreciates my opinion. Mags, let's go," he said, rising to his feet with an air of entitlement.

"Now?" Christian blurted out, his heart pounding with frustration. "She just won a big contest. This is her moment."

"It's just a pie-making contest," Bobby replied dismissively, waving his hand as if swatting away a pesky fly. "And I need to get back to help a patient walk again. I'm sure you can discern which is the more pressing matter," he continued, his voice dripping with condescension. Bobby's gaze narrowed. "Do you have a problem with me taking *my girlfriend* home, Mr. Starrycard?"

Christian's chest tightened. Anger surged within him like a wildfire. "Yeah, I have one hell of a problem," he snapped, his voice low and dangerous. His fists clenched as he fought to keep his composure. "And it's not *just* a pie-making contest."

Maggie bolted to her feet. "I left my apron inside Christian's family's paper company," she stammered, her bottom lip trembling.

"We can get you another apron, Mags," Bobby replied, staring at his cell.

"No, this one came from an antique store. I want to get it. It's important to me. Christian, can you let me in so I can retrieve it?"

"Yeah, of course," he said, reading between the lines. She was fighting tears and wanted a minute alone with him. And he sure as hell needed time with her away from this guy.

Bobby's phone pinged again. "Mags, we need to leave. I'm parked across from the town hall. Here," the man said, slipping a business card and pen from his pocket. He scribbled on it and handed it to Christian. "You can ship it to us. That's *our* address— for now."

"No, I need to get that apron," Maggie blurted out. "I won't be long. I'll meet you at the town hall." Without waiting for Bobby's response, she hurried toward the shop.

Christian followed a step behind, but once they were out of Bobby's view, he reached for her hand and gathered her into his arms.

She inhaled a shaky breath and sobbed against his chest. "Christian, I'm sorry...I never meant to do this to you. You must think I'm a horrible person. I had a boyfriend, and I fell in love with someone else. My mind is spinning. Those were pictures of me, and I have no recollection. Nothing. I don't even remember my grandparents. And I—"

He tightened his hold on her. She was on the cusp of a panic attack, and he couldn't allow her to spiral. "Breathe. Maggie, look at me and breathe."

She lifted her head, her warm hazel eyes glistening with tears.

"Every storm passes," he said, trying to comfort her with her grandfather's words. "This is not your fault. There was no way you could know that you had…" The word boyfriend caught in his throat, feeling foreign and unreal as if speaking it would solidify a reality he wasn't ready to accept. A knot formed in his belly as the situation hit home. Part of him had always dreaded the thought that someone might be missing her. Maggie was incredible. How could anyone not fall for her? But this man didn't love her the way she deserved to be loved. Still, there was no denying it—he was in her life, a part of her world.

She buried her face in his chest and wept, dampening his shirt with her tears. "I don't know what to do. I want to remember my life. I want to know who I am. But I don't want to leave you. I love you. What should I do? What am I supposed to do? What do we do?" she asked, trembling, tears slipping down her cheeks.

What did he want?

That was easy.

He wanted to whisk her into his arms and return to the ranch. He wanted to close the gate and never allow anyone, or anything, the chance to spoil what they had. He wanted to block out her past and keep her safe in his arms and in his bed. But that wasn't fair. This was what the selfish part of him wanted—the part that believed she'd come to ease his pain and fill the emptiness after baseball. But he wasn't that bitter man anymore, and he wasn't focused only on his pain and suffering.

She deserved every chance to reclaim her past. What if her memories returned along with feelings for Bobby? What if he was the love of her life? Holy hell, it didn't feel like it. But he couldn't deny that he was biased in this matter. Yeah, the guy seemed self-centered, and the comment about Maggie's baking being a *little hobby* made him want to kick his ass, but she'd spent five years with him. If he talked shit about this guy, he'd be talking shit about her choice. And he wasn't about to make her feel any more pain. Still, he wasn't about to put up a white flag and surrender.

Fuck no.

"What are you thinking?" she asked, touching his face.

"I'm thinking that I love you. I love it when you blush. I love it when I catch you humming to yourself as you bake. I love every part of you. But you can't ignore this part of your life. This might be how you get your memories back. It sounds as if you loved your grandparents very much. I only met your grandfather once, but I can tell you with one hundred percent certainty that he was a good man. A kind man. A supportive man. All the things you are. And that makes me think your grandmother must have been just as wonderful and loving. I want you to have that piece of your life. I don't know if I can give that to you, but maybe Bobby can."

"But I'm not some divine angel you dreamed about. I'm just some girl you saw when you were in terrible pain and at your lowest moment," she said, her voice trembling as she sniffled, tears brimming in her eyes.

His heart shattered at the sight of her pain. He cupped her face in his hands. "Maggie, I love you. I don't care that we know how you appeared in my subconscious. You will always be my dream girl. I want what's best for you. But do not think for a second that means I won't fight for you. I will always fight for you." He removed the ring from his pocket.

Her eyes widened in surprise, the tears momentarily forgotten. "Is that what I think it is?" she asked, her voice barely a whisper.

"Yes," he nodded, his voice filled with quiet determination. "This is for you. This is how committed I am to you. There will be a right time to ask you to be my wife. I know it. I feel it. But it's not today. I love you too much to let you sacrifice the opportunity to get your memories back. I couldn't live with myself without giving you the chance to see if you're meant to be on a different path. All I want is for you to be happy." His voice cracked as he returned the ring to his pocket, the weight of the moment pressing down on him. He pulled out his phone, his hand still trembling. "Take my cell. If you need anything, call my grandpa Rex. I'll borrow his phone, and I'll keep it close, just for you. Whenever you need me, whether it's tomorrow, next week, a decade from now, day or night—I'll be there in a heartbeat. You are my world, Maggie. I'm yours, always and forever. I love you so much that it breaks my heart to think of you leaving, but I can't ask you to stay. I can't ask you to sacrifice your chance to regain what you've lost. All I want is you, but I love you too much to hold you back."

"What are you saying?" she asked, her words barely audible through her sobs.

Christian's heart clenched as his tears spilled onto his cheeks. "I have to let you go."

Twenty

CHRISTIAN

CHRISTIAN STOOD in the back of Starrycard Creek Elementary School's second-grade classroom as Finn's fiancée introduced the next guests. McKenzie glanced back at him, gave him two thumbs-up, and mouthed, "You did a good job, Uncle Chris."

"Thank you," he mouthed back, then signaled for her to pay attention to the next group of classroom guests invited to help celebrate Donnelly Days at the school—guests he knew well. He nodded to the group as his grandfather's phone vibrated silently against his hip. He positioned himself near the room's coat closet. This location obscured his tall frame and gave him a little privacy. It didn't matter where he was or what he was doing. He wasn't missing any calls these days.

He peered at the cell's screen, and a rush of warmth flooded his body.

Maggie: Hi, Number Eleven, what's up?

His heart swelled as he typed a reply.

Christian: Hey, TBD. I just finished telling the story of when Seamus wrestled the mountain lion to McKenzie's class for their Donnelly Days lesson.

Maggie: Hailey's class?

Christian: That's right. The woman runs a tight ship.

Maggie: I don't doubt it. I adore her and Izzy.

He looked up momentarily as the classroom burst into laughter. Despite missing Maggie like he'd lost a piece of his heart, he couldn't help but smile as his college baseball coach, Clark Redmond, pretended to trip and select a book titled *Goldie Locks and the Three Queens* from a sparkly basket. But Coach wasn't here in a coaching capacity. Today, his coach was the fabulous Ms. Ruby Wrinkles. Dressed in sparkling red from head to toe, she was joined by her drag queen friends Diamond Dentures, Jade Jowls, and Sapphire Sags, members of the Geriatric Gemstones Drag Ensemble.

His phone buzzed, and again, his heart swelled.

Maggie: Did you bring the tooth to show the kids?

Christian patted his jacket pocket containing the item.

Christian: I sure did. I took it out for them to touch. They loved it. Now they're having Drag Queen Story Time. My college baseball coach and a few of his friends are reading to the kids. Their bus made it to Starrycard Creek. The children are having a ball.

Maggie: It sounds wonderful.

He glanced at the smiling children, his gaze lingering on McKenzie as she giggled with her friends, before turning his attention to his coach and the other Gemstones, who were putting on a theatrical rendition of the tale with a sparkling, glitzy twist.

Christian: The Gemstones would be crazy about you. I haven't gotten to chat with them yet. They came in right as I finished my talk. We'll catch up after. They're staying with me at the ranch.

Maggie: I would have loved to have met them.

Christ, he would have loved that, too. Coach Redmond was the reason he'd gained the skills to become a Major League ballplayer. He loved the man like a second grandfather—or glamazon grandmother when he took on Ruby's persona.

Christian: How are you? Have you remembered anything new? Another recipe? A part of your past?

He waited for her reply, his pulse racing. Texting was how they'd communicated these last couple of days. He'd wanted to give her space to see if time with Bobby would spark her memories to return, but when a text came in on his grandfather's phone from his cell at 11:11 p.m. the night she left with the message *Hey, Number Eleven, are you up?* He'd wept tears of joy.

During that first exchange, he'd learned she was sleeping in Bobby's guest room—thank Christ. He might not have been able to restrain himself if the guy had suggested sleeping in the same bed. She'd also conveyed that nothing felt familiar and being there was like somehow going backward. While he was no fan of her spending time with Bobby Junior, he wanted her to remember, and he didn't want her anxiety to get the best of her. He couldn't bear the thought of her feeling guilty or confused. The situation was fraught enough.

Pulsing dots appeared on his screen, and he waited, a thrill of anticipation coursing through him.

> Maggie: I'm still in a fog. I've taken a few walks, and Bobby's driven me around Rocky Mountain City, but no memories have returned.

> Christian: I'm sorry.

> Maggie: I'm

He read the word and waited for another text. Nothing came.

> Christian: What is it? You can tell me.

> Maggie: Bobby's been hinting about surprising me with something.

A muscle twitched in his jaw. That guy gave him a bad feeling, and it had only intensified over the past three days.

> Christian: What kind of surprise?

> Maggie: I think he wants to take me to Fiji. He mentioned wanting to go a few times since we got to Rocky Mountain City. But I feel like it's the wrong thing to do. I don't want to leave the state. Still, what if it helps me remember?

His heart was in his throat. He couldn't bear the thought of the woman he loved being stranded on a remote island with a guy who made his skin crawl.

> Christian: You sound unsure. What do you need? What can I do?

> Maggie: You're doing what I need. Just
> messaging with you makes me feel more like
> myself. I hope you don't mind this.

"Oh, hell no," he said under his breath, hammering out a reply.

> Christian: Never. I'm not going anywhere. I will
> fight for you, but I also don't want to get in the
> way of you reconnecting with your past. The
> right time will come. I promise. I will always love
> you. Always.

Was he worried she may regain her memories and recall her love for Bobby? Yeah, he'd be lying if he said that outcome hadn't crossed his mind. But fear and aimlessness hadn't taken hold like they had when he'd lost his ability to play baseball. And that was solely because of Maggie. Thanks to his dream girl, he had something more powerful than those destructive emotions.

Now, he had hope.

He'd written her name on a piece of Starrycard Creek paper. And heaven help him, he prayed she was meant for him to love and cherish.

His phone buzzed.

> Maggie: I have my stone with me.

He smiled and patted his pocket.

> Christian: Me too.

> Maggie: I better go. Bobby just got back from
> the hospital. He wants to take me to a bistro for
> drinks. It's supposed to be one of my favorite
> spots in town.

> Christian: Maybe that will trigger your memories. I hope it does. Remember, I'm always here. Text me anytime.

He watched the screen, his heart hoping for more dots, more time with her, but his last message had gone unread.

"You could get detention for being on your phone during class," Eliza whispered as she slipped into the classroom.

He glanced at the phone. Maggie still hadn't replied. She'd probably left with Bobby.

He mustered a grin for his sister as the children's joyful giggles filled the room. "I already did my part. But the Gemstones are showing me up with their act."

Eliza glanced at the phone. "Were you texting with Maggie?"

"Yeah."

"How is she?"

He pictured Maggie's face. Her smile. That blush. "She's trying to figure out how to get her memories back."

"Any luck with Doctor Bad News Boyfriend?" Eliza asked, her expression puckered as if she'd just tasted a sour lemon.

"Who?"

"Kenz calls Bobby Doctor Bad News Boyfriend. You're the Baseball Card Boyfriend. She believes you and Maggie belong together."

His entire family knew what had gone down at Donnelly Days. He'd told them the whole story because he wasn't going back to his old destructive coping mechanisms. He wasn't alone. And that meant trusting the people he loved and letting them support him.

"I agree with McKenzie, but Bobby is part of Maggie's past. I have to be patient," he said, his voice calm but his heart so damned heavy.

"You need to go to her," Eliza urged.

"That's all I want, but it's not time, not yet. You've got to trust me."

"Sitting on the pitch, eh?" his sister replied, raising an eyebrow.

"Stop the presses! Eliza Starrycard-Dunleavy knows something about baseball," he teased.

She didn't laugh. "That's what you're doing, aren't you? Waiting for the right moment to clobber the hell out of that guy and get Maggie back?"

"Something like that, hopefully, minus the violence. It's a little like waiting for a sign. A ripple of energy and change in the wind. I'll know it when it happens."

"Because you love her."

"Yes."

Worry clouded Eliza's gaze. "What if she remembers she loves Doctor Bad News?"

He lifted his chin, his resolve holding him up. "I can't think like that. I won't let myself go there."

His sister nodded approvingly. "I know that look."

"What look?"

"That calm self-assurance. I was worried you'd spiral with Maggie leaving."

For the space of a breath, after watching Maggie leave with Bobby, he'd considered taking up residence on the couch in the still room and drinking himself into oblivion. But he hadn't done that. He'd stayed until the festival ended to help run her pie booth. When he'd returned to the ranch with Lucky, he'd bypassed the moonshine room and headed into the kitchen. He'd stood in the center of the space, closed his eyes, and inhaled the heady scents of cinnamon, pumpkin, and molasses. The rich aroma of the piñon nuts and cloves still mingled with the hints of juniper from the Stumble Juice. Maggie was there—her energy and gentle spirit lingered. And he wasn't alone.

And while she'd left him with hope, he had something else to fortify him. Deep down, he remained a son of Starrycard Creek folklore and a superstitious ballplayer.

He'd written her name on that scrap of Starrycard Creek paper. More than that, actually. He'd written his hope for her.

When he opened his eyes, the first thing he noticed was the rolling pin she'd used to craft dozens of perfect pie crusts. Like he'd done with his bat as a young boy, he'd grabbed that old wooden cylinder and placed the baking tool on her pillow when he'd gone to sleep these last two nights.

Strange?

Absolutely.

But it wasn't any stranger than wearing his underwear backward for an entire season.

And he was waiting for a sign.

He locked eyes with his sister. "I won't spiral. I won't fall into that pit again. I've got to be strong and ready for when Maggie needs me."

The whisper of a knowing grin graced Eliza's lips—the same expression his mother and grandmother made when they knew a person's words were the truth, straight from the heart. But as quickly as that sly grin bloomed, her demeanor turned more elusive. "In the meantime, could you be *strong* for me?"

"What's up?"

"Jack can't pick up Kenz today—an emergency case at his office. Could she hang with you and the Gemstones for a few hours? We have a staff meeting after school. Otherwise, I'd keep her with me."

"One does require strength when spending time with the youngest Starrycard," he joked.

Eliza rested against the wall. "You're telling me. That child is—"

"The spitting image of you," he shot back, barely able to hold back a grin.

His sister sighed deeply, the sound carrying the weight of her exhaustion. "When that child hits her teen years, I'll need a steady supply of Stumble Juice sent to the house."

"Consider it done, and yes, I can watch McKenzie."

"Actually," Eliza continued, "can you keep her overnight? We've got an all-day teacher training tomorrow. Kids don't report to school. Jack's working in the morning, but he'll be off by one tomorrow. The man's got so many dog butts to probe, according to Kenz."

He chuckled. "She's always welcome with me."

"You're a lifesaver, Chris," she replied, then checked her watch. "I've got to go. Dismissal is in a few minutes. I need to go be *principally*. You good?"

He cocked his head to the side. "Principally?"

"Yes," she answered in her don't-mess-with-me principal voice, "it means in the matter of being and acting as the principal."

He knew better than to challenge an educator on word usage, even if he knew she was totally bullshitting. "If you say so."

"You're the best," she whispered, then slipped out of the classroom, her footsteps fading as she headed down the hallway.

Before he could blink, the children erupted into enthusiastic applause. He flicked his gaze to the front of the classroom, where the Gemstones exchanged hugs and high fives with the children.

"All right, boys and girls," Hailey called, then clapped in rapid succession.

The children froze, their attention snapping back to their teacher like she'd conjured a spell.

Hailey gifted the classroom guests with a wide grin. "We're very grateful to have had Mr. Starrycard, Ruby Wrinkles, Diamond Dentures, Sapphire Sags, and Jade Jowls visit our classroom today. Thank you for sharing your time and talents with us. Now, second graders," she continued, "let's get our coats and backpacks and line up in the hall. We've got one minute until dismissal." She clapped again, and the children sprang into action, gathering their things and forming a line outside the classroom.

His coach caught his eye and then gestured to Hailey. "She could run the entire RMU Athletics Department."

Hailey chuckled, donning her coat. "I appreciate the compliment, Ruby Wrinkles, but I'll stick to seven-year-olds," she replied, then turned to Christian. "Is McKenzie going home with you today? I noticed Principal Starrycard-Dunleavy popped in."

"Yeah, Kenz is coming with me."

"Woo-hoo!" McKenzie cheered.

Hailey slipped a folder into McKenzie's backpack. "Have fun with your uncle and the Gemstones. Don't get into too much trouble."

"Us, get into trouble?" Diamond Dentures purred.

"We'll be on our best behavior," Christian replied.

The bell rang, and Hailey joined the children in the hallway.

"I loved the way you acted out the story, Miss Ruby Wrinkles, or should I call you Coach like Uncle Chris does?"

Ruby took a knee to be at McKenzie's level. "When I'm in my fancy red clothes, I'm Miss Ruby Wrinkles, and when I'm in jeans and a sweater, I'm Coach. Does that work for you?"

"Yes, ma'am, Miss Ruby Wrinkles," the child exclaimed. "Uncle Chris?" she continued, skipping to his side.

"What's up, Kenz?"

"Can I play outside for a little bit?"

He surveyed the Gemstones. "Do you mind hanging around the playground before we head to the ranch?"

"Are there any swings?" Diamond Dentures asked with a cheeky grin.

"The best swings in all of Colorado. They're super squeaky," McKenzie answered, bright-eyed.

"We will never turn down a super-squeaky swing. Lead the way, you little powerhouse," Sapphire Sags declared with a bejeweled wave of her hand.

McKenzie, Diamond, Sapphire, and Jade headed to the playground while he and Ruby hung back.

Ruby looked him over as they walked down the brightly colored hallway. "How are you doing, All-Star?"

"Better, healing. The pain is minimal. The exercises help. And love," he added and pictured Maggie.

"Love, huh?" Ruby replied, a curious lilt to her voice.

They walked in a comfortable silence and stepped out into the brisk fall air.

"Do you miss the game?" Ruby continued.

"I do, but I've found a new perspective. I'm needed here at home."

Ruby nodded as the Gemstones joined them, and McKenzie remained on her swing.

"Well, this ass doesn't fit on an elementary school swing anymore," the beautifully rotund Sapphire Sags lamented.

"Honey, did it ever?" Diamond teased, then set her sights on Christian. "Did Ruby inquire about our Little Miss Cry-In-Her-Pie?"

Christian narrowed his gaze. "I don't understand."

"Let me rephrase. Did a sweet little thing named Maggie ever make it to your door, honey?" Diamond asked pointedly.

Christian nearly fell over. "What did you just say?"

Diamond shared a curious look with Ruby. "I asked if Maggie, a young woman with strawberry-blond hair and a thing for pies and sporks teeming with Coxsackievirus, met up with you."

"She was on our bus a couple of weeks ago, and we struck up a conversation with her," Ruby added, still watching him closely.

Christian's mouth fell open in astonishment as his gaze darted between the drag queens. "Yeah, she made it. How did you know she was looking for me?"

"She told us," Jade Jowls explained. "She was headed to Starrycard Creek to see you to deliver a rock and your baseball card. It was an errand from her dearly departed grandfather. He asked her to do it in a letter. It was his last wish."

"Except the woman saw a dog stuck on the railroad tracks not far from your ranch. She ordered the bus driver to stop. She ran off to save the poor thing and left everything behind. The driver said he couldn't wait, and that was the last we saw of her," Ruby explained.

"I...I saw her. I ran to her. We saved the dog together, but she fell and hit her head just after that. She passed out, and when she woke up, she didn't remember anything. The doctor diagnosed her with amnesia," Christian said, his words laced with astonishment.

"Are you sure a bonk to her head did that and not brain-eating bacteria? I told her that spork was trouble," Diamond huffed.

"No, her brain is fine. They did a bunch of scans. We only knew her name because it was on her apron. I've been with her night and day since she arrived in Starrycard Creek, and we fell in love."

"You fell in love?" Ruby asked, her wide eyes sparkling with curiosity, a hint of excitement in her voice.

"Yes, she's my everything."

"Isn't that something! I can give you this. It's for Maggie," Jade Jowls said, handing him a card. "We peeked at her wallet and learned her last name is Michaels. I made a call, and it turns out my nephew's estate business is the company that purchased Maggie's grandparent's home and all items in it. They can be hers if she wants them. The items, that is. The house sold to a young family. And I have another piece of information for her. I did a little research on the pink pie plate she had with her on the bus. My friend's an expert in that field and says it's worth a small fortune."

Holy shit.

"We'd love to see her. Maybe we could help jog her memories. Where is she now, Christian?" Diamond asked.

His heart sank. "She's with her boyfriend."

"Her boyfriend?" the queens exclaimed, disgust twisting their painted faces.

"I thought you said you loved her?" Ruby pressed.

"I do, but her boyfriend, Bobby, showed up. She left with him to go back to Rocky Mountain City. We thought it was the best chance to help her recover her memories. He had pictures of her and her grandparents on his phone. They'd been together for five years. He said they were in love."

"That lying sack of Coxsackievirus," Diamond hissed.

"Did he apologize for cheating on her?" Ruby demanded.

A cold knot formed in Christian's stomach. "He cheated on her?"

"When we met her, she was sobbing into a pumpkin pie. She'd lost her grandmother two years ago, lost her grandfather quite recently, her dog had died, the rescue dog she and this *boyfriend* were supposed to foster had already been adopted, and then the poor dear, after going broke, selling off all her possessions to pay her grandfather's medical bills, baked a pie for her boyfriend on the day she was supposed to move in with him only to walk in on the scumbag screwing another woman against the wall."

Christian ran his hands through his hair and paced. "I had a terrible feeling about that guy," he said, his blood boiling.

"Did this boyfriend see you and Maggie together?" Diamond asked.

"I don't know. He could have. Why would that matter?"

"He'd play hot and cold with her. She mentioned that he'd reel her back in anytime she was doing well. It's manipulative, and that's not love," Ruby said, her cheeks burning scarlet, clearly disgusted that Maggie had been treated with such cruelty.

"No, it most certainly isn't love," Christian said, fury building inside him as he recalled Kieran mentioning that a guy had been lingering around Maggie's pie booth during Donnelly Days. That had to have been Bobby Junior.

"Maggie was in a fragile state when we met her," Sapphire continued, heartfelt concern on her face. "She'd endured multiple traumas in a relatively short period of time. It's no wonder a bump to her head triggered amnesia. As a former mental health clinician, I'd say that her mind probably couldn't take the stress of waking up in a strange environment. The amnesia became a protective mechanism."

"Christian, you need to call her," Ruby said, urgency lacing through her words.

He pulled out his cell, but his heart sank as a realization set in like a gut punch. "He'll lie. Her boyfriend is a liar and a cheat."

Diamond shook her head. "He's not her boyfriend, honey. He's just—"

"Fucking Bobby," Christian muttered, recalling how Maggie's spirits had brightened when he'd lightened the mood with that exact phrase after their encounter with Bob from accounting at the hospital. Deep inside, her subconscious had known her so-called boyfriend, Bob, well, Bobby, was bad news. He stopped pacing. "Maggie needs to regain her memories. The doctor believed that they could return at any time. Still, we don't have time to waste. Something could trigger them to return. She needs to know the truth about Bobby. He wants to take her away. We can't let that happen," Christian said, then grimaced as another truth hit him.

"What is it, son?" Ruby asked gently.

"Maggie's been back in her old life since Saturday night, and her memories still haven't returned."

"Perhaps it's her mind continuing to protect her, especially if she's with the man who's hurt her and broken her trust," Sapphire offered.

"What could bring her back?" Christian murmured, his thoughts churning.

Ruby snapped her gem-covered fingers. "The pie plate."

"The pie plate," Diamond repeated, a wide grin stretched across her face.

"The one she had with her on the bus? The one that's worth a fortune?" Christian pressed.

"That exact one," Ruby answered.

Christian studied his mentor. "Why do you think it would work?"

"Maggie loved her grandparents deeply. She told us the story of how her grandfather proposed to her grandmother and why he'd given her that exact pie plate. You see, her grandfather loved to make her grandmother blush and—"

"Blush?" Christian blurted out, cutting off Ruby.

She nodded. "Yes, he loved the color of her cheeks when he made her blush. He'd found a pink pie plate at a flea market that matched them. He placed an engagement ring in the center of it and gave it to her when he asked her to marry him."

"Where is it now? Did you keep her things? Do you have them with you?" Christian asked, the words rushing past his lips.

"No, the bus driver said we couldn't take them. Company policy. He told us they had to go into lost and found," Diamond replied.

A kernel of hope burned in Christian's heart. "Where? Which lost and found?"

"The Starrycard Creek Bus Depot. We figured Maggie would have known to check there, but if she didn't even remember how she arrived in town…" Sapphire began.

"She wouldn't know her things were there," Christian finished.

"Come on, Uncle Chris. Let's go, Gemstones. We're gonna race to the bus depot," McKenzie cried, popping up out of nowhere.

Christian practically jumped out of his skin. "Jeez, Kenz, how long have you been here?"

"Long enough to know that we have to go so we can get Maggie to remember. We have to get her away from Doctor Bad News. Hurry!" the child called, darting away at lightning speed.

"McKenzie, don't run across the street!" Christian cried, taking off.

"Honey, you do not want to get splattered like a bug!" Diamond called, breaking into a run.

Christian looked from side to side as the Geriatric Gemstones matched his pace.

"I need to improve my conditioning," he breathed, struggling to keep up with four senior citizens dressed in full drag, all chasing after McKenzie.

"Where's the fire, Kenz?" his grandpa Rex called, rounding the corner with Judge Ironside, Judge Wolcott, and Judge Haynes.

"Come with us. We're getting Maggie back," McKenzie called, kicking up her pace, and sweet Christ, the kid could move.

"What do they feed these children in Starrycard Creek?" Diamond Dentures huffed between strides.

"What happened to Maggie? Is she okay?" his grandfather called, doing a damned fine speed walk.

"The boyfriend is a liar and a cheat," Ruby answered.

"Nobody messes with our Maggie," Judge Ironside bellowed, falling into stride with the gemstones as Wolcott and Haynes joined Rex in a brisk walk.

The light at the intersection across from the bus depot turned red, and McKenzie skidded to a halt.

"Kenz, you can't run off like that," Christian said, catching his breath.

"Why not? Don't you want to get Maggie back? She's supposed to be with you, Uncle Chris, not Doctor Bad News."

"The kid has a point," Ruby agreed as Rex and the speed-walking judges caught up to them.

A horn honked, and Kieran rolled down his SUV's window. "Do I even want to ask what's happening here?"

"Hey, Uncle Kier, we're getting Maggie away from the turd burger. Oops, that's a twelve-year-old word. We're getting Maggie away from Doctor Bad News."

The walk symbol lit up, and the kid bolted across the street toward the bus depot.

Kieran pulled over, exited his vehicle, and jogged to join the group. "Kenz, language."

"Sorry, Uncle Kier," she hollered over her shoulder.

His brother pinned him with his gaze as the eye-catching crowd reached the other side of the street. "Christian, what are you doing?"

"We told you, Uncle Kier. We're rescuing Maggie."

"Is this some sort of game, or is McKenzie serious?" Kieran pressed.

"It's serious," Diamond answered. "Maggie's boyfriend is— like McKenzie says—a bad news turd burger. Bobby lied to her when he said they were happy and in love. The day she arrived in Starrycard Creek, she'd walked in on him cheating on her—in the act."

Kieran balked. "In the act?"

"Against a wall," the drag queen supplied. "The poor dear just lost her grandfather, had to sell everything to pay off his medical bills, and was supposed to be moving in with the guy that day. She was bringing him a pie and found him in a compromising position."

"He also wants to take her to Fiji, then God knows where else," Christian continued. "He mentioned moving out of state for work. He told her that she wanted to go with him. He's a real scoundrel."

"Fuck Bobby," Kieran said under his breath.

"Fuck Bobby," Christian repeated his new mantra.

"I know a thing or two about scoundrel exes. What's the plan? Why are we at the bus depot?" Kieran asked as they entered the waiting area.

"Hopefully, an item that will jog her memory is in the lost and found," Christian answered.

"Hey, Flo," McKenzie chimed, skipping toward a scowling woman seated at the ticket booth. A lit cigarette hung from her hot pink lips as she paged through a magazine. Kenz turned to the group. "That's Flo. Her sister runs the animal rescue, and she and her sister helped Uncle Finn surprise Hailey with kittens, *and* she's helping them plan their wedding."

"And she's breaking the law by smoking in a place of business," Judge Wolcott added sternly.

Flo looked the judge up and down, then exhaled a few smoke

rings from her flaming pink lips. "You want to work the three to eleven shift at the bus depot? Be my guest, handsome."

They couldn't piss this woman off. She stood between him and the items in lost and found.

Christian gifted the woman with a warm grin. "Flo, we didn't come here to harass you. We simply need to see if something we require is in your lost and found."

"Is that so?" Flo purred with a hint of mischief, her fingers languidly gliding over the magazine as she flipped the page.

Damn, Flo was one cool operator.

"Yes, I'm looking for anything belonging to Maggie Michaels —and if there's a pie plate with her things, you'll have my eternal gratitude."

She offered him a shit-eating grin. "Are you Maggie Michaels, doll?"

He shifted his stance. "No, ma'am, I'm Christian Starrycard. You might know of me. I used to play baseball for the Rattlers and played college ball at RMU."

She shrugged and exhaled a stream of smoke. "I'm not really into sports. If you're not Maggie Michaels, I can't give you her things."

"But Flo," McKenzie lamented, "My uncle Chris really loves Maggie. Like a lot, a lot. And a bad man in an old fancy car that was real loud took her from Starrycard Creek."

"Was this old and loud fancy car red?" came a familiar voice with a rolling Italian accent.

Christian spun around. "Nico, what the hell are you doing here?"

And where the hell did he come from?

"My car would not start after I returned from Italy. I'm having it towed, so I took the bus from Rocky Mountain City Airport to Starrycard Creek. Now, McKenzie Starrycard-Dunleavy, *bella*, tell me more about this car."

What was so important about this car?

"The license plate said *bone doctor*," the child answered.

"Are you sure it didn't say *boned her*?"

Christ, the guy was back to this.

"Nico," Christian began, "I don't think that—"

"It had the letters *B-O-N-E-D-R*," McKenzie continued, talking over him. "In school, we learned abbreviations for stuff like mister, that's capital *M*, lowercase *r*, and a period. And doctor is capital *D*, lowercase *r*, and a period. I'm a super spy, and when Maggie was walking away from Donnelly Days and met up with Doctor Bad News, I followed her and watched her get in a red car. The Bone Doctor car."

"Bobby is an orthopedic surgeon, like his father. He's a bone doc," Christian exclaimed.

Nico gasped. "Yes, yes, McKenzie, that is the car I saw. But I did not read it correctly. The person in this car pushed Lucky out while the vehicle was still moving and sped off."

"That's animal cruelty," Judge Ironside barked.

"And animal abandonment," Haynes added.

"And the egregiousness of this crime would merit felony charges, punishable by three years in prison," Judge Wolcott finished.

"And Nico saw it happen," McKenzie said.

"And I took a picture," the man added, showing McKenzie the image on his phone.

"That's it. That's Doctor Bad News' car, Uncle Chris," his niece confirmed.

He turned to Flo. "Please, we need your help. The woman I love lost her memory. She's been diagnosed with amnesia. She's with her awful ex-boyfriend, but she doesn't know he's awful on account of—"

"The amnesia," Flo supplied, wide-eyed. "This town is like a soap opera with you Starrycard people." She ground her cigarette in an ashtray and leaned forward. "You love this amnesia-plagued chick?"

"I do, ma'am."

"Do you want to marry her?"

"Yes," he answered, conviction coating the word.

Flo leaned back and lit a fresh smoke. She gestured at him with her cigarette. "You hire me on as your wedding planner, and I'll let you sift through lost and found. And spoiler alert. I might have noticed a pie plate in there. I might have even rinsed it off so it wouldn't get moldy."

Bingo!

Christian's borrowed phone buzzed. He pulled it from his pocket and read the text.

> Maggie: Bobby has tickets. We leave for Fiji tonight. A car is coming to get us in three hours.

Three hours.

Christian inhaled deeply, then released a slow, steady exhale. It was time to get in the zone. The air around him hummed as if the very essence of Starrycard Creek—the legends, the whispers of magic, and the weight of every dream he had ever held—wrapped around him. He scanned the group—their faces full of concern, loyalty, and love for Maggie and for him, too.

Three hours. It was an eternity for a ballplayer who'd once measured his life in seconds, in the split-second decisions that had defined his career. His mind settled on Maggie—her laughter, the soft warmth of her touch, her blushing pink cheeks, and the way her gentle smile had led him through his darkest hours.

He was meant to give her the world—to give her everything.

Everything.

The word echoed in his mind as he focused, and a plan to get back his dream girl crystallized.

Next steps: execute the plan and fucking succeed.

His gaze snapped to Flo, like when he was a batter, sizing up a pitcher on the mound. "Flo the Wedding Planner," he said, confident and ready to knock it out of the park.

Flo arched an eyebrow, her lips curling into a smirk as she exhaled a thin stream of smoke. "Yes, doll?"

He flicked his gaze to Ruby, and an understanding passed between them. "I'm ready to swing," he said, his voice steady and resolute.

"You sure are, All-Star."

Flo cocked her head to the side. "Help a gal out. What does that mean?"

Christian's smile broadened as Donnelly grit and Starrycard determination fueled him. He locked onto Flo's gaze. "It means," he said, pausing to allow the anticipation to build, "you're hired."

Twenty-One

MAGGIE

"MAGS, give me the name of another fancy type of pumpkin pie. Derek messaged me—his wife is loving how much you know about pies. He says she's a foodie looking to wow his family at Thanksgiving this year."

Maggie peered across the table at the man she'd been dating for the last five years. "Who's Derek?" she asked. Bobby had been talking nearly nonstop since she'd gotten into his car and said goodbye to the town and the man she loved, but she hadn't been able to focus. She could barely breathe.

"Who's Derek?" Bobby shot back, a sharp annoyance threaded through his reply.

She nodded.

"He's our future. I'm on the shortlist to join his practice. We've only talked shop, but when he mentioned his wife was stressing over Thanksgiving desserts, I found my in with him. I need another suggestion fast. So far, we've given her maple pumpkin pie and cheesecake pumpkin pie."

Maggie stared at the table, her unease settling in like a heavy fog. Everything felt wrong. She was trying to fit into a life—supposedly, her life—but nothing made sense. From the second she'd left Christian's embrace, the warmth and safety of life in

Starrycard Creek vanished, replaced by a cold emptiness. Her hands trembled as she reached for her cup of tea, but even that motion felt unnatural.

Nothing clicked, not the words she spoke, not the smile she forced, not even the room she sat in. Of course, it didn't help that she still couldn't remember a thing about her life, but the energy here was negative, and all she wanted to do was escape.

Bobby tapped the table. "Mags, come on. Derek's waiting. I need another pie."

"Stumble Juice Pumpkin Pie," she stammered, staring out the window. A subtle calm settled over her as she recalled the rich flavor and the piñon nut crust.

"Mags!"

She gasped and met his disparaging gaze. "What's wrong?"

"Stumble Juice Pumpkin Pie sounds like something hillbillies with missing teeth eat. Don't you have anything more refined? These are highly educated people. I know that might be tricky for you because you didn't go to college or finish culinary school. But I need you to start thinking and acting like a doctor's girlfriend again."

She watched as he flicked his gaze back to his cell. How could she love this man? Who was Pre-amnesia Maggie? A snob? A gold digger? No, simply the thought of using someone tied her stomach in knots.

"Come on, Mags," he urged.

"Um…ricotta pumpkin pie."

"Nice one," he crooned, hammering out a text, then hit send.

Ping.

"Fuck, yes, Bobby, you are the master," the man announced, pumping his fist as he obsessed over the screen.

"Fuck Bob," she murmured, recalling how Christian had eased her anxiety with that teasing phrase. But there was more. It had felt like a small, rebellious victory when she'd spoken those words.

"What did you say?" Bobby asked, still glued to his cell.

"Nothing," she mumbled.

"Okay, Derek's wife wants the recipe. We are so in. Who would have thought your little baking hobby would be so helpful? This NYC partnership is going to work out. I can feel it. I'll get out from under my father's shadow and make a name for myself."

"In New York," she repeated, taken aback.

"Yeah, I thought I mentioned that to you," he answered, then checked his watch. "Are you packed? The car to the airport will be here soon. I put your passport on the desk in the bedroom."

"I saw it. I've got it."

"And you don't need to take those pills," he said, gaze locked on his cell's screen.

"The anxiety meds?" she asked, her voice wavering as she felt a knot tighten in her stomach.

"You don't need them," he said dismissively, still focused on his phone.

"I disagree."

"Mags, I'm a doctor," he stated flatly, as if that alone should silence her doubts.

"And a doctor prescribed them, and they're helping me," she countered, her eyes narrowing as she tried to read his expression, feeling a growing unease.

"Some doctor practicing in Bumblefuck, Colorado," he muttered, finally looking up.

She took a steadying breath. "I'll consider it."

He returned to his phone. "Make sure to bring a jacket. I'm changing our tickets. When we leave Fiji, we'll head straight to New York so I can have some face time with Derek. Everything is riding on fostering this relationship."

Her pulse kicked up as her breathing grew shallow. "What's the rush? And I don't know if a move will help me get my memories back."

"The rush?" he snapped. "This is my career, and it's going

nowhere in Colorado, thanks to a bullshit *issue* with one of the nurses at the hospital."

"An issue?" Maggie repeated, her voice soft but her mind racing.

He waved her off. "You know women. Everybody wants to bag a doctor."

This man was so full of himself.

She stared at him.

"But I only have eyes for you, Mags," he added like it was an afterthought. "And you want to move. You wanted a change of scenery after losing your grandparents," he added, donning a smile that was a touch too wide.

"I said those words?"

He cleared his throat and glanced away. "You knew that several practices across the country showed interest in bringing me on as a partner. You support me. That's who you are," he added, widening his syrupy grin.

Her heart clenched as a quiet resolve built inside her. "What did I want to do?"

"I don't understand," he replied, irritation creeping into his tone.

"What were my plans for wherever we decided to settle? My path?"

He shrugged and went back to fiddling with his phone. "What does that matter? I'm a doctor. I make plenty of money."

"No," she said, more to herself as she spoke the word.

"Yes," he countered smugly. "I'll be making bank, babe. I'm thinking of getting another Corvette. Maybe a seventy-one ZR2. My dad doesn't have one of those."

"I'm not talking about money. I'm talking about me," she said, then slipped her hand into her pocket and felt the cool starry quartzite stone, its touch grounding her in the moment. She sighed, and the weight of her decision settled over her. As much as she wanted to remember, she couldn't continue this charade. "I can't do this, Bobby. I can't be with you," she added, rising from the chair.

Without waiting for his response, she went into the bedroom and grabbed her suitcase and purse. She headed for the door, her mind made up.

But before she could leave, he stood in front of her, blocking the exit, his expression darkening. "What will you do? Run back to Christian Starrycard? Find another man to pay your bills?" he said, his words dripping with contempt.

Maggie met his gaze, her eyes unwavering. "I don't think I'm that kind of person," she said quietly, her voice carrying a newfound strength—a strength she'd discovered in Starrycard Creek.

"You don't know who you are, Maggie," he barked. "That's why we need this time away. You're stressed and confused, and I'm losing sleep trying to find a new practice. The moment we're sipping rum punches under the Fiji sun, everything will make sense again. I hear it's paradise."

"You *hear* it's paradise?" her voice trembled with disbelief. "I thought you wanted to take me there because it's where you told me you loved me."

"Yes…it is. I misspoke. I'm under a lot of pressure," Bobby stammered.

Maggie shook her head. "I can't do this. It doesn't feel right."

"Maggie, I'm your best chance to get your memories back. Isn't that what you want? Don't you want to remember your grandparents? They loved you. How could you do this to them?" His voice was smooth, but the way he leaned in, almost too close, made her skin crawl.

Her heart ached, but something deep within her told her to listen to her instincts. "I want that more than anything, but I can't keep denying what I feel inside. And right now, my gut is telling me that I've been ignoring my intuition when it comes to you— maybe I always have, but I see you clearly, Bobby, and your path is not my path."

"Maggie, stop it," Bobby hissed, his tone sharpening. "This isn't you."

Her gaze hardened as she looked him in the eye. "Who do you think I am?"

"You're not a risk taker," he shot back, his tone dripping with condescension. "You play it safe because you know you can't handle the real world on your own. You're too anxious and too weak to make it out there without someone like me. You need me because, without me, you'd crumble."

She lifted her chin. "I did all right over the last few weeks."

"With another guy supporting you," he replied with a scoff.

"Yes, you're right," she admitted, a surprising calm settling over her.

"Now you're coming to your senses." He smirked, certain he'd won.

"Christian did support me. He believed in me. No, he believes in me. He loves me, and I love him," she said, her voice gaining strength.

"You're confused. You're suffering from head trauma. I know this. I'm a doctor."

"I'm not confused," she replied, her voice steady and sure. "I don't know who I was before I had amnesia, but I know who I am now."

"Who are you now?" Bobby asked, pinching the bridge of his nose, his tone tinged with exasperation.

Her mind drifted to the moments that mattered—the comforting weight of her hand in Christian's, the confidence she'd felt standing before Judge Ironside, the warmth that filled her as she baked at the ranch. Her gaze grew glassy, but what bubbled to the surface wasn't exactly a memory. It was an echo. A sureness from deep within. A gentle hand on her back. She blinked away the tears, determination coursing through her veins. "I'm a baker. I'm a friend. I'm a dog mom, and I'm in love with a man who builds me up. I'm Maggie TBD."

"TBD?" Bobby spat. "You're Maggie Michaels. What nonsense is this TBD crap?"

She glanced from the entryway into the sterile kitchen. The place was devoid of warmth—or a heart. There was no sign of her here. "TBD stands for to be determined. My path is *to be determined* by me."

"Well, your path leads to the airport today. I can't get a refund on these tickets," Bobby snapped, trying to bully her.

She tightened her grip on her suitcase. "I'm not going to the airport."

He exhaled a frustrated sigh. "You didn't use to be this difficult. And, FYI, this man you say you love is a washed-up baseball player. And when I say washed-up, I mean it. I saw his shoulder X-rays. He's done. He'll never be a famous athlete again."

Bobby didn't get it. He'd never get it.

"That's not what I love about him," she replied, her voice calm but resolute. "Now step aside."

"Where are you going? You don't have any money. You don't have anything," he yelled, his voice rising as he tried to assert control over her.

She set down her bag and opened her purse. "That's not true. I have some of the money I made selling my pies." The table had gotten so busy that instead of adding the funds to the lockbox, she'd pocketed the cash. She retrieved the bills and counted them, tears coming to her eyes. "I have one hundred eleven dollars."

Number eleven.

She laughed as a lightness took over, then paused and grew silent as a faint, rhythmic thrum cut through the stillness.

Bobby shook his head. "What's so funny? A little over a hundred bucks is nothing."

"You're wrong, Bobby. It's everything," she replied as the sound grew louder and more insistent. "Do you hear that?"

"It's probably just some news helicopter covering traffic or some bullshit like that," he answered with a dismissive wave.

It wasn't just some traffic copter.

Her heart pounded with anticipation as she grabbed her things, nudged past him, and opened the door.

"What are you doing?" he barked.

She looked over her shoulder as she descended the porch steps. "I'm believing in myself. I'm trusting my heart. I'm going with my gut."

"You don't have anyone, Maggie. Don't you understand that? I'm what you've got. And if you play your cards right and help me land this New York job, I'll be set for life. I'll be rich."

She didn't have to have her memories to deduce that whatever they had, it was always about him. His path. His goals. His dreams.

Dreams.

Her gaze shifted upward as a helicopter appeared over the treetops, its dark shape looming larger with each passing second. The rhythmic *whup-whup-whup* of the rotors grew deafening, making the very air around her pulse with its intensity.

It was headed straight for the street in front of Bobby's house.

She peered down the street as the helicopter began its descent. Police cars had cordoned off the road, their lights flashing in a blur of red and blue. The helicopter hovered briefly, the downdraft whipping her hair across her face before it touched down with a controlled thud. The rotors wound down. The roar of sound tapered off, and her spirits soared.

Her heart skipped a beat as the helicopter pilot exited the aircraft. She soaked in the sight of the man with broad shoulders and a boyish half-grin. She glanced at Bobby, who stood wide-eyed and dumbstruck beside her.

She pressed her hand to her heart and held Christian's gaze. "I'm not alone, Bobby. Not even close."

"HEY, TBD," Christian purred, striding toward her in jeans, a Starrycard Creek Paper Company T-shirt, and a pair of aviators. The man was like something out of a dream—her dreams.

"Hey, Number Eleven. Are you allowed to park your helicopter in the middle of the road?" she teased through happy tears.

"Normally, no. But today, the city made an exception." He glanced at the police presence. "It turns out I've still got a lot of friends here in Rocky Mountain City."

"Is this some stunt?" Bobby grumbled.

Christian eyed the man. "Hey there, Bobby Junior. We'll get to you in a second. I'm here for my girl," he said, holding her gaze and using that commanding tone that sent a delicious shiver down her spine. "Are you going somewhere, TBD?"

"We're leaving for—" Bobby began, but she stopped him.

"No, I'm leaving *him*," she corrected.

Bobby scoffed. "She's confused."

Christian took a step toward her ex. "Maggie knows her heart. I doubt she's confused."

"What are you doing here?" Bobby demanded, but the shake to his voice revealed his unease.

Christian took off his aviators and pegged Bobby with his

gaze. "I'm here to support Maggie, and I brought back up—people she met right after she left Rocky Mountain City and just before she lost her memory."

"Just before?" Bobby's voice cracked, his smug grin faltering.

"Yes, Bob, right before," he repeated, his gaze softening as it settled back on her. "But before that, Maggie's got a special delivery from a certain pup, a little girl, and a retired papermaker," he added, gesturing toward the helicopter. In the fading twilight, the figures inside were barely visible, but her heart knew who was coming her way.

"McKenzie, Rex, Lucky!" she called as the trio approached.

McKenzie held up a box—one of the plain pink ones she'd used for her pies during Donnelly Days. But this one was different. It had an image and something written on it.

"It says 'My Blushing Baker,'" McKenzie read, presenting it like a gift.

"It does, indeed," she replied, studying the box. *My* and *Blushing* were printed in a jovial cursive font above a darling illustration of a pie with stars dotting its surface. The pie plate featured a little face with rosy, pink cheeks and the word *Baker* was printed in the same whimsical cursive below it.

She accepted the box and then knelt to pet an excited Lucky. The animal licked her face, then sniffed Bobby and growled.

"Come on, now, Lucky," Rex coaxed, reining in the dog's leash. The patriarch of the Starrycard family winked at her, then patted Lucky's head. "Don't worry, boy. We'll get to him."

We'll get to him? What was that all about?

"What's inside the box is yours, Maggie, and Miss Sapphire Sags says that you should sit down before you open it," McKenzie instructed.

"Sapphire who?" she asked.

The child beamed. "Your Gemstone friend."

"I'm sorry. I'm a little confused."

"Hopefully, we're about to change that," Christian said as he jogged to the porch and retrieved one of the patio chairs. "Here, TBD, have a seat."

She settled in the chair and peered at the box. "What's in here?"

"Something we think will trigger your memories. Something your grandfather gave to your grandmother," Christian explained.

She held his gaze as a lump formed in her throat. "You know this for sure."

"We do," Christian confirmed. "You shared the history of this object with the people you met on a bus. One of them happens to be a retired mental health professional. I explained your memory loss to her. She believes the traumas you've endured over the last handful of years caused your mind to forget because it hasn't been ready to absorb your current reality."

"What?" she asked, searching his face for answers.

He knelt in front of her. "Your brain's been...sitting on the pitch, waiting for the right moment to unlock your memories."

"Sitting on the pitch," she repeated, emotion building in her chest.

He brushed a tear from her cheek. "Yes, and I'm here because I love you, and I want you to feel safe and secure when you open that box."

"We love you, Maggie," McKenzie chimed. "Isn't that right, Great Grandpa Rex?"

"We do. The entire town of Starrycard Creek cares about you," the man said gently.

Maggie exhaled a shaky breath. "I'm nervous," she whispered, staring into Christian eyes and drinking in the soothing shade of sage green.

He took her hands in his and rested them on top of the pie box. "The storm always passes. And if this doesn't work and your memories don't return, we'll figure it out. I've got you. We're a team," he said, giving her hands one last squeeze before releasing them.

She concentrated on the pie box and traced the darling *My Blushing Baker* logo with her index finger. Slowly, she lifted the lid and was met with an object in the same shade of pink as the box. "It's a pie plate," she noted. "It looks vintage, like an antique."

"That's right," Christian said gently.

Her fingers trembled as she reached inside, carefully lifting the pie plate from its bed of white tissue paper. The cool ceramic against her skin felt familiar. The soft pink glaze shimmered in the low, dusky light. The faint imperfections etched into its surface spoke of countless years filled with love and use. The edge was intricately scalloped, each curve adorned with a delicate pink ceramic star that seemed to sparkle with its own light. In the center, a sea of smaller stars spiraled around a larger center star, creating a pattern as mesmerizing as the night sky in Starrycard Creek.

She closed her eyes and traced the rim of the pie plate, feeling the little bumps and points of each ceramic star. Blurry images and sensations rose to the forefront of her mind. It was as if she were tuning an old hand-held radio, searching through static until the music came through at top volume. And she recognized that little radio she'd imagined. She saw it on the counter next to a pie plate. This pie plate—the one in her hands. She gasped as the scent of cinnamon and freshly brewed coffee enveloped her senses. She was in the kitchen tucked inside her grandparents' house—her house. She could hear Grandma Connie humming along to the radio as she baked. She could see her grandpa Fred seated at the table, his name printed on his overalls above the words RMU Maintenance Staff. He held a mug and grinned tenderly as he watched her grandmother place tiny stars atop a pumpkin pie.

"Talk to me, TBD," Christian said softly.

She opened her eyes, and tears streamed down her cheeks. "My grandfather bought this pie plate for my grandmother for eleven dollars at a flea market."

Tears welled in his eyes as he cupped her face in his hands. "Do you remember them?"

"I do," she whispered, the blank pages of her life suddenly filled with warmth and love. "I remember everything—the kitchen, my swing hanging off the old oak tree in the backyard. I remember my room with lace curtains my grandmother and I made together. I remember how my grandfather would roll my socks into little tubes when he helped me put away my laundry. I remember trips to the park and walks through the farmer's market. And baking. I remember my grandmother teaching me to carefully line the pie plate with the rolled-out crust, making sure it was centered and gently pressing it into the pan. I was loved, Christian, so very loved by my grandparents," she sobbed, holding the pie plate to her chest.

"You *are* so very loved," he said tenderly, brushing the tears from her cheeks.

"Just breathe, Maggie. Let the memories return at their own pace. It's okay to feel whatever comes up. You're safe, and you don't have to face this alone." The voice wasn't Christian's, but she recognized it. She looked over his shoulder as three drag queens accompanied by Judge Ironside approached.

"Who the hell are you people?" Bobby balked.

"Watch your tone, kid. I'm Maggie's honorary uncle, the Honorable Judge Morris T. Ironside."

"And we're—" the woman in sparkling red began.

"The Geriatric Gemstones—Ruby Wrinkles, Diamond Dentures, and Sapphire Sags," Maggie supplied, smiling through her tears.

"Who?" Bobby barked.

"We're her family," Diamond Dentures announced in all her sparkling grandeur.

"Maggie doesn't have any family," Bobby shot back.

"Oh, how wrong you are. We're her glamazon grandmothers," Diamond replied with a theatrical wave of her ring-adorned hand.

"A helicopter in my street and drag queens? This is too much.

I'm done," Bobby mumbled, irritation thick in his tone, but his gaze lingered on the group, his eyes darting around like a cornered rabbit.

"You're not going anywhere *yet*," Diamond seethed. She reached into her glittery bag and produced a spork. "This sad excuse for cutlery might just be teeming with Coxsackievirus. Make another move, and I'll jam it into your mouth. If anyone deserves raging diarrhea, it's you," the drag queen roared.

And holy moly, her drag queen glamazon grandmas came onto the scene guns blazing, or in their fabulous cases, rhinestones shining.

Maggie rose to her feet with the pie plate carefully cradled in her arms. "Ruby, Diamond, Sapphire, it's so good to see you again."

The queens embraced her in a bedazzled group hug.

"Our Little Miss Cry-In-Her-Pie," Diamond cooed, beaming.

Maggie looked from Christian to Ruby. "You're Christian's old baseball coach from RMU, aren't you?" she asked, connecting the dots.

"I don't know how I feel about the word *old*, but yes, Christian and I go way back to when I coached him in college."

She wiped away fresh, happy tears. "Christian, I'm sure they told you we met on the bus I was taking to Starrycard Creek because that morning..." Maggie froze, then zeroed in on Bobby —her cheating creep of an *ex*-boyfriend. Her memories of their relationship had also returned. She glared at the man. "You don't love me. You've made me doubt myself and my value for years. You must have only wanted me because you saw me with Christian in Starrycard Creek or noticed me at my pie stand and couldn't bear to see me happy and making something of myself. And you cheated on me. I walked in on you on the day I left for Starrycard Creek. I saw it with my own eyes."

"Mags, that was a hiccup," he answered with a dismissive wave, his lips curling into a smug smile. "We've been together for five years. You've forgiven me before."

"Not this time," she said sharply, as the extent of his deception materialized. "And you didn't even take me to my grandparents' place. We drove by some random house, and I've never been to any of the restaurants you said were my favorites. And I've never even been to Fiji. You told me you loved me over the phone during a break in your weekly squash match with your dad. And you only did it to get me back after dumping me. You never wanted to help me get my memories back because it benefited you to keep me in the dark. You must have seen me at Donnelly Days, didn't you?"

"You're right. He saw you. Kieran noticed him," Christian confirmed.

"So what!" the man exclaimed like a sullen toddler.

"And when you'd learned I'd lost my memory, even then, you couldn't show an ounce of kindness or concern for my welfare," she pressed, laying into the man.

"Are we done?" he huffed. "Unless you're going to give me the recipe for ricotta pumpkin pie, I should be on my way. I deserve a vacation for putting up with this bullshit."

"You're a terrible person, Bobby Driscoll," she said, strength surging through her veins.

He scoffed. "That's where you're wrong. By virtue of my work, I can't be a terrible person. I'm an orthopedic surgeon—a bone doctor," he answered and gestured to the license plate on his Corvette parked in the driveway.

"Speaking of *bone doctors*," Judge Ironside began, a sly twist to his lips, "would this happen to be your car?" the man asked, pointing to Bobby's restored vehicle.

"A real Sherlock here. Yeah, she's mine," Bobby replied, his voice dripping with arrogance.

"Thank you for confirming that piece of evidence," the judge said smoothly.

Evidence?

"Maggie, *bella*," came a booming voice as Nico exited the helicopter.

She glanced at Christian. "How many people fit in that thing? Anyone else hidden in there?"

He wrapped his arm around her. "Nobody else is inside, but you'll want to pay attention to what's about to happen."

She turned back to Nico. "It's good to see you. What are you doing here?"

Nico's vibrant mood shifted, and his expression grew somber. "I'm here to identify a suspect."

"A suspect?" she repeated.

Judge Ironside motioned toward the officers stationed at the end of the road. Three vehicles rolled forward, then halted. Six men in blue emerged, arms folded tightly across their chests, eyes locked on Bobby.

"Are they here for me?" Bobby stammered. "Because you can't arrest me for cheating on my girlfriend. And I didn't kidnap her either. I might have stretched the truth a smidge, but she came with me willingly," the man continued, but the shake to his voice couldn't be denied.

The judge nodded to an officer—a man who looked rather familiar.

"Robert Driscoll, Junior, I'm from the Creek County Sheriff's Department. You're being charged with animal cruelty, animal abandonment, and reckless endangerment."

What was happening?

Maggie's jaw dropped.

"That first charge alone comes with three years behind bars," Ironside announced.

"What?" Bobby eked out.

"We know what you did to Lucky. I saw it happen. I took a video. Your license plate was visible," Nico stated, and immediately, she knew what this was about.

If she loathed Bobby before, now she utterly despised him.

"Lucky is the dog I was supposed to foster. You promised me you'd pick him up while I was meeting with the estate people.

Why would you get him and then push him out of a moving car? Why didn't you return him to the rescue?"

Bobby shrugged. "It would have been…inconvenient."

"Inconvenient?" she shot back.

"Yeah, after I got him in the car, I got a text about the New York opportunity. We couldn't foster a dog when there was a chance we'd be moving, and I didn't want to drive all the way back to the rescue. Plus, it's just a dog."

"Did you get that, Officer?" the judge asked.

"Yes, sir, my body cam is recording."

Judge Ironside crossed his arms. "I see an open and shut case with a confession like that. Good luck getting a job anywhere, Mr. Driscoll. Take him away, Officer Gandy."

"Officer Gandy!" Maggie exclaimed, now recalling how she knew the man. He was their arresting officer.

"Good to see you, ma'am," the man said with a nod. "I'll be transporting Mr. Driscoll back to Creek County to face charges."

"It's *Doctor* Driscoll," Bobby whined as the cuffs clicked around his wrists.

"Whatever, man. Let's go," the officer ordered as a tow truck pulled up next to the vintage Corvette.

"What's happening to my car?" Bobby cried.

"It was used in the commission of a crime. Naturally, we're hauling it in," the judge supplied.

"No," Bobby wailed, bawling like a spoiled brat.

"Hey, Doctor Bad News," McKenzie called. "I'm not supposed to say this till I'm twelve, but I'm gonna say it anyway. You're a super-big *TURD BURGER!*" The little girl glanced around. "Am I in trouble?"

"No, Kenz. You're exactly right, kid," Rex replied, patting McKenzie on her shoulder.

"That was for you and Lucky, Maggie," McKenzie said, smiling from ear to ear.

"Thanks," Maggie replied, looking on as Officer Gandy put Bobby into the back of the squad car.

Christian gazed down at her. "How are you holding up, TBD?"

"I'm…" she said as her gaze moved from the police cars to the helicopter to the pie plate and then to Christian, the man who had captured her heart so completely. She stared up at him.

"Don't worry, Maggie," Rex teased with a twitch of a grin. "We Starrycard men often render the women we love speechless."

"I'll keep that in mind," she replied, still reeling from the whirlwind of events that had unfolded.

"Is that your stuff?" Christian asked and nodded to her suitcase and purse.

"Yes."

"We'll take care of loading it onto the helicopter," Nico said, collecting her things.

"You two might want to take a breather. I'll get everyone on the chopper," Rex added before leading the others toward the waiting aircraft.

She rested her forehead against Christian's chest and sighed, grateful to be alone with him. "Thank you for coming for me," she whispered, her voice catching as another wave of emotion washed over her.

He tilted her chin and placed a feather-light kiss at the corner of her lips. "I will always come for you, no matter what. I will always fight for you, and I'll always be there to support you. I promise you this with my whole heart."

This man.

This good, kind, loving man.

She wanted to forget about her time with Bobby and immerse herself in his love. But one question wouldn't leave her mind. How could she have let Bobby mistreat her for so long?

"I can't understand what I ever saw in Bobby. I can't believe I dated him for five years. Maybe I was too weak to walk away," she said, her voice tinged with regret.

Christian's eyes blazed with intensity. "Maggie, the last thing you are is weak. The Gemstones shared what you'd told them with me. Here's what I know. You met Bobby after your grand-mother had surgery. You cared for her. She passed, and then your grandfather got sick. Bobby took advantage of a young, vulner-able woman who had to be strong for the people she loved. And then you woke up with no memories, and in a matter of days, you won over a town, and you stole my heart. You're remarkable. I am in love with a remarkable, strong, caring woman." Christian's voice softened as he took her hand, squeezing it gently. "And I'd like to take this remarkable, strong, and caring woman home, where she belongs—with me."

"I want that, too," she whispered. She glanced back at Bobby's house, and a phrase came to her.

Every storm passes.

Her grandfather's wise words echoed in her mind, and she felt a sense of closure. Her stormy relationship with Bobby was over —it had passed. She'd endured and had come out stronger.

"And one other thing," Christian said, a coy grin curling the corners of his mouth.

"What's that?"

His grin widened as the last rays of light highlighted his beau-tiful face. "Fuck Bob."

She laughed, a weight lifting from her shoulders. "Fuck Bob," she repeated, then sighed, allowing the lightness to take over. "I knew there had to be a reason that felt so good to say."

He reached out and stroked her cheek. "Are you ready to head home, TBD?"

"I'd like that more than anything. But I do have one question," she added with a sly smirk.

He matched her expression. "Let's hear it."

"Are we really going back to Starrycard Creek in a helicopter?"

He chuckled and picked up the pink pie box. "We could walk to the bus station and buy a one-way ticket home, but I'm not sure Rocky Mountain City or the neighbors would appre-ciate a helicopter sitting idle in the middle of the road—and then there's the matter of the five senior citizens, one dog, one muscle-bound Italian, and one seven-year-old. I promised them pie once we got back to Starrycard Creek, and these people take the promise of dessert seriously. And they certainly don't want to wait."

"Who's making the pies?"

"Wolcott and Haynes. They wanted to test out the new ovens."

"In the senior center?" she asked, surprised the renovation had moved so quickly.

"Not exactly. You ready?"

She watched him for a beat, her heart swelling with affection. "What do you have planned?" she asked as they headed to the chopper, her curiosity piqued.

"Starrycard stuff," he replied with a mischievous grin.

"That's my favorite kind of stuff. But before we go, I need to say something." She tightened her hold on his hand and the pie plate. "I need to speak the words."

"I'm listening."

"I love you, Christian Starrycard. I never doubted your love for me, not for a second. And..." she continued, feeling her cheeks heat.

"And?" he echoed, a curious lilt to his voice.

"Having my awful ex hauled off to jail was not a bad way to sweep a girl off her feet."

"I'm glad you approve because I love you, and I won't let anyone hurt you. Anyone who tries will have to go through me."

"That's pretty fierce and determined, Number Eleven."

"You bring that out in me," he responded, a smile tugging at his lips as he tapped the door of the helicopter's cockpit. "You're riding up front with me, TBD," he said, guiding her inside with a gentle hand on her back. "Let me adjust this for you," he whispered, carefully fitting the headset over her ears before closing the door. He took his place in the pilot's seat and secured his own headset. "All set back there?"

Maggie looked over her shoulder as their headset-wearing

companions each offered a thumbs-up, and Lucky released a spirited *woof*.

"All right, folks, we're taking a little detour before we head back home," he said, his words clear and steady through the headphones.

Christian gripped the controls, and the helicopter roared to life, its rotors whipping the air as it lifted off the street. The ground fell away in seconds, and the city shrank beneath them as they soared into the sky. Darkness had fallen, and the lights from Rocky Mountain City twinkled below. Maggie relaxed, observing the city like a bird in flight. But just as she was about to be lulled into a meditative state, she edged forward, peering at a familiar bend in the road below.

"Does that place look familiar?" Christian asked.

She touched the glass. "That's my old house. How did you know where it was?"

"The Geriatric Gemstones have our ways," Diamond said, her voice purring through the headset. "We retrieved the pie plate along with the things you left on the bus—including your ID."

Maggie squinted. "There's a car parked in the driveway."

"We learned your house sold quickly to a young family," Christian explained. "We were told they were ecstatic to be starting their life there."

Her heart swelled with a serene contentment. "I'm glad. That little house holds lots of love. It'll be good to them." She peered ahead. "What about the contents of the house? Did the family buy them, too?"

"No, the contents were purchased by another buyer."

She nodded. "I'm glad someone will get some use out of them. They might be old, but they're sturdy, tried and true," she replied, grateful her grandparents' things hadn't ended up in a landfill.

"I still have an apartment here. We can come back whenever we want," Christian said, then pointed at a building below. "We're coming to the Rocky Mountain City Rec Center. I'm told that's where you learned to swim when you were in preschool."

She reared back and gawked at the man. "Yes, it is. How would you know that?"

"Ruby here on the headset. I made a few calls to people I used to work with in the Athletics Department at RMU. They connected me with a few of your grandfather's colleagues. They say he always had stories about his precocious granddaughter."

"Oh, no," Maggie said, chuckling as she recalled the man's talkative ways and rich, rolling laughter.

"Yeah, Maggie," McKenzie added, her little voice sounding so cute through the headset. "This one lady said that your grandpa told a story about when you were a little girl. You didn't want to wait to change into your swimsuit before swimming lessons, so you ran out of the locker room totally naked, and your grandma had to bribe you with pie to get you out of the pool."

"Terrorizing community centers at a young age? That explains a lot," Ironside said dryly, but Maggie could hear the smile in the judge's voice.

She laughed, her eyes filling with tears of pure joy.

"Now, we're coming up on the diner where your grandparents met. I'm told it's a little coffee shop now," Christian said.

She pressed her hand to her heart. "That's right. That's it," she said, peering down at the top of the building on a sleepy corner of the city.

Christian reached over and squeezed her hand. "Are you okay?" he mouthed, keeping the exchange private.

She gave his hand a squeeze. "I've never been better."

"Look, everyone, it's the RMU baseball fields and locker room facility," Ruby exclaimed.

"That is where I had that chance encounter with your grandfather, and..." Christian continued, veering east. "Here's where we met, where we first locked eyes, and you became the light in my life and the girl of my dreams."

"Aw," came a chorus of voices over the headset as they passed over The Rattlers' ballpark.

"And now, folks, sit back and relax," Christian said, checking the instruments on the console, "we'll follow the train tracks and head home."

"Don't get any ideas, Lucky. No train adventures for you, poochie-poo," Diamond crooned, garnering a round of laughter.

"We've got about half an hour. You all know what to do," Christian added with a subtle curl to his lips.

Maggie watched the man. "What do they have to do?"

"Just more Starrycard stuff."

He really was planning something, but she was content to let the Starrycard surprises reveal themselves in their own time. As she looked down at the pie plate resting in her lap, her fingers traced the scalloped edge, and a wave of déjà vu stirred a mix of emotions. This treasured item had been with her at the beginning of her journey to Christian's hometown, a journey that began with a pie plate in her lap and tears in her eyes. But now, the tears welling up weren't born from sorrow, loss, or desperation. These tears were different. They were tears of joy, renewal, and hope. They fell because she'd never imagined she could experience such deep acceptance again, and yet here she was, surrounded by that very love.

She released a slow, steady breath and relaxed into the seat. The bright city lights faded, and no one spoke as pockets of light from the small towns below dotted the darkened terrain like stars scattered across the night sky.

After twenty-five minutes, McKenzie's voice bubbled with pure excitement, ending the stretch of silence. "I see my house, and there's the creek. I see the paper shop next to the creek, and there's town hall and my school."

"Good eyes," Christian remarked and headed for the center of town.

Maggie surveyed the scene. "You're landing the helicopter in the square?"

"Yeah, I am. I have a little more pull with the mayor in this town. No one will mind if I leave the chopper parked there for a bit."

He deftly set the helicopter down in the middle of the square, the blades slowing as they came to a gentle stop.

"I'll take Lucky. See you there," McKenzie called as the passengers disembarked and headed down Main Street, clearly sure of their destination.

"Aren't we going with them?" Maggie asked.

Christian placed his headphones on a hook. "We are. But I wanted some time alone with you before…"

"Before…" she repeated.

"Let me help you out," he said, grabbing the empty pie box and then exited the cockpit.

"What kind of Starrycard stuff awaits us, Number Eleven?" she asked, stepping out of the aircraft.

They walked down the street, and he held out the box. "What do you think of the name, My Blushing Baker, and the logo?" he asked, stopping beneath a streetlight so she could get a good view.

She touched one of the stars. "I love it. My grandfather liked it when he made my grandmother blush—like you do to me. It's something I loved about them, and I love about us."

He nodded, and that boyish grin appeared. "I love that we share that with your grandparents."

"Did you make the logo?"

"No, Caroline designed it," he replied, his voice warm and steady as he gently guided her down the sidewalk.

She relied on him to lead the way, her fingers lightly clutching his arm as she kept her gaze trained on the image. "It's perfect, Christian. It's exactly what I'd want if I had my own…" Her voice trailed off, her breath catching in her throat as she froze, her eyes widening in disbelief as she peered ahead. "What am I looking at? What is this?" she asked, her voice trembling.

"Margaret Kathleen Michaels," Christian said, his eyes sparkling with a blend of pride and affection, "this is your bakery."

Twenty~Three

MAGGIE

"COULD YOU SAY THAT AGAIN?" Maggie asked, her voice tinged with wonder as she stared at the banner stretched across the front of the quaint brick building off Main Street. Bathed in the streetlight's warm glow, the logo was a replica of the one on the box. The crisp fall air kissed her cheeks, but the intensity of Christian's love wrapped around her heart and warmed her from within. And then there was something else. For the space of a breath, she felt a calming presence. She glanced up at the night sky. The stars seemed brighter tonight, twinkling like a thousand tiny blessings from above.

"What you're looking at is your very own bakery," Christian replied, his tone filled with pride.

"My bakery." She peered through the window. The pink walls matched the pie box perfectly. Soft lighting made the space feel inviting and peaceful. Her heart fluttered as she took in the lively scene inside. Christian's family, the Gemstones, the judges, and Nico all laughed and chatted while Lucky weaved happily between them, his tail wagging a mile a minute. She swept her gaze over the group again, then paused, spotting someone she didn't know. "I recognize everyone except the older woman with bright pink lipstick and an unlit cigarette in her hand. Who is she?"

"That's Flo, and if my luck continues, I have a feeling we're going to become quite familiar with her."

"Okay," she murmured, her mind reeling from the day's surprises, trying to make sense of the breathtaking marvels that had suddenly become her life.

She had a bakery.

She was a real baker.

"Are you absolutely certain this is my bakery?" she asked again, her voice tinged with a mix of wonder and disbelief.

"I'm one hundred percent sure." He opened the door to the shop and held it for her. The moment they stepped inside, the room erupted in cheers, the sound filling every corner of the shop with buzzy bliss.

"Welcome home, Maggie!" Goldie called, her voice ringing out above the cheers.

"It's so wonderful to have you back, dear. We heard your memories returned," Maeve cooed, her eyes glistening with emotion.

"We couldn't be happier to see you both," Owen added, his smile broad and welcoming.

"Pie for everyone!" Rex bellowed. "Wolcott, Haynes? How are we doing on the dessert front?"

"Pies are cooling and will be ready to be cut in five," Judge Haynes called from the back of the bakery.

"Was this place recently renovated?" Maggie asked, surveying the cozy space as the scent of pumpkin pie and fresh paint lingered.

"It sure was. And don't touch the walls. We finished painting ten minutes ago," Finn replied and motioned to Hailey, Izzy, Eliza, and Jack, each holding a paintbrush. "This used to be a café," Finn continued, resting his hands on his hips above his tool belt. "Converting it into a bakery was easier than expected, especially with everyone pitching in. There's still work left to do, but Chris wanted you to see what this space could become—for you."

"When did you start working?" Maggie asked.

Finn glanced at the group. "About four hours ago—right after Chris called to tell us he was heading up to Rocky Mountain City to get his dream girl."

"And he asked me to print up a few of these," Owen said, handing her a business card.

"Maggie TBD, The Blushing Baker and Certified Pie Freak," she said, reading the words embossed onto the rectangle.

"I couldn't help myself," Christian said.

She peered up at the man. "I can't believe you did this for me."

"Don't you get it?" he said, drinking her in. "I would do anything and everything for you."

She stroked his cheek, then turned to the group. "Thank you. I'm overwhelmed by your kindness," she said, her voice barely a rasp.

"So...you like it?" Christian asked, a boyish sweetness to the question.

"I love it. There aren't even words to describe how much I love it—how much I love you," she answered, her eyes shining with unshed tears.

"Now, pie!" McKenzie called, then frowned. "Or is this the kissing part? Maggie, maybe you should kiss your baseball card boyfriend."

Maggie cocked her head to the side. "My what?"

"After you left, I decided to call mean old Bobby, Doctor Bad News, and call Uncle Chris your baseball card boyfriend. But now I can just call Bobby a turd burger," McKenzie replied with a cheeky grin.

"McKenzie Fiona Starrycard-Dunleavy!" The voices of over a half dozen Starrycards echoed in the room while Rex and Goldie giggled at the child's words.

"Okay, no kissing part, just pie," the child chimed, then high-tailed it to the back of the shop.

Kieran cleared his throat, maintaining a composed expression as the people in the room fell silent. "Cool your heels, McKenzie. There will be no pie—or kissing—until Maggie addresses a pressing legal issue."

"Legal issue?" Maggie stammered as everyone's gaze fell on her.

Kieran leaned in toward her. "I'm currently in attorney mode, as you can observe from my muted demeanor. However, I felt it important to express that while my behavior may not convey my enthusiasm for your presence, I'm delighted to see you and Christian together. Please, have a seat," he said and gestured to a chair at a small table in the center of the space.

She set the pie plate beside a folder on the table, her fingers lightly tracing a faint, familiar line in the wood, then gasped. "I know this table. This is my table. It's from my grandparents' kitchen." Her gaze swept across the shop, soaking in every detail. She peered into the back and concentrated on the baking equipment. "That's my grandmother's mixer. And those are her pie plates." She froze as a familiar *tick, tick, tick* caught her attention. She found the source of the noise and gasped again. "And that's my clock." She turned, her heart swelling as she recognized every piece of décor—her décor. The vase that once sat on her bedside table now held lavender beside the cash register. The little dish her grandparents used for their car keys was beside it. Her knick-knacks and keepsakes adorned the room. Even the lace curtains from her bedroom were there.

"Everything here is from my home. How did I miss that?" she said softly, her voice tinged with disbelief.

"I was wondering how long it would take you to notice," Christian said, offering her a maddeningly sexy, slightly cocky, and completely Christian Starrycard grin.

This man.

Maggie turned to him, a thousand questions swirling in her head. "How did you get it?" she asked, touching the vase, needing to make sure it was real.

"I bought it."

"You're the buyer?"

His grin widened. "I know someone related to the estate seller you worked with."

"Who?"

"That would be me," Jade Jowls announced. "You sold your house and everything in it, save for a few personal items, to my nephew's company," the drag queen explained. "And you were one smart cookie to hold on to that pink stardust pie plate. It's worth over one hundred thousand dollars."

One hundred thousand dollars?

Maggie's knees nearly buckled as she clutched Christian's arm. "I hope I'm not hurting you because I don't think I can let go. Did Jade say one hundred thousand dollars?"

Christian quickly set the box on the table and wrapped his arm around her, drawing her close. "She did. And I've got you."

"Are you serious, Jade?" she pressed, her gaze ping-ponging between the ceramic pie plate and the drag queen. "My pink starry pie plate—the one my grandfather bought for eleven dollars—is worth that much money?"

"It sure is. My friend came down from Denver to authenticate it. You know that little *EB* scratched on the side?"

"Yes, I showed it to you when you asked for a closer look when we were on the bus," Maggie replied, her voice barely above a whisper as she worked to process the information.

"Eleanora Brighton was the artisan behind that pie plate. She created it in this part of Colorado in the late eighteen hundreds. Her distinct crockery is considered works of art by collectors, and this rare piece is part of the Stardust Collection, one of her earliest works," Jade explained as she removed her phone from the pocket of her sparkling green gown. She tapped the screen and held it for Maggie to see. "Check this out. My friend found it. It's a photo of Eleanora holding your plate."

"And she's standing next to my ancestor, Fiona Donnelly-Starrycard," Christian added.

Maggie could barely believe her eyes. "That's incredible."

"Your pie plate was inspired by this region, and I'd be willing to bet, thanks to that old photograph, it was made with water and clay from the creek in this very town," Jade continued, her voice softening with the weight of the history she was revealing.

"The stars aligned and brought us together," Christian said. "Starrycard Creek was always meant to be your home. And I was meant to love and care for you the way your grandparents would have wanted." He picked up the pie plate, kneeled, and reached into his pocket. He placed the ring—the pink diamond engagement ring—into the center of the pie plate. "I promised that there would be a right time to do this. And that time is now, surrounded by our friends and family and with this pie plate, the same one your grandfather used to propose to your grandmother." He grinned up at her. "With that said, Margaret Kathleen Michaels, will you—"

Kieran cleared his throat, halting the proposal. "I'm sorry, but before Maggie agrees to enter into a legally binding union, it is imperative that she fully understands the implications of such an agreement."

Maggie looked up, her brows furrowing in confusion. "Oh, I'm good with legally binding unions."

"I insist you review these documents. You need to understand your situation," Kieran pressed.

"Is this about the bakery space? Do I need to sign a lease?" she asked, trying to make sense of the unexpected turn in events.

"No, there's no lease," Kieran replied as he retrieved the papers from the folder, his tone measured. "Once your signature is on these forms, you'll own this building outright, as well as another piece of property."

"I'll own this building and something else?" she repeated as she looked to Christian for answers.

What was happening?

Christian pointed to the ring. "Keir, I was in the middle of proposing."

"I understand, however, Maggie's situation is about to change, and she must be made aware of such alterations before committing to any legal obligations that may affect her rights, responsibilities, and interests."

"Um…okay?" Maggie said, sharing a perplexed look with Christian.

"Just go with it, guys," Izzy remarked, beaming at her husband. "This is Kieran's love language. He's showing you both he wants what's best for you."

"All right, Kier, it appears that we're doing paperwork now," Christian said, but the man didn't look put out by the disruption. No, he appeared giddy.

"You know about this?" she asked, watching Christian closely.

Without uttering a word, he gifted her with that smile—the one that always made her heart skip a beat, just like the one on his baseball card.

"Christian asked me to prepare the documents," Kieran answered.

"More Starrycard stuff, Number Eleven?" she asked, eyeing the man.

"Something like that, TBD."

"Maggie," Kieran continued, "pursuant to the terms and conditions set forth in these agreements, the title and ownership of this building and Donnelly Ranch shall henceforth be vested to you."

Her jaw dropped. "You're giving me the ranch and this building?" she asked, staring up at Christian, who was now grinning ear to ear.

"He is," Kieran replied, answering for his brother. "And these assets are yours, even if you choose to decline my brother's offer of engaging in a marital union."

"Enough with the legalese," Izzy called. "English, babe."

Kieran nodded. "Everything Christian has will be yours, Maggie."

What?

She rested her hands on Christian's chest and studied the man. "You don't have to do this. I love you. All I want is to be with you, to be part of your family, and to belong to this community. You gave me back my memories. You've already done so much for me." She glanced around the room. "You all have given me so much."

Christian gently placed his hands over hers. "You know what I've got tattooed on my chest above my heart, right?"

"Give what you love everything you've got," she replied, the words echoing through her soul. A soul that deep down had known it was entwined with his from the moment she'd woken up in the hospital.

Christian nodded, his gaze unwavering. "Maggie Michaels, you are what I love. My heart, my life, what's mine, and every part of me belongs to you." He released her hands and removed a pink pen from his pocket.

Shaking her head, she couldn't help but feel stunned for what felt like the hundredth time in the last hour. "Pink? You've really committed to this."

He shrugged as that sweet half-grin lit up his face. "It's my new favorite color. But FYI, the ink is black."

"Maggie, this ink requirement is per my instructions. While there are no laws against signing in colored ink, black and blue are preferred on legal documents," Kieran interjected.

"I think that's dumb. I think you should be able to pick any color of the rainbow. I bet some turd burger made up the only black or blue rule," McKenzie mused.

"Language, Kenz," the Starrycards chimed in unison.

Maggie chuckled, loving everything about this place and the people. "Am I dreaming?" she asked Christian, her voice barely a whisper.

"This is real, TBD. We're real. Our love is the real thing."

She focused on the pen, not ready to take it. "I have to ask one more time. Are you sure about giving me the ranch? I know how much it means to your family."

"And that's why it's such an honor to entrust it with you," Rex said as the other family members nodded and murmured in agreement.

Christian's expression softened. "Yes, I'm sure. I've never been more certain in my life, and as you can see, everyone here agrees with my decision. We love you. We're your family. Sign the papers, TBD." He pressed the pen to her palm and curled her fingers around it.

She grinned up at him with tears in her eyes. The love in this space was palpable. It filled the room, warm and familiar, much like the love she felt from her grandparents when she'd stand in their little kitchen, surrounded by the scent of freshly baked pie. Starrycard Creek was where she was meant to be, where her grandparents would have wanted her, and where she was home.

Steady and sure, she signed on the line.

She looked up and caught Ruby's eye. "Looks like Little Miss Cry-In-Her-Pie found her path," she said, so grateful the Gemstones could be a part of their moment.

Ruby nodded, tears shining in her eyes. "I agree wholeheartedly. And your journey led you to where you belong."

"All right, all right, let the man propose," Diamond Dentures wailed, her voice thick with emotion as a river of tears streamed down her face, smearing her mascara.

"Diamond might be sassy, but she's a real sucker for love," Jade said, patting the drag queen's back.

"And we love you, but you're no longer Little Miss Cry-In-Her-Pie. You, dear Maggie, are our blushing baker," Ruby declared with a broad smile.

Christian carefully set the engagement ring on the pie plate's center star, his movements deliberate and full of purpose. "I want to do this right. I know your grandfather proposed with this pie plate. I want to make them a part of my proposal. Am I missing anything?" he asked, his gaze flicking up to meet hers.

There was one more thing—something she hadn't shared with the queens. "My grandmother didn't answer with words after my grandfather proposed. She didn't have to. My grandfather knew her answer because…"

"She blushed," Christian finished as the realization settled over him.

"That's right."

"So, this is a challenge," he purred, his tone taking on that teasing edge she loved so much.

She couldn't help but play along, her lips curling into a coy smile. "Looks like it is. Luckily, I know you like a challenge."

The air crackled with anticipation.

He glanced at the clock. "It's straight up eleven minutes past the hour. That's my number. I do love a challenge, and you know how I enjoy breaking records."

She bit back a grin. "I do."

"What do you think, everyone?" He checked the time again. "Do you think I can make Maggie blush in under forty seconds?"

The crowd erupted into cheers, and Christian stood there, radiating that unmistakable self-assurance she loved so much.

"Better get going. You've only got thirty seconds now," Owen called.

Christian smirked, the corners of his mouth lifting in that way that sent her pulse racing. "I'm good. I've got my lucky rock," he said coolly, placing it on the pie plate with the ring.

"I've got mine, too," she added, her voice soft but steady as she placed her rock beside his.

"And for a little extra luck, we'll add some Starrycard Creek paper," he said, placing his college baseball card in with the treasured items. He settled his sage-green gaze on her. "Here we go, TBD. Blush or bust."

Heaven help her! She loved this man.

"Blush or bust," she repeated, her breath catching in her throat.

The room buzzed with electric silence. Excitement thrummed beneath the ticking clock, every second dragging out the sweet tension.

"Margaret Kathleen Michaels," he began slowly, speaking deliberately in that commanding purr of a voice that made her toes curl.

"Uh-huh," she exhaled, barely managing to get the sound out as every nerve in her body lit up. The anticipation was maddening, and her self-assured man was savoring every second.

"Let's add something to that string of pretty names."

"What are you thinking?"

"Ten seconds to go," someone called, but Christian didn't break their connection.

"How do you like the sound of Margaret...Kathleen...Michaels...Starrycard?" he asked, his voice low and intimate. The heat from his gaze sent a flush spreading from her heart through her veins, igniting that telltale warmth.

She didn't move a muscle.

She didn't say a word.

She didn't have to.

"That's a yes! Maggie's blushing. That's a yes with five seconds to go," McKenzie announced, her sweet voice cutting through the charged atmosphere.

Christian's lips curved into a satisfied smile. "Still got it."

And heaven help her. This man.

He tipped up her chin gently. "Look at that," he murmured.

"What?" she breathed, her voice barely more than a whisper.

"My favorite shade of pink coloring the cheeks of my future... *wife*," he said softly, his words wrapping around her heart.

Surrounded by the warmth of family, friendship, and the comforting scent of pumpkin pie, he slid the ring onto her finger with a tenderness that brought tears to her eyes. "This is our path. This is our forever," he whispered against her lips, his breath mingling with hers as he sealed their love with a kiss.

Epilogue

CHRISTIAN

"I'M glad you're here, Number Eleven…and alone," Maggie purred as she sauntered toward him with something hidden behind her back.

He closed the bedroom door. "What do you have there, TBD?"

Of course, he knew her last name was no longer *to be determined*, but he was a ballplayer. And once a nickname took hold, it was locked in. And…anytime she started with the *Number Eleven* business, he had to match her sass.

Also, number-eleven talk usually meant she was feeling naughty.

"With the excitement of hosting Thanksgiving, I forgot to show you something that arrived," she said, playing the innocent.

He tipped up her chin and gazed into her hazel eyes. "And what would that be?"

She watched him for a beat, a sexy smirk on her lips. "Sit down and close your eyes."

"Will I like this?" he asked, drinking her in, so fucking in love with his dream girl.

Her eyes glittered with mischief. "Oh, you'll like it. Now follow directions."

He nodded, keeping his gaze locked on her as he took a few steps backward and settled on the edge of their bed.

"Eyes," she chided.

"Somebody woke up bossy," he mumbled, complying, but it was an act. He loved seeing her confidence grow and loved watching her take on her role as a small business owner. He loved everything about the woman who grounded him and got him so worked up that he could barely wait to make her body tremble against his each night.

He listened to the soft rustle of denim, the faint purr of a zipper, and the quiet drop of her jeans and sweatshirt hitting the floor. A lusty smile stretched across his face. "I agree. I have a feeling I'm really going to like this. Do you know how hard it's been to keep my hands off you for the last twenty-four hours?"

Yesterday morning, his family had arrived, their energy taking over the ranch as they prepped for today's Thanksgiving feast. They were hosting the group for the long weekend. And while he'd loved having everyone at the ranch, he'd gotten spoiled rotten having Maggie all to himself these last couple of weeks.

Not to say they hadn't been busy.

He'd set up his office in town hall and had begun brainstorming with Kieran and his mother. And when he wasn't with them or enduring good-natured ribbing from the seniors during the Rise and Fucking Shine Mobility class (adding the expletive, his first act in his new position, had tripled attendance), he was at My Blushing Baker, helping Maggie transform the space for its December grand opening.

This new pace provided a steady stream of meaningful work. It wasn't the grind of Major League Baseball but a different rhythm altogether. And thanks to the love of his life, it was everything his heart needed. He'd found the path meant for him—a path never to be traveled alone.

And speaking of alone—the clock on their private time was ticking away.

Since their guests arrived, Maggie had spent most of her time in the kitchen baking and prepping dishes while he'd arranged hikes, games, and entertainment—and doing laundry. Yep, laundry. Nobody could fold a fitted sheet faster. He was the damned master of linens. Okay, did that sound insane? Sure, but he still had a competitive side. He just applied that drive differently now. And that competitive side is what got them both up at the crack of dawn today. He'd set the table and dug out all the board games while she'd put the turkey in the oven.

"Open your eyes," she said softly.

The sultry edge to her words sent a jolt of pure animal desire surging through him and had him rock-hard in the space of a breath. Steadying himself, he opened his eyes, and sweet Christ, he was the luckiest man alive.

Maggie stood before him in an apron—and nothing else.

She did a sexy little twirl. "Blame this little interruption to our early morning prep on my perma-horny brain."

"Can you confirm with Dr. Ironside that perma-horny brain is a lasting affliction?"

"My perma-horny condition is only brought on by you, Number Eleven."

"Damn right," he growled.

She swayed her hips and cradled her full breasts in her hands. "I need your opinion. I like where the logo is placed. And I think the fit is just right," she added, running her hands down her abdomen. She gazed at him through her lashes. "What do you think, Number Eleven? Do you like the fit?"

He licked his lips. "I think my blushing baker looks tastier than one of her pies. And that's saying something because I love to *devour* her pie."

She raked her gaze over his body. "You look a little hungry now."

"I've never been more famished." He stood, peeled off his T-shirt, and let it fall to the floor next to her clothing.

She glanced at the clock. "It's six eleven."

"That's my lucky number." He glanced at the door to McKenzie's room. "And we have nineteen minutes until our neighbor wakes up."

"That's not much time."

He kicked off his shoes and lost his jeans and boxers. "Not much time? You know what I can do in one minute and eleven seconds." He closed in on her, naked as the day he was born, his cock glistening with his arousal.

She blushed that perfect shade of pink, matching her apron and the giant rock on her finger. "Oh, I know what you can do."

He trailed his index finger along the edge of her apron, savoring the velvety softness of her porcelain skin. "I'm about to wrinkle the fuck out of that apron."

"It's supposed to be wrinkle-proof."

"Is that a challenge?"

"Oh, it's a challenge."

He dropped his hands to his sides. "You're missing something."

"Am I?"

He went to the dresser and removed a little box. "This was supposed to be a Christmas gift, but I want to see it on you. I don't want to wait." He removed a dainty gold chain with a number eleven charm intricately crafted from starry quartzite. The flecks shimmered, holding a secret shared only between them.

"It's beautiful," she said as he hooked the clasp.

"I had them make it from a piece of the stone your grandfather wanted you to return to me. You have a piece of us both and…"

"And…" she repeated.

"Everyone will know your heart belongs to number eleven."

"Isn't this enough?" she asked, raising her left hand adorned with the sparkling pink diamond ring. But the tears in her eyes revealed how profoundly his gesture had touched her.

He offered a teasing shrug. "I like to be thorough in claiming what's mine. Now," he continued, his voice gravelly and commanding, "turn around and walk into the bathroom. I need another view of that pretty little ass."

She traced the charm with a light touch, her fingers moving with a sensual rhythm, and her deliberate movements damn near drove him out of his mind.

"So...you want to watch me do something like this?" she asked, pushing onto her tiptoes as she owned the room, strutting toward the bathroom.

He followed behind. "Have you considered a clothing-optional bakery model?"

"I wonder what the town would think of that. I'm sure Nico would be on board," she mused with a wry grin, catching his eye in the mirror's reflection.

"Fuck that," he answered, his voice low and rough as he moved in on her. "I changed my mind, TBD. My *naked* blushing baker is an at-home only activity."

He came up behind her and kissed her neck as he slipped one hand between her thighs. He massaged her sweet bud, and she hummed a dirty purr of delight.

"This is how you want it," he said against the shell of her ear.

She closed her eyes and arched her back. "Yes."

He felt her breasts through the soft cotton, her nipples tightening into perfect pearls that pressed into the fabric. He couldn't get enough of her. Her arousal fed his desire. His pulse quickened, sensing her need for release intensifying. The blush on her cheeks consumed her neck. He rubbed his cock against her ass and inhaled a tight breath, reveling in the friction between their bodies.

"I want to feel you. Please, let me feel you," she whispered, gasping as he increased the pressure and pace. He slipped a finger inside her and found her hot, wet, and aching for his cock.

He gripped her waist and lifted her, setting her on the edge of the sink. She wrapped her arms around his neck, and he claimed her mouth. The apron bunched at her waist as he kissed her and palmed her ass. He slid into her slowly, languidly, savoring the moment as they became one.

"You feel so good, so perfect," he said and drew his tongue across the seam of her lips.

She rewarded him by clenching her core. He tightened his grip on her ass and tilted her hips, making love to her in long, fluid strokes. At this angle, he could fill her tight, wet heat to the hilt and create delicious friction against her sensitive bundle of nerves. He focused on her, fixated on her pleasure as raw desire took over, and his need to make her come hard on his cock had him near delirious. He pistoned his hips. With each punishing thrust, her breasts heaved beneath the pink cotton, a sensual scene that had him on the precipice of release.

She tightened around him. "Christian, Christian..." she moaned, flying over the edge in a glorious cascade of breath and sweat and pulsing energy.

"Take it...take everything. It's yours," he gritted between shallow breaths, kissing her, tasting her, so in sync with her body, he had no idea where he began and she ended.

Lost in a sea of ecstasy, she threaded her fingers into the hair at the nape of his neck and pulled. That sweet bite of pain was his undoing. He joined her, hurdling into the abyss, awash in her scent, her touch, and their rasping breaths mingling in the slice of space between them.

He held her close and supported her as she wound down from her euphoric spiral. The necklace's charm dangled against her back. He marveled at the sight of his number caressing her skin, his ring securely on her finger, and his heart wholly in her hands. "I love you, Maggie," he whispered as he gently rested his chin on the crown of her head and smiled the warm, sated grin of a man who had everything that mattered.

She looked up at him, and he stroked her cheek. "Margaret Kathleen Michaels Starrycard," he said softly, drinking her in.

"What are you doing?" she asked, staring at him in all her pink-cheeked perfection.

"I like to say it. I love the sound of it."

"Me too."

"Me too!" McKenzie called—from the other side of the door.

"Kenz?" he exclaimed, the mood snapping from tender to panicked. "What are you doing out there?" he called as he and Maggie scrambled, grabbing towels and wrapping them around their bodies. Thank God he'd shut the bathroom door.

"I just came into your and Maggie's room through our door."

"How long have you been there?" he asked, cringing.

"I heard you saying Maggie's name. Are you gonna make her spell it? That's what Miss Higgins does in our second-grade class."

"No, not right now," he said, turning to Maggie and giving her the international look for *what the fuck are we supposed to do?*

"It's early, Kenz, and it's a holiday. You should be sleeping in," Maggie said, securing the towel around her apron-clad body.

"It's Aunt Caroline. She needs us. I need to tell everyone."

Oh shit!

"Is she okay?" he called, but the child didn't answer. All he could hear was a stampede of steps as she booked it out of the room.

Bam, bam, bam, bam, bam!

"It's an emergency! Everybody, get up!" she called, going door to door, banging like she was leading an FBI raid.

The stillness of the early morning was shattered by rising voices echoing through the hall as his family gathered outside their guest rooms.

"But Caroline's not even here," Maggie said, worry laced into her words.

"She must have called or emailed McKenzie," he replied as they hurried out of the bathroom, then came to an abrupt stop in the hallway. "What the hell is this?" he asked, taking in the spectacle.

The entire group stood in the hallway, clad only in towels.

"We were...deciding who would take a shower first," his father said sheepishly.

"Everybody except Uncle Owen was in the bathroom when I went knocking on doors. You guys must really like to fight over who gets to shower first. Is that why you're all naked?"

Christian parted his lips to speak, but nothing came out. *Was everyone getting it on?* He shared a look with Maggie, then realized she still had on the apron below the towel.

Oh, no!

"But Maggie isn't naked. I like the new apron. Why are you wearing it without clothes?" the child asked, cocking her head to the side.

"Because..." Maggie eked out, looking to him, eyes pleading for him to bail her out.

"She wanted to test to see if it would get wrinkled," he supplied, feeling pretty damned good about that save.

"Get wrinkled doing what?" his precocious niece pressed.

"Yeah, doing what?" Eliza chirped with a sly Starrycard grin in place.

"Probably bathroom yoga like you and Daddy do, Mommy," Kenz answered, not missing a beat.

"Touché," Jack said, biting back a grin as his wife hung her head.

Christian's gaze landed on Owen, and his jaw nearly hit the floor. "What the actual hell are you wearing?" he blurted out, his eyes wide with disbelief.

Owen glanced down at his ensemble, completely unfazed. "They're flannel footed pajamas. They're warm and cozy. What about them?"

Finn burst into laughter, shaking his head in mock horror. "I think I figured out why you can't find anyone to date," he teased, his grin widening. "That's straight-up serial killer stuff, man."

"Finn, I thought you were an axe-murderer mountain man when we met," Hailey countered, her eyes twinkling with amusement.

"But those are hot," Finn answered. "Mister Flannel Footie over here is—"

"Uncle Finn, stop worrying about Uncle Owen's baby onesie pajamas, and look at this!" McKenzie interrupted, her voice high-pitched with urgency as she held out her phone.

"Baby onesie pajamas?" Owen muttered under his breath, clearly miffed, but his attention quickly shifted to the child.

"Caroline's Future depends on what you do next," his father read, sharing a concerned look with his mother.

"Aunt Caroline's been kidnapped!" McKenzie cried, her eyes wide with fear.

Owen immediately crouched down to her level. "No, Kenz, I don't think so. Don't get upset," he reassured her, taking the phone from the child's trembling hands. "Caroline's Future is the name of a project. This is an e-greeting card site. I know it because Caroline keeps sending me this stuff, telling me we need to expand in what we offer at Starrycard Creek Paper Company. It looks like a proof to approve a design."

"Is she okay?" Rex asked, worry creasing his brow.

"Yeah, I believe so…but…" Owen eyed McKenzie.

Christian picked up on his brother's apprehension. "Hey, Kenz," he said casually. "I hear Lucky downstairs. I bet he needs to go out. Could you run down and keep an eye on him?"

McKenzie's gaze swept over the group, her eyes lingering on each adult before she nodded.

"We'll tell you if Caroline needs help. I promise," he said, reassuring her.

"Okay, Uncle Chris," she replied and bounded down the staircase.

As soon as she was out of earshot, the reality of their situation hit him like a ton of bricks. He was nearly naked, surrounded by almost everyone in his family and their significant others—also nearly naked. It was bizarre, to say the least.

"What's the deal with the towels? Weren't you people sleeping?" Owen asked, his confusion evident as he glanced around at the group.

"We were showering, separately, like grown-ups do, honey," Maeve answered smoothly.

"We weren't," Rex replied with a wide grin as he cast a loving look at his wife.

"No, sir, we were not," Goldie cooed. "And Christian, the new mattresses you purchased for the guest rooms are pure bliss for making love."

Oh, Christ on a cracker!

"Goldie! Grandpa! Ew!" Christian lamented.

Finn clapped a hand over his mouth, his face twisted in horror. "Stop talking, Goldie," he begged, his voice muffled.

"My ears will bleed if I hear any more," Eliza added, her expression one of mock disgust.

"What?" Goldie replied, grinning. "Who doesn't want to get in a little pre-meal hanky-panky? That's certainly not happening after I've eaten my weight in turkey, mashed potatoes, and pie. I'll tell you that."

"I wish you hadn't told us anything," Kieran murmured as Izzy giggled beside him, clearly enjoying the Starrycard chaos.

Ping!

Ding!

Ping!

Everyone glanced toward their rooms.

"Whatever McKenzie received from Caroline has likely hit our in-boxes. My guess is she mistakenly included everyone's email when she requested a proof of an e-card she was working on," Owen explained.

The family huddled around McKenzie's phone.

"Is it safe to open and click?" Izzy asked.

Owen nodded. "Yeah, I've checked out this site before. I'll do it." His brother tapped the screen, then tapped again. "It's an e-Christmas card with a picture of Caroline and...some dude."

"Who's the dude?" Kieran asked, leaning in closer.

Christian narrowed his gaze. "I don't recognize him."

"Look, it says tap to approve Caroline's Future holiday message," Maggie offered.

"Here goes. I'll read it aloud," Owen said, tapped again, then frowned.

"What is it?" Maeve pressed.

"It says, 'Everyone's favorite train wreck of a Starrycard has got herself a lightning-hot career and a sexy boyfriend who's a beast in the sack. Merry Christmas, and see you soon, Turd Burgers! Love and kisses, Caroline.'"

The hallway fell silent for a split second before erupting into a cacophony of voices.

"Well, that's..." Goldie began, sharing a curious look with her husband.

"One hell of a Christmas greeting," Rex finished as the family continued to buzz with a mix of disbelief and amusement.

"Is this a stunt?"

"Maybe she needs cash?"

"Caroline has a boyfriend?"

Christian wrapped his arm around Maggie, taking in the scene. He had a strong hunch that his little sister was about to desperately wish she could become invisible.

"Is Caroline all right?" Maggie asked softly as his family continued to discuss the youngest Starrycard's welfare.

He chuckled. "Buckle up, TBD. This coming Starrycard Christmas looks like it's going to be a wild one."

The Farm to Mabel Duet

A brother's best friend romance set in a small-town

Book One: Farm to Mabel

Book Two: Horn of Plenty

Farm to Mabel: The Complete Duet

The Langley Park Series

A suspenseful, sexy second-chance at love series

Book One: The Road Home

Book Two: The Sound of Home

Book Three: The Beginning of Home

Book Four: The Measure of Home

Book Five: The Story of Home

Box Set (Books 1-5 + Bonus Scene)

Own the Eights Series

A delightfully sexy enemies-to-lovers series

Book One: Own the Eights

Book Two: Own the Eights Gets Married

Book Three: Own the Eights Maybe Baby

Box Set (Books 1-3)

STANDALONES

The Kiss Keeper

A toe-curlingly hot opposites attract romance

Not Your Average Vixen

An enemies-to-lovers super-steamy holiday romance

Sign up for Krista's newsletter to get all the up-to-date Krista Sandor romance news.

Learn more at www.KristaSandor.com

Acknowledgments

First and foremost, a huge thanks to Becky, who helped me turn Starrycard Creek into something magical.

Carrie, you are an absolute saint for being the first to tackle my wild and untamed manuscripts. Your sharp eye, endless patience, and unwavering support keep me grounded. I trust you implicitly—my stories will always have to land in your hands (or on your Kindle) first.

Marla and Tera, thank you for your thoughtful proofing—seriously, the red pen is a force to be reckoned with in your hands.

Najla and the incredible team at Qamber Design, you outdid yourselves with this cover. It's perfection.

Leah, your swag designs are absolutely on point—thank you for making readers feel like part of this story's world with your creations.

To my husband, David, thank you for being my rock through every high and low, always cheering me on, and loving me unconditionally. And when I inevitably declare that I'll never finish a book (which happens every time), thank you for listening patiently—and for bringing me chocolate and Diet Coke—the true foundation of a strong marriage.

Finally, to you—the readers. You are the heart, the soul, and the reason romance lives. Thank you for diving into these pages and letting my characters into your lives. Without you, this book would just be a dream in my head.

About Krista Sandor

If there's one thing Krista Sandor knows for sure, it's that romance saved her. After she was diagnosed with Multiple Sclerosis in 2015, her world turned upside down. During those difficult first days, her dear friend sent her a romance novel. That kind gesture provided the escape she needed and ignited her love of the genre. Inspired by strong heroines and happily ever afters, Krista decided to write her own romance series. Today, she's living life to the fullest. When she's not writing, you can find her running 5Ks with her husband or chasing after their growing boys in Denver, Colorado.

Never miss a release, contest, or author event! Visit www.KristaSandor.com to sign up for her romance newsletter.

www.ingramcontent.com/pod-product-compliance
Lightning Source LLC
Chambersburg PA
CBHW051438190726
48289CB00001B/247